Praise for **GODS**

"A spellbinding fairy tale rooted in Mexican mythology, *Gods of Jade and Shadow* is a magical fairy tale about identity, freedom, and love, and it's like nothing you've read before." —*Bustle*

"[A] dazzling fairy tale . . . a whirlwind tour of a 1920s Mexico vivid with jazz, the memories of revolution, and gods, demons, and magic." —*NPR*

"Beautifully rendered in the most gorgeous, evocative prose . . . A rip-roaring adventure set in 1920s Mexico, featuring dueling Mayan death gods, a secondary cast of ghosts, spirits, and warlocks and, caught in the middle of it all, an eighteen-year-old who peers longingly at the stars and constellations she's named after." —*Locus*

"Set in a lushly rendered and gorgeous world, this is historical fantasy at its best: a fresh, feminist coming-of-age tale that lets the ancient and the new meld and clash in a book you can't put down." —S. A. Chakraborty, author of *The City of Brass* and *The Kingdom of Copper*

"An evocative and moving modern Indigenous fairy tale filled with quiet moments of vulnerability and honesty. Oh, my heart!" —Rebecca Roanhorse, Hugo and Nebula award–winning author of the Sixth World series

"Snappy dialog, stellar worldbuilding, lyrical prose, and a slow-burn romance make this a standout. . . . Purchase where Naomi Novik, Nnedi Okorafor, and N. K. Jemisin are popular." —*Library Journal* (starred review)

"A magical novel of duality, tradition, and change ... Moreno-Garcia's seamless blend of mythology and history provides a ripe setting for Casiopea's stellar journey of self-discovery, which culminates in a dramatic denouement. Readers will gladly immerse themselves in Moreno-Garcia's rich and complex tale of desperate hopes and complicated relationships."

—*Publishers Weekly* (starred review)

"Casiopea is not a damsel in distress, but rather a young woman coming of age in a time where music, myth, art and exploration thrum colorfully around her. . . . Readers will be floored by Moreno-Garcia's painstaking attention to detail. Her descriptions of the emotionally charged interactions between realistic human characters and otherworldly gods, witches and demonic forces are unforgettable, as are as the fairy-tale and folktale aspects of the plot."

—*BookPage* (starred review)

"Moreno-Garcia has a talent for taking Mexican folklore, customs, and mythology, twisting them around, and turning out fascinating stories. . . . Fans of lush, evocative language will be thoroughly delighted."

—*Booklist*

"Simultaneously heartbreaking and heart-mending, *Gods of Jade and Shadow* is a wondrous and magical tale about choosing our own path. I felt weepy and happy and hopeful when I finished—everything you want to feel at the end of a great story."

—Kevin Hearne, *New York Times* bestselling author of The Iron Druid Chronicles and *A Plague of Giants*

GODS
OF
JADE
AND
SHADOW

GODS
OF
JADE
AND
SHADOW

Silvia Moreno-Garcia

Del Rey New York

2020 Del Rey Trade Paperback Edition

Published in the United States by Del Rey,
an imprint of Random House, a division of
Penguin Random House LLC, New York.

DEL REY and the HOUSE colophon are registered
trademarks of Penguin Random House LLC.

Originally published in hardcover in the United States by Del Rey,
an imprint of Random House, a division of
Penguin Random House LLC, in 2019.

This book contains an excerpt from the forthcoming
book *Mexican Gothic* by Silvia Moreno-Garcia. This excerpt has
been set for this edition only and may not reflect the final
content of the forthcoming edition.

LIBRARY OF CONGRESS CATALOGING-IN-PUBLICATION DATA
Names: Moreno-Garcia, Silvia, author.
Title: Gods of jade and shadow: a novel / Silvia Moreno-Garcia.
Description: New York: Del Rey, 2019.
Identifiers: LCCN 2019007450| ISBN 9780525620778 (trade paperback) | ISBN
9780525620761 (ebook)
Subjects: | BISAC: FICTION / Fantasy / Historical. | FICTION / Fairy Tales, Folk Tales, Leg-
ends & Mythology. | GSAFD: Fantasy fiction.
Classification: LCC PR9199.4.M656174 G63 2019 | DDC 813/.6—dc23
LC record available at https://lccn.loc.gov/2019007450

Printed in the United States of America on acid-free paper

randomhousebooks.com

20 19 18 17 16 15 14 13 12

Book design by Elizabeth A. D. Eno

Para mis abuelas, Goyita y Rosa. Otros mundos, otros sueños.

But what the lords wished was that they should not discover their names.

—*Popol Vuh*, translated into English by
Delia Goetz and Sylvanus Griswold Morley
from the work by Adrian Recino

GODS
OF
JADE
AND
SHADOW

Chapter 1

Some people are born under a lucky star, while others have their misfortune telegraphed by the position of the planets. Casiopea Tun, named after a constellation, was born under the most rotten star imaginable in the firmament. She was eighteen, penniless, and had grown up in Uukumil, a drab town where mule-drawn railcars stopped twice a week and the sun scorched out dreams. She was reasonable enough to recognize that many other young women lived in equally drab, equally small towns. However, she doubted that many other young women had to endure the living hell that was her daily life in grandfather Cirilo Leyva's house.

Cirilo was a bitter man, with more poison in his shriveled body than was in the stinger of a white scorpion. Casiopea tended to him. She served his meals, ironed his clothes, and combed his sparse hair. When the old brute, who still had enough strength to beat her over the head with his cane when it pleased him, was not yelling for his grandchild to fetch him a glass of water or his slippers, her aunts and cousins were telling Casiopea to do the laundry, scrub the floors, and dust the living room.

"Do as they ask; we wouldn't want them to say we are spongers," Casiopea's mother told her. Casiopea swallowed her angry reply because it made no sense to discuss her mistreatment with Mother, whose solution to every problem was to pray to God.

Casiopea, who had prayed at the age of ten for her cousin Martín to go off and live in another town, far from her, understood by now that God, if he existed, did not give a damn about her. What had God done for Casiopea, aside from taking her father from her? That quiet, patient clerk with a love for poetry, a fascination with Mayan and Greek mythology, a knack for bedtime stories. A man whose heart gave up one morning, like a poorly wound clock. His death sent Casiopea and her mother packing back to Grandfather's house. Mother's family had been charitable, if one's definition of charity is that they were put immediately to work while their idle relatives twiddled their thumbs.

Had Casiopea possessed her father's pronounced romantic leanings, perhaps she might have seen herself as a Cinderella-like figure. But although she treasured his old books, the skeletal remains of his collection—especially the sonnets by Quevedo, wells of sentiment for a young heart—she had decided it would be nonsense to configure herself into a tragic heroine. Instead, she chose to focus on more pragmatic issues, mainly that her horrible grandfather, despite his constant yelling, had promised that upon his passing Casiopea would be the beneficiary of a modest sum of money, enough that it might allow her to move to Mérida.

The atlas showed her the distance from the town to the city. She measured it with the tips of her fingers. One day.

In the meantime, Casiopea lived in Cirilo's house. She rose early and committed to her chores, tight-lipped, like a soldier on a campaign.

That afternoon she had been entrusted with the scrubbing of the hallway floor. She did not mind, because it allowed her to keep abreast of her grandfather's condition. Cirilo was doing poorly;

they did not think he'd make it past the autumn. The doctor had come to pay him a visit and was talking to her aunts. Their voices drifted into the hall from the nearby living room, the clinking of dainty china cups punctuating one word here and another there. Casiopea moved her brush against the red tiles, attempting to follow the conversation—expecting to be informed of anything that went on in the house in any other way was ridiculous; they never bothered talking to her except to bark orders—until two shiny boots stopped in front of her bucket. She did not have to look up to know it was Martín. She recognized his shoes.

Martín was a youthful copy of their grandfather. He was square-shouldered, robust, with thick, strong hands that delivered a massive blow. She delighted in thinking that when he grew old, he would also become an ugly, liver-spotted wretch without teeth, like Cirilo.

"There you are. My mother is going crazy looking for you," he said. He looked away when he spoke.

"What is it?" she asked, resting her hands against her skirt.

"She says you are to go to the butcher. The silly codger demands a good cut of beef for supper. While you're out, get me my cigarettes."

Casiopea stood up. "I'll go change."

Casiopea wore no shoes and no stockings and a frayed brown skirt. Her mother emphasized neatness in person and dress, but Casiopea didn't believe there was much point in fretting about the hem of her clothes when she was waxing floors or dusting rooms. Still, she must don a clean skirt if she was heading out.

"Change? Why? It'll be a waste of time. Go right away."

"Martín, I can't go out—"

"Go as you are, I said," he replied.

Casiopea eyed Martín and considered defying him, but she was practical. If she insisted on changing, then Martín would give her a good smack and she would accomplish nothing except wasting her time. Sometimes Martín could be reasoned with, or at least tricked into changing his mind, but she could tell by his choleric expression that he'd had a row with someone and was taking it out on her.

"Fine," she said.

He looked disappointed. He'd wanted a scuffle. She smiled when he handed her the money she needed to run the errands. He looked so put off by that smile, she thought for a moment he was going to slap her for no reason. Casiopea left the house in her dirty skirt, without even bothering to wrap a shawl around her head.

In 1922 Governor Felipe Carrillo Puerto had said women could now vote, but by 1924 he'd faced a firing squad—which is exactly what you'd expect to happen to governors who go around delivering speeches in Mayan and then don't align themselves with the correct people in power—and they'd revoked that privilege. Not that this ever mattered in Uukumil. It was 1927, but it might as well have been 1807. The revolution passed through it, yet it remained what it had been. A town with nothing of note, except for a modest sascab quarry; the white powder shoveled out was used for dirt roads. Oh, there had been a henequen plantation nearby once upon a time, but she knew little about it; her grandfather was no hacendado. His money, as far as Casiopea could tell, came from the buildings he owned in Mérida. He also muttered about gold, although that was likely more talk than anything else.

So, while women in other parts of the world cut their hair daringly short and danced the Charleston, Uukumil was the kind of place where Casiopea might be chided if she walked around town without her shawl wrapping her head.

The country was supposed to be secularist after the revolution, something that sounded fine when it was printed as a decree, but was harder to enforce once push came to shove. Cristero rebellions bubbled down the center of Mexico whenever the government tried to restrict religious activity. That February in Jalisco and Guanjuato all priests had been detained for inciting people to rise against the anti-Catholic measures promoted by the president. Yet Yucatán was tolerant of the Cristeros, and it had not flamed up like other states. Yucatán had always been a world apart, an island, even if the atlas assured Casiopea she lived on a verdant peninsula.

No wonder in lazy Uukumil everyone held to the old ways. No wonder, either, that their priest grew more overzealous, intent on preserving morality and the Catholic faith. He eyed every woman in town with suspicion. Each diminutive infraction to decency and virtue was catalogued. Women were meant to bear the brunt of inquiries because they descended from Eve, who had been weak and sinned, eating from the juicy, forbidden apple.

If the priest saw Casiopea he would drag her back to her house, but if he did, what of it? It was not as if the priest would strike her any harder than Martín would, and her stupid cousin had given her no chance to tidy herself.

Casiopea slowly walked to the town square, which was dominated by the church. She must follow Martín's orders, but she would take her time doing so. She glanced at the businesses bunched under the square's high arcades. They had a druggist, a haberdasher, a physician. She realized this was more than other towns could claim, and still she couldn't help but feel dissatisfied. Her father had been from Mérida and had whisked her mother off to the city, where Casiopea was born. She thought she belonged there. Or *anywhere* else, for that matter. Her hands were hard and ugly from beating the laundry against the stone lavadero, but her mind had the worst of it. She yearned for a sliver of freedom.

Somewhere, far from the bothersome grandfather and impertinent coterie of relatives, there would be sleek automobiles (she wished to drive one), daring pretty dresses (which she'd spotted in newspapers), dances (the faster, the better), and a view of the Pacific sea at night (she knew it courtesy of a stolen postcard). She had cut out photos of all these items and placed them under her pillow, and when she dreamed, she dreamed of night swimming, of dresses with sequins, and of a clear, starlit sky.

Sometimes she pictured a handsome man who might partner with her for those dances, an amorphous creation glued together by her subconscious using the pictures of movie stars that appeared between the print ads for soap and bobby pins, and which she'd also preserved, safe at the bottom of the cookie tin that contained every precious item she owned. Despite this, she did not engage in the gleeful whispering and giggling of her female cousins, who spoke their dreams. She kept her mouth tightly shut; the pictures were in the tin.

Casiopea purchased the items she needed and began circling back home, her steps leaden. She stared at Grandfather's house, the best house in town, painted yellow, with elaborate wrought-iron grilles at the windows. Grandfather's home was as pretty as El Principio ever was, he claimed. That had been the famous hacienda nearby, a huge building where dozens and dozens of poor workers had toiled in misery for decades before the revolution freed them and sent the old owners fleeing abroad, though it didn't improve the workers' conditions.

A big house, as fancy as one could get, filled with the same valuables a hacendado might have, this was Cirilo Leyva's house. With his money the old man could have kept his family in Mérida, but Casiopea suspected he longed to return to Uukumil so he could parade his wealth before the people he'd grown up with. It was the opposite journey Casiopea wished to make.

How beautiful this yellow house!

How much she hated it.

Casiopea rubbed away the beads of sweat above her upper lip.

It was so hot Casiopea felt her skull was being baked. She ought to have taken the shawl to protect herself. Yet, despite the heat, she dallied outside the house, sitting under a Seville orange tree. If Casiopea closed her eyes she might smell the scent of salt. The Yucatán peninsula, Uukumil, they were distant, isolated from everything, and yet the scent of salt was always nearby. This she loved, and she might miss in a distant, landlocked city, although she was willing to make the trade.

Finally, knowing she could not wait any longer, Casiopea went into the house, crossed the interior courtyard, and delivered the provisions. She saw her mother in the kitchen, her hair in a tidy bun, chopping garlic and speaking with the servants. Her mother also worked for her keep, as the cook. Grandfather appreciated her culinary abilities, even if she had disappointed him in other respects, mainly her marriage to a swarthy nobody of indigenous extraction. Their marriage produced an equally swarthy daughter, which was deemed even more regrettable. The kitchen, though busy, was a better place to spend the day. Casiopea had helped there, but when she turned thirteen she had hit Martín with a stick after he insulted her father. Since then, they'd had her perform meaner tasks, to teach her humility.

Casiopea stood in a corner and ate a plain bolillo; the crusty bread was a treat when dipped in coffee. Once Grandfather's meal was ready, Casiopea took it to his room.

Grandfather Cirilo had the largest room in the house. It was crammed with heavy mahogany furniture, the floor decorated with imported tiles, the walls hand-stenciled with motifs of vines and fruits. Her grandfather spent most of the day in a monstrous cast-iron bed, pillows piled high behind him. At the foot of the bed there lay a beautiful black chest, which he never opened. It had a single decoration, an image of a decapitated man in the traditional Mayan style, his hands holding a double-headed serpent that signaled royalty. A common enough motif, k'up kaal, the cutting of the throat. In the walls of old temples, the blood of the decapitated was sometimes shown spurting in the shape of snakes. The image etched on the lid, painted in red, did not depict the blood, only the spine curving and the detached head tumbling down.

When she was younger, Casiopea had asked Grandfather about that singular figure. It struck her as odd since he had no interest in Mayan art. But he told her to mind her own business. She did not have a chance to ask or learn more about the artifact. Grandfather kept the key to the chest on a gold chain around his neck. He took it off to bathe and to go to church, since the priest was strict about forbidding any ornamentation during his services.

Casiopea set her grandfather's supper by the window and, grunting, he stood up and sat at the table where he had his meals every day. He complained about the salting of the dish, but did not yell. On the evenings when his aches particularly pained him, he could holler for ten whole minutes.

"Do you have the paper?" he asked, as he did every Friday. The two days when the railcar stopped by the town, they brought the morning daily from Mérida.

"Yes," Casiopea said.

"Start reading."

She read. At certain intervals her grandfather would wave his hand at her; this was the signal that she should stop reading that story and switch to something else. Casiopea doubted her grandfather cared what she read, she thought he simply enjoyed the company, although he did not say this. When he was fed up with her reading, Grandfather dismissed her.

"I heard you were rude to Martín today," her mother told her later, as they were getting ready for bed. They shared a room, a potted plant, a macramé plant hanger for said plant, and a cracked painting of the Virgin of Guadalupe. Her mother, who had been Grandfather's most darling daughter as a child.

"Who said so?"

"Your aunt Lucinda."

"She wasn't there. He was rude to me first," Casiopea protested.

Mother sighed. "Casiopea, you know how it is."

Mother brushed Casiopea's hair. It was thick, black, straight as an arrow, and reached her waist. During the daytime she wore it in a braid to keep it from her face and smoothed it back with Vaseline. But at night she let it loose, and it cloaked her, hiding her expression. Behind her curtain of hair Casiopea frowned.

"I know he is a pig, and Grandfather does nothing to curb him. Grandfather is even worse than Martín, such a mean old coot."

"You must not speak like that. A well-bred young woman minds her words," her mother warned her.

Well-bred. Her aunts and her cousins were ladies and gentlemen. Her mother had been a well-bred woman. Casiopea was just the poor relation.

"I want to tear my hair out some days, the way they talk to me," Casiopea confessed.

"But it's such pretty hair," her mother said, gently setting down the hairbrush. "Besides, bitterness will only poison you, not them."

Casiopea bit her lower lip. She wondered how her mother ever gathered the courage to marry her father, despite her family's protestations. Although, if the nasty rumor Martín had whispered in her ear was true, the marriage had taken place because her mother had been pregnant. That, Martín declared, made her almost a bastard, daughter of a worthless Pauper Prince. And that was why she had hit him with a stick, leaving a scar upon his brow. This humiliation he would never forgive her. This triumph she never forgot.

"Did you go over that reading I marked for you?"

"Oh, Mother, what does it matter if I can read or write or do sums?" Casiopea asked irritably.

"It matters."

"I'm not going anywhere where it would matter."

"You do not know that. Your grandfather has said he'll give us one thousand pesos each upon his passing," her mother reminded her.

In Mexico City, a shop worker at a reputable store could get five pesos for a day's wages, but in the countryside half of that, and less, was more realistic. With one thousand pesos Casiopea might live in Mérida for a whole year without working.

"I know," Casiopea said with a sigh.

"Even if he doesn't give us all that, I've got my savings. A peso here and a peso there, maybe we can figure something out for you. Once you're a little older, a year or two older, perhaps we might think of Mérida."

An eternity, Casiopea thought. *Maybe never.*

"God sees your heart, Casiopea," her mother said, smiling at her. "It is a good heart."

Casiopea lowered her gaze and hoped this was not the case, for her heart was bubbling like a volcano and there was a tight knot of resentment in her stomach.

"Here, give me a hug," her mother said.

Casiopea obeyed, wrapping her arms around her mother like she'd done when she was a child, but the comfort she derived from this contact in her youth could not be replicated. She was upset, a perfect storm inside her body.

"Nothing ever changes," Casiopea told her mother.

"What would you like to see change?"

Everything, Casiopea thought. She shrugged instead. It was late, and there was no sense in rehashing the whole thing. Tomorrow there would come the same litany of chores, her grandfather's voice ordering her to read, her cousin's taunts. The world was all gray, not a hint of color to it.

Chapter 2

The soil in Yucatán is black and red, and rests upon a limestone bed. No rivers slice the surface in the north of the peninsula. Caves and sinkholes pucker the ground, and the rainwater forms cenotes and gathers in haltunes. What rivers there are run underground, secretive in their courses. The marshes come and go at their whim during the dry season. Brackish waters are common, giving a habitat to curious, blind fish in the depths of the cave systems, and where limestone meets the ocean, the shore turns jagged.

Some cenotes are famous and were once sacred places of worship where the priests tossed jewels and victims into the water. One near Mayapán was said to be guarded by a feathered serpent that gobbled children. Others were supposed to connect with the Underworld, Xibalba, and finally there were those that were suhuy ha, the place where virgin water might be gathered.

There were several cenotes near Casiopea's town, but one farther away, an hour's ride on a mule-drawn carriage, was reckoned to possess special healing properties. Once a month Grandfather had them make the trek there so that he could soak himself in its waters, hoping to prolong his life. A mattress was dragged onto the cart to ensure that Grandfather would be comfortable, and food was packed for them to eat by the cenote after Grandfather's soak. Grandfather would then take his midday nap, and they would head back when the sun had gone down a bit and the air was cooler.

The monthly trip was one of the few occasions when Casiopea had a chance to enjoy the company of her family members and a deserved respite from her chores. A day of merriment. She looked forward to it like a child anticipates Epiphany.

Grandfather spent most of his days in bed in his nightshirt, but on the occasion of the trip to the cenote, as with any visit to church, he would pick a suit and a hat to wear. Casiopea was in charge of Grandfather's clothes, of washing and brushing them, of starching his shirts and ironing them. Since they left the house early, this meant a day or two of preparations were necessary for the trip to the cenote.

The day before their departure, Casiopea had almost finished with her list of chores. She sat in the middle of the interior patio of the house, a joyful patch of greenery with its potted plants and fountain. She listened to the canaries chirping in their cages and the random, loud screeches of the parrot. It was a cruel animal, this parrot. As a child, Casiopea had tried to feed it a peanut, and it had bitten her finger. It spoke naughty words, which it had learned from the servants and her cousin, but for now it was quiet, preening itself.

Casiopea hummed as she shined Grandfather's boots. It was the last task she needed to accomplish. Everyone else was napping, escaping the midday heat, but she wanted to get this done so she could read for the rest of the day. Her grandfather had no interest in books and much preferred the newspaper, but for the sake of appearances he had purchased several bookcases and filled them with thick leather tomes. Casiopea had convinced him to buy a few more, mostly astronomy books, but she had also sneaked in a few volumes of poetry. He never even looked at the spines, anyway. On good days, such as this one, Casiopea could sit for several hours in her room and lazily flip the pages, run her hands down the rivers of the old atlas.

The parrot yelled, startling her. She looked up.

Martín strode across the courtyard, heading in her direction, and Casiopea immediately felt irritated—he was intruding upon her silence—though she tried not to show it, her fingers twisting on the rag she was using to apply the polish. He ought to have been sleeping, like everyone else.

"I was going to go to your room and wake you up, but you've saved me the trip," he said.

"What did you need?" she asked, her voice curt despite her attempt at keeping a neutral tone.

"The old man wants you to remind the barber he needs to come and clip his hair this evening."

"I reminded him this morning already."

Her cousin was smoking, and he paused to grin at her and let the smoke out of his mouth in a puff. His skin was pale, showing some of the European heritage the family valued so highly, and his hair curled a little, the reddish-brown tone he owed to his mother. They said he was good-looking, but Casiopea could not find any beauty in his sour face.

"My, aren't you being industrious today? Say, why don't you clean my boots too, since you have the time. Fetch them from my room."

Casiopea cleaned floors when it was necessary, but the bulk of her obligations were to her grandfather. She was not Martín's servant. They employed maids and an errand boy who could shine his shoes, if the oaf couldn't figure out how to do it himself. She knew he was asking in order to encroach on her personal time and to irritate her. She should not have taken the bait, but she could not help her fury, which stretched from the pit of her stomach up to her throat.

He had been at her for several days now, starting with the moment she'd had the audacity to tell him she wanted to change her clothes to run the errands. It was a tactic of his, to wear her down and get her in trouble.

"I'll get to it later," she said, spitting the words out. "Now let me be."

She ought to have simply said "yes," and kept her voice down, but instead she'd delivered the answer with all the aplomb of an empress. Martín, a fool but not entirely stupid, noticed this, took in the way she held her head up high, and immediately smelled blood.

Martín crouched down, stretched out a hand. He clutched her chin, holding it firmly.

"You talk to me with too much sass, eh? Proud cousin."

He released her and stood up, wiped his hands, as if he was wiping himself clean of her, as if that brief contact was enough to dirty him. And she was dirty, polish on her hands, it might have gotten on her face, who knew, but she was aware it was not about the dirt under her fingers or the black streaks of grease.

"As if you had anything to be proud of," her cousin continued. "Your mother was the old man's favorite, but then she had to run off with your father and ruin her life. Yet you walk around the house as if you were a princess. Why? Because he told you a story about how you secretly are Mayan royalty, descended from kings? Because he named you after a stupid star?"

"A constellation," she said. She didn't add "you dunce," but she might as well have. Her tone was defiant.

She ought to have left it at that. Already Martín's face was growing flushed with anger. He hated being interrupted. But she could not stop. He was like a boy pulling a girl's pigtail and she ought to have ignored him, but a prank is not any less irritating because it is childish.

"My father may have told tall tales, and maybe he did not have much money, but he was a man worthy of respect. And when I leave this place I will be someone worthy of respect, just like him. And you will never be that, Martín, no matter how many coats of polish you apply to yourself."

Martín yanked her to her feet, and instead of trying to evade the blow he would surely deliver, she stared at him without blinking. She'd learned that cowering did no good.

He did not hit her and this scared her. His rage, when it was physical, could be endured.

"You think you are going to go anywhere, huh? What, to the capital, maybe? With what money? Or maybe you are thinking the old man will leave you the one thousand pesos he is so fond of mentioning? I've seen the will, and there is nothing there for you."

"You are lying," she replied.

"I don't have to lie. Ask him. You'll see."

Casiopea knew it was true, it was written on his face. Besides, he didn't have the imagination to lie about such a thing. The knowledge hit her harder than a blow. She stepped back. She clutched her can of shoe polish like a talisman. Her throat felt dry.

She did not believe in fairy tales, but she had convinced herself she'd have a happy ending. She'd placed those pictures under her pillow—an ad showing an automobile and another one with pretty dresses, a view of a beach, photos of a movie star—in a childish, mute effort at sympathetic magic.

He grinned and spoke again. "When the old man passes away you'll be under my care. Don't shine my shoes today, you'll have plenty of chances to polish them every day, for the rest of your life."

He left and Casiopea sat down again, numbly rubbing the cloth against the shoes, her fingers streaked black. On the floor next to her lay his cigarette, slowly extinguishing itself.

The consequences were swiftly felt. Mother informed her of the punishment while they were getting ready for bed. Casiopea slipped her hands into the washbasin upon the commode.

"Your grandfather has asked that you stay behind tomorrow," her mother said. "You are to mend a couple of his shirts while we are out."

"It's because of Martín, isn't it? He's punishing me because of him."

"Yes."

Casiopea raised her hands, sprinkling water on the floor.

"I wish you'd stand up for me! Sometimes I feel like you have no pride, the way you let them walk all over us!"

Her mother was holding the hairbrush, ready to brush Casiopea's hair as she did every night, but she froze in place. Casiopea saw her mother's face reflected in their mirror set by the washbasin, the hard lines bracketing her mouth, the lines upon her forehead. She wasn't old, not really, but right that instant she seemed worn.

"Perhaps someday you'll learn what it is to make sacrifices," her mother said.

Casiopea recalled the months after her father died. Mother tried to make a living with her macramé, but more money was necessary. First Mother sold the few valuables they owned, but by the time the summer came, most of their furniture and clothes were gone. Even her wedding ring was pawned. Casiopea felt ashamed of herself then, realizing how difficult it must have been for Mother to go back to Uukumil, to her harsh father.

"Mother," Casiopea said. "I'm sorry."

"It's a difficult situation for me too, Casiopea."

"I know it's hard for you. But Martín is so mean! Sometimes I wish he'd fall down a well and break his back," Casiopea replied.

"And would that make your life any happier if he did? Would it make your chores shorter and lighter?"

Casiopea shook her head and sat down on the chair where she sat every night. Her mother parted her hair, gently brushing it.

"It's unfair. Martín has everything and we get nothing," Casiopea said.

"What does he have?" her mother asked.

"Well . . . money, and good clothes . . . and he gets to do anything he wants."

"You shouldn't do everything you want just because you can," her mother said. "That is precisely why Martín is such a terrible man."

"If I had grown up with his money, I promise I wouldn't be terrible."

"But you'd be an entirely different person."

Casiopea did not argue. She was bone-tired and Mother was constantly serving her a meal of platitudes instead of any significant answers or action. But there was nothing else to do but to accept this, to accept the punishment and carry on day after weary day. Casiopea went to sleep with her head full of quiet resentment, as she must.

When her family left the next morning, Casiopea went to her grandfather's room and sat on the edge of the bed. He'd piled his shirts on a chair. Casiopea had brought her sewing kit but upon the sight of the stupid shirts she tossed the sewing kit against the mirror atop the vanity. She would not ordinarily have allowed herself such a visible demonstration of her rage, but this time the anger was too overwhelming and she thought she'd catch on fire. She must cool down. Afterward, she would be able to take a deep breath and push the thread through the eye of the needle, stitching new buttons in place.

Something metallic rattled and slid off the vanity. With a sigh she rose and picked it up. It was grandfather's key, which he normally wore around his neck. Since he'd gone to the waterhole he'd left it behind. Casiopea stared at the key resting on her palm and then at the chest.

She'd never opened it, never dared to attempt such a thing. Whatever lay in there, whether it was gold or money, it must be valuable. And she recalled that the old man was going to leave her nothing. She had not stolen from Grandfather; it would have been idiotic since he would notice it. But the chest . . . if it was gold coins, would he truly notice the absence of a couple of them? Or better yet, should she take *all* of them, would he be able to stop her from running off with his treasure?

Casiopea endured, patiently, like her mother asked her to, but the girl was no saint, and every mean remark she swallowed had accumulated like a bloated tumor. If the day had not been so warm, with a heat that scrambles the senses, the kind of heat that makes a tame dog bite the leg of its owner in an act of sudden betrayal, she might have eluded temptation. But she was feverish with her quiet anger.

She slashed at the cycle of her pitiful existence and decided that she'd look inside the chest, and if there was indeed gold inside, damn it all to hell, she'd take off and leave this rotten place behind. If there was nothing—and most likely there was nothing and this was but a quiet act of rebellion, which, like the tossing of the sewing kit, would serve as a tepid balm to her wounds—then she would at least satisfy her curiosity.

Casiopea knelt in front of the chest. It was very simple, with carrying handles on each end. No decorations except for the one image painted in red, the decapitated man. When she ran her hand along its surface, she discovered shapes that had been carved and painted over. She could not tell what they were, but she could feel them. She gave the chest a push.

It was heavy.

Casiopea rested both hands on the chest and for a moment considered leaving well enough alone. But she was angry and, more than that, curious. What if indeed there was money locked away in there? The old man owed her something for her suffering.

Everyone owed her.

Casiopea inserted the key, turned the lock, and flipped the lid open.

She sat there, confused at the sight of what lay inside the chest. Not gold but bones. Very white bones. Might it be a ruse? Could the prize be hidden beneath? Casiopea placed a hand inside the chest, shoving the bones around as she tried to uncover a hidden panel.

Nothing. She felt nothing but the cold smoothness of the bones. This was her luck, of course. Black.

With a sigh she decided enough was enough.

Pain shot through her left arm. She pulled out her hand from the chest and looked at her thumb only to see a white shard, a tiny piece of bone, had embedded itself in her skin. She tried to pull it out but it sank deeper in. A few drops of blood welled from the place where the bone had splintered her.

"Oh, what foolishness," she whispered, standing up.

Blacker than black her luck. The daykeepers would have laughed predicting her life, yet as she rose, the chest . . . it groaned, a low, powerful sound. But surely *not*. Surely the noise had come from outside.

Casiopea turned her head, ready to look out the window.

With a furious clacking the bones jumped in the air and began assembling themselves into a human skeleton. Casiopea did not move. The pain in her hand and the wave of fear that struck her held the girl tight to her spot.

In the blink of an eye all the bones clicked into place, like pieces in a puzzle. In another instant the bones became muscle, grew sinews. In a third blink of the eye they were covered in smooth skin. Faster than Casiopea could take a breath or a step back, there stood a tall, naked man before her. His hair was the blue-black of a sleek bird, reaching his shoulders, his skin bronzed, the nose prominent, the face proud. He seemed a warrior-king, the sort of man who could exist only in myth.

Unnaturally beautiful the stranger was—this was beauty sketched from smoke and dreams, translated into fallible flesh—but his dark gaze was made of flint. It sliced her to the core, sliced with such force she pressed a hand against her chest, fearing he'd cut through bone and marrow, to the very center of her heart. There was a song the girls of her town sometimes sang; it went "Now there, mother, I've found a man, now there, mother, I'll dance along the road with him, now there I'll kiss his lips." Casiopea did not sing it because, unlike the girls who smiled knowingly, who smiled thinking of a specific young man they'd like to kiss or whom they'd kissed already, Casiopea knew few names of boys. She thought of that song then, like a pious person might have thought of a prayer when caught in a moment of turmoil.

Casiopea stared at the man.

"You stand before the Supreme Lord of Xibalba," the stranger said. His voice had the chill of the night. "Long have I been kept a prisoner, and you are responsible for my freedom."

Casiopea could not string words together. He had said he was a Lord of Xibalba. A god of death in the room. Impossible and yet, undeniably, true. She did not pause to question her sanity, to think she might be hallucinating. She accepted him as real and solid. She could see him, and she knew she was not mad or prone to flights of fancy, so she trusted her eyes. Her preoccupation was, then, very simple. She had no idea how to address a divine creature and bowed her head clumsily. Should she speak a greeting? But how to make her tongue produce the right sounds, to pull a breath of air into her lungs?

"It was my treacherous brother, Vucub-Kamé, who tricked and imprisoned me," he said, and she was grateful for his voice, since she'd lost her own. "From me he took my left eye, ear, and index finger, as well as my jade necklace."

As he spoke and raised his hand, she realized he was indeed missing the body parts he had mentioned. His appearance was so striking one could not notice the absence at first. Only when it was highlighted did it become obvious.

"The owner of this abode assisted my brother, enabling his plan," he said.

"My grandfather? I doubt—"

He stared at her. Casiopea did not utter another word. It appeared she was meant to listen. So much for thinking of proper greetings or feeling poorly about her clumsy silence. Her teeth clacked together as she closed her mouth.

"I find it fitting that you have opened the chest, then. A proper circle. Fetch me clothes; we will journey to the White City," he said. It was a tone she was accustomed to, the tone of a man directing his servant. The familiarity of such a command managed to rouse her from her confusion, and this time she delivered a whole sentence, however stilted.

"Mérida? We, meaning the two of us . . . you want *both* of us to go to Mérida."

"I dislike repeating myself."

"Pardon me, I do not see why *I* should go," she said.

The retort came unbidden. This was how she got in trouble with Martín or her grandfather. A scowl here, an angry gesture there. She could control herself most of the time, but after a while dissatisfaction would boil in her belly and escape, like steam from a kettle. It never failed. However, she had not talked back to a god. She wondered if she might be struck by lightning, devoured by maggots, turned to dust.

The god approached her and caught her wrist with his hand, raising it and making her hold her palm up, outstretched.

"I shall explain something to you," he said as he touched her thumb. She winced when he did, a nerve plucked. "Here lodges a shard of bone, a tiny part of me. Your blood awoke and reconstituted me. Even now it provides nourishment. Every moment that passes, that nourishment, that life, flows out of you and into me. You will be drained entirely, it shall kill you, unless I pull the bone out."

"Then you should remove it," she said, immediately alarmed, and forgot to add a proper "please" to the sentence. This was probably the minimum expected of a mortal.

The god shook his head majestically. You'd have thought he was decked in malachite and gold, not naked in the middle of the room. "I cannot, for I am not whole. My left eye, ear, and index finger, and the jade necklace. These I must have in order to be myself again. Until then, this shard remains in you, and you must remain at my side, or perish."

He released her hand. Casiopea looked at the hand, rubbing the thumb, then back up at him.

"Fetch me clothes," he said. "Be swift about it."

She could have complained, wailed, resisted, but this would have merely been a waste of time. Besides, there was the bone shard in her hand, and who knew if her fear of death by maggots might have some truth to it. Assist him she must. Casiopea tightened her jaw. She threw the doors of her grandfather's armoire open and scooped out trousers, a jacket, a striped shirt. Not the latest fashion, though the shirt's detachable white collar was brand new. Death, thin and lanky, went the refrain, and the god was indeed slim and tall, meaning the clothes would not fit him properly, but it was not as if she could ask a tailor to stop by the house.

She fetched a hat, shoes, underwear, and a handkerchief to complete the ensemble. She'd performed such tasks before, and the familiarity of handing out clothes won over any misgivings.

The god knew how to dress himself, thankfully. She'd had no idea if he had any experience with such garments. It would have been even more mortifying to have to button up the shirt of a god than it already was to watch him get dressed. She'd seen naked men in mythology books, but even Greek heroes had the sense to wear a scrap of cloth upon their private parts.

I shall now go to hell, she thought, because that was what happened when you looked at a naked man who was not your husband and this one was handsome. She'd probably burn for all eternity. However, she amended her thought when she recalled that she was in the presence of a god who had spoken about yet another god, which would imply that the priest had been wrong about the Almighty One in heaven. There was no one god in heaven, bearded and watching her, but multiple ones. This might mean hell did not exist at all. A sacrilegious notion, which she must no doubt explore later on.

"Indicate to me the quickest way to reach the city," the god told her as he adjusted his tie.

"The tram. It is almost eleven," Casiopea said, glancing at the clock by the bed and holding up the suit jacket so that he might put it on. "It stops in town twice a week at eleven. We must catch it."

He agreed with her, and they rushed across the house's courtyard and out into the street. To reach the tram station they had to cut through the center of the town, which meant parading in front of everyone. Casiopea knew exactly how bad it looked to be marching next to a stranger, but even though the pharmacist's son turned his head in her direction and several children who were chasing a stray dog paused to giggle at them, she did not slow down.

When they arrived at the pitiful tram station—there was a single bench where people could sit and wait under the unforgiving sun for their transport—she recalled an important point. "I have no money for the fare," she said.

Maybe their trip would not be. That might be a relief, since she did not understand what they were supposed to do in the city, and oh dear, she wasn't ready for any of this.

The god, now dressed in her grandfather's good clothes and looking very much the part of a gentleman, said nothing. He knelt down and grabbed a couple of stones. Under his touch these became coins. Just in time, as the mule came clopping down the narrow track, pulling the old railcar.

They paid the fare and sat on a bench. The railcar had a roof, somewhat of a luxury, since the vehicles that made the rounds of the rural areas could be very basic. There were three others traveling with them that day, and they were uninterested in Casiopea and her companion. This was a good thing, as she would not have been able to make conversation.

Once the railcar left the station, she realized the townspeople would say she had run off with a man, like her mother did, and speak bad things about her. Not that a god who had jumped out of a chest would care about her reputation.

"You'll give me your name," he said as the station and the town and everything she'd ever known grew smaller and smaller.

She adjusted her shawl. "Casiopea Tun."

"I am Hun-Kamé, Lord of Shadows and rightful ruler of Xibalba," he told her. "I thank you for liberating me and for the gift of your blood. Serve me well, maiden, and I shall see fit to reward you."

For a fleeting moment she thought she might escape, that it was entirely possible to jump off the tram and run back into town. Maybe he'd turn her into dust, but that might be better than whatever horrid fate awaited her. A horrid fate awaited her, didn't it? Hadn't the Lords of Xibalba delighted in tricking and disposing of mortals? But there was the question of the bone shard and the nagging voice in the back of her head that whispered "adventure."

For surely she would not get another chance to leave this village, and the sights he would show her must be strange and dazzling. The pull of the familiar was strong, but stronger was curiosity and the blind optimism of youth that demanded *go now, go quickly*. Every child dreams of running away from home at some point, and now she had this impossible opportunity. Greedily she latched on to it.

"Very well," she said, and with those two words she accepted her fate, horrid or wonderful as it might be.

He said nothing else during their journey to Mérida, and although she was confused and scared, she was also glad to see the town receding in the distance. Casiopea Tun was off into the world, not in the way she had imagined, but off nevertheless.

Chapter 3

Martín Leyva. Twenty and good-looking, in a blunt sort of way, with honeyed eyes and a sharp tongue. The only son of Cirilo Leyva's only son—although the old man had daughters aplenty—was, due to this accident of birth, heir to the Leyva fortune, his sex allowing him to prance around town like a rooster. With his fine boots and silver belt buckles and his monogrammed cigarette case, he struck such a picture that no one doubted his position in society or his magnificence.

No one, that is, except for his cousin Casiopea. Her skeptical gaze was like a splash of acid in the young man's face. "Why couldn't you be a boy?" Grandfather had told Casiopea one time, and Martín had never been able to forget that moment, doubt sewn into his soul.

Martín Leyva, the magnificent and contemptuous Martín Leyva, stomped into the sitting room like a child, and like a child he sulked, sitting in one of the overstuffed chairs. His mother, his aunts, and two of his sisters were there that day, busy with their embroidery.

"Mother, do you have any cigarettes left?" he asked with an irritated sigh.

Although the newspapers carried advertisements advising women to substitute cigarettes for sweets, Martín's mother, Lucinda, doled them out with caution, partly because she was old-fashioned and partly because she was miserly.

"You smoke too much; it's bad for your breath. And what happened to your cigarettes?" she asked. "Did you go through a pack already?"

"It's been days since I smoked anything, and I wouldn't ask if Casiopea ran errands like she's supposed to," he replied, angry that he was being questioned.

"Has she been skimping on her chores again?"

"She's taking forever to run to the store, and she's simply rude," he said. If his mother could find fault in Casiopea, then she wouldn't find fault in him, and his overconsumption of tobacco would be ignored.

"I see."

Lucinda had hair of a reddish tint and a neck so divine a poet had composed a sonnet in her honor. She had married Cirilo Leyva's only son, a soft, quiet young man whom she didn't much like, because poets can seldom pay the rent. She enjoyed the luxuries of the house at Uukumil, the status that being a Leyva conferred on her around these parts, and most of all she enjoyed fawning upon her only son. After Casiopea hit him with a stick, she had regarded the girl with narrowed eyes, convinced the child was foul.

Lucinda reached for the velvet purse she carried with her at all times and took out a cigarette, handing it to her son.

"I'll have to mention this to your grandfather," Lucinda said.

"If you wish," Martín said. He had not meant to get Casiopea in trouble, but if this was to be the final outcome, he did not care. He reasoned that if she'd hurried back home he wouldn't have been forced to beg his mother for the cigarette; therefore the girl had been the one in the wrong. He used such reasoning often. Seldom was he the cause of his own misfortune.

He went to smoke in the interior patio, watching the parrot in its cage as it ate, and then, bored, slipped back to his room for a nap. He engaged in an indolent existence punctuated by the most expensive treats and drinks he could find in town. When Martín awoke, he pawed around his bed for his pack of cigarettes and remembered Casiopea was supposed to bring them back. He cursed under his breath, because she had not bothered to hand them to him yet.

He waited for her in front of Grandfather's room until she came out, newspaper tucked under her arm. She saw him as soon as she stepped into the hallway and looked at him with very dark, very dismissive eyes.

"Wherever have you been? I told you to fetch me cigarettes and you never came back."

"I was doing my chores, Martín. Bringing the beef to the cook."

"What about me?" he asked.

"I thought the most important thing was to get the meat for Grandfather's supper."

"Oh, and what, *I'm* not important?"

"Martín," she said and reached into her skirt's pocket and held out the cigarettes for him. "Here."

This, like many of her gestures, was dismissive. Not that she had said anything particularly bad. It was her tone of voice, the movement of her head, even the way she breathed. Quiet and defiant at the same time, driving him to irritation. He thought she plotted against him, or she would if she could.

Martín snatched the pack of cigarettes. The girl walked away, and once she was out of sight he forgot he'd been angry at her, although she quickly got on his bad side again with her impertinence about the boots. Was it so difficult to simply do as he asked without a complaint or curt look?

Of course he tattled on her, told Grandfather Casiopea was being disrespectful again, and after that was accomplished he went in search of entertainment, as if to reward himself. There was a single, lackluster cantina in town. He did not frequent it because it was unseemly for the grandson of the most important man in Uukumil to show his face there. Instead, he socialized with what passed as the cream of the crop of their town. The pharmacist and the notary public, who also served as the haberdasher, organized games of dominoes at their homes on certain nights of the week, but Martín was often bored when he attended these gatherings. Casiopea could play both chess and checkers, but she was better than him at these pursuits, and since he did not like to be beaten by anyone, especially a girl, he did not deign to play with her.

He made up his mind and walked to the pharmacist's home. With mechanical rigidity he sat around the table with the other men, watching as one of them emptied the box with the game pieces.

Rather than being upset at the monotony of this game, he was soothed by the familiar faces and rituals. Unlike Casiopea, who had grown disenchanted with the town, with the sameness of expressions, he was comforted by its familiarity.

By the time Martín went back home and saw Casiopea walk across the interior patio, headed for bed, no doubt, he was in a hazy, pleasant state of mind, and being the kind of drunk who naturally engages in multiple apologies when inebriation erodes his defenses, he spoke to her.

"Casiopea," he said.

She raised her head. She didn't look at him with a question in her eyes, like others might, but stared at him instead.

When he'd been a boy Martín had feared the monster that dwelled under his bed, pulling his covers up to his chin to stay safe. Martín had the nagging suspicion that as a child his cousin had feared nothing, and that she feared nothing now. He thought this was unnatural, especially for a girl.

"Casiopea, I know the old man is punishing you, and I have to say it's a raw deal. Do you want me to ask him to let you come with us tomorrow?" he asked.

"I don't want anything from you," she spat back.

Martín was incensed. Casiopea loved to push against him, to disobey him, to speak in that insolent tone of hers. How could he be kind when she was this willful? It had been wrong to even consider extending her this courtesy.

"Very well," he told her. "I hope you enjoy your chores."

He left her with that. He did not consider that his attempt at an apology had been insufficient, nor that Casiopea had a reason to be curt with him. He simply catalogued this conversation as another mark against his cousin's character and went to bed without regrets. If she wanted to martyr herself while the rest of the household enjoyed a day of merriment, let her be.

Chapter 4

It was T'hó before the Spaniards stumbled upon the city—once glorious, then ruined, as all earthly things must be ruined—and named it Mérida. The vast sisal plantations made the hacendados rich, and great houses rose to mark the size of their owners' fortunes, replacing mud-splattered streets with macadam and public lighting. The upper-class citizens of Mérida claimed the city was as fine as Paris and patterned Paseo Montejo after the Champs-Élysées. Since Europe was considered the cradle of sophistication, the best clothing stores in Mérida sold French fashions and British boots, and ladies said words like *charmant* to demonstrate the quality of their imported tutors. Italian architects were hired to erect the abodes of the wealthy. Parisian milliners and dressmakers made the rounds of the city once a year to promote the latest styles.

Despite the revolution, the "divine caste" endured. Perhaps no more Yaquis were being deported from Sonora, forced to work the sisal fields; perhaps no more Korean workers were lured with promises of fast profits and ended as indentured servants; perhaps the price of henequen had fallen, and perhaps the machinery had gone silent at many plantations, but money never leaves the grasp of the rich easily. Fortunes shifted, and several of the prominent Porfirian families had married into up-and-coming dynasties; others had to make do with slightly less. Mérida was changing, but Mérida was still a city where the moneyed, pale, upper-crust citizens dined on delicacies, and the poor went hungry. At the same time, a country in flux is a country padded with opportunities.

Casiopea tried to remind herself of this, that here was her chance to see the city of Mérida. Not under the circumstances she had imagined, but a chance nevertheless.

Mérida was busy, its streets bustling with people. Everyone walked quickly. She had little time to take in the dignified buildings. It was all a blur of color and noise, and sometimes clashing styles, which testified to the tastes of the *nouveau riche* who had built the city: Moorish, Spanish, quasi-rococo. She wished to grip the god's hand and ask him to pause to look at the black automobiles parked in a neat row, but did not dare.

They passed the city hall, with its clock tower. They crossed the town square that served as the beating heart of Mérida. They went around the cathedral, which had been built using stones from Mayan temples. She wondered if Hun-Kamé would be displeased by the sight of the building, but he did not even glance at it, and soon they were walking down side streets, farther from the crowds and the noise, leaving downtown behind.

Hun-Kamé stopped before a two-story building, painted green, restrained and proper in its appearance. Above its heavy wooden door there was a stone carving, a hunter with a bow aiming at the heavens.

"Where are we?" she asked, feeling out of breath. Her feet hurt and her forehead was beaded with sweat. They had not eaten nor traded words during their trip. She was more exhausted than alarmed at this point.

"Loray's home. He is a foreigner, a demon, and thus may prove useful."

"A demon?" she said, adjusting her shawl. It was filthy with the dust from the road. "Is it safe to see him?"

"As I said, he is a foreigner and so he acts as a neutral party. He will not have any allegiance to my brother," he replied.

"Are you certain he is home? Perhaps we ought to return later."

Hun-Kamé placed a hand against the door, and it opened. "We enter now."

Casiopea did not move. He walked ahead a few paces and, noticing she was not following him, turned his head.

"Do not sell him your soul and you'll be fine," he said laconically.

"That sounds simple," she replied, with a tad of a bite to the words.

"It is," he said, either not registering the sarcasm in her voice or not caring.

Casiopea took a deep breath and stepped inside.

They went down a wide hallway, the floor decorated with orange Ticul stone, the walls painted yellow. It led into a courtyard, a vine-entangled tree rising in a corner and a fountain gurgling at its side. They walked into a vast living room. White couches, black lacquered furniture. Two floor-to-ceiling mirrors with ebony frames. White flowers upon a low table. The only word to describe the room was *opulent*, though it was not like her grandfather's home. She thought it bolder, minimalist.

A man sat on one of the couches. He wore a gray suit and gray tie, with a jade lapel pin for a note of color. His face was finely chiseled and he had a gallant, youthful appearance—one could not guess him more than thirty-two, thirty-three—though the eyes dispelled that impression. His eyes were much older, an impossible shade of green. On his right shoulder there sat a raven, preening itself. She knew the bird and man to be supernatural, similar to the god she traveled with and yet of a different vintage.

The green-eyed man smirked and threw his head back, staring at the ceiling.

"How is it that you are here? There are wards on the doors and windows," the man said.

"Neither locks, nor wards, can keep a Lord of Xibalba out. Death enters all dwellings."

"Death has no manners. I thought your brother banished you."

"Imprisoned me," Hun-Kamé said in a monotone. "It was unpleasant."

"Oh, well, you are free now. And dragging a soiled parcel, I see. That girl is more dust and grime than girl."

The green-eyed man looked at her, his arm draped over the back of the couch. Casiopea felt her face grow hot with mortification, but she did not reply. She'd heard worse insults.

"Loray, Marquess of Arrows, I present the Lady Tun," Hun-Kamé said with a motion of his hand.

The use of the word "lady" surprised her. Casiopea stared at Hun-Kamé, not knowing why he'd called her that. For a moment she felt like folding against herself, like a fan.

The demon smiled at this, and then Casiopea straightened herself and looked him in the face. Martín had told her she was haughty. She saw no reason to attempt modesty at this point. She sensed that would have been the wrong choice with Loray.

"A pleasure to meet you," she said, extending a hand to him.

Loray stood up and shook it, despite her dirty and sweaty palms. "I am delighted to meet the lady. Delighted to see you again, too, Hun-Kamé. Sit, please, both you and your companion."

They did. Casiopea was grateful for the respite. She wanted to take off her huaraches and rub her feet: she had a blister on her toe. Her hair, under the shawl, was in disarray.

"I suppose you aren't here for wine and a cheese platter, although, should you fancy that, there are always drinks in this household. What do you need from me?" the demon asked, sitting down and stretching his legs.

"I am missing certain elements of myself and must retrieve them. You know my brother and have traded with him. Perhaps in your dealings he has revealed a secret or two. Or else you've dug those secrets out from other parties, as you are wont to do."

"Dear Hun-Kamé, you might have forgotten this detail, being absent for as long as you've been: I am but a demon and do not trade with your brother," Loray said, pressing a hand against his heart theatrically.

"You trade with everyone."

"Everyone," the raven repeated, hopping down to rest at Loray's side. The demon tipped his head, glancing at the bird.

"I speak with everyone. It's not the same at all."

"Spare me the intricate definitions you apply to yourself," Hun-Kamé said. "You survive by selling secrets. Sell me one. Or are you going to disappoint me and tell me you've lost your touch?"

"Lost his touch," the raven agreed and flew off to the other end of the room, sitting on top of a sleek white liquor cabinet.

Loray raised an eyebrow at that and chuckled, pausing to give the bird an irritated look. "Well. You might be disappointed to hear I know where only one of your missing body parts lies, Hun-Kamé."

Loray rose and poured himself a glass of a dark liquor he took from the white cabinet. Technically Yucatán was one of the few "dry" states in the country, but the application of the law was haphazard, and it was no surprise a fancy house like Loray's came equipped with plenty of booze.

"Are you thirsty?" he asked.

She shook her head no. Hun-Kamé also rejected the drink. The demon shrugged and sat down again, the glass in his left hand.

"I know where you can find your missing ear, but that is all. The issue, however, is the price of my assistance, and the matter of your brother's wrath if he hears I have helped you."

"As if you feared the gods or the night, archer," Hun-Kamé replied. "But name your price."

"Archer. How formal we've become. Well, as you know, I am restricted in my movements, bound to this city. A ridiculous spell someone set on me," Loray said.

"By your own doing. If you didn't want to be here, you shouldn't have followed those Frenchmen into their petty war of conquest."

"The mistakes of my youth! It takes a century or two to learn better. Give me leave to travel this land. Open the Black Road of Xibalba so that I may walk it."

"Open," the raven repeated, imitating his master.

Hun-Kamé looked at the demon. His angular face had a fixedness to it that was unpleasant, but then he tipped his head, a slight nod.

"When I regain my throne, you may walk the roads of Xibalba, beneath the earth, but Middleworld is not my domain," the god reminded him.

"That will be sufficient, since from Xibalba I may find my way back to Middleworld easily enough," the demon replied. "I will tell you who has your ear, but you may not like the answer. It is with the Mamlab, unfortunately, and you know what that entails, gentle rain or hard thunder, who can say. I despise weather gods. They are too moody."

Loray downed his drink, his eyes resting on Hun-Kamé. Whether he expected Hun-Kamé to be disappointed or pleased with the answer, she did not know, but she did note that the god's expression was leaden. He revealed nothing.

"Do you know where he is now?"

"Which one?"

"The youngest, for it could be none other than him. Speak, then. Where?"

"You are correct, it is the youngest. And I thought your brother was the diviner!"

"Marquess, vanish your mirth," Hun-Kamé said, his voice clipped.

Loray sighed. "Precisely? It is hard to tell. Again, that is the problem with weather gods. But it is almost time for Carnival and I wager he will be in Veracruz. You'll have to take a ship from Progreso to get there, but these days there are many vessels moving in and out of that port, so it should not be a problem. I can arrange your passage if you wish," the demon said, polite as polite could be. "You might even be able to leave by tomorrow. It'll give you a chance to rest."

Rest, yes. Whether it was the trip, the shock of walking next to a god, or the bone shard in her hand, Casiopea felt the desperate need to curl up in bed and sleep.

"Come. You'll like the guest rooms," Loray said, guiding them through his house.

Loray was right. Her room was large and airy, with plenty of light filtering in. But she did not pause to look around much, instead falling upon the bed and sleeping as soon as her head touched the pillow.

When Casiopea woke it was to the smell of coffee. Tentatively she opened her eyes and stared at the fine, high ceiling, then lifted herself up, leaning on her elbows.

"Good morning, miss," a maid said.

"Good morning," Casiopea repeated.

The maid handed her a tray and cutlery. Casiopea, who until this point was used to serving others, regarded the breakfast with wary eyes.

"Mr. Loray has asked several employees from the Parisian to stop by this morning."

"What is that?" she asked.

The maid frowned. "It is a shop. They are bringing dresses for you. You'll have to take a bath."

Casiopea ate the breakfast, hardly chewing. The maid hurried her, saying the dressmakers would arrive any minute now. She was essentially shoved into the bathroom. It was very different from the simple shower she was used to. It had a big bathtub with iron-clawed feet and on shelves there sat dozens of bottles with expensive oils and perfumes.

She filled the tub to the brim and proceeded to pour from a few of the bottles of oils. Roses and lilacs and other sweet-smelling things. At home, she would clean her neck and face in the water basin each morning and was allowed a shower on Sundays, before church. Grandfather said they should not use the hot water, that a good cold shower was what young people needed to keep their heads clear of noxious ideas. Casiopea made sure to leave the hot tap open until the bathroom was clouded with steam. Then she slid into the tub so that the water reached her chin. She had a knack for quiet insurrection.

Once she was done washing away the grime of the road, the water in the tub rendered murky, she splashed out and wrapped herself in a huge towel. She wrung out and combed her hair. When she stepped out of the bathroom, she found an extensive number of boxes were scattered around her room, from which three women were pulling dresses, skirts, and undergarments. The women spoke about Casiopea in a direct, unflattering fashion. They knew her, at a glance, a country girl and judged her for it.

"You'd think she'd never worn a corselet," one woman said.

"Or garters," another replied.

"Or even stockings. She has a peasant's legs, quite bare, but at least that means there's little to shave," a third concluded.

"What is there to shave?" Casiopea asked, but her question was not answered, and instead the women demonstrated the proper wearing of hosiery and kept talking as if she were not there, or worse, as if she were a doll they were dressing.

The women handed her item after item and asked what she thought. Casiopea, who owned one good dress for church, had a hard time making an assessment, and several times the women chuckled at her stammered answers. She ended up donning an ivory dress with a bright green contrasting sash, so light it frightened her, the hem shorter than anything she'd ever worn. It hit her mid-calf. Grandfather thought the ankle was the proper length for a skirt, but these women insisted this was the fashion.

It looked like the things girls wore in magazines. Reckless, as was this whole voyage.

Charmeuse, voile, gingham in bold colors were heaped on the bed as the maid began to fold the items Casiopea had picked, or at least acquiesced to, placing them in a suitcase. Another maid walked in and said Loray wanted to speak to her.

Casiopea went back to the living room, glad that she did not have to stare at silk brassieres with side laces any longer. The demon smiled as soon as he saw her and, walking toward her, lifted her hand. His raven was not at his shoulder this time; it rested on the back of a chair, cocking its head at them.

"There you are and looking well."

She nodded, unsure of his intent. He held her hand and kissed it, like gentlemen used to do in the old days. He clasped her hand between his.

"You must forgive me for what I said before. I was rude to you. It is a fault of mine, I can be boorish."

"It's fine. Although I wonder why you've bothered giving me nice clothes," she replied, pulling away from his grasp and lightly tugging at the sash adorning her hips. It felt so odd to be attired like this, and she wondered how much he'd spent on her.

"I thought you could use a change of outfit, and I was correct," Loray said, appraising the girl with a smile. "Besides, it might help us become better friends."

He was trying to charm her, but Casiopea was not used to being charmed. The village boys scarcely paid attention to her. Had she been a common servant they might have wooed her and stolen kisses, but since she was a member of the Leyva family, however nominally, they did not dare. She had little practice in this arena.

For this reason, rather than blushing or lowering her lashes, she replied with earnest vehemence.

"Somehow I don't think demons and gods have many friends," she said.

"You are correct. But I'm willing to make an exception for you, seeing as I have a soft spot for mythmaking. Do you understand the journey you are about to embark on?"

"I know I have to help Hun-Kamé if I am to help myself."

"Of course, but do you understand what is at stake?" he asked.

She had no idea. A somnambulist, she was placing one foot in front of the other and following whatever path Hun-Kamé traced. It was not a lack of initiative on her behalf: she was utterly confused, unsure any of what was happening was quite real, and reacted based on instinct. She was, however, curious.

"Tell me," she said, knowing a story lay ahead, as fine as any of the legends and tall tales her father had spun for her.

"Thousands upon thousands of years ago a stone fell upon the earth. It cracked the land, left a scar. And when an event of such intensity takes place, something remains," Loray told her, and seemed pleased in the telling. "Power, embedded in the peninsula, radiating from it. There is much magic here. In other parts of the world the ancient gods have gone to sleep, for although gods do not die, they must slumber when their devoted cease in their prayers and offerings.

"But here the gods still walk in Yucatán. They can move deep into the jungles, into the isthmus, or they can wander farther north, where the rattlesnakes curl in the desert, though the farther they walk from the place of their birth, the weaker they become. Yucatán is a well of power, and the Supreme Lord of Xibalba can tap into that power."

"Power," the raven said.

Loray raised his hand. The raven flew across the room to rest upon his wrist and the demon stroked its feathers.

"Through a series of unfortunate events I've found myself chained to this city and wish to escape it. If I can descend into Xibalba, I could transcend the bonds that hold me here . . . tunnel my way out, so to speak. But I can't walk around Xibalba without permission."

"Which Hun-Kamé will grant you," she said.

"It is a gamble, of course. Hun-Kamé may fail, and if he does, I will find myself in trouble. His brother is harsh."

Again here was a detail Casiopea had not considered, what it might mean to defy a god. She had followed Hun-Kamé because she thought it necessary, but a desire for freedom—even a "peasant" who has never owned a pair of garters can sense the call for adventure—had also pushed her forward, making her ignore the dangers she might face. Now that Loray spoke, it was obvious there was much to worry about. It was not only the words the demon said, but the way he said them, quietly, and she noticed that at no point had he spoken the name of Hun-Kamé's rival.

Vucub-Kamé, she thought, and held the name in her mouth.

"I want insurance. That same insurance would prove beneficial to you," Loray said.

"I don't understand," she replied.

"Inside you there is a strange thing, is there not? A piece of him, the seal of the underworld upon you."

"A bone shard."

She opened her hand and looked at her fingers. Whether Hun-Kamé had volunteered this information or Loray had found out by some other means she could not know.

"The Lords of the Underworld cannot walk Middleworld freely. They must use messengers to speak with mortals or else manifest during the nights, and then only for the briefest of periods. A single hour."

"But we traveled in the daytime."

"Because Hun-Kamé is not entirely a god. Because your human blood mixes with his immortal essence, cloaking him from the sun. It nourishes him too. Without it he would be lost, weakened as he is."

She closed her hand into a fist and felt the shard there. It was like a living thing, hidden beneath the murmur of her blood.

"He said it would kill me, the bone shard."

"It will. If it is not removed. But of course he cannot remove it, nor would he wish to in his state. And yet he must. The more life he absorbs from you, the more human he must become. It is a bad bargain for both of you, but there is no other way," Loray said, his face serious.

The raven nodded his head, as if emphasizing this point.

"Yet this bargain may also be our salvation, if the tide turns and Hun-Kamé fails in his quest." A smile formed on his lips.

"What do you mean?" she asked.

"Should he be unable to recover his missing elements, should his brother catch up with you and the situation be dire, cut your hand," Loray said simply.

"What?"

He made a motion, as if he were holding a machete and slicing off his own arm.

"Cut it. It will sever the link to Hun-Kamé."

"How will that solve anything?"

"It will help us. He will be thoroughly weakened."

How easily he said "us," as if they were old acquaintances. Any mortal would have been dazzled by the demon's voice, the smile, his looks. Casiopea had enough common sense to be wary. Life had taught her to be untrusting. Dreamers and romantics like her father did not fare well, and though she had dreamed in Uukumil, she'd done so quietly, in secret. If someone chanced by, she closed the book she was looking at. She hid desires inside an old tin can. She never told anyone what she hoped for.

"The reigning Lord of Xibalba will look kindly at the woman who helped defeat his brother," Loray said.

"And I will be without a hand," she replied.

"Sacrifices have to be made at times. If it comes to it, cut your hand, not a big deal."

"And injure him."

"That is the point."

"Why aren't you trying to cut my hand?" she asked.

Bold, the question. She grew brazen, and quickly.

"Dear girl, if I pressed a blade against your skin, it would accomplish nothing. You'd be right as rain in a heartbeat," he said, brushing past her, brushing her arm for a second, as if to emphasize his point. "No enemy can wound you, nor coerce you into wounding yourself, not when a Lord of Xibalba walks beside you. Not even one who has lost his throne. It must be by your hand and your hand alone. Free will."

"Nothing of this makes sense."

"Only know this final option is available to you. It might save you, and me," he said.

There was amusement in the demon's face, as if he enjoyed speaking these words. Under his politeness she detected a quiet malice.

"Vucub-Kamé would forgive you if you tell him you advised me to do this?"

She said the name to test his boundaries, since Loray was afraid of uttering it. And when she said it the demon did not seem amused.

"Perhaps," he muttered.

"What if I cut my hand right this instant?"

"Too soon. Hun-Kamé might win his throne back." He stood before the white liquor cabinet, throwing it open, and looked over his shoulder at her. "Besides, you have an unfortunately brave and kind heart."

"How do you know what heart I have?"

"You'd make a poor card player, dear. Can't hide yourself."

She did not understand what he meant; it was her cousin who played games of chance, not her, although here now she'd stepped into a rather intricate game.

Loray poured himself a drink, and as he raised it to his lips Hun-Kamé walked into the living room in a white linen suit, a smart straw hat in his hands and a black handkerchief knotted around his neck. Again it was difficult to perceive the lack of an eye, the ear. Yet it was not as if he concealed himself. He was much too striking. Preternatural beauty; it made Casiopea dip her head and look down for a heartbeat.

"Good day," Loray said, his voice cheerful. His raven had migrated again to his shoulder.

"Good day," the raven said, echoing the greeting.

"I trust you obtained passage for us, Marquess," Hun-Kamé said. "I do not wish to dally."

Businesslike and to the point, but polite. Grandfather yelled, stamped his cane against the floor to make himself heard. Martín threatened her into obedience. This type of authority was alien to Casiopea.

"Would I fail you in this matter?" Loray said, sounding a tad annoyed. "There is a vessel departing from Progreso this evening. It is fast. You'll reach Veracruz in a couple of days."

"My tracks must remain hidden."

"I will do what I can, but your brother has his ways. He may already be looking for you," Loray warned him.

"I wove an illusion. It will conceal my escape, for a while."

There was gravity to their exchange, but the demon punctured it by holding up his glass.

"Good! Drink with me. I won't have you say I am not hospitable. We must toast. Our fortunes will soon change, and let's hope for the better."

"I will drink with you once I have recouped my throne."

The answer was not what the demon had expected, but the god softened it somewhat. "The clothing you've provided is a thoughtful detail," Hun-Kamé added. An oblique way of saying thanks.

"I thought you might like it. New fashions. The top hat is gone and not a moment too soon. You might find the music amusing. The dances are livelier. The old century was too prim."

"What do I care which dances the mortals dance?" Hun-Kamé said.

"Don't be dull. You'll scare the lady away," Loray told him.

Again there was that slight glint of malice in the demon's face. He filled a second glass and handed it to her, leaning down and whispering so lightly she might have imagined his voice in her ear.

"Remember what I told you," he said. "If you should be on the losing side, there may be a chance to side with the victor. Whoever that may be."

Then he clinked his glass against hers, a smile across his face. Casiopea took a sip.

Chapter 5

Nine levels separate Xibalba from Middleworld. Although the roots of the World Tree extend from the depths of the Underworld up to the heavens, connecting all planes of existence, Xibalba's location means news does not travel fast in this kingdom. It is therefore hardly surprising that Vucub-Kamé, sitting on his fearsome obsidian throne, set upon a carpet of bones, was not immediately aware of his brother's escape from his prison.

And yet, even at such distance, a warning echoed in Vucub-Kamé's chamber. He thought he heard a note, muffled, like a flute being blown; it sounded once and he dismissed it, but the second time he could not.

"Who speaks my name?" he said. He felt it, like a volute of smoke brushing against his ear, a white flower in the dark.

The god raised his head.

His court was as it always was, busy and loud. His brothers—there were ten of them, five sets of twins—reclined on cushions and ocelot pelts. They were not alone. The noble dead who went to their graves with treasures and proper offerings, who were buried in their finery and jewels, were allowed safe passage down the Black Road and a place in the Black City of Xibalba (sometimes, for their amusement, the Lords of Xibalba had turned back or tricked these noblemen, instead picking a common peasant to join them, but not often). Thus, courtiers milled about, their bodies painted with black, blue, or red patterns. Women wearing dresses with so many jade incrustations it was difficult for them to walk whispered to one another while their servants fanned them. Priestesses and priests in their long robes talked to scholars, while warriors watched the jesters cavort.

Xibalba can be a frightful place, with its House of Knives and its House of Bats and many strange sights, but the court of the Lords of Death also possessed the allure of shadows and the glimmer of obsidian, for there is as much beauty as there is terror in the night. Mortals have always been frightened of the night's velvet embrace and the creatures that walk in it, and yet they find themselves mesmerized by it. Since all gods are born from the kernel of mortal hearts, it is no wonder Xibalba reflected this duality.

Duality, of course, was the trademark of the kingdom. Vucub-Kamé's brothers were twins: they complemented each other. Xiquiripat and Cuchumaquic caused men to shed their blood and dressed in crimson, Chamiabac and Chamiaholom carried bone staffs that forced people to waste away. And so on and so forth.

Vucub-Kamé and Hun-Kamé had walked side by side, like the other gods did, both of them ruling together, even if, unfairly, Hun-Kamé was the most senior of all the Lords of Xibalba and ultimately Vucub-Kamé did his will.

They were alike and yet they were not, and this is what had driven Vucub-Kamé into bitterness and strife. Spiritually, he was a selfish creature, prone to nursing grievances. Physically, he was tall and slim and his skin was a deep shade of brown. His eyelids were heavy, his nose hooked. He was beautiful, as was his twin brother. But while Hun-Kamé's hair was black as ink, Vucub-Kamé's hair was the color of corn silk, so pale it was almost white. He wore headdresses made from the green feathers of the quetzal and lavish cloaks made from the pelts of jaguars or other, more fabulous animals. His tunic was white, a red sash decorated with white seashells around his waist. On his chest and wrists there hung many pieces of jade, and on his feet were soft sandals. On occasion he wore a jade mask, but now his face lay bare.

When he rose from his throne, as he did that day, and raised his hand, the bracelets on his wrist clinked together making a sharp sound. His brothers turned their heads toward him, and so did his other courtiers. The Supreme Lord of Xibalba was suddenly displeased.

"All of you, be silent," he said, and the courtiers were obediently silent.

Vucub-Kamé summoned one of his four owls.

It was a great winged thing, made of smoke and shadows, and it landed by Vucub-Kamé's throne, where the lord whispered a word to it. Then it flew away and, flapping its fierce wings, it soared through the many layers of the Underworld until it reached the house of Cirilo Leyva. It flew into Cirilo's room and stared at the black chest sitting in his room. The owl could see through stone and wood. As it cocked its head it confirmed that the bones of Hun-Kamé rested inside the chest; then it flew back to its master's side to inform him of this.

Vucub-Kamé was therefore assuaged. Yet his peace of mind did not last. He played the game of bul, with its dice painted black on one side and yellow on the other, but this sport did not bring him joy. He drank from a jeweled cup, but the balché tasted sour. He listened to his courtiers as they played the rattles and the drums, but the rhythm was wrong.

Vucub-Kamé decided he must look at the chest himself. It was night in the land of mortals, and he was able to ascend to the home of Cirilo Leyva. Cirilo, who had been in bed, asleep already, woke up, the chill of the death god making him snap his eyes open.

"Lord," the old man said.

"You'll welcome me properly, I hope," Vucub-Kamé said.

"Yes, yes. Most gracious Lord, I am humbled by this visit," the man said, his throat dry. "I'll burn a candle for you—no, two. I'll do it."

The old man, diligent, struck a match to ensure two candles burned bright by his bed. The god could see in the darkness, he could make out each wrinkle wrecking Cirilo's face; the candles were a formality, a symbol. Besides, Vucub-Kamé, like his brothers, enjoyed the flattery of mortals, their absolute abeyance.

"Had I known the Great Lord was coming I would have prepared to better receive him, although my hospitality could never be sufficient to satisfy the tastes of such an exalted guest," Cirilo said. "Should I pierce my tongue and draw blood from it to demonstrate my devotion?"

"Your blood is sickly and thin," Vucub-Kamé said, giving Cirilo a dismissive glance. This man had been as strong as an ox before he morphed into this distended bag of bones.

"Of course. But I can have a rooster killed, a horse. My grandson has a fine stallion—"

"Hush. I forgot how dull you are," Vucub-Kamé said.

He raised his lofty hand, quieting the man, his eyes on the black chest. It looked unchanged, just as the god had left it. He could detect no disturbance.

"It is not a trivial visit that I perform. I have come to gaze at the bones of my brother," the god said. "Open the chest."

"But Lord, you told me the chest must not be opened."

This simple sentence, which truly did not hint at defiance, was enough to make the death lord's serious face turn indignant. The mortal man noticed the change, and although Cirilo was old and pained by his age, he managed to turn the key to the chest and open it with an amazing alacrity.

The chest was empty, not a single bone left behind. Vucub-Kamé realized his sorcerous brother had crafted an illusion to make it seem like he was contained inside his prison. He also realized the portent had come to pass.

Vucub-Kamé, who had the power of foresight, had glimpsed this event, the predetermined disappearance of his brother. It was predetermined because fate had placed its seal upon him, ensuring in one way or another Hun-Kamé would be set free. Fate is a force more powerful than gods, a fact they resent, since mortals are often given more leeway and may be able to navigate its current.

Fate had therefore decreed Hun-Kamé would be set free one day, although it had not marked the day. Vucub-Kamé had prepared for this. That does not mean he would not have wished for more time to face his troublesome brother. Nor does it mean he was not upset.

"Oh, Lord, I do not understand," Cirilo began, meaning to adopt the pose of the supplicant. He was not proud when it came to the matter of keeping his limbs attached to his body.

"Silence," Vucub-Kamé said, and the old man shut his mouth and remained still.

Vucub-Kamé stood in front of the chest and stared at it. It was made of iron and wood; Xibalbans have no love of iron. Like the axe that had cut off Hun-Kamé's head, this item had been crafted by mortal hands, which would have no problem grasping the metal.

"Tell me, what happened here?" Vucub-Kamé said, commanding the chest.

The chest groaned, the wood stretching and rumbling. It vibrated like the skin of a taut drum, and it had a voice. "Lord, a woman, she opened the chest and placed her hand upon the bones. A bone shard went into her thumb, reviving Hun-Kamé, and together they have escaped," it said in a deep voice.

"Where to?"

"T'hó, to the White City."

"And who was this woman?"

"Casiopea Tun, granddaughter to your servant."

Vucub-Kamé turned his eyes toward Cirilo, who had begun to shake all over.

"Your granddaughter," Vucub-Kamé said.

"I did not know. I swear, oh, Lord. That silly girl, we thought she ran off with some no-good fool, like her mother did. Good riddance, we thought, the stupid tart and—"

Vucub-Kamé looked at his hands, at his palms, which were dark, blackened by burn marks. He had suffered and labored for this throne. His brother could not have it.

"I want her found. Fetch her for me," he ordered.

"Lord, I would, but I do not know how. I am feeble. I have grown old," Cirilo said, grasping the mattress and attempting to lift himself back to his feet, making more of a show of his frailty than he should, for he had no intention of leaving his home to look for anybody.

The death lord beheld the wrinkled man with disdain. How brief were the life of mortals! Of course the old man could not chase after the girl.

"Let me think, let me think. Yes . . . I have a grandson, lord. He is young and strong, and besides, he knows Casiopea well. He can recognize her and he can bring her to you," Cirilo suggested after he managed to stand and find his cane, pretending that this had not been his first thought.

"I would speak to him."

"I will fetch him promptly."

Cirilo went in search of his grandson, leaving the god to contemplate the room. Vucub-Kamé ran a hand across the lid of the chest, feeling the absence of his brother like a palpable thing. The girl had left no imprint, he could not picture her, but he could imagine Hun-

Kamé reconstituted, in a dark suit, the kind mortals wore, traversing the country.

The old man waddled back in. He had with him a young man who looked like Cirilo had once been, his face vigorous.

"This is my grandson, my lord. This is Martín," Cirilo said. "I have tried to explain to him who you are and what you need of him."

The god turned toward the young man. Vucub-Kamé's eyes were as pale as his hair, paler, the color of incense as it rises through the air. Impossible eyes that gave the young man pause, forcing him to look down at the floor.

"My brother and your cousin seek to do me wrong. You will find the girl and we will put a stop to them," the god said. "I know where they will be headed, as they will no doubt try to retrieve certain items I've left in safekeeping."

"I want to assist, but your brother . . . sir, he is a god . . . and I am a man," Martín said. "How would I accomplish such a thing?"

He realized the boy was unschooled in magic, unschooled in everything. Raw like an unpolished gemstone. This might have been a source of irritation, but then Cirilo had been much the same and had played his role.

Besides, he could taste the mordant laughter of fate in this affair. That it should be Cirilo's granddaughter who would assist his brother and in turn it should be the grandson who would assist Vucub-Kamé. Folktales are full of such coincidences that are never coincidences at all, but the brittle games of powerful forces.

Vucub-Kamé shook his hand dismissively. "You will be my envoy and I shall endeavor to assist you in your journey. You need not do anything too onerous, merely convince her to meet with me."

"That is all?" Martín asked.

"Take this."

Vucub-Kamé slid a heavy jade ring from his middle finger and held it up, offering it to the mortal man. Martín hesitated, but he took the ring, turning it between his fingers. Skulls were engraved all around its circumference.

"Wear this at all times, and when you wish to summon me, say my name. But I will come to you only after the sun has set, and you must not call on me for foolish matters. You will find the girl and convince her to meet with me. Take care that my brother does not discover you are around."

"Your brother will not suspect I am following him?"

"Let us hope not. I will arrange for transportation for you; await my word."

Cirilo had begun to speak, but Vucub-Kamé shushed him. He stood directly in front of the young man and read in his eyes fear and pride and many wasted human emotions, but he focused on his hunger, which was considerable.

"I raised your family to wealth after your grandfather assisted me. Do this properly and you will not only continue to enjoy a privileged position, but I shall raise *you* very high, higher even than your grandfather was ever raised," he said.

The young man had the good sense to nod, but he did not speak.

"Fail and I will shatter you like pottery against the pavement," the god concluded.

Again, the young man nodded.

Vucub-Kamé then descended back to his realm quick as the wind, having said all the words he wished to say. Middleworld had chafed Vucub-Kamé that night, the mockery of the empty chest, the missing bones, rubbing the god raw.

Alone, in his chambers, the god drew a magic symbol upon a wall and the wall opened, allowing him to enter a secret room. It was pitch-black in the room, but Vucub-Kamé said a word and torches on the walls sputtered into life.

Upon a stone slab there lay a bundle of black cloth, fringed with yellow geometric patterns. Vucub-Kamé slowly extended a hand and pulled away the cloth to reveal the iron axe he had swung years before, severing his brother's head. Symbols of power adorned the blade and the handle. He had entrusted a mortal sorcerer, Aníbal Zavala, to have it forged, because no artisan of Xibalba could produce such a thing. Their weapons were of obsidian and jadeite. Iron came from far away: it was the metal of the foreigners. And it could pierce the body of a god like the strong jadeite blade could not.

Wielding such a weapon, made of noxious iron and tattooed with powerful magic, had burnt Vucub-Kamé's palms, left him with scars, but it was a small price to pay for a kingdom. Now he contemplated the weapon, which he'd not seen in many years, and bent down, passing his hand over it without touching it. He felt the threads of power embedded in it, like static electricity, and pulled his fingers back.

Yes, its magic and its blade were sharp. It would allow him to succeed a second time.

Vucub-Kamé had been smart, he had scattered his brother's organs across the land. He'd also built something. Far in the north, in Baja California, there awaited a tomb fit for a god.

Gods may not be killed, but Vucub-Kamé had found a way, just as he had found a way to imprison his brother in the first place, a feat that few would have ever dared to contemplate.

Chapter 6

Progreso's lofty name did not initially match the nature of the port city, north of Mérida. It had started as a quiet town with houses made of mud and stone, and roofs of palm tree fronds. But then the government sketched a railroad between Mérida and Progreso, a telegraph line was installed, and a new pier was built. It became the chief point through which henequen moved out of the peninsula. The new Progreso sported a municipal building with marble stairs, and all kinds of ships streamed in and out, full of cargo. This meant there were plenty of ships willing to take two passengers who found themselves in need of transportation, and plenty of captains who did not care to ask why they needed such speedy service.

Loray had obtained for them passage on a fast, reliable vessel that was headed to Veracruz, carrying mostly bales of henequen. Casiopea and Hun-Kamé were to share a stateroom with two berths. The beds had clean, crisp sheets, but aside from a washstand, a chair, and a mirror, there was nothing more to say about their accommodation. The ship had no smoking room, no lounge. It was a bare-bones operation.

"We'll be rather crammed in here," she mused.

"We will look for proper lodging in Veracruz," he replied, sliding his suitcase under one of the beds, strapping it in place.

"But you and I . . . a man and a woman," she said, a reflex. The teachings of the priest, her mother, grandfather, repeated without thought. Bad, bad, bad. Immoral, really, to be alone with him behind closed doors.

"I'm not a man," he said simply and sat in the one chair. It had a wicker back and seemed rather comfortable. He set his hands upon its arms in a kingly gesture that was as reflexive as her own. He was used to sitting in a throne.

She looked at him and thought it was easy enough to say the words, but he *looked* like a man. And should anyone ask, what should she say? No, he is a *god*, you see. No sin there, despite how beautiful he may be.

If sins were about to be tallied, Casiopea realized she might be in trouble. At this point she'd probably have to pray about five hundred rosaries. Running away from home, talking to a demon, seeing a man naked . . . best not to dwell too much on this.

Casiopea set down her suitcase and placed it next to his own.

To keep herself from recalling the town priest's angry face, she sat on the bed and began peeling an orange. She'd bought a bag of them when they were walking around the port as a precaution. She did not know what kind of meals they'd be served or at what time of the day.

"Do you want one?" she asked Hun-Kamé. "Or do you not eat?"

"I don't need to eat this kind of food in Xibalba, but I am not quite my old self at this moment," he replied.

"Well, you can have one."

She held up the orange for him. He extended a hand slowly and grabbed the fruit. At first he simply palmed it and did not attempt to peel it, but then, watching her fingers upon her orange, he began to strip the peel away.

"How'd you end up in that chest, anyway?" she asked, orange juice dripping down her chin. She wiped it off with the back of her hand.

"Treachery."

"What kind? And how was my grandfather involved?"

"Mortals prayed to us and gave us sacrifices, they composed hymns and burned incense. They don't anymore. When your grandfather lanced his skin and drew blood, and begged me to pay him a visit, reciting the proper words, I was curious. I went. The greatest sacrifices are always in blood and from a mortal's own volition. Unfortunately, it was a trap. He was working for my brother."

Outside of their room the air crackled with the shouts of the captain, ordering the men to finish loading the cargo so they might sail away. To and fro the sailors went. They'd be off any minute now. Travel by water did not alarm Casiopea; in fact, it was soothing for her nerves. She could understand water. She'd slipped into the cenotes since she was a toddler. Had travel by train been necessary she might have been more reluctant or more excitable.

"How long did you spend in that chest?" she asked.

"Fifty years. Your grandfather was a young man then."

"Were you aware of what was going on?"

"I slept, but it's not the sleep of mortals."

She remembered what Loray had told her, how gods could not die. Instead they slept. Casiopea frowned.

"How many gods are there?"

"I have eleven brothers."

"And beyond that? I go to church every week, and well . . . the priest says if you are good you'll head straight to Heaven, but is Heaven real, then? Is there one God up there or many?"

It was another sin to ask this. Four, five, how many was that? Oh, did it matter? She wanted to know.

Although he had carefully peeled his orange, Hun-Kamé was not eating it. He held it in the palm of his hand. "Chu'lel," he said. "It is the sacred life force that resides around you. In the streams, in the resins of trees, in the stones. It births gods and those gods are shaped by the thoughts of men. Gods belong to the place where the chu'lel emanated and birthed them; they may not travel too far. The god of your church, if he is awake, does not live in these lands."

She spit out the seeds from her orange, cupping them in her hand. There was a wastebasket next to the washstand. She tossed them in there.

"Why wouldn't he be awake?" she asked, frowning.

"The prayers and offerings of mortals feed gods, they give them power, just as they give them shape. But when the prayers cease, the chu'lel that bubbled to the surface may sink back into the earth, and the gods must sleep. But they remain and may flower again."

Finally Hun-Kamé took a section of the fruit and placed it in his mouth. If he enjoyed the taste of the food, his face did not show it. Whatever foods the gods sampled in their abode would be much more enticing than an orange.

She thought back to the tale of the Hero Twins, when they defeat the Lords of Xibalba and decree that no sacrificial blood will ever be offered again to them, and she wondered if that was the moment when the gods had lost their worshippers, or whether it happened later. Perhaps she might ask about them at some point, but now a more urgent question assailed her.

"How can you be here, then, when mortals do not pray to you?"

"There are wells of power, secret places unlike others, where the land is fertile and strong, and gods may remain. My dominion is vaster than others because a stone weaved through the heavens and cleaved the oceans, the earth itself. Kak noh ek. A boiling kiss upon this world."

"You mean an asteroid," she said, finally understanding. "You were born from an asteroid."

How silly that she had not caught Loray's meaning before! Yes, an asteroid. She had not paid them too much heed when perusing astronomy books, being more interested in distant stars.

"But then, the moon would be filled with gods, would it not?" she asked.

"Have you not heard a word I said? Mortals gave us our form," he told her.

Like a furnace? she wondered. Did mortals sculpt the forms of gods? And if so, did those forms change? Or were gods inviolable, their visage, once imagined, forever remaining in its original shape?

Then her mind turned to the chunk of rock that had delivered the gods onto her continent. How could that have been the raw material from which the dark-haired god arose?

"Is that why my ancestors built observatories and looked at the night sky? Did you want them to look at the place you came from?"

"What funny thoughts you have," he said. "What would I care about the heavens when I reside in the Underworld?"

"I would care. All I could do sometimes was stare at the sky," she admitted.

"Whatever for?"

"Because it made me think one day I'd be free," she told him.

She had looked up at the night sky far too often, trying to divine her future in the face of the pockmarked moon. Casiopea was a realist, but her youth also made it impossible to remain rooted to the earth every second of the day. Once in a while she sneaked a line of poetry into her heart, or memorized the name of a star.

"Free of what?"

"My grandfather was terrible. I do not miss him or his house," she admitted. Her mother she did not miss yet, either. She knew that would come. For now, the excitement and newness obliterated those feelings, though she realized she must pen Mother a letter. At least a postcard. She would send one from Veracruz.

"Then it is a good thing I rescued you," Hun-Kamé said.

"You did not rescue me," Casiopea replied. "I opened that chest. Besides, I wasn't a princess in a tower. I knew I'd get away one way or another, and I was not waiting for a god to liberate me. That would have been both silly and unlikely."

"You appear very certain of yourself for a girl without a penny in the world who had not even seen what lay a kilometer away from her home until a couple of days ago."

"Well, now I have a god by my side."

"Just watch how you speak to me, stone maiden," he said, pointing at her.

He did not sound angry, but she disliked the words all the same. After having been ordered by her family to mind her tongue and her manners, she was loath to allow a man to so quickly dictate her speech patterns.

"My grandfather and my cousin slapped me when I was impertinent. Will you do that too?" she asked, and she couldn't help but to cut her words with a tad of defiance.

He gave her an odd look, which wasn't quite disapproval. And he didn't quite smile even if his lips curved, teeth showing.

"No. I would not. I also can't imagine it would do any good, since their blows did not curb your spirit. That is worthy. My brother did not break me, either."

She chided herself for not considering the cruel imprisonment he'd suffered. He was at turns quiet and a tad rude, but then he had not spoken to anyone in many years, locked in a place of blackness, left alone.

As much sorrow as Casiopea had known, she had still an understanding of kindness.

"I'm sorry about that. What my grandfather and your brother did to you," she said, her voice soft.

"Why would you be sorry?" he asked in surprise. "It had nothing to do with you."

"Yes, but if I had known, I'd have let you out long ago."

His gaze fixed upon her. She thought he had not looked at her yet, and only in that instant did she materialize before him. It was an uncomfortable sensation, because his gaze was cool, and yet it burned, made her look down at the folds of her skirt and feel like she might blush, an uncommon occurrence.

"You are gracious, stone maiden," he said.

"Why do you call me that?" she asked.

He was perplexed. "Is that not your name? Casiopea Tun."

"Oh, my surname," she said. Of course, it meant stone.

"And are you not a maiden?" he inquired.

This time she did blush, her cheeks very hot, and if she could have she might have crawled under the bed and stayed there for an hour, utterly mortified.

"Casiopea . . . it's better if you call me Casiopea," she said.

"Lady Casiopea," he replied.

"Not lady. You said that at Loray's house. You said 'lady' as if . . . I scrub pots on Saturdays and starch my grandfather's clothes. I'm not a lady," she said, rubbing her hands together.

"Loray would not know a lady from a snail. I had to correct him."

"But—"

"Courage is the greatest of virtues," he told her, holding up his hand and extending his index finger. "You have been brave. I thought a mortal, faced with my abrupt appearance and an equally abrupt quest, would have broken into sobs and abject fear. You have not.

There is merit in this, as it would have been very vexing to drag you around in such a state."

It was a bizarre compliment, and she could only nod her head at him.

"I will call you Casiopea if you wish it."

"That would be nice," she said.

The matter settled, he leaned back in his chair and finished eating his orange, his movements precise as he tossed the peel away. She watched him with interest. Exactly what human mind had conjured him? What had been the basis of him? Had a mortal turned her head toward the heavens and thought "hair as black as a moonless night" and evoked him? And then had this person given him a name just like that?

"Hun-Kamé," she said, trying his name experimentally.

He raised an eyebrow at that, hauteur in the gesture. "Lord of Xibalba," he corrected her.

"I can't go around calling you that. Do you think if we are in the street I can cry 'oh, Lord of Xibalba, could you come here?'"

"I am not a dog for you to call me," he replied, standoffish.

Casiopea made a scoffing noise; it lodged in the back of her throat. She scratched one of the oranges with a single nail.

He was quiet, and she imagined they would spend the remainder of the trip in silence, just as they'd traveled in silence to Mérida and then to Progreso. He minced his words, as though they were precious stones, probably thinking her unworthy of them. She had rationed her words too, having to conceal her thoughts in the presence of her family members, but this was not her nature. It was an act born of sheer necessity.

"I suppose you do have a point," he said, surprising her.

Casiopea raised her head, thinking she'd heard him wrong.

"Hun-Kamé you may call me, while we are in Middleworld."

"That is very generous of you," she said sarcastically.

"I realize that," he replied in earnest.

She was unable to suppress a chuckle. "You don't have a sense of humor, do you?"

"What good would that do me?"

His voice was flat and she smiled, feeling the rest of the trip might not be all silent stares after all. It was her first trip by boat, her first trip by anything, as a matter of fact, and she did not particularly relish the thought of spending it pretending she was a nun who had made a vow of silence.

"Do you have more fruit?" he asked.

Casiopea grabbed another orange and tossed it at him. He caught it with his left hand.

The crew had finished securing all the bales and the ship slid out of Progreso, on its way to Veracruz. She did not even realize when this happened, as she was too engrossed in their conversation and had forgotten she was supposed to feel nervous about being alone with him.

Chapter 7

"There, in the cabinet. Get me a brandy," Cirilo ordered.

Martín obeyed, opening the cabinet that contained some of his grandfather's favorite trinkets. It also housed a wonderfully expensive set of glasses with a matching decanter, decorated with a row of hexagons and stylized ferns. Grandfather had said Martín could have it as a gift on his wedding day.

He poured the old man a drink and handed it to him. His grandfather had slid back into bed, pulling the covers up, and drank his brandy slowly. Martín was not ordinarily invited to share a nightcap with the old man, but he was rattled and did not bother asking him for permission, pouring himself a drink too. When he was done, he sat on a chair by the side of the bed and chuckled.

"Christ," Martín said. "Fucking Christ."

"Watch your blasphemous mouth," Grandfather said.

"I'm sorry, but I've recently met a god," Martín snapped back.

Despite his impertinent tone, Martín stared down at the floor, unable to look at the old man. He, like everyone else in the house, regarded Cirilo as an intransigent stone idol who must be meticulously obeyed, lest they incur his wrath.

"Why didn't you ever tell me about this? A lord of the Underworld, a chest filled with bones. Nothing," Martín muttered, feeling cheated.

"I didn't think you were ready. And I believed I had more time."

For all his aches and pains and complaints, despite leaning more heavily on his cane these days, the old man was indestructible. His eyes shone bright and alert in his weathered face and his teeth, yellow with time, remained sharp.

"Well . . . will you tell me now?"

"What do you want, Martín? A bedtime story?"

"An explanation."

"What is there to explain?"

Cirilo busied himself with a pillow, trying to make himself more comfortable, and then deciding that he couldn't, or wouldn't do it, gestured for his grandson to finish the task. It was the kind of request that Casiopea would have fulfilled, but she was gone. Martín placed another pillow behind the man's back, frowning.

"Grandfather," Martín said when he was done, hoping the man would deign to answer his question. Cirilo looked irritated, but he spoke all the same.

"I was a nobody, with no prospects, minding my own business and carrying on as best I could, when one day this woman came to see me. She was very beautiful, unhumanly beautiful, and she told me I'd been born on the appropriate day, of the appropriate month."

"Appropriate for what?"

"Sorcery. A spell to trap a god."

"And you agreed?"

"Not immediately. I thought she was mad. Then I met her associates, and it turned out they were all legitimate. A pair of sorcerers, the Zavala brothers. And Vucub-Kamé, of course. All conspiring against the Lord of Xibalba."

"What happened?" he pressed on.

"What do you think? I played my part. It was simple. I was merely supposed to serve as bait, they were busy with the rest. And they managed it, lopped his head off, stuffed his body in a chest." The old man snapped his fingers twice. "Pour me another drink."

Martín obeyed, carefully grabbing the decanter and filling his grandfather's glass. "Why would they leave the chest with you? Here? In Uukumil?"

"Vucub-Kamé couldn't take it with him. The chest needed to remain above ground. Hun-Kamé was a Lord of Xibalba, and the earth was his mother, so burying it was impossible. But Middleworld is not the land of the Xibalbans. Middleworld owes them no favors and no blessings."

Cirilo wet his lips with the brandy before continuing. "He could have given it to one of his associates, but he didn't. Anyway, it needed to remain here, in Yucatán, and he entrusted it to me. It was not as if there are bandits in Uukumil. I thought it would be safe enough. Until your cousin opened it."

"You could have taken better precautions," Martín replied.

For a moment Martín thought his grandfather was going to get up from his bed and beat him with his cane, like he'd done when he was little. He wouldn't put it past him. But instead the man glared at him.

"I took the damn precautions," he sputtered. "First two years I slept with a shotgun by the bed, in case intruders came at night. I hardly did anything except watch the damn thing. But then more years went by, and it became obvious it was a wasted effort. No one was looking for it."

Grandfather had leaned forward as he spoke, clutching the glass tightly. He relaxed his grip and tossed the glass on his side table as if it were a cheap jug made out of coarse clay.

"Vucub-Kamé came by in those first few years. I don't know if to gloat or why. But then he stopped visiting, and after a while . . . well, after a decade had gone by, I began to think I'd dreamed it."

"You thought you'd dreamed it," Martín repeated.

"That's what I said. I did not open the damn chest, so it's not as if I could refresh my memory about what was inside."

"If you thought you'd dreamed it, why didn't you open it?"

"It's best not to know certain things, and besides, it no longer mattered. Real. False. Life was what it was."

Martín, who had a rather atrophied imagination, incapable of considering for long periods of time anything that was not directly in front of him as worthy of interest, could understand this reaction.

"What did you get in exchange for your assistance?"

"What do you think?" Cirilo replied, extending his arms and pointing to the cabinet, the curtains. "All of this. He paid me off. I was nobody and then I was someone."

"You might have told me."

"Told you what? That I had a strange dream? That I believed in sorcery? I know you all, you vipers, you'd have had me committed."

Martín thought about his aunts and his father. He wouldn't put it past any of them to drag Cirilo to the insane asylum if he gave them the chance. His father was meek and soft, but he had never gotten along with the old man. As for Martín's sisters, their husbands, and his assortment of cousins, they were all vying for power, clawing at each other.

"Well," he said. "It didn't do you any good to keep quiet about it. Not with that traitor running around. You gave her access to this room, to your things, and she's not even a real Leyva."

"That's precisely why she had access to my room and my things. Do you think I could have trusted you to take care of me, Martín?" the old man said with a chuckle. "You are careless and lazy, but you must shape up now. The family has need of you."

"I'll do what I must and go where I must," Martín replied.

"Do not muck it up, as you are wont to do."

He did not enjoy the look his grandfather gave him. The old man did not much like Martín, although this was not terribly surprising, since he seemed to like no one. But he had never been more aware of Cirilo's distaste. None of this was his fault, so why was he being judged so harshly?

"When have I mucked it up? I've only ever done as you've said," he protested.

"Listen, boy," Cirilo said, reaching for his cane, which rested by the bed, and slamming it hard against the floor, making Martín wince. "You may think I'm unkind to you and harsh, but you do not know *him*."

The young man recalled Vucub-Kamé. When his grandfather had woken him up and roughly ordered him to get dressed, haltingly explaining they had a divine guest, he'd simply thought him mad— Cirilo was right, such revelations would lead a man to the asylum— but one quick look at Vucub-Kamé and poor Martín had to admit to himself that no man could have eyes like the stranger did, nor the hair to match. And there had been too the shimmering sense of power, crackling around them, that made Martín sheepish despite his enormous pride.

"Your idiocies, they won't do with him. You must serve him and serve him well. Bow low, address him properly, flatter him, and most of all do as he says so that we may not be cursed."

"Cursed."

"Yes. What, do you think we will keep all this if Vucub-Kamé fails and his brother regains his throne? Would you like to be a pauper, begging for coins on a streetcorner? Worse even, serving Casiopea? Imagine if Hun-Kamé should reward her and punish us."

Martín panicked at the thought of his cousin ending up with the house at Uukumil, all of his expensive boots and his fancy belt buckles and the silver cigarette case snatched from his grasp.

"Fine, fine," Martín said, running a hand through his hair. "Then tell me how I should address him and any other tidbits you may know. Christ, I may need them."

Cirilo gripped his cane with one hand, but let it rest against the wall and began talking.

Chapter 8

Every state, and sometimes every city, earns itself a reputation. The people from Mexico City are haughty and rude. The people from Jalisco are brave, sometimes to the point of foolhardiness. But the people from Veracruz, they are all laughter and joy. Reality and rumor do not always match, but Veracruz, lately, had been trying to build up its happy façade. In 1925, two years before, the local authorities had instituted a carnival.

Oh, there had been a carnival before, despite the mutterings of the Church. But it had been a sporadic, tumultuous affair, flaring up and cooling down. Its purpose and its organizers had been different. Now the carnival was modernized, molded by civic leaders who saw in it a chance to quietly insert useful post-revolutionary values into the community, amid all the glitter and dances. The newspapers said this was a festivity for "all social classes," exalting the beauty of the women on display—models of Mexican femininity, filled with softness and quiet grace. A few years before prostitutes had been engaged in civil disobedience, protesting rental prices. Unions had been busy agitating workers, buzzing about bourgeoisie pigs. But Carnival smoothed out differences, brought people together, pleased the organizers. There was also, most important, money to be made.

Casiopea and Hun-Kamé arrived in Veracruz a day before Carnival. This meant the hotels were bursting at the seams and there was little chance of proper lodging to be had. After a few inquiries they managed to find a run-down guesthouse that would take them in.

"I have two rooms. I don't see no wedding rings on your fingers, so I imagine that is what you need," the owner of the guesthouse said with a frown. "If that is not the case, off you go. This is an honest home."

"That will be fine. This is my brother," Casiopea said. "We've come from Mérida to see the parade and do some shopping."

Underneath the shadow of his hat and with the sun glaring so fiercely around them, it was difficult to discern Hun-Kamé's features. This, along with the ease of Casiopea's lying tongue, smoothed the old woman's concerns.

"The door of my house closes at eleven. I don't care if there are revelries outside, if you come by later, you'll have to sleep on the street," the woman told them, and they followed her to their rooms.

The rooms were more than modest, and the woman was overcharging, but Casiopea knew there was no point in complaining. She placed her suitcase by the bed and paused before a painting of the Virgin, which served as decoration upon the sterile walls. Ordinarily she would have made the sign of the cross upon coming in contact with such an image, but now she considered it futile to engage in genuflections in front of a deity, who, very likely, did not reside in her vicinity.

It also made it a lot easier to fly down the hallway and knock on Hun-Kamé's door, bidding him to go out with her. There was a city to see, the Villa Rica de la Vera Cruz, the most important port in the country. Always beleaguered, poor Veracruz; when Sir Francis Drake had not been assailing it, the French looted it, and then the

Americans seized it. It was tenacious, one must say that about Vera-cruz: it weathered Spanish conquistadors, British buccaneers, French soldiers, and American marines. Perhaps that was why its inhabi-tants were said to be so cool and collected, dressed in their guaya-beras and laughing the night away to the music of the harp and the requinto. When war has knocked on one's front door that many times, why should the minuscule daily ills matter?

They went for supper. There were many places offering elaborate seafood dishes near the arches of the downtown plaza, but Hun-Kamé avoided the larger restaurants. Too much noise there, too many people, and no tables to spare. The air smelled of salt and if you walked down the malecón you could glimpse the sea, but it wasn't the Pacific Ocean from the postcard which she longed to gaze at. It seemed fun, though, this port. They said it resembled Ha-vana, and there were frequent dances for the younger set at the Lonja Mercantil. Or else, sweethearts from middle-class families walked around and around the main plaza under the watchful eye of their older relatives: courtship still followed strenuous rules.

Since they were not courting and they had no nosy relatives to trail behind them, Casiopea and Hun-Kamé wandered around with-out direction, heading wherever they pleased. They took a side street and ended up sitting in a café, all whitewashed outside, like most buildings in the city, where the patrons smoked strong cigarettes and drank dark coffee, safe from the muggy heat that assailed the port.

The café offered a minimal menu. It was not the kind of place where one had a decent meal; instead it sold coffee with milk, poured from a kettle, and sweet breads. To summon the waitress, one clinked a spoon against the side of a glass and the glass would be refilled with coffee and steaming milk. The patrons could also avail themselves of a café de olla, sweetened with piloncillo.

Casiopea, imitating the other customers, clinked her glass and summoned a waiter this way, ordering bread and coffee for both of them, although, as usual, her companion was uninterested in their meal.

Hun-Kamé took off his hat and she noticed, for the first time, that he had acquired a black eye patch that contrasted with the whiteness of his clothes. Though white was not his color—she suspected he had elected to blend in with the other men in town who outfitted themselves in this fashion—he looked rather fine. He always did and yet the novelty of him never ceased.

Casiopea stirred her coffee while he ran a finger around the rim of his glass. The table they were sharing was so small that if she moved a tad forward she might bump her elbow with his or knock his glass to the floor. Others had come earlier and secured bigger tables, and now they were playing dominoes.

"How will we find the Mamlab? Where is he?" she asked.

"The Huastec people are cousins to the Mayans, and their gods are cousins of mine. The Mamlab are not one god, but several."

"Loray spoke as though he was referring to one."

"Oh, he is referring to *one*. The Mamlab live in the mountains, where they play music, drink, and make love to their frog wives. But some of them venture into town to partake in festivities and seduce enticing women. And the youngest, he is more insolent than the rest, and that cousin of mine has my ear."

She knew of Chaac, who carried his stone axe and beat the clouds to release the rain. And there was the Aztec Tlaloc, with his heron-feather headdress, but the Mamlab she did not recall.

"And he, this god, he has a name, then?"

"The Mam is called Juan," Hun-Kamé said laconically, sipping his coffee.

"Juan? What kind of name is that for a god?" she asked, dismayed to discover deities had names taken out of the Santoral. It hardly seemed creative, or appropriate.

"Sometimes he is Juan, sometimes he is Lord Thunder, sometimes not. Are you not Casiopea, Lady Tun, a Stone Maiden, and other permutations? And beyond these is there not some secret name in your heart, which you keep under lock and key?"

Casiopea's father, he'd called her kuhkay—firefly—because the little bugs carried lights from the stars, and she was his little star. She wondered if he meant this, if this might be her long-lost name.

"Maybe," she conceded.

"Of course. Everyone does."

"Do you have a secret name?" she asked.

His arm stilled, the glass freezing in midair. He placed it down, carefully, on the table. "Do not ask silly questions," he told her, his tongue whip-hard.

"Then I'll ask a smart one," she said, irritated by his scalding tone, hotter than the coffee they were drinking. "How will we find your cousin? The city is large."

"We will let him find us. As I've explained, he is fond of pretty young women he can seduce. You will do for bait."

He looked at her with a certainty that would accept no excuses, the certainty of a god before a mortal, yet she felt compelled to protest. Casiopea had a gap between her two front teeth and heavy-lidded eyes; neither trait had ever been declared attractive. The papers were full of ads for whitening creams that would yield an "irresistible" face. She was dark and made no effort to rub lemons on her skin to acquire what people said was a more becoming shade.

"You must be joking," she told him.

"No."

"You claim he is fond of pretty young women, and I am not a pretty young woman."

"You have never gazed at your reflection, I suppose," he replied offhandedly. "Blackest of hair and eyes, black like the x'kau, and as noisy."

She could tell he wasn't trying to flatter her; he had remarked on her looks like he might remark on the appearance of a flower. Besides, he'd insulted her in the same breath.

He did not mean it as a compliment. He couldn't have meant it like *that,* she thought.

"Even if he'd look at me—"

Hun-Kamé rested a hand flat against the wooden surface of the table.

"Some of my essence drifts in your body. This means some of my magic rests upon your skin, like a perfume. It strikes a strange note, which will surely attract him. The promise of something powerful and mysterious cannot be ignored," he said.

It puzzled her to imagine death as a perfume that clung to her and, rather than striking the sour note of decay, could be as pleasant as the scent of a rose. But she did not give this too much thought because she was busier summoning her outrage.

"I do not want to be seduced by your cousin," she countered. "What do you take me for, a woman of ill repute?"

"No harm will come to you. You will lure him, bind him, and I will deal with him," Hun-Kamé said.

"Bind him? You are mad. How? Won't he know—"

"Distract him with a kiss, if you must," he said, sounding impatient. Clearly they had been discussing the point far too long.

"As if I would be going around kissing men at the drop of a hat. You kiss him."

She stood up and in the process almost toppled the table. Hun-Kamé steadied it and caught her arm, lightning fast. He stood up.

"I am the Supreme Lord of Xibalba, a weaver of shadows. What will you do? Walk away from me? Have you not considered my magic? It would be foolish. Even if you managed it, the bone shard will kill you if I do not remove it," he whispered.

"Perhaps I should hack off my hand," she whispered back.

Casiopea realized she should not have said this, alerting him to her knowledge of this exit clause, but she'd spoken without thinking, needled by his haughtiness. She wanted to bring him down a peg, and though it is impossible to humble a god, her youth allowed her to naïvely think it might be done.

"Perhaps. But that would be unkind," he replied.

His gaze was hard as flint, ready to strike a spark. Despite her outburst of boldness, Casiopea was now forced to lower her eyes.

"It would also be cowardly, considering you gave me your word and pledged your service to me. Though it might merely reflect your heritage: your grandfather was a traitor and a dishonorable man. He knew not the burden of patan, nor its virtue."

She closed her hands into fists. There was nothing she had in common with her grandfather: it was Martín who inherited all his virtues and his vices. Casiopea liked to believe herself a copy of her father or closer to her mother, even though she did not feel she possessed the woman's kindness. Like many young people, ultimately she saw herself as a completely new creature, a creation that had sprung from no ancient soils.

"I'm no coward," she protested. "And when have I pledged anything to you?"

"When we left your town. 'Very well,' you said, and accepted me. Is that not a promise?"

"Well, yes . . . but I meant—"

"To cut your hand off at the first chance?" he asked, taking a step forward, closer to her.

She echoed him, taking a step too. "No! But I'm also no fool to . . . to blindly do your bidding."

"I do not consider you a fool, although you do raise your voice louder than an angry macaw," Hun-Kamé said, gesturing toward

their table and its two chairs. His movements were those of a conductor, elegant and precise.

"It might be that, in my haste, I have been crude," he said. "I do
not wish to give you a poor impression. At the same time, I must
emphasize that we are both united by regrettable circumstances and
must proceed at a quick pace. Had I been given a choice, I would
not have inconvenienced you as I have. Yet your assistance is quite
necessary, Casiopea Tun."

On a table nearby, old men shuffled their dominoes with their
withered hands, then set down the ivory-and-ebony pieces. She
glanced at the game pieces, lost for a moment in the contrasting
colors, then looked back at him.

"I'll help you," she said. "But I do it because I feel sorry for you,
and not . . . not because you are 'supreme lord' of anything."

"How would you feel sorry for me?" Hun-Kamé asked, incredu-
lous.

"Because you are all alone in the world."

This time his face wasn't flint, but basalt, cool and devoid of any
menace or emotion, though it was difficult to pinpoint emotions
with him. Like the rivers in Yucatán, they existed hidden, under the
surface. Now it was as if someone had dragged a stone upon a well,
blocking the view. Basalt, unforgiving and dark, that was what the
god granted her.

"We are all alone in the world," he said, and his words were the
clouds when they muffle the moon at night, they resembled the earth
gone bitter, choking the sprout in its cradle.

But she was too young to believe his words and shrugged, sitting
down again, having accepted his invitation. He sat down too. She
finished her coffee. The slapping of dominoes against wood and the
tinkling of metal spoons against glass around them was music, possessing its own rhythm.

"You said you'd bind him. How?" Casiopea asked.

"A piece of ordinary rope."

"A piece of ordinary rope," she repeated. "Will that work with a god?"

"It's the symbolism that matters in most dealings. I'll speak a word of power to the cord, and it will be as strong as a diamond. It will hold him, and I will do the rest. Do not be frightened," he concluded.

"It is easy for you to say. I bet gods don't need to fear many things while regular people have an assortment of fears to choose from," she replied.

"You are not a regular person, not now."

For how long, she wondered. And she had to admit to herself that part of what kept her next to him was not just the promise of freeing herself of the bone splinter or a sense of obligation, but the lure of change, of becoming someone else, someone other than a girl who starched shirts and shone shoes and had to make do with a quick glimpse of the stars at night.

"Do not be frightened, I say," he told her and took her left hand with his own.

It was not a gesture meant to provide comfort, at least not the comfort that can be derived from the touch of another person. This would have required a trace of human empathy and affection. It was a demonstration, like a scientist might perform. And still her pulse quickened, for it is difficult to be wise and young.

"Feel here, hmm? My own magic rests in your veins," he said, as if seeking her pulse.

He was right. It was the tugging of a string on a loom, delicate, but it ran through her, and when he touched her it struck a crystalline note. Upon that note, another one, this one much more mundane, the effect of a handsome man clutching a girl's hand.

She pulled her hand free and frowned. She was not *that* unwise.

"If your cousin frightens me, I'll run off, I don't care," she swore. "Angry macaws bite, you know?"

"I shall have to take my chances."

She tapped her spoon against her glass, summoning the waitress, who poured more coffee and milk for them.

"Do you like it? This drink?" he asked her after the glass was refilled, a frown upon his brow.

"Yes. Don't you?"

"It's too thick and awfully sweet. The milk disrupts the coffee's bitterness."

"We must not disrupt the purity of the coffee bean," she said mockingly.

"Precisely."

She chuckled at that, and he, of course, did not find it amusing. Not that it would be likely that a god of death would be very merry, not even in Veracruz, where no one must wear a frown, and not even during Carnival, when every trouble must be thrown to the air, left to be carried off by the winds.

Thus they sat there, together in the café, the dark, serious god and the girl, as the night fell and the lights were turned on in the streets.

Chapter 9

How short their hair was! Casiopea watched all the fashionable young women with their hair like the American flappers, serving as "ladies in waiting" for the Carnival queen. In Casiopea's town no one dared to sport such a decadent look. Even face powder might be cause for gossip there. In Veracruz, during Carnival, there were plenty of painted faces and rouged cheeks and unabashed looks to go around. If her mother had been there, she'd have told Casiopea that such shamelessness should be met with scorn, but seeing the girls laughing, Casiopea wondered if her mother was mistaken.

The queen, after being crowned, waved at the crowds, and thus began the formal masked balls at the Casino Veracruzano and other select venues. But the revelers were not confined to the insides of buildings, and those who could not afford the masked ball tickets made their own fun in the streets and parks, drinking, dancing, and sometimes engaging in mischief. Lent would arrive soon, the moment to say farewell to the flesh. So now was the time to throw caution to the wind and carouse. No one would sleep that first night of Carnival, and sometimes they wouldn't sleep for days, too preoccupied with floats, parades, and music to bother heading to bed. A thousand remedies would be available the next morning to fix the hangover many locals would suffer from. One local solution was the consumption of shellfish for breakfast, although others contented themselves with aspirins.

The buildings down Cinco de Mayo Street were decorated with streamers and flags, and the cars that ventured into the streets sported flowers and colorful banners. Revelers set off firecrackers and shared bottles of booze. Inside restaurants and hotels, folkloric dancers twirled their skirts and musicians played the danzón, a Cuban import that was wildly sensual but also wildly popular.

Veracruz had an African legacy. In this port, the slaves had been hauled off the European ships and forced to toil in sugar plantations. Descendants of these slaves clustered in Yanga and Mandinga but had influenced the whole region, leaving a mark on its music and cuisine, and like everyone else they attended Carnival, flooding the streets. There were black-skinned men dressed as skeletons, indigenous women in embroidered blouses, light-skinned brunettes playing the part of mermaids, pale men in Roman garb. Once Carnival was over, the fairer skinned, wealthier inhabitants of the city might look with disdain at the "Indians" and the "blacks," but for that night there was a polite truce in the elaborate game of class division.

Casiopea watched all this with amazement and trepidation as they joined the crowds of masked and disguised revelers. Hun-Kamé had rented two costumes for an exorbitant price that morning. He was decked soberly in a black charro suit, with a silver-embroidered short jacket, tight trousers decorated with a long line of buttons on the sides, and a wide hat upon his head. He cut a dramatic, attractive figure and looked as though he were ready to leap upon a stallion and perform the typical tricks of these horsemen, especially apt given that he carried a rope on his right arm. She matched him, attired as a charra, with a jacket and a skirt and a great deal of silver embroidery, except her clothing was white. Unlike him, she lacked a hat.

Earlier that day, at the guesthouse, she had pressed the embroidered jacket against her chest and curiously stood in front of a mirror. "Have you never seen your reflection?" he'd asked her.

Thus she looked at herself. Not the quick, darting glance Casiopea was allowed in the mornings, but a long look. Vanity, the priest in Uukumil had warned her, was a sin. But Casiopea saw her black eyes and her full mouth, and she thought Hun-Kamé might be right, that she was pretty, and the priest was too far away to nag her about this fact. Then she grabbed a brush and pinned her hair neatly in place.

Casiopea and Hun-Kamé walked together down the busy streets, the earthy sound of the marimba spilling out from a nearby building, urging her to dance.

"Where are we headed?" she asked.

"To the busiest, most crowded part of the city," he replied.

A sea of revelers greeted them, thicker than the throng they had passed. It was a chaos of horns and drums, people dressed as devils and angels, the scents of tequila and perfume mingling together. Above them, people in balconies threw confetti and children tossed eggshells filled with glitter, while a few men, either drunk or full of spite, emptied a bottle of rum onto the pedestrians.

There, in the midst of this mess of feathers, sequins, and masks, Hun-Kamé stopped.

"Walk around here," he told her, handing her the rope, "and remember to tie his hands when you have the chance."

When Casiopea's father died, her mother attempted to make a living for them doing odd jobs. For a while she tried her hand at macramé and taught her daughter the trade. Casiopea could tie sev-

eral knots, but she did not know if they would be fit for supernatural beings, even though Hun-Kamé had assured her any simple
knot would do.

"Where are you going?" she asked, because he was turning away
from her.

"He shouldn't see me with you."

"But—"

"I'll be watching and I will follow you. Whatever he says, do not
release him and do not leave his side either."

"How will I know what he looks like?"

"You'll know."

"Wait!" she said as he stepped away.

He stopped, his cool hand brushing hers, and her hold on the
rope slackened.

"I'll be behind you," he said. It wasn't an attempt at reassurance,
it was a fact.

With that, he was gone. She was scared, abandoned among all
these strangers. In Uukumil, the biggest event of the year was the
peregrination of the local saint, which was hauled from the church
and carried around the town. This, this was so much bigger! There
were women in terrifying masks and a boy who kept banging a
drum, and Casiopea thought of simply running off.

She tightened her grip around the rope and bit her lower lip.
She'd said she'd do this and she would. She began walking, pushing
her way next to dancers who were paired together and shuffling
their feet right in the middle of the street. She slid past two harle-
quins who tossed confetti at her and evaded three rowdy men who
were bumping into people and yelling obscenities.

"You wouldn't happen to have matches, would you?" a man
with a melodious voice asked her.

He was a dark fellow, broad-shouldered, good-looking, and

strong. He was dressed like a pirate, with a blue coat, a sash upon his waist, and tall boots. The way his teeth gleamed and the way he stood drew Casiopea in.

This is him, the Mam, she thought.

It is likely that having already met one god, she was able to quickly identify another. Or else it was Hun-Kamé's essence, caught under her skin, that allowed her to see there was an extraordinary element about this stranger.

"No," she said, looking down at her shoes, not in modesty, but because she didn't want him to read the recognition in her eyes.

"A pity. What are you doing all alone on a night like this?"

"I came with my friends, but I seem to have misplaced them," she said, lying again with panache. She had, it seemed, a talent for it.

"That is terrible. Maybe I could help you find them?"

"Maybe," she agreed.

He took out a cigarette and a lighter and placed an arm around her waist, guiding her through the street.

"I thought you needed matches," she said.

"I needed an excuse to talk to you. Look, you sweet thing, how nicely you blush," he said, his voice honeyed.

He said a number of things to her in that cloying tone of his, things of little importance, because a minute or two later she could not recall them. Compliments, enticements. His words were electric, charged like a cloud pregnant with rain. She followed him away from the revelers, down an empty alley. There he pressed her against a wall and ran a hand along her chest, smiling, the touch making her shiver. Was this what women and men did in the dark? The indecencies the priest muttered about? Books were coy on the specifics of seduction.

"What would you say, hmm, about giving me a kiss or two?" he asked, tossing away his cigarette.

"Now?"

"Yes," he told her.

Casiopea nodded. The man leaned down to kiss her. She'd never been kissed before and didn't particularly know if she wanted to start with him. She turned her head.

Her fingers on the rope relaxed for a moment, then she grasped it tight.

She'd been nervous before, but now she grew still and calm. She pushed him away, gently, coyly, so that he smiled. His hands fell on her waist. And she gave him another gentle shove; she raised the rope and attempted to tie his hands but it proved difficult because one of those hands was now roaming down her stomach, pinching at the buttons of her costume. Casiopea let out an irritated sigh and held his wrists together.

"What are you doing?" he asked.

"You want that kiss, then you'll let me do it," she said, although she intended nothing of the sort.

"What a perverse thing you are! What game are we playing?"

"You'll see," she said. "Now, if you will. Be still."

He laughed as she tied a sturdy knot. When she was done, he tried to kiss her on the lips, and she turned her head and slapped him soundly. Even then he thought she was playing, but when he tried to pull a hand free, he could not.

His face changed: it grew stormy.

Casiopea slid away from him. His eyes were bright as lightning, and when he spoke it was a hiss, like the wind through the trees.

"Who are you?" he asked. "How did you do this? I will give you a thrashing, girl."

"You will not," she replied, stepping away from him as he fumbled and tried to undo the knot, even going as far as putting it in his mouth and gnawing, which accomplished nothing. Frustrated, he spat on the floor and began circling her.

"You come here and undo this now, girl! You do it quick and I won't drown you in the river and play music on your bloated corpse."

He ran toward her, trying to pin her against the wall, and Casiopea moved aside, the god crashing against it, loosening a few bricks in the process. He turned around and opened his mouth as if to let out a scream, but instead out came a warm gust of wind, which shoved her back two, three steps, and got under her clothes. It felt like someone had rubbed a hot stone against her skin.

She blinked and considered how ridiculous it was to be standing in an empty alley with an angry god when she ought to have been running in the other direction, far and away, back to the guesthouse, and maybe all the way back to her home. But Hun-Kamé had said not to release the man or leave his side, so she brushed the hair away from her face and crossed her arms.

"Well, must I crush your every bone, you idiot?" he asked, looking ready to charge at her like an angry bull.

"How disrespectful you are," Hun-Kamé said.

He was there all of a sudden, right by her side, like a fallen piece of the velvety sky, like a nocturnal plant that unfurled and greeted her, his hand touching her shoulder, shielding her from any threats with that quick gesture.

Juan, the Mam, smiled, his attention jumping from her to him. He laughed, riotous, sounding like a man in his cups.

"Hun-Kamé, my cousin. So it is you who has set such a soft trap for me. What a surprise," he said, his toothy smile bright.

"Not too big a surprise, I'd think. Hasn't my brother sent his owls to inform you of my escape and to warn you I'd come looking for my property?" Hun-Kamé replied, unsmiling.

"Maybe he has. I wouldn't know. I move between the hills and the streams. I am difficult to find."

"Not too difficult, treacherous cousin," Hun-Kamé said.

"Treacherous? I? For guarding the property of the lord Vucub-Kamé?"

"For keeping my ear, you dog. As if you didn't know who it belonged to."

Hun-Kamé's face was cold, but a sliver of anger colored his words, red hot, like the embers of a cigarette.

"I did know it was yours. Then again, I also know the Supreme Lord of Xibalba is now Vucub-Kamé. Can I be chided for doing the bidding of the ruler of nine shadow regions?"

Juan made a mocking gesture, bowing down low before Hun-Kamé and then jumping up to his feet.

"You can be chided for changing your allegiances in the blink of an eye," Hun-Kamé said.

Juan shook his head. "I follow the direction of the wind, and I cannot be blamed if a new wind begins to blow. Vucub-Kamé gave me your ear, yes, and I bent my knee, not because I have love for your brother, but because one must follow the order of things. The order and the reign now belong to Vucub-Kamé."

As he spoke, Juan circled Hun-Kamé and Casiopea, slowly, a smile gracing his lips. The smile grew wider.

"These bonds won't hold me for too much longer," he said, rubbing his hands together, testing the rope. "What do you intend to do then?"

"As if the bonds mattered. What I wanted was your attention," Hun-Kamé replied.

"You have it."

"Return to me the item Vucub-Kamé entrusted you."

"And disobey the orders of the Supreme Lord of Xibalba? You are not to have it back," Juan said, shaking his head.

"Disobey the orders of the false Supreme Lord and please the righteous one."

The Mam shrugged. "Those are such confusing terms. False? Righteous? I am not a betting man, cousin. Today Vucub-Kamé has the throne. Tomorrow you may have it, maybe not. I wouldn't want to face your brother when he is angry. Conflict between us is tiresome and unnecessary."

Despite his words, the god opened his mouth wide, the corner of his lips distended. He unleashed another gust of wind, stronger than before, which might have indeed broken Casiopea's bones as he'd previously promised, except that in the blink of an eye Hun-Kamé had raised a hand and the shadows on the floor rose like a wave, a cocoon, against which the wind crashed and shattered.

The Mam coughed and opened his mouth again, but Hun-Kamé spoke.

"Don't try that with me or I'll think you uncivil," he said.

The god smiled and shook his head, his voice hoarse. "I thought we were playing! We have a rope to skip, and your friend can be Doña Blanca and we'll dance around her. I wouldn't seriously—"

"Be quiet."

Hun-Kamé's face had the grimness of the grave. It rubbed the insolence off the other god's smile, sobering him a tad.

"If you do not return what belongs to me, you will find yourself in a very unpleasant situation. The bonds, as you say, may not hold long, but they will hold long enough for me to ruin your merry week of feasting. And when I sit on my throne, I will make sure to sour your nights. No drumming down the river, no imbibing of spirits, no laughter for you and your brothers."

"And what if you do not regain your throne?" Juan asked, with mock innocence.

"Would you like to chance it, cousin? Remember who I am, remember my magic and my might. Remember also that my brother has always been the weaker one," Hun-Kamé said, speaking in a low voice.

Juan's smile was eclipsed completely. Although the night had been warm, Casiopea felt a chill go down her spine and rubbed her arms. The coldness seeped up from the earth, as if the ground had frozen beneath their feet. In Xibalba it was said there was a House of Cold where it hailed, and the hail cut your hands as sharply as a blade, and she thought perhaps this was the cold they felt. Whatever its source, it was unnatural and had an immediate effect on the god.

"This . . . this chill. I like the nights warm, cousin," Juan said, and his teeth chattered, a plume of smoke escaping from his lips.

"Oh? I feel nothing. Casiopea, do you feel anything?" Hun-Kamé asked smoothly.

She shook her head and the Mam chortled, but the tips of his fingers were turning white, a delicate frost lacing itself across them.

"I respect you, Hun-Kamé. You know as much," Juan said.

"Truly? I was beginning to doubt it."

"I would not wish you as my enemy."

"Swear to return my property and I will consider you blameless."

Although Casiopea had been awed by Hun-Kamé when he appeared before her, and although she had been frightened too, she had not understood the whole extent of him. It was only watching the gods speak that she realized the weather god was intimidated, and she began to wonder about Hun-Kamé's nature and his might.

Death, she walked next to Death, and Death wore the face of a man. So she spoke to Death like a man, raised her voice to him, she might even defy him, but of course he was no man. She'd seen drawings of Death in dusty books. It was depicted as a skeleton, its vertebra exposed, black spots on its body symbolizing corruption. That Death and Hun-Kamé seemed entirely different from each other, but now she realized they could be the same.

She glimpsed, for the very first time, the naked skull beneath the flesh. And if a god feared Death, should she not fear him too, rather than share oranges and conversation with him?

"I swear by air and water, and by the earth and fire too, if need be. Let me go and I'll hand it over," Juan said.

The frost now covered his whole chest and had worked itself up to his neck, turning his voice into a whisper, but Hun-Kamé spoke a word and the ice crystals melted off, though a chill infected the air.

He loosened the rope around the Mam's hands and the god, in turn, reached into his pocket and took out a wooden box, inlaid with iridescent mother of pearl. Hun-Kamé opened it. In it lay a human ear, perfectly preserved. Hun-Kamé pressed it against his head, cupping it in place, and when he drew away his hand the missing ear was attached to his flesh, as if it had not been cut off.

Hun-Kamé inclined his head at the other god, gracious.

"I will assume you remain my beloved cousin, then," Juan said, rubbing his hands together, "and that I may be allowed to leave now."

"Go. Enjoy the night."

The Mam nodded, but now that the frost had melted he quirked a mischievous eyebrow at them.

"I might enjoy the night better if I'd had a chance to taste the sweetness of your pretty girl. Would you not let her dance with me?" the god asked, turning his sly eyes toward Casiopea. "How I love mortal women, you know that, and since we are friends again, it would be a nice gesture to grant me this one to warm me up. I think we both agree I could use some warming up after—"

"Oh, I'll slap you twice if you even think it," she declared.

"I like a good slap now and then. Come here," he said, holding his palm upward and crooking his finger at her.

The death god stood stiff as a spear, and his hand fell upon Casiopea's shoulder. "Look elsewhere for diversions," Hun-Kamé said drily. "And apologize to the lady for being crude tonight."

"How prickly you are! I was trying to be friendly, but instead I'll be off, then. There is no point in offending Death and his hand-maiden any further. My apologies, miss. Be well, cousin."

The weather god took out a cigarette and he lit it, chuckling as he walked down the alley and disappeared from sight, heading back toward the music and the raucous crowds. The night grew warmer, again the ordinary tropical night of the port, and Hun-Kamé lifted his hand from her shoulder.

"Thank you," she told him.

"You should not thank me for such small things," he replied.

Casiopea supposed he was correct, since he needed her and if he had stood up for her, it was because she was valuable to him. Nevertheless she considered it a nice gesture. No one had ever defended her when Martín bothered her, and she could not help but to feel grateful and to look kindly at him. Thus, minutes after she thought she might want to fear him, be wary of him, she was again forgetting his true nature and seeing a man.

"Lady Tun, if you'll come with me, we have work to do," Hun-Kamé said, heading in the opposite direction from the one the Mam had taken.

"What kind of work?"

"Now that I have my ear back I can listen to the voices of the psychopomp and the dead. Let us find a proper crossroad."

"I don't know what you mean."

"You shall see," he said.

Chapter 10

They walked away from the downtown area, the crowds growing thinner until there were only a few people around them, then none. They walked for a long time. The white houses on each side of the street were silent as tombs. The silver in their costumes caught a ray of light here and there, like a stray spark.

They reached a crossroad. There were no more houses, not a single lonely shack on the side of the road, only the narrow path they'd been following. Casiopea glanced up at the stars, looking for Xaman Ek, which the Europeans called Polaris. This star was the symbol of the god with the monkey head, to whom the resin of the copal tree is offered at the side of the road. She wondered if he was as real as Hun-Kamé, and whether he truly had the head of an animal.

A moth flew by, and Hun-Kamé stretched out his hand, as if calling for it. The moth obeyed him, gently settling upon his palm, and he closed his fingers, crushing it. Had Hun-Kamé been mortal, he would have needed a more substantial sacrifice—a dog would have been suitable—to engage in this sorcery of the night. But since he was a god, and a god who had regained his lost ear and with it a smidgen of his magic, the moth sufficed.

Hun-Kamé opened his hand, sprinkling gray-and-black dust upon the ground.

He said several words that Casiopea could not understand. It was a strange tongue, very old. Where the dust had fallen, smoke began to rise, as if a charcoal brazier had been lit. The smoke had a shape, that of a dog, but then it shifted and it was a man, and then a bird, until one could not precisely define the nature of the apparition. The more she tried to pin it down, the more jumbled it became, threatening to give her a headache.

"I greet you and thank you for obeying my call," Hun-Kamé said. "Do you know me?"

"Prince of the Starless Night, Firstborn Son of Xibalba. You are a god without a throne. I know you," the smoke said. Its voice was low; it resembled a smoldering fire.

"Then you realize you must obey my command," Hun-Kamé said with the hauteur of a king, a hand pressed against his chest. "I wish to know where my essence is hidden."

"To you I owe three answers, and three I will give."

The smoke rose, the dog, the bird, the shape, towering above them. It had two black eyes, two black pinpoints, which shone despite its blackness. Casiopea, standing next to Hun-Kamé, felt it looking at her. It was a fabulous thing, this creature, which brought with it the scent of incense and dead flowers. It made her wonder what other impossible beasts the Lords of Xibalba commanded.

The smoke opened its jaws and spoke.

"The city on the lake, the impossible city, Tenochtitlán. Deep in the arid wastelands, El Paso," it said.

Then the apparition shook its head and stared at the ground, evasive. It was clear it did not wish to say any more.

"Where else?" Hun-Kamé demanded.

The apparition curled out its tongue. "In Baja California, by the sea, find Tierra Blanca. Find your destiny, Lord of Xibalba, but find your doom, for your brother is more cunning and more powerful than you ever imagined," the smoke-creature said, and its voice was now the crackling of burning wood.

"Do not lecture me, messenger," the god replied.

"I speak the truth."

"Who has what belongs to me? Where do they reside?"

"You must ask the ghosts, or sorcerers, or some other who can aid you, oh Lord, for I have given you three answers and a warning, which is the most even a god such as you may command of me."

"Then I dismiss you and will take your answers with me."

The smoke creature grew larger, then it bowed, its body folding upon itself, its forehead touching the ground. The smoke seeped into the earth, like the rain sinks into the soil, and was gone. Around them the night trembled, bidding the apparition goodbye.

"You have heard where we will journey," Hun-Kamé told her. "Tomorrow we depart for Mexico City."

He could have said they'd depart for Antarctica and it wouldn't have mattered much; she couldn't muster the energy for a reply and her forehead ached.

They walked back to the guesthouse. It was very late and the front door was closed, but Hun-Kamé opened the door with ease. They went to their rooms and Casiopea, exhausted by the excursion, fell upon the bed without bothering to change out of her clothes, dressed in silver and white. The wonders of the night did not keep her up, and she slept soundly.

The next day, they caught the evening train to Mexico City. Had they taken an earlier train, Casiopea might have been able to gaze out the window and observe the landscape, the marshes and the scrub growth and the rows of palm trees. Huts with walls of bamboo, old men sitting in worn chairs, children chasing stray dogs. She might have been able to see the train climb up from the low hills of Veracruz and approach the mountains, their tops dusted with snow. But the night was like spilled ink upon the page, blotting out all vegetation and natural features.

Casiopea did feel the train, though. It lumbered onward, away from the humid heat of the coast. She had never been on such a contraption. She felt as if she rested in the belly of a metal beast, like Jonah who was swallowed by the whale. This image in her family's Bible had often disconcerted her, the man sitting inside a fish, his face surprised. Now she sympathized with him. She could not see where they were headed, nor the place where they'd come from, and thus felt as though time and the world around her transmogrified, became unknowable; it was as if she were traveling in a dream.

She listened to the metallic click of the wheels along the steel rails while Hun-Kamé leaned back in his chair. They were sharing a sleeping car and it was small, so when he sat like that, his legs stretched out, he seemed to take up all the space. She did not mind, though, curled up against the window, the stars and the sky absorbing her thoughts. She associated her father with the smell of musty books or ink, the rustle of paper—he'd been a clerk, those had been the tools of his trade. But most of all she associated him with the stars, which he loved.

"You can speak with ghosts?" she asked, breaking the silence in their compartment.

"And other things that roam the night, as you may have noticed," Hun-Kamé replied.

"Would you be able to speak with my father? He passed away when I was small."

He turned his head, looked at her with disinterest. "Ghosts generally attach themselves to the stones, to a single place; rarely they may be shackled to a single person. I could not, from here, summon your father. Besides, he may not be a ghost. Not everyone who dies binds himself to the land. If your father perished quietly, then quietly he will have left this mortal realm."

"Would he be in Xibalba?" she asked.

"Most mortals stopped worshipping the gods of Xibalba long ago, and since their belief calcified, they do not venture down our roads anymore. Your father is not my subject."

For a moment she had thought she might be able to see her dear old father's face, to listen to his voice. Disappointed, she turned toward the window.

"I suppose it's for the best," she said with a sigh.

"What do you mean?"

"Xibalba is a terrible place. There is a river of blood, and the House of Bats and the House of Gloom. I would not want my father to be in such a frightful land." But here she paused and tapped a finger against the glass, frowning. "But then, the Hero Twins kill you in the story I heard, yet here you are. I wonder if all of it is true. Perhaps it is not as bad as that."

"Mortals like to speak their stories and do not always tell the true tale," Hun-Kamé said disdainfully. He had taken his straw hat off and was inspecting it, his fingers carefully touching the fibers.

"What is Xibalba like? What is the true tale?"

The straw hat interested him more than her question, and since he did not always provide an answer, she had almost given up on an explanation when he spoke with that cool, collected voice, which was drained of emotion.

"The Black Road leads to Xibalba, and at its heart there sits my palace, like a jewel upon the crown of your kings. It is very large, and decorated with colorful murals. It has almost as many rooms as the year has days. It is surrounded by other fine buildings, so elegant no human construction may approximate them. Picture a jewel, yes, but one without a single imperfection, balanced upon your palm."

He leaned forward, the hat dangling from his fingers. His face had become more animated. "My palace can be found by a series of ponds of blue-green waters, and in the ponds swim the strangest, most curious fish from the coldest depths, blind, but beautiful. They all glow with an interior light, like the firefly glows. There are trees around these ponds. Trees like the ceiba tree, but their bark is silver and their fruits are silvery, and they shine in the dark."

"Do you miss it?" she asked, because there was longing in his words, and his kingdom sounded quite astonishing, not like the shadowy place of sorrow she'd been told about.

"I belong there," he said.

She thought it might be a good thing to possess such certainty. She had never known quite where she belonged, a Leyva but not really a member of the family. And Uukumil had been stifling. It worried her; he knew exactly where he'd be headed, and she realized she could not return to her hometown.

What would she do when Hun-Kamé regained his missing organs? This line of thought in turn made her consider his health.

"How does it feel?" she asked. "The ear."

Casiopea touched her own ear as she spoke. The process of reintegrating it had appeared effortless, but it might not truly be so.

"What?" he asked.

"Does it pain you?" she said.

"No."

"My hand hurts sometimes," she admitted.

"Let me see."

"It doesn't hurt now," she clarified. "But yesterday, it did. Like grit in your eye, you know? But not in my eye, of course."

Hun-Kamé stood up and went to her side, lifting her hand and holding it up, as if to get a better look at it, even though there was nothing to look at. Maybe he could see the bone shard, hidden inside her skin.

"If it hurts again, let me know," he told her.

She raised her head and stared up at him. He was still wearing the black eye patch.

"Is the opposite true? Does it hurt where your eye is missing?"

"The absence disturbs me," he said, and the words were heavy, stones sinking into a river.

"I'm sorry," she said.

Since he was still holding her hand she gave it a light squeeze. She did not expect him to say thank you, since such trivialities were not very godly, but she did not think he'd frown like he did, staring down at her fingers.

"Why are you touching me?" he asked.

"Oh. Well . . . *you* were the one who touched me," she said.

"No. Just now."

"Sorry."

He'd set his hand on her shoulder before. It had not seemed an issue. She had not considered that reaching out for him might be offensive, a mortal coming in contact with the divine rather than the divine coming in contact with the mortal.

She attempted to draw her hand back, but he did not let go of her, and Casiopea wondered if they were going to play tug-of-war.

"You can let go," she said. "I didn't realize—"

"Such insolence."

"Keep squeezing my hand then and complaining at the same time, you'll see some real insolence," she sputtered. It didn't seem fair for him to start acting like she'd insulted him when all she'd attempted was to be kind.

Hun-Kamé laughed and released his grip on her. It was a full laugh: it bounced around the compartment like a startled bird. She smiled, responding to the display of mirth.

"Why do you laugh?" she asked. He had not done this before.

"You are a funny thing," he told her. "It's like having a playful monkey."

It was not quite an insult. It *sounded* like an endearment, but she frowned all the same. Her annoyance, however, did not last. She could forgive quickly when it suited her. Besides, he'd gone back to his seat and was again resting there quietly, so there really wasn't much to be angry about.

She'd almost forgotten he was with her when he finally spoke.

"What do you keep looking at?" he asked.

"The stars," she replied. "There's a thousand of them out to-night."

"There are a thousand every night."

"Maybe," she whispered, leaning her head against her arm and naming them in her head, as she'd done since she was a child, one of the games she played before going to bed.

Eventually, Casiopea stretched on the upper berth and closed her eyes, falling into a deep sleep. The train kept moving slowly forward, its wheels clacking. On the lower berth a lord of Xibalba did not sleep, but instead listened to the rhythm of the train. The laughter that had escaped from his lips was unusual, and he allowed himself to consider what it meant for a couple of minutes. Since he was a proud god, this matter did not occupy more than those two minutes, and then he dismissed it.

But rest assured that in the underground kingdom of Xibalba, another lord had heard Hun-Kamé's laughter and could discern its meaning.

Chapter 11

The imagination of mortals shaped the gods, carving their faces and their myriad forms, just as the water molds the stones in its path, wearing them down through the centuries. Imagination had also fashioned the dwellings of the gods.

Xibalba, splendid and frightful, was a land of stifling gloom, lit by a cheerless night-sun and lacking a moon. The hour of twilight did not cease here. In Xibalba's rivers there lurked jade caimans, alabaster fish swam in ink-black ponds, and glass insects buzzed about, creating a peculiar melody with the tinkling of their transparent wings. There were bizarre plants and lush trees, though no flowers bloomed in the soils of the Underworld—perhaps some had, at one point, but they'd long withered.

These were all bits of dreams that had taken physical shape, but the nightmares of mortals also abounded in the fabulous landscape of Xibalba.

There were vast tracts of land where the terrain was barren and gray, and men walked through this desert in despair, crying out for mercy. There were also swamps where a thin fog clung to the ground, noxious vapors rising from the waters, skeleton birds resting on dead trees shrieking loudly. There was a limestone outcropping, with many caves, like a honeycomb, and here lived the souls of confused mortals, who raised their hands in the air and tore their hair from their skulls, for they had lost the memory of themselves and did not remember the purpose of their journey. Beasts and fabulous creatures born of delirious ravings roamed the jungles, scaring the fools who ventured there. It was safest to stay close to the Black Road of Xibalba, that long ribbon that cut through the city where the gods resided. Stray from the path and it was easy to descend into chaos and terror.

In the beginning there had only been the city, Xibalba, but around it had sprung the swamps, the jungles, the caves, and the rest of the curious topography of the Underworld, so that now the borders of Xibalba were much vaster than at the time of its origin. People called all of this Xibalba, rather than refer only to the single city by that name. The city proper became the Black City and the lord's palace in turn was called the Jade Palace.

Hun-Kamé had reigned over this kingdom, and spent many moments in the gardens of his palace, but Vucub-Kamé preferred to dwell in his vast, windowless chambers, the walls painted yellow and red, multicolored cushions strewn upon the floor. He was resting upon these cushions when one of the four owls from the Underworld swooped into his room. He had sent it off into the world, to spy on the roads and spy on his brother.

The owl had found Hun-Kamé. The bond of kinship, which renders the blood of one mortal man similar to that of another member of his family, held true between the great lords of Xibalba. It was truest for Hun-Kamé and Vucub-Kamé. They were twins, very much alike. Same of height and build, differentiated by the color of their hair and eyes. Hun-Kamé had come into the world first, his black eyes like the depths of the waterhole. Seven heartbeats later Vucub-Kamé had opened his pale eyes, the color of ash, though they sometimes turned silver when he was in deep thought, and sometimes they became almost translucent, like the sastun, the divining stone.

The owl, well acquainted with the psychic essence of Vucub-Kamé, flew through Middleworld, searching for a similar essence. It was inevitable he would find Hun-Kamé.

When the owl returned to Xibalba, it bore a gift in its beak.

The gift was Hun-Kamé's laughter, which the owl had heard and captured in a white seashell it now dropped on its lord's open palm. Vucub-Kamé pressed the seashell against his ear and listened to the laughter. It was unpleasant to be aware of his brother's voice after such a long absence, and he crushed the shell between his fingers as soon as the echo of the laughter died off. Then he rose from the cushions, retrieved a ceremonial obsidian knife, and ventured outside the palace.

Ordinarily, when Vucub-Kamé left his palace, he was carried on a golden litter, hoisted upon the shoulders of his most exquisite courtiers. Singers walked ahead of him, proclaiming the beauty and wisdom of their lord, while behind followed his brothers and the rest of his retinue, burning incense or holding up cups filled with zaca. He was vain, Vucub-Kamé, as gods always are, and loved to be exalted.

That day, however, he exited the palace in silence, without alerting any of his servants. He did not wear a headdress, nor fine robes, but was attired in a simple white cloak. Alone he walked the streets of his city until its buildings were behind him, until the black ribbon of a road was nowhere in sight, and he reached a swamp.

Caimans, like the ones found in generous numbers in the swamps of Yucatán, swam there, snapping their jaws in the air. But these caimans were like the ghosts of caimans: their scales were alabaster and gold. He called forth one of these, which was greater in size than all the caimans who float in Middleworld, like a man might

call to his dog, and sat on the creature's back. He rode in this manner across the swamp.

The mangrove trees knitted their roots tightly below the water,
glistening eerily. Skeletal birds perched on meager branches and
stared at the death lord with their empty eye sockets, while he
reached the edge of the swamp and ascended the steps to the House
of Jaguars. Sometimes Vucub-Kamé sent men to the house to be
torn to shreds by the fierce animals, a punishment and an amusement, since, being dead already, they could not truly die and would
be reconstituted in time.

The jaguars were far from tame. But when Vucub-Kamé walked
in, the cruel beasts bent their heads and licked his hands as tenderly
as kittens.

Vucub-Kamé petted one of the jaguars, his fingers running upon
its fur. He admired its yellow eyes. Then, having made his choice, he
cut off the great cat's head. He opened its chest and retrieved its heart.
It fell to the ground, the heart, and the jaguar's blood traced an odd
pattern, which the god read, like men may read letters upon paper.

This was Vucub-Kamé's gift: prophecy. With the bright red seeds
of the Coral Tree he could keep track of days and divine what might
be, or scry into an obsidian mirror for answers. With such sorcery
Vucub-Kamé had foreseen his brother's escape from his prison,
though he had not known when or who would save him. He had
known, too, that when he escaped, Hun-Kamé would have necessity
of a mortal's assistance. Like a parasite, he would feed on the life of
the mortal until he could recoup his absolute essence, and, since he
would be tied to the mortal, he would be able to walk Middleworld
with the freedom the Lords of Death were not ordinarily granted.
Yet a toll must be paid. The mortal vitality that gave him strength,
that allowed him to roam the lands of men, would slowly pollute
him. It would turn Hun-Kamé more and more mortal each day,

until, if he could not restore his powers, Hun-Kamé would snatch the last heartbeat from the human heart and, with it, the whole of the mortal's essence. And he would become almost completely a man, no longer a god.

Vucub-Kamé counted on this process to take place. He had built the hotel in Tierra Blanca knowing it would happen, assuring himself victory.

Hun-Kamé's laughter proved that he was indeed turning human.

It is not as if the gods do not express anger, envy, and desire. But these are like compartments that may be opened and closed with iron keys, and often the gods exist in a state of placid indifference. Their laughter, when it surfaces, is not born in the heart, but the head. Hun-Kamé's laughter, however, had been cooked in the furnace of his heart. It was bright and vigorous.

This puzzled Vucub-Kamé. He did not expect his brother to become human quite so quickly. Indeed, he was not prepared for this to happen yet. Hun-Kamé needed to reach Tierra Blanca when he was close to his final descent into mortality, at which point he would be weak, a shell of his former self. Yet this laughter did not hint at weakness, its joy indicated unknown strength. What was happening? What had changed?

Vucub-Kamé, concerned, had therefore decided he needed to read the blood of the jaguar—for all the sacred truths are rendered in blood—in order to discern the future, to ensure his plan was secure.

But what Vucub-Kamé read in the blood did not reassure. It made him frown. The jaguars, sensing his irritation, twitched their tails.

Vucub-Kamé pressed his nail against the blood and drew a symbol there, then another. Three times his nail scratched the blood until he straightened up. His gray eyes caught a flicker of light in the jaguars' chamber, and for a moment they were burnished.

He walked out of the House of Jaguars, climbed down its white steps, and reaching the caiman that had borne him there, he cut off its head with his wicked knife. The caiman's blood colored the water, and Vucub-Kamé read the crimson signs.

Again he was disappointed.

Finally, the god took the knife and sliced his palm with icy determination, letting his blood fall upon the water. The blood was black as ink, and when it fell, it caused the water to bubble and swirl for a few seconds. Vucub-Kamé peered down at its surface.

"What is this trickery?" he whispered, his voice a hiss.

He could not read the signs properly. Before, he had foreseen Hun-Kamé's escape, and prepared to meet him in Tierra Blanca. Now he could see this future, but other paths branched off and were hidden to him. When he tried to peer into these rivulets he was confronted by the face of a woman he'd never met, but whom he assumed was Casiopea Tun. Her human essence tainted Hun-Kamé's own immortal substance, making it difficult to differentiate the future, to extricate her from him.

It was as if Vucub-Kamé had been blinded. No longer could he observe his moment of triumph. This troubled him because, if Hun-Kamé's escape was ordained by fate, Vucub-Kamé's dominion of Xibalba had never been sealed in such a way.

The death god stood by the shore of the swamp, his mind festering with the darkest of thoughts, and in the trees the skeletal birds, sensing his anger, hid their heads under their wings.

The god closed his palm into a fist, and when he opened it his hand was healed, as if no knife had cut it. He could not be harmed this way. The burn marks he carried were unusual, just as the beheading of his brother had been an outrageous anomaly born of iron and spiteful magic.

Vucub-Kamé called for two of his owl messengers. He had four and they were all terrifying creatures, feasting on the troubled dreams of men when they were free to roam Middleworld. Chabi-Tucur was the fastest and smallest of the four, and the one who had followed the trail of Hun-Kamé. Huracán-Tucur was the largest, so massive a man might ride atop its back, but too great to hide its magic from Hun-Kamé. Even though his brother was missing an eye and could not see the winged creatures, he might sense Huracán-Tucur's flapping wings. Vucub-Kamé could not risk this. Therefore, he gave instructions to the small owl that he should return to Middleworld and spy on Hun-Kamé.

Then he spoke to the larger owl. He instructed it to fly to Middleworld and find the mortal man, Martín. The owl would transport the man to Mexico City, where Martín could await the arrival of his cousin. There was no doubt this was the trajectory Hun-Kamé was following, attempting to reconstruct himself as quickly as possible.

If Martín succeeded in intercepting Casiopea, Vucub-Kamé would be able to enjoy an undeniable victory. Should she evade him or, worse, refuse to meet with Vucub-Kamé . . . well, the death god had left little to chance. Even if chance had somehow infiltrated his plans, even if the future concealed itself from the god's gaze, he would achieve his goal.

Seven heartbeats had separated the brothers. Hun-Kamé, the firstborn, claimed the crown, the throne, the realm of Xibalba, because of the span of those heartbeats. Afterward there emerged Vucub-Kamé, trailing after his siblings, holding the long black cloak that covered Hun-Kamé's shoulders. For a while their kingdom had expanded, growing in beauty and power, their other brothers appearing to complete their court, siblings born from charred bones and nightmares. Then there had come the phantasmagoric buildings of the Black City, the monsters in the plains made of ashes, the ever-increasing sighs and prayers and thoughts of mortals giving their world its colors.

And then, silence, decay. The prayers dwindled. Hun-Kamé, as if to match the indifferent times in Middleworld, had become an indifferent master, both selfish and spoiled. Vucub-Kamé had urged his brother to travel with him to Middleworld, not because he cherished mortals and their cities, but because he worried about the changes occurring on the peninsula. He worried about Xibalba. Hun-Kamé ventured up through the centuries, but even as sorcerers from across the sea disembarked near T'hó, bringing with them demons and spell books and even a ghost or two pressed against their backs, the Lord of Xibalba shrugged.

Vucub-Kamé had taken the kingdom because he must. He, as the superior brother, had been constantly cast as the inferior, and yet he would be the savior of Xibalba. He was the son Xibalba required, its future and its one chance.

Hun-Kamé had been given the mastery of illusions, but wasn't Vucub-Kamé a great sorcerer in his own right? Was he not more cunning than his brother? Was he not worthier of the black throne?

Yes, the god assured himself. All of this was true. All of this was known. One day mortals would make songs about his victory, narrating how death killed death and carved himself a magnificent new kingdom. An impossible task. A thousand years they'd sing and a thousand more.

Vucub-Kamé let a smile graze his lips. It was a terrible smile, and his very white teeth threatened to grind bones to dust. But then, one must not expect tenderness of death.

The god summoned another caiman and rode it back toward his palace, while the body of the creature he had decapitated sank slowly into the muck.

Long after the god had abandoned the swamp did the birds in the trees dare to lift their heads and emitted their shrill cries, but haltingly, afraid of their lord's anger.

Chapter 12

exico City has never inspired much love. "At least it's not Mexico City!" spills from the lips of anyone who resides outside the capital, a shake of the head accompanying the phrase. Everyone agrees that Mexico City is a vile cesspool, filled with tenements, criminals, and the most indecent lowbrow entertainment available. Paradoxically, everyone also agrees Mexico City exudes a peculiar allure, due to its wide avenues and shiny cars, its department stores filled to the brim with fine goods, its movie theaters showing the latest talkies. Heaven and hell both manifest in Mexico City, coexisting side by side.

Until 1925 Mexico City had been relatively free of the foreign influence of the flapper. Then, all of a sudden, the streets were inundated with bataclanesco imagery, courtesy of a troupe of dancers who'd come to perform at the most expensive clubs in the city. The slender, languid, androgynous female dominated the capital's billboards. Though some capitalinos, attached to their delicate morals, shook their head at these "painted women," many embraced the new ideal eagerly, glancing with distrust at the lowly "Indians" who came from other parts of the country and did not make any effort to hide their tanned skins under face powder, nor don the stylish dresses of the Jazz Age.

If the Porfiriato had been all about imitating French customs, Mexico City in the 1920s was all about the United States, reproducing its women, its dances, its fast pace. Charleston! The bob cut! Ford cars! English was sprinkled on posters, on ads, it slipped from the lips of the young just as French phrases had once been poorly repeated by the city folk. A bad imitation of Rudolph Valentino, hair slicked back, remained in vogue, and the women were trying to emulate that Mexican wildcat, Lupe Vélez, who was starring in Hollywood films.

As Casiopea and Hun-Kamé left the train station, hailed a cab, and journeyed downtown, she observed this prismatic, contrasting city. If she'd thought in Mérida people moved quickly, the pace was absolutely insane in Mexico City. Everyone rushed to and fro, savage motorists banged the Klaxon looking for a fight, the streetcars drifted down the avenues packed with sweaty commuters, newspaper vendors cried out the headlines of the day at street corners, and billboards declared that you should smoke El Buen Tono cigarettes. Kodak film and toothpaste were available for sale in the stores, and, near an intersection, a poor woman with a baby begged for coins, untouched by the reign of progress and modernity.

There were many places where someone with money could stay. Hun-Kamé decided on the Hotel Mancera, with rooms starting at five pesos a night, a price that Casiopea found terribly high. It had been the baroque home of aristocrats before it was vastly remodeled and turned into a venue that now boasted about its beds with box springs and Simmons steel furniture. High ceilings, chandeliers, wood paneling, and a handsome bar completed the ensemble. It was, in one word, luxurious, and had been purchased by the leader of a union, the Confederación Regional Obrera Mexicana. They said he'd paid for it in gold, that he organized numerous orgies, and that he'd gone through a million pesos meant for disaster relief. This was all likely true.

So far, their trip had been scarce on grand accommodations, and Casiopea felt intimidated as they walked into the lobby, having no idea even how she was supposed to greet the person behind the front desk. Hun-Kamé, however, knew what he was doing, or at the very least had no problem commanding attention.

He secured for them two rooms, though they did not have a chance to unpack, because Hun-Kamé immediately set out to conduct errands with her. Or so he told the hotel staff as he instructed them to take their bags to the rooms without them.

They did indeed go outside, and it was not hard to find the things Hun-Kamé wanted: matches and scissors. Curious, Casiopea inquired about this purchase, and Hun-Kamé said he would explain back at the hotel. Since she was hungry and wanted to get a bite, she let it go.

"I must summon a ghost," Hun-Kamé told her when they were back in her room, as he closed the heavy curtains.

"You need scissors for that?" she asked.

"Yes. To cut your hair. A good chunk of it will have to go," he said and touched her hair, indicating how much of her long mane he needed: he meant to cut it below her chin.

She thought she hadn't heard him right. "My hair," she said carefully.

"Yes."

She did not even know what to tell him. All she wanted to do was yell a loud, emphatic no, and yet she was not even able to open her mouth, too outraged to phrase her objections.

"Let me explain," he offered, his voice very calm. "I am in need of information regarding the whereabouts of my missing elements, and I will employ ghosts for this purpose. The summoning of ghosts can be done using human hair, bones, or teeth."

"But . . . but you called that other thing in Veracruz and you didn't need my hair," she protested.

"That was a psychopomp, a creature of Xibalba over which I have some power, by virtue of my birth. If we were in my realm I would indeed be able to summon the dead without offerings. But, since I am in your world and since I am not . . . quite myself at this moment, I must find another solution."

He was being serious. She had hoped it was a jest, even if she didn't think him capable of jesting.

"You cannot use me as . . . as . . . a stupid puppet," Casiopea said. "You can't take whatever you want and—"

"If you calm down, you will realize this is the most rational way to proceed."

"Can't we . . . what if we pay a barber for some hair? They sweep it away into the garbage, anyway," she insisted.

"Symbolism is important. It should be offered willingly," he said, speaking low.

She had not been one for tantrums as a child, but when she did pitch a fit, it was a sight to behold, and right then she felt that if she didn't sit down, calm herself, and close her eyes, she was going to smack the god of the dead across the face. She'd hit Martín one time when she'd been like this. "Devil's got into her," her mother said when her temper flared.

"You and your symbolism! I do not know why I even came with you to this city!" she yelled, because he was being so damn calm and measured, and his voice was but a whisper.

There was a table by a window and on it a glass ashtray, rather heavy. She clutched it between her hands and wished to pelt him with it, but then, thinking better of it, she sat on the floor and tossed it aside.

"You came with me because we are linked together, unfortunately, and you need me to remove the shackles that bind us," he said. "And maybe because it's greater than you or I, this whole tale."

Casiopea stubbornly stared at her shoes. "I don't care," she said in a low voice.

He leaned down, as if to get a better look at her.

"We could try to do this another way, which would involve having to get a shovel and see if we can find a suitable corpse at the cemetery, but when it comes to necromancy, I am guessing you prefer to keep it simple, especially since time is ticking."

He spoke so serenely, so nicely. It made her feel petulant and silly, and it made her want to wail. So she bit her lip hard, because if she didn't she was going to really, truly, smack him across the face.

"Why not you? Why is it always *me* that has to make an offering?" Casiopea asked.

"Because, my dear, you are mortal and I am a god. Gods make no offerings of this sort," he said with a tone that was not condescending but had a delicate flatness to it.

She grew angrier, not exactly at him anymore, but at the whole universe, which, as usual, demanded that she be the lowest rung of the ladder. She had thought her position had changed when she'd left Uukumil, but it had not. She was Casiopea Tun, the stars aligned against her.

"Give me the scissors," she said, the cold fury of this thought granting her the strength to go through with the task.

She planted herself in the bathroom, glaring at the mirror, and at him, since he stood behind her. She made quick work of it. Although Casiopea attempted to maintain a steady hand, she butchered her hair. The dark strands fell to the floor, her long mane savaged by her own hand. For a moment she was fine. Another moment and she had tossed the scissors away and was crying, sitting on the edge of the bathtub.

She couldn't help it. The tears rolled down her cheeks even as she tried to blot them out. "It was the one thing . . . the only thing anyone ever told me was 'you have pretty hair,' " she whispered.

He looked at her with cool detachment and she felt embarrassed, sitting there with her eyes red, sniffling. She'd learned to keep her tears at bay; Martín teased her so much she had to. It was uncomfortable to behave like a child when she prided herself on her mettle and common sense. Hun-Kamé reached into his pocket and pulled out a handkerchief, handing it to the girl. She wiped her eyes roughly.

"You should start your summoning," she said, handing him back the handkerchief. There was no point in mourning her lost mane.

He gathered the hair, and they headed back to the bedroom. Hun-Kamé retrieved a metal wastebasket sitting by the desk, deposited the hair in it, then placed the wastebasket in the middle of the bedroom. He struck a match, setting the hair on fire, the sharp smell of it making her eyes watery again. All this occurred in perfect silence.

"Hold my hand," he told her. "Do not let go, even if you are frightened. And do not look into their eyes, do you understand?"

"Why?"

"Ghosts are hungry," he said simply. "Repeat with me: I shall hold on to your hand and I will not look into their eyes."

Casiopea thought she had no business holding any man's hand for an extended length of time, but then, she didn't like the word "hungry" paired with "ghosts."

"I'll hold on to your hand and I will not look into their eyes," she muttered, and she laced her fingers with his, feeling a little bold, but he did not complain.

Hun-Kamé spoke a few words. It was the same unknown language he'd spoken at the crossroads, only now she wasn't even sure it was a language. Just a sound, a hum.

The temperature plummeted and she felt goose bumps on her arms. It was not the same cold that they'd experienced in Veracruz. That had been like touching hail, while this was the cold of things that are long dead and rot in the sour earth.

Nothing else happened at first. Then she noticed that the shadows in the room had grown somewhat . . . darker. Light was streaming in from outside, beneath the curtains, and yet everything was grayer, the shadows like pools of ink. Then they shivered, the shadows, they stretched down the floor, growing larger, changing their shape. And they rose. They became solid. Yet they were not solid: it was as if someone had punched holes in the room and where something should have been there was darkness.

The shadows resembled people. They had arms, a torso, a head. They moved, darting across the room, ruffling the curtains, whispering among themselves.

In the middle of the room, the hair burned very bright, too bright, its glow the remaining source of illumination now because the shadows dominated everything, not a single stray ray of light creeping in from the outside. An endless darkness and the shadow people standing in front of them, very close, the dim fire revealing that they had no features, their faces were smooth as pebbles.

Hun-Kamé had told her to hold his hand, but instead she squeezed it tight. The room's expensive furniture, the massive bed, the oil paintings on the walls, they all had faded. What was left was merely darkness. She was not even sure if there was a floor beneath their feet. Hun-Kamé alone anchored her in place.

"You called for us," one of the shadow persons said, though none of them had a mouth.

"I thank you for attending me. I am Hun-Kamé, Lord of Xibalba, who searches for his stolen essence. Somewhere in this city a piece of myself has been hidden. Do you know where it might be?"

"Answers have a price."

"Rest assured, it shall be paid," Hun-Kamé said and tossed strands of her long hair, which he held in his free hand, at them.

The shadows gurgled and scrabbled, snatching bits of hair and eating them. They did have mouths, after all, and long, gray tongues, which rolled out onto the floor, and they had eyes that glowed blue-green, slits of color floating in the dark. Casiopea felt her body turn into iron, and now she didn't only hold the death god's hand, she shifted very close to him.

"This is nothing, these are scraps," one of the shadows said.

"Careful," Hun-Kamé said, "mind your words. I am kind now, but I could be harsher and wring the truth from you."

"Refuse and filth, bits and pieces and nothing whole," the shadow said. "Give us fresh meat and bones instead. Give us *her*."

All the blue-green eyes turned toward Casiopea in unison, and they were fearsome, and one of them held her gaze.

Had she been able to distinguish their faces, even if they looked like rotten corpses, she might not have been so scared. But in the dark the shadows had the outlines of childhood monsters and they held her in their thrall, their blue-green glow making her think of evil dreams. They smelled bad, too, sickly-sweet; the aroma of wilted flowers.

She raised her hands to cover her mouth, fearing she'd scream, and when her fingers touched her lips she realized she had let go of Hun-Kamé. She looked around, trying to hold on to him, but he was gone. The room was gone. The fire was dying away. There were only the dark pillars that shuffled closer and closer to her, their glowing eyes growing more vivid, their tongues brushing the floor.

"Oh, her heart, we'll chew it twice and then spit it and chew it again," one of the shadows said.

"And the marrow, the marrow too. We'll drink from her veins," replied another.

A tongue snaked in Casiopea's direction, brushing her foot, and she gasped and stepped away from it, but the circle of shadows grew tighter, they closed in around her like a noose. North and south and east and west. They were everywhere.

She pressed her hands against her mouth again, panicked, and for one moment she suspected the god had intended to leave her with these things all along. That it had been a ruse and she was to be their meal. But there was the bone shard in her finger. He wouldn't.

The shadows were so close, and their putrescence made her want to gag. They opened their mouths, and their breath curled out, cold and humid and blue-green, making her wince.

If only she'd held on to his hand!

"And . . . and not looked into their eyes," she whispered.

But she was looking! She realized then that she had not stopped looking at that one shadow that had caught her gaze. She drew a deep breath and closed her eyes, and felt her body sway, and there was the grip of hands on her shoulders.

"Casiopea, look at me," a voice said.

"No," she replied, her eyes closed tight.

She felt warm breath from human lips as he leaned down to speak into her ear. "It is me, Hun-Kamé," he said.

She snapped her eyes open and looked up at him, and he looked down at her, slowly taking her left hand between his. The shadows grumbled and sighed around them; a couple of them spat on the floor. She could see the outlines of the room again and the wastebasket with the burning hair.

"We are famished!" they said. "We are hungry!"

"Oh, she nearly forgot herself," wailed another.

"Quiet, you degenerate fiends, and attend me," Hun-Kamé said, his voice cutting through their muttering like a blade. "Your eyes, on the ground, don't you dare raise them again."

The shadows hissed, and their blue-green glow grew narrow until they had no eyes. Blind they stood before both of them.

"Now, tell me what I need to know."

The shadows spoke to one another in animated whispers, bowing their heads, as if conferring among themselves. Their tongues lolled out and in of their mouths. The matter decided, they spoke again.

"Head to Xtabay's abode," a shadow said. Perhaps the same one that had caught her eye before, perhaps another. Casiopea could not tell them apart.

"Where does she reside?"

"Nearby, see here," the shadow said and a spark of fire, from the burning hair, lifted itself into the air and traced a line, a shape.

"My thanks," Hun-Kamé said and tossed the last bits of hair to the shadows, which fell onto one another to devour them. And as they fell, blending, becoming one, the cold from the room ebbed, the darkness changed, and they were standing in the middle of a normal room, a tendril of smoke rising from the wastebasket, the bustling city again outside their window.

"I told you not to look at them," Hun-Kamé said, letting go of her hand. He sounded grim, and she felt silly for the whole episode. First she'd wept, then she'd lost hold of him. And she'd been so scared, like a girl.

"I know," she muttered.

The hair he'd tossed on the floor and the burnt hair in the wastebasket had vanished, but a sulfuric stench lingered in the room. He opened the windows to allow light and air in, and Casiopea was grateful for this gesture because the air inside was charged and stale.

Casiopea breathed in slowly. She felt supremely tired, her legs threatening to buckle beneath her. Her hand throbbed and she rubbed it, bending down at the same time, as if a heavy stone had been deposited on her shoulders. She straightened herself quickly enough, but he had noticed.

"I apologize thoroughly. This was taxing for you," he said, and now he didn't seem grim, just sober and measured.

"I . . . I'm not even sure . . . what were those things?" she asked.

"Ghosts."

"I didn't imagine ghosts were like that."

Not that she had pictured ghosts as people wearing sheets, with two holes cut out for their eyes, or as wispy, floating apparitions. She hadn't thought they'd be as frightening as they'd been. Nor that they might try to eat her.

"Certain ghosts. There are others, like those who haunt the roads and devour children, for one," Hun-Kamé said with a shrug. "You should rest."

"I'm not sure I want to nap," she said, suddenly afraid of all the creatures that lurk in the dark and the shadows that might invade the room if she drew the curtains.

"And I assure you, you should. I do not say this idly. When I cast magic, I draw from your strength."

She stared at him. "Like . . ."

"I feed off you. You know this."

"Not like this, not—"

"Every minute of every hour, and when I use my magic, even more. Come, lie down," he said, clasping her hand and drawing her toward the bed, then gesturing for her to sit.

Casiopea sat at the head of it, clutching a decorative pillow between her hands. She had wanted to see Mexico City, and when she did she had not expected she would be frightened by ghosts. Nor did she think she'd spend her first evening there asleep because a god had used her hair and her energy to conjure said ghosts. She'd imagined a nebulous sort of fun. But there was little fun to be had; even Carnival had not been enjoyed, merely observed from afar.

"It's not right," she said, frowning and toying with the pillow's tassels. "It isn't fair. I'm food for them or . . . or for you."

"And who ever told you life was fair?"

"Maybe I thought it would be fairer with a god at my side."

"That is rather naïve," he said. "I'll have to dissuade you about this. Who said this to you?"

He seemed so utterly serious—not cruel, just serious and concerned, as if he'd just discovered she didn't know how to count to ten—about this matter that it made her chuckle.

"What amuses you?"

"Nothing. I suppose I might nap for a bit," she told him, rather than explaining herself. She didn't think he'd understand. "I guess you'll want to sleep too."

"I do not sleep."

They had shared their quarters on the boat and the train, but she had not checked to see if he slept. He certainly lay on his berth. She had assumed he must rest too.

"But you said you slept in the chest, and Loray, he told me some gods sleep," she said, remembering that detail.

"I also said it was not like your sleep, and as you can imagine, it was under extraordinary circumstances that I engaged in this activity."

She considered this, nodding and placing the pillow back on the bed, behind her. "That means you don't dream," she said.

"Dreams are for mortals."

"Why?"

"Because they must die."

Somehow this made a perfect sort of sense. The volume of Aztec poetry she had read was full of lines about dreams and flowers, the futility of existence.

"That's sad," she said, finally.

"Death? It is unavoidable, not sad."

"No, not death," she said, shaking her head. "That you don't dream."

"Why would I need to dream? It means nothing. Those are but the tapestries of mortals, woven and unwoven each night on a rickety loom."

"They can be beautiful."

"As if there's no other beauty to be had," he said dismissively.

"There's little of it, for some," she replied.

She thought of the daily drudgery at Uukumil. Rise, get grandfather's breakfast to his room, take the dishes back to the kitchen, sweep a floor or scrub it clean. Each evening a meal with her mother, each night a prayer to her guardian angel. Sundays at church, the clothes clinging to her skin, the day too hot. The secret time to peruse the pages of her father's book. Her mother, brushing her hair and smoothing her worries. And again, this cycle.

"Is that why you stare at the stars?" he asked. "Are you searching for beauty or dreaming with your eyes wide open?"

"My father was an astronomy enthusiast. He knew the names of the stars and he'd point them out. I try not to forget them."

She also tried to retain the sound of his voice when he told her legends before bedtime, but truth be told she'd forgotten. This made her sad, but she attempted to clutch the other remains of his memory even more tightly, holding with special reverence a book of poems by Francisco de Quevedo with pages falling out, like a withered daisy, which had rested by her father's bedside when he passed away.

"My grandfather was so angry when he heard they'd called me Casiopea. Grandfather wanted a good Christian name, not some Mayan nonsense, and threatened to cut off contact with my mother if they went with that. Then they named me Casiopea. 'It's Greek nonsense, now,' my father said."

She remembered the priest's face when he'd heard she had no proper Christian name. He insisted on calling her María, and when that didn't work, "the Leyva girl," eliminating Tun. Now that she thought about it, that's what most people called her, even though she had girl cousins, and any of them might have been "the Leyva girl." There had been talk that some of those cousins ought to go to a boarding school, but Grandfather was old-fashioned and believed a woman's place was at home, where she could focus on learning to be a proper wife. Martín had gone to a school when he'd been younger, but fed up with the rules and lessons there, he'd got himself expelled. Grandfather did not bother sending him back again.

"My grandfather didn't appreciate the wittiness of the statement. He cut her off anyway. Then my father died and we had to go live in Uukumil," she said. "Had I known you were trapped in that chest, I would have released you years ago, to spite him."

"I would have been very grateful," he replied. "As for those stars of yours and your dreams, I suppose they've kept you company, and there is no folly in them."

She pressed a cheek against the bed's padded headboard and glanced up at him. Her eyelids felt heavy but she didn't want him to go yet, she wanted him to stay by the bed, looking down at her, his hands in his pockets, an eyebrow quirked.

"It's odd to imagine the stars keeping someone company, as if they were ladies in waiting," she said, unable to suppress a yawn despite her best effort.

"I certainly wouldn't pick stars as my attendants, but then I am not mortal."

"What attendants do you have?" she asked.

"What kind of attendants do you picture?"

Casiopea imagined skeletons and bats and owls—all manner of creatures that haunt the night, since those were the elements that embroidered the tales of the realm of Xibalba.

"Frightful ones," she said tentatively. "Am I wrong?"

"Dead ladies, noblemen, and priests who bought passage into my kingdom centuries ago, attired in their finery."

He smiled, as if recalling his throne room and his courtiers, and although she truly did not wish to gaze upon this world of his, she smiled too, because the memory of Xibalba brought him joy. He looked at her, then, and noticing her exhaustion—or another detail that gave him pause—he set a hand against his chest and dipped his head politely.

"I'll let you sleep," he said.

She nodded, placed her head against the very white pillows, not even bothering to get under the covers.

She heard his footsteps as he moved away, and then they stopped.

"Rest assured, your vanity can remain safe," he told her.

Casiopea lifted her head and frowned. He was by the connecting door, looking down at the floor, as if in deep thought. She wasn't sure she hadn't imagined the words, since he wasn't looking at her.

"I'm sorry?"

"You were worried about the hair. You said it was the only becoming feature you possess," Hun-Kamé said.

"It doesn't matter. A hat—"

"It's not the only one," he said.

It was a simple utterance, which she might have accepted graciously had his gaze not fixed on her with an austere sincerity that made her panic and gape at him like a damn fool.

"Thank you?" she mumbled at last.

He closed the adjoining door and Casiopea stared at it for a long time, the sleep that had been courting her having vanished. She wondered what those becoming traits were. He'd said once before that she was pretty, but she hadn't quite believed him. He was merely being kind, she told herself. But even if he was, it was both nice and odd to experience such chivalry.

Chapter 13

They ordered room service, which Casiopea had never done before, but the hotel clerk had mentioned it when they checked in, so she'd gone downstairs to inquire how this service might be obtained. They probably thought her a country bumpkin, asking such a thing, but Casiopea had never been reluctant to learn.

There were a myriad of food options, but she opted for bread rolls and marmalade, knowing little of what one was supposed to purchase in such a place, plus hot coffee. Shortly thereafter a hotel employee knocked at her door, wheeling in a cart and depositing two dishes on the table.

Hun-Kamé and Casiopea discussed their schedule for the day, eating by the open window. Hun-Kamé wanted to go to a jewelry store, which Casiopea thought odd.

"What would you need from there?" she asked, dipping the bolillo in her coffee.

"A necklace, very likely. If we are to see Xtabay tonight we cannot head there empty-handed."

"I thought gods did not make any offerings."

"It's not an offering, it's a gesture of goodwill. Besides, I won't be carrying it, you will," he said airily.

Casiopea pointed at him with the butter knife. "You consider me your maid."

"My ally, dear lady," he replied, sipping his coffee slowly, as if he was still reluctant to taste earthly dishes.

She frowned, picking at the center of the bolillo, extracting the soft bread from the harder shell. She didn't have the luxury of eating the soft part of the bolillo back home, having to munch whatever was available under the watchful eye of her mother. Now she could do as she pleased, and she rolled bits of soft bread, tossing them into her mouth.

"You could spin a few jewels out of rocks," she said.

"I can't do that."

"I've seen you turn stones into coins," she reminded him.

"I cannot alter the nature of an object. It is merely a play of light and shadow, an illusion."

"Will the illusion wear off?"

"Illusions always wear off."

They asked the concierge about jewelry shops. There were suitable shops all down Madero—stubborn capitalinos still referred to it as Plateros, unwilling to accept the name change that honored a murdered president—but he emphasized La Esmeralda, which had been the darling of the Porfirian aristocracy. La Esmeralda was looted in 1914 by Carranza's troops, but that seemed like a lifetime ago. It had been renovated seven years before, grew more splendorous, and advertised itself as a place for "art objects and timepieces," selling all sorts of wildly expensive baubles.

The store was grand, but like many newer buildings in Mexico it was also a mishmash of styles, French rococo mixing with neoclassic, a little vulgar if one looked at it closely. Most capitalinos did not realize that the architectonic pretensions of the building were more *nouveau riche* than Art Nouveau, and, had this been explained to them, they would have denied the building had any deficiencies.

The store's name was boldly emblazoned across the front, a clock marking the hour above it. Before its iron skeleton was erected a more modest three-story building had stood there, made of red tezontle, best suited for the soft Mexico City soil that had been, after all, a city of canals before the Spaniards filled up its waterways. But then Hauser and Zivy had that old house smashed and established the Esmeralda in its place, a store in which the distinguished consumer could order Baccarat crystal and elaborate music boxes. Inside, the building was all marble, glass, and dark wood, gleaming crystal and profuse decorations.

Hun-Kamé knew what he wanted, focusing on gold necklaces. Casiopea, meanwhile, looked at a heavy silver bracelet with black enamel triangles, of the "Aztec" style, which was much in vogue and meant to attract the eye of tourists with its faux pre-Hispanic motifs. It was a new concoction, of the kind that abound in a Mexico happy to invent traditions for mass consumption, eager to forge an identity after the fires of the revolution—but it was pretty.

"You should try it on," said the saleswoman, smelling a commission.

"I couldn't," Casiopea said.

"I'm sure your husband will think it pretty."

"He is not my husband," she replied.

The saleswoman gave her a funny look, and Casiopea realized she must think she was Hun-Kamé's mistress. How embarrassing!

Casiopea tugged at her hair, self-conscious. She had informed Hun-Kamé she'd have to go to a hairdresser that same day, since her work with the scissors had been poor. She'd look like a flapper now and they'd think her a loose girl. The saleswoman probably judged her a tart already.

It was very important not to be a tart. But she was already wearing skirts that showed her legs. What were the other requirements for such a designation? Did it matter if she wasn't one but merely looked the part?

"If you like it, you should take a closer look at it," Hun-Kamé said, hovering next to her.

"It's expensive."

"I already bought an expensive necklace, a bracelet is no concern."

She tried it on and then he asked. "Would you like it?"

"Truly?" she replied.

"If you wish it," he said, signaling to the saleswoman, who took the bracelet and began to place tissue paper in a box.

"If I wore it in Uukumil they'd say it's gaudy and the priest would chide me."

"You're not in Uukumil."

Casiopea smiled at him. The saleswoman placed the lid on the box and she gave Casiopea a curious look. She was probably confused, trying to determine if Casiopea was a mistress already or a would-be one, meant to be seduced with nice jewelry.

"Thank you," Casiopea said when they left the store. "I've never owned anything of value and nothing this pretty."

In the middle of the street a policeman was directing traffic, looking bored, while she looked nervously at the semaphore and the multitudes around them, trying to determine at which point it was safe to cross the street. She eyed the streetcars fearfully and the automobiles in wonder, and someone behind shoved her aside, eager to get to the other side of the street. She was confused by the city and its incessant activity, but also happy and grateful for Hun-Kamé's company. She thought of him as her friend.

It was not the gift that had prompted this, but their daily interactions, his politeness, which were quickly endearing him to her. This was hardly surprising considering how few friends Casiopea had.

There was her mother, who with her never-ending optimism helped the young woman face each day. Casiopea's female cousins tended to ignore her. When she was younger she had been able to play with the children of the maids and the other boys and girls in town, but as she matured everyone grew distant. Her grandfather was the cause of this, since he didn't want any grandchild of his, however nominal, in the company of "rabble."

Casiopea, caught in this in-between state, focused on her chores instead of socializing. In her spare time, she looked to books or the stars for company.

To have someone at her side was alien and yet a delight. There was joy in the quest, now, the joy of her nascent freedom and his company.

"It is of no consequence," he replied.

"It is to me," she said. "And I want to say . . . of course I want to say thank you, even if I have no idea why you even bothered with it."

She smiled. In return, he gave her a smidgen of a smile, so tiny she felt she might have to cup it in her hands to keep it safe, or the wind might blow it away.

The Lord of Xibalba did not smile often, and he did not laugh. This does not mean he did not find amusement in certain things. It was a dry sort of amusement, which was not polluted by mirth. That he smiled now was because he was dislocated, altered and altering, and due to the mortality creeping in his veins. But it was also because, like Casiopea, he had been alone for a very long time and found an amount of comfort in the company of another being.

He drew nearer to her, the smile growing, becoming careless. Abruptly he remembered himself. The smile faded. She did not notice, too busy turning her head, looking down the avenue.

"I should find a hairdresser," Casiopea told him as they crossed another street.

"Would you like me to accompany you?" he asked.

"I can manage," she said, not wanting to seem a child who must be guided at every turn.

"Then I will see you back at the hotel," he replied, handing her several bills.

She looked at the money. "Won't it turn into a puff of smoke when you walk away?"

"Don't worry. Loray gave me real money; I have not been casting illusions in order to obtain sufficient legal tender. Though he'll have to wire more if we want to pay people in these delightful bills rather than sticks and stones. A nuisance. Were I in Xibalba, I'd simply command my servants to bring me the jewels and treasures of the earth. Were I in Xibalba I'd show you truly fine jewelry to wear, necklaces of silver moths and the blackest pearls you've ever seen, darker than the darkest ink."

"This bracelet is more than fine," she said simply, running her fingers along its surface, for she did not want to begin wishing for impossibilities and great treasures.

She set off, then, first to find a post office. Casiopea had thought to write her mother a letter explaining herself, but she considered better of it. She decided a letter would be too problematic. She would not know where to begin or end her narrative. Instead, she opted for a pretty postcard. Casiopea kept her words brief, saying she was in Mexico City and was doing well, that she would write more later and send her address. She guessed that by now everyone in town thought she'd run off with a lover, and she did not bother to mention the presence of her companion. Besides, she could hardly say "and I am with a god at this time."

After the post office Casiopea found a hairdresser who looked at her curiously, wondering if she'd tried to bob her hair by herself. Casiopea lied and said that had been the case.

"Yes, bobbed hair is all the rage," the hairdresser told her. "My husband doesn't like it much, but it makes for good business. You're not from here, are you? Your accent . . ."

And so on and so forth, the hairdresser trailed on, making small talk. She informed Casiopea that the best place to go dancing, if she was looking for such fun, was the Salón Mexico, though it was important that she pay for the first-class section.

"You want to be in the 'butter,' not the 'lard' or the 'tallow,'" the hairdresser explained, because that's what they nicknamed the sections. "The butter is where the decent men in suits and ties go to dance."

The lard, the hairdresser told her, was where small-time employees, maids from fancy houses, and secretaries congregated. The tallow was the lowest of the low, and no decent lady should head there. It was full of whores, she was warned.

But when Casiopea looked in the mirror and saw her bangs and her short hair grazing her cheek, she thought she looked like the whores they'd warned her about. And yet her hair seemed quite nice. This might mean that the whores were not as bad as they'd said. Or maybe it meant something else entirely. Like most questions that had assaulted her during her journey, Casiopea had an impressive ability to mark them down as topics she should process later, but that she could not be bothered to consider at the time.

She exited the hairdresser's shop and for a block or two, she walked very slowly, fearful that people would point at her, even ridicule her new hairstyle. But the pedestrians kept walking, the policemen directed traffic, the motorists banged their palm against the horn. Mexico City was too busy to notice a young, provincial girl with her black hair cut short. She gave a beggar a smile and asked a woman for directions, and neither person seemed shocked by her appearance.

Casiopea let out a sigh of relief, realizing no one was going to stop her because she looked different. Just as she was smiling, however, a heavy hand fell on her shoulder.

"Casiopea, we have to talk," a voice said.

She knew that voice well. It was her cousin Martín.

Chapter 14

Our *Father, who art in heaven,* he told himself, repeating the Lord's prayer inside his head. But then he switched from prayer to curses, and back again. The curses were all destined for Casiopea.

He kept his eyes closed tight, fearing he might fall and dash his body against the ground, and the owl flapped its wings quickly. It was a gigantic creature, its talons large enough to lift a man in the air, and Martín kept thinking it would either throw him off his back or rend him with its beak and devour him whole.

The night wind toyed with the young man's hair and he squeezed his eyes harder, he held tight to the feathers and the flesh of this supernatural creature. When the owl landed on the roof of a building, Martín could hardly contain his joy. He almost burst into tears.

"Your cousin will be at the Hotel Mancera," the owl told him.

Or at least he thought it was the owl who had spoken, although it might have been Vucub-Kamé making himself heard through the animal, since the bird's voice had a flintlike quality that made Martín bow his head, respect instinctive in the presence of the unnatural.

"You will tell the girl the Lord of Xibalba wishes to speak with her," the owl said. "But do not scare her. It is best to make an ally than an enemy."

"Of course," Martín said, although he frankly thought it might be better to slap some sense into his cousin. "What if she refuses?"

"Then we will determine another way to proceed. Do nothing else without the Supreme Lord's consent," the owl said, before it batted its wings and flew off into the night.

Martín was left alone on the roof of a building he did not know, in a city he had never visited before. It was the middle of the night, and he was afraid of being robbed by ruffians. He was also dreadfully cold; the trip on the owl's back had left him sniffling and tired. Martín checked himself into a hotel near Casiopea's lodgings and went to sleep because there was little he could do until the morning and he needed a pillow under his head and a hot bath.

He hoped for good dreams. Instead, he dreamed of Uukumil, his childhood, and his hateful cousin.

In dreams, she hit him with the stick and Grandfather laughed.

Martín Leyva was indolent, proud, and cruel. His faults were not solely the result of an inherent nature. They had been honed and coaxed by his family, through explicit action and through lapses in judgment.

As a man he already saw himself as worthy of praise. As a Leyva, child of the wealthiest family in town, his ego grew inflated. There was little he could not do, from berating the servants to lording over his female cousins and his sisters as if he were the ruler of a principality. His grandfather was a bitter tyrant, and Martín copied his mannerisms, feeling disappointed with his father, who was a much more placid fellow, meek, gray, and subdued by the patriarch. Rather than imitate the father, then, he took after the grandfather. He considered himself the future Man of the House, the undisputed macho of the Leyva clan.

Nevertheless, sometimes cracks showed in his narcissistic façade. Martín was sent off to a good school but expelled. He'd had a hard time fitting in at the institution. Not only were the intellectual demands too much for his limited, closed brain, but he could discern scorn in the faces of the other pupils. The Leyvas were kings of Uukumil, but not kings of Mérida. He felt like an outsider, diminished. Unable to be the center of attention, he managed to get himself packed back to his hometown and refused to return to the school.

But home did not offer the respite he might have expected, mainly because Casiopea was living with the family.

At first, Martín had not quite known how to react to the girl, who was two years his junior. He was aloof, but his cool indifference turned to outright anger the more he observed her. First of all, there was Casiopea's personality, which irritated him.

The day he returned from school, the letter narrating his expulsions clasped between his hands, she'd been with Grandfather to observe his humiliation . . .

His sisters and his other girl cousins were mild, quiet creatures who knew better than to defy him. But Casiopea was made of sterner stuff. She did as she was told, but sometimes she'd protest. She'd rebel. And even if she said nothing, he read mutiny in her eyes.

Then there was the matter of her intelligence. Martín thought books were for fools. If a man could do long division and read the headlines of the newspapers, that was all that was required. For a while he had read the paper for his grandfather, stumbling over big words, until the man, exasperated, assigned the task to the younger girl. Lo and behold, she could read well, could write in a neat hand, and did her sums with surprising quickness. Her mother had taught the child, and then the child continued to teach herself more. Martín believed this was suspicious, unfeminine.

"Why couldn't you be a boy?" Grandfather said, eyes on Casiopea, and Martín almost broke into tears . . .

Hostile, he circled around the girl, issuing orders, seeking to dominate her, finding pleasure in this power. Yet he held back an inch. There was the slim veneer of civility to his actions. He spoke unpleasantries, but in the tone of a gentleman.

This changed when she hit him. He had been goading her for a while and did not think she'd break. But then Martín told her that she was almost a bastard: her mother had been pregnant when she married, round with child. Casiopea grabbed a stick and swung it against the boy's head.

She almost took out his eye. In pain, hollering, thinking he had been dramatically injured, Martín had wept until his mother and the other members of the family ran out to see what was wrong.

Casiopea pretended she hadn't heard the words, ducking her head, but she'd heard and Martín had heard . . . Why couldn't you be a boy?

The beating Casiopea received from Grandfather did not satisfy Martín. Nothing could satisfy him. He quivered in his bed as the doctor examined him and rubbed an ointment on his face. A man, overcome by a girl. Because at fifteen he had considered himself a man already, and suddenly he was reduced back to infancy. He saw the disgust in his grandfather's face, the veiled smiles of the servants, the scorn there, hidden and quiet and real, and he felt such utter shame.

He hated her from then on. It was not animosity or the scuffles of youth; he could not stand her.

Although, if he admitted it to himself, the trouble had started before, that day when he returned from school. But he did not like to think of it. Somehow the physical beating was a better start to the animosity. It justified it more neatly. She'd started it.

In dreams, she hit him with the stick and Grandfather laughed. Martín twisted and turned and muttered in his bed, her name on his lips.

Martín disliked the city when he saw it at night, and his impression did not improve once the sun was out. He thought it was too large and indifferent to him, that here he was nobody, while in Uukumil he was Young Mister Leyva, people tipping their hats at him when he walked by.

Martín's brain was rather dismal in its ability to imagine anything that was not solid and palpable, but he did fantasize about success. These were coarse dreams of money, nebulous power, undisputed respect. In Mexico City Martín felt the metropolis dwarfing him and his desires. He did not enjoy it.

Early he rose and went to station himself outside the Hotel Mancera, thinking he might wait to see if Casiopea would come out. She did and walked in the company of a man in a navy jacket, dark-haired. It was Hun-Kamé, no doubt. They went into a store and then separated—which suited Martín's purposes perfectly—at which point she headed to the hairdresser.

He caught her when she came out, her hair shockingly short. He disliked her look at once and even more the way her eyes darted up to his face, concerned but not as afraid as she ought to have been.

"What are you doing here?" she asked.

"I could say the same thing," he told her. "Your mother's been worried sick, you did not even leave a note, and Grandfather will not shut up about you."

This much was true, but he said it in order to admonish and mollify her, not because he cared to inform her about the state of affairs in Uukumil. He thought if he could make her feel guilty, he might get her to agree to the meeting.

"I'm sorry if I've made anyone uneasy," Casiopea said, and she did look honestly pained, but then she frowned. "How did you know I was here? I've told no one."

"You didn't think you could steal—"

"Steal? I didn't steal anything," she replied, interrupting him.

"You did, you stole some bones that were locked in an old box and now we've got hell to pay for it."

They were standing in the middle of the street. Martín maneuvered his cousin aside, so that they were now under the awning of a store, which offered more privacy.

"What do you mean?" Casiopea said.

"The Lord of Xibalba, Vucub-Kamé, is upset. He's angry at Grandfather, at your mother, at me, at every single Leyva."

"You had nothing to do with it."

"Try telling that to a god."

His words were having the expected effect. Casiopea lowered her eyes, her lips pursed.

"I'm sorry. But I don't see why you are here," she muttered.

"*He's* sent me."

"Vucub-Kamé?"

"Yes, of course. Didn't you wonder what would happen to us when he learned what you'd done?"

"I . . . I had no choice," she protested. "But if you must blame someone, you can blame me."

"What good do you think that might do? He is upset."

"But—"

"However, Vucub-Kamé did say he'd be willing to listen to your side of the story."

Someone came out of the store and elbowed Martín away. He frowned, and would have barked a nasty word or two at the fool who dared to push him like that, but there was no chance of it. Blasted city with its rude citizens, Martín would swear no one could recognize him as a man of good breeding in this place, not with this smelly stew of unsuitable people.

"My side of the story?" Casiopea repeated.

"Yes. He wants to speak to you. Casiopea, you must say yes. If you decline, who knows what ruinous future awaits us. Grandfather served Vucub-Kamé, and that is how we came to be so well positioned in Uukumil. He is our protector."

"He's certainly never behaved like my protector," Casiopea replied.

"Cousin, I realize we've done you a bad turn. But I promise you that if you talk to him, all of that will be in the past, and upon your return home, with me, you'll have a rightful place in Uukumil, as it should have been from the beginning."

Although not terribly imaginative, Martín did have a natural talent for pushing people's buttons and understanding their moods. He was a manipulator at heart, and though he had a difficult time establishing true intimacy with others, he could pretend it. Therefore, he had considered what the best way to speak to his cousin might be, and he had decided he must be firm, but also promise a reward that could soften her. The lure of a social position, a place in the family, those were to him the most natural appeals. After all, he was highly aware of the pecking order and he imagined others were as well.

"I am sure Vucub-Kamé could be made to understand that we are innocent, that we have not willingly betrayed his trust. Grandfather will be very grateful if you make the Lord of Xibalba see this."

"Hun-Kamé is the Lord of Xibalba," she said.

"He was. Not anymore. Casiopea, you do not owe him anything, but you owe the family your loyalty. You are a Leyva," he concluded.

The girl was stunned by the speech. He saw her shrink, her shoulders falling, her whole frame becoming smaller. Martín smelled success. Years bullying Casiopea had done the trick, made him aware of how to shove the girl around. But then she raised her head, eyes brighter than they should have been.

He had not recalled—had not wanted to recall—the rebellious streak that marked his cousin, how once in a while she talked back at him or muttered under her breath. That rebellion was in full bloom now as she straightened up and threw him a cold, determined look.

"Hun-Kamé needs my help," she said.

"And we don't? You'll treat us as if we were rubbish?"

"You are the one who has treated me like rubbish, and now that you need me you are willing to offer me the things I've wanted. I wanted so much to be liked by you and the family, to make Grandfather proud, but nothing I've ever done has been good enough."

The brat! Talking to him with a brazen tone, the way no woman should talk to a man. She was imperious, like he was somehow beneath her when she ought to have fallen on her knees and begged for forgiveness. She should have agreed without hesitation to do as he said. He was so shocked he could not even begin to speak.

"You will pick him over us?" Martín asked, outraged, when he managed to recover his wits.

"He has shown me more respect and kindness in a few days than you ever showed me my entire life," Casiopea said, her words slow and deliberate. "I do not care about your crumbs."

Crumbs! What a ridiculous thing to say when he was offering her the greatest honor imaginable. Brat and bitch. Ungrateful bastard. He wanted to hurl insults at her, but the girl had already stepped away, done with him. The gesture was even worse than her speech. He'd always dismissed Casiopea, he said when their conversation was over. She was supposed to do as he said, when he said it.

"Where do you think you're going?" Martín demanded, and he clutched her arm.

She froze, lips open, and looked so utterly tiny he almost felt sorry for her. Almost.

Suddenly she clasped her mouth shut, raised her chin, and gave him a shove. He lost his balance and the wicked creature took off, leaping away like a hare. Martín tried to follow her, pushing people aside, but she was swift and small, and waded between pedestrians with much more ease than he did.

"Stop!" he demanded, giving chase. "Stop!"

She looked over her shoulder at him, but she did not slow down. A boy on a bicycle, a basket with bread balanced atop his head, was blocking the way and he thought, *Aha, I've got you!* Martín rushed forward, his fingers gripping her sleeve, but she elbowed him away and pushed the boy on the bicycle aside, sending sweet breads flying around.

The boy groaned, climbing off the bicycle to pick up the bread that had fallen on the ground, and Martín almost collided with him.

There was an intersection up ahead, and the traffic light was about to change. He thought she wouldn't chance it.

She dashed across the street.

Damn her!

Martín prepared to go after her, but the light turned green and cars were streaming by, the traffic like a river separating them. Anyway, she'd turned a corner and he couldn't see her anymore, lost among multitudes. He took off his hat, clutching it between his hands in frustration.

A beggar sat at the corner with a tin cup in his lap and a cardboard sign at his feet that said "ALMS." He was an old man, the deep creases on his face flecked with dirt, his white hair greasy. When he opened his mouth one saw a maw with nary a tooth. Where there had been a left arm, there dangled an empty flap of clothing.

The beggar raised his cup and rattled it, trying to attract Martín's attention. The young man looked down at the poor wretch and instead of offering the man a few coins, he kicked his cardboard sign away.

"Motherfucker!" the beggar yelled.

Martín did not reply. He stomped all the way across the street. The beggar stood up and kept yelling, "Motherfucker, mother-fucker!" When Martín disappeared, the man grabbed his sign and set it back in place, then he sat down again with a loud grumble. The pedestrians, having seen such spectacles before, returned to their routine, heads down, eyes on the newspapers, or else they in-spected their watches and the billboards advertising face creams and detergents.

Chapter 15

"And what did you tell him?"

"What do you think I told him? Told him to take a hike," Casiopea said.

She kept walking in circles, sick with worry. Hun-Kamé, on the other hand, was leaning back in a plush chair. Nice suit, black hair slicked back, he looked more bored than anything else.

"Doesn't it bother you? Your brother has tracked us down," she said.

"I imagined he'd track us down, sooner or later. I'm glad you did not agree to speak to him, though," he replied. "Nothing good would come of it."

"He tried to explain that I'd be welcome back at home. As if that might ever happen. Oh, why are you looking so calm?"

Because he did look far too calm. Carved in stone. Apparently, he did not wish to partake in her agitation, which disturbed her even more. It was as if a mirror refused to give back her reflection.

"Would it please you if I ran around like a headless chicken, as you do?" he inquired.

He seemed to be fond of comparing her to animals. She wondered what he'd come up with next. A turtle? A cat? She might be an entire zoo to him, both funny monkey and pretty bird.

"You are scared of what, precisely?" he asked her before she could become properly incensed by the comment.

"Well, I'm . . . I'm scared of your brother, of course. He's found us."

"I do not think it is what frightens you. Is it your cousin that has you in such a state?"

Casiopea stopped moving for a second, her hands clasped under her breast. Although she wished to tell him that no, Martín had nothing to do with this, the truth was he had everything to do with her current agitation. But it wasn't him. When she reached deep into herself, she found a slightly different answer.

"I don't want to go back to Uukumil," she whispered.

She missed her mother, she felt unsure of herself outside of the safety of her town, and she had no idea where their adventure would eventually lead them, but she did not wish to turn back, for turning away from a quest felt to her akin to sacrilege.

"When I saw him . . . for a moment, I thought he'd make me go back. He always gets his way and I have to do as he says. And I keep thinking . . ." She trailed off. She did not understand herself.

"What if you are shackled to the loser in this contest?" Hun-Kamé said, his voice dry. "What if your cousin is the smarter one, sitting in the victor's corner."

"What if I'm only free for a few days?" she replied, the disquiet of a butterfly fearing it will be trampled.

Hun-Kamé had been looking around the room, distracted. Now he gazed at her. The god's age was unknowable; it eluded a specific bracket. He was not old, yet he did not give the appearance of youth. One may count the rings of trees to know the time of their birth, but there were no lines on his face to offer such clues. There was a sense of permanence in him that rendered such inquiries null.

When he looked at her, however, Casiopea noticed he was boy-ish, which she'd never realized before. Of course, this was because he had never been young before. But in that moment he reflected her, sympathy and the same apprehension masking him. Somehow this capacity to understand her also brought forth the strange change in his countenance. No longer ageless, he was a young man. Twenty-one, twenty, a passerby would have guessed.

"I ask myself the same question," he told her, and his voice was equally young, jade-green, the color of the ceiba tree before it reaches maturity.

As soon as he'd spoken, the youth dissipated, as if he'd remembered his full nature and the extent of his roots. Hun-Kamé's face grew still, whatever ripple that had stirred it fading. He was again ageless, polished like a dark mirror. The change was so startling and so quick, Casiopea was not certain it had taken place.

Hun-Kamé turned his head again, looking in the direction of the window. The wind was stirring the curtains.

"We need to speak to Xtabay," he said, smoothing his hair and standing up. He reached for the box with the necklace, which he'd left atop a coffee table.

"I've heard she is a demoness," Casiopea said, glad to change the topic. Ghosts that devour people and monsters of smoke were much easier for her to consider than her family and the fears knotted under her skin.

"Not a demoness. Who said that to you? Your town's priest?" he asked.

The stories had not come from the priest, but from the gossip of the servants. The priest would not have abided such talk, complaining as he did about the Yucatec propensity for superstition, magic, and legends, the peasants whispering about the aluxo'ob while they learned their catechism.

Xtabay was a figure she had discovered with the assistance of the cooks and pot scrubbers, intently listening to their tales. Like all legends, the stories contradicted themselves, and it was hard to know who was wrong and who was right. Some said Xtabay was a mortal woman who, due to her cruelty and indifference, returned to the land of the living to steal men's souls. Others claimed she was a demoness. She lived near the ceiba tree, no, in the cenotes. She would appear in the middle of the jungle, and run away when a man approached her, luring him until he was forever lost. But other stories said she tossed them into cenotes, where they drowned. And yet others insisted she strangled the men or ate their hearts. They said she used her beautiful singing voice to ensnare them, while the cook had told Casiopea it was her sheer beauty that served as the lure, and there were those who said it was her hair, which she combed with a magical comb, that attracted her victims. The Xtabay seduced, she lied, she tempted, peeking through the leaves of the trees and smiling her red smile.

Since she was no man and thus immune to her spell, Casiopea did not fear the tales.

"I don't remember," Casiopea said, shrugging.

"She is a spirit. You've met a demon already. They are not the same."

"What is the difference?"

"She was human and was altered. A hungry ghost who grew more powerful and became something new. Spirits, unlike ghosts, may travel the roads instead of being nailed to a single spot."

"Then she is a type of ghost. But I thought men could sleep with her, how—" Casiopea blurted out and was instantly mortified by her frank comment.

It was wrong, outright wrong, to discuss whatever went on between men and women in bed. The priest had drummed into the young girls of Uukumil the importance of chastity. Despite this, Casiopea had witnessed secret kisses between the servants. On one occasion, a traveling troupe had come to town with a film projector. Against a white sheet, Casiopea had had the chance to gaze at Ramón Novarro, the "Latin lover" who had Hollywood agog, and watched him embrace a gorgeous woman, promising her his undying affection. And there were books too, which her grandfather never cared much to read, but which she had perused. Poetry speaking of love and fleeting desire.

This knowledge was forbidden and was never to be spoken of.

"As I said, she is something else, alive and not, a creature of flesh who may also be unfleshed," he replied. "A seductress who consumes men."

Of course, once he said "flesh" and "seductress," her mind, instead of drifting toward less profane matters, immediately focused on the amorous pursuits of supernatural beings. If spirits could lie with men, she wondered what that meant when it came to demons. Or . . . gods, since the Mamlab clearly had no problem chasing after women. The legends were of no assistance in this matter—the Hero Twins were the product of a virgin birth, and not denizens of the shadows—but Casiopea had read enough Roman and Greek mythology to recall that Hades had indulged in these pursuits, snatching Persephone and seducing her with bits of pomegranate. Zeus enjoyed the company of nymphs and goddesses alike. And then there were all those mortal women, not goddesses. Leda, supine, with the swan against her breast, an illustration that she'd found rather absorbing.

She considered this in an abstract way. Gods and goddesses. Gods and mortals. However, with a god standing in front of Casiopea it was impossible that her mind not make another leap and connect Hun-Kamé to the matter of these pairings.

It was immoral to even think it, to stare at him and wonder . . . well. Did he ever seduce a woman, tempt her with pomegranate seeds? Ridiculous question! As if there were any pomegranates nearby. Although that was not the point, the point was—

The point was her cheeks were burning, and Casiopea had the good sense to bite her tongue back and not voice such an impudent train of thought.

"You seem upset," he said.

Casiopea shook her head, evasively, unwilling to commit to words. This had the unexpected effect of making him move closer to her, as if to get a better look at her, like a physician who must examine the patient. Casiopea wanted nothing more than to shrink against the wallpaper and disappear. She couldn't look him in the eye for fear he'd guess what she'd been wondering about.

And what would she say if he guessed? Pardon me, but you are handsome, and if you are handsome, then I assume you must have chased spirits of your own near the waterholes.

She did not want to know the answer, did not want to know a single thing right now, and this was precisely why the priest admonished them to keep their thoughts on the works of Christ and the saints who judge everyone from the heavens. If she'd done that, she wouldn't be dying of mortification, but she knew more names of stars than names of saints.

"What is the matter with you?" he asked, frowning.

The words were green once more. He was young for the span of a moment. Fortunately, this deepened his confusion, made it a different sort of puzzlement, and it threw him off.

Casiopea regained her composure. She decided she was being ridiculous. Enough was enough.

"We shouldn't waste any time," she said. "Let's go meet Xtabay."

He nodded, himself again, and Casiopea had no idea where they were headed, but she led the way out of the room and out of the hotel because it had become too stuffy in there. The dirty city air never felt so refreshing. She practically sprinted across the street.

When they reached the corner, Hun-Kamé placed a hand on her arm and steered her in the right direction, which turned out to be toward a taxi. They headed to the Condesa.

"You'll have to get us in to see her," Hun-Kamé said as the taxi rolled down the street.

"Me?"

"The handmaiden provides the introductions and delivers the gifts."

"What kind of introductions?"

"It does not matter as long as we are allowed in," he said.

On her lap Casiopea carried the box with the necklace. She rested her fingers on its lid and nodded.

The Condesa was in motion, was modern, was being filled with Art Deco buildings. The neighborhood had been part of a vast hacienda that had belonged to the Countess of Miravalle. There the Porfirian elite held horse races on a vast track. Now, a delightfully modern park was rising in its heart. There were no haphazard alleys and tenements in this colonia but a perfectly orchestrated collection of boulevards and trees.

The houses and apartment buildings in the Condesa were of sturdy concrete, sharp geometric patterns decorating their façades, tribute to the "primitivism" that was in vogue. Zigzags evoked notions of Africa, while certain colorful tiles tried to paint a fantasy image of Middle Eastern mosaics.

It was hip, the Condesa, the place to be for the young and the rising stars. An urban triumph, the architects told themselves, even if the colonia was not quite finished, structures half completed, lots empty. It was like watching cocoons that have yet to reveal butterflies.

Hun-Kamé and Casiopea headed toward one of these newer structures, a four-story building with stained double-glass doors depicting sunflowers. Hun-Kamé unlocked the door, and they walked through a lobby filled with potted plants. They boarded a cage elevator, very grand, all glinting copper, with geometrical motifs and flowers running up and along its sides. Hun-Kamé pressed the button for the top floor and up they went.

Hun-Kamé slid the door open with a rattle of metal and they stepped out. The elevator opened onto a well-lit hallway.

A single knock on a sturdy door, and a severe man immediately greeted them.

"We bring a gift for the lady of the house, and we are hoping for an audience," Casiopea said. She'd had time to prepare a speech while riding in the taxi.

"Has the lady said you might visit today?" the man asked, raising an eyebrow at her.

"No, but she will be pleased to see my lord."

"She is busy," the man said and would have closed the door in their faces, but Casiopea would not allow it; she shoved the door open, making the man's eyebrows go up even higher. She had not rehearsed this, but she was quick to improvise.

"If you do not obey me or make us wait, you will regret it very much. My lord is a great lord and very kind, but trust me, you would not want to sour his day," she said. "Now, let's try this again. We bring a gift; *take it to her*."

Casiopea bowed and extended the box with the necklace toward the man, who snatched it from her hands and wordlessly walked away, leaving them to wait at the threshold.

"I suppose that is one way to get someone's attention," Hun-Kamé mused.

"It's the kind of thing *you* would say," Casiopea replied.

"It is indeed," he replied, sounding pleased.

The man came back, guiding them to a room that might have been best fit for a Hollywood fantasy. The floor was checkered, black-and-white, like a chessboard; gauzy burgundy curtains fluttered slightly, teased by a gentle breeze, revealing colored window-panes. Potted plants and vases with flowers were profusely set upon any available surface—multiple coffee tables, side tables, cabinets, all made of fashionable Bakelite. Dwarf palm trees were arranged against a wall, enormous black pots held luxuriant plants, and baskets with ferns dangled from the ceiling, as if the owner of this apartment meant to snatch a piece of the jungle and toss it between four walls.

In a corner a parrot rested inside a circular chrome cage, which dangled from a thin metal stand. It eyed them as they walked in. The parrot in Uukumil was mean, and Casiopea regarded this bird as a bad omen.

In the center of the room there was a burgundy couch that matched the curtains. On it lay a woman in an elegant white satin dress, so fine and delicate each curve of her body was visible under the material. Her neck was adorned with a long strand of pearls, which dipped between her breasts. Her nails were red, as were her lips, and her dark hair was swept back with a silver-and-ruby embroidered headband. She looked like a movie star rather than a dangerous spirit.

"Let me speak," Hun-Kamé told Casiopea. "There, stand there."

Hun-Kamé motioned for Casiopea to stand close to the entrance, next to a row of potted plants, while he approached the woman. Xtabay held in her right hand the necklace they'd brought, idly, her eyes falling on Casiopea for a second and fixing on the god.

"Greetings, Lady Xtabay," he said.

"My, but could it be the lord Hun-Kamé? Without a proper retinue and only one handmaiden at your side?" the woman said, making Casiopea wonder if in Xibalba he was followed by a dozen royal guards and servants holding parasols. And she thought, yes, that must be the case.

"And yet I found a proper gift."

"Thank you for the pretty trinket, but it might have been even better if you'd told me you were coming. Unannounced visits can be such a hassle."

Her voice was very beautiful, as was her face. It was not human beauty, every angle, every feature, too flawless, too polished. The room had an artificial quality and so did she. She had the allure of the snake, of the jaguar, and she was also every stray fantasy men have ever dreamed. Prismatic, she changed. From one angle her lips were full and her face rounded, yet from another that face became thin, the cheekbones sharp, as if she sought to please any and every onlooker.

It was easy to imagine how many men had been lured by her into the jungle, striving to catch a strand of her hair between their hands, only to drown in a waterhole instead. Casiopea touched the leaves of a large potted plant. She was nervous. If he'd assigned her a proper role—to guard the door, for example—she would have felt better, but to merely stand there seemed silly. Yet back in his palace he might have a multitude of people to do precisely that: handmaidens to stand behind him, servants to line up in front of him for no good reason, like decorative items. And women as attractive as this one to speak to. It was only because he'd been brought low that he now traveled in the company of a single, bumbling mortal girl.

Casiopea let go of the leaf and frowned.

"I am certain I was expected," Hun-Kamé replied.

The woman smiled, placing the gold necklace she had been holding on the couch. She sat up, resting a hand against the hollow of her throat. Her movements and her voice were practiced, reinforcing the idea this was an actress often on display.

"Your brother might have hinted you'd be here," she admitted.

"You know why I have come."

"Of course. To intimidate me. To force me to surrender that precious piece of your essence that you must regain. But, dearest Hun-

Kamé, we all know one thing: you are not quite yourself right now. I'm not afraid."

The woman smiled at him. Her teeth were flawless, the smile most delightful. But sharp too, the smile of a predator, the allure of the carnivorous flower. By the couch lay a zebra skin, serving as a rug, and the woman ran a naked foot across the black-and-white stripes. Back and forth she moved her foot, her eyes on the god.

"I thought you'd be wise," he replied.

"I am. And it would be unwise to surrender to you."

"My brother must have made you an offer."

"Which you cannot match," Xtabay said.

"What is the offer?"

Xtabay stood up and shrugged. She circled Hun-Kamé, brushing a hand across his back as she did, the other hand busy touching her strand of pearls, as if she meant to count them. She sighed.

"A place beside his throne. I am to be his consort."

"He cannot raise you to godhood."

"You are very misinformed and out of date. The world is changing."

"You've fallen for Vucub-Kamé's dream? His ridiculous notions of power?"

Xtabay laughed. Her pretty voice had a musical quality to it, but the laughter was not pleasant. Hollow. As polished as the rest of her, as shiny as the metal and Bakelite furniture adorning the room. She pressed her hands together. She wore rings on many fingers; her bracelets clinked. And when she shook her head, there was the flash of expensive earrings. It must be nice, Casiopea thought, to wear such finery every day and have the constant favor of gods.

"You have been quite ridiculous too, Hun-Kamé. Existing so quietly in your kingdom of shadows, happy to think of former glories. You are like a dog eager to eat scraps," she said languidly, managing to make the insult sound impersonal.

"Everything has its time. The gods do not walk the land for a reason," he said, his voice subdued. The insult had not stirred him.

"The chu'lel can be harnessed."

The dress swished as Xtabay walked in front of him. The white satin rippled, and Xtabay stretched out a hand, brushing Hun-Kamé's face as her dress brushed the cool checkered floor. Knots of power, invisible, tied themselves around the god. Casiopea could not possibly see them, but a shiver went down her spine and the plants around her shivered too, making a low, low sound.

"Ah, Hun-Kamé, do not be upset with me, I couldn't bear it. You know I have always been fond of you. You are so much more intelligent than your brother, so much stronger and more handsome," the woman declared.

"You say that only because it is me standing before you, and not him, right this instant," he told her, but his voice was odd, he slurred his words.

Casiopea noticed that Hun-Kamé had closed his eye and his shoulders drooped. She knew the legends of the Xtabay but had not thought she could affect him. Ordinarily, Casiopea would have been correct in her assessment: Xtabay could have no power over a god. Then again, Hun-Kamé was not exactly a god at this time, his immortal essence mixed with Casiopea's human self. He was vulnerable.

Casiopea watched him carefully. She did not know about magic, but she did know about bad feelings, and she was certain now that the parrot had indeed been a terrible omen.

"What are you doing?" she whispered, and she wondered whether she should approach them. Last time she had not followed his instructions a ghost had almost snacked on her bones. Did she interrupt them? Would that make things worse?

Behind her there was a soft rustling, but she was too worried trying to listen to the conversation to pay it heed.

"I would much rather sit by your side than his. Wouldn't that please you? It would not be too difficult to manage," Xtabay said.

"I . . . can see your point."

Each word the woman spoke made Hun-Kamé drowsier. Xtabay moved closer to him, placing her hands on his chest.

The rustling continued. Casiopea looked behind her, annoyed. One of the potted plants had extended long tendrils, reaching toward her. Before Casiopea could flinch, it wrapped itself around her legs. Another tendril whipped her in the face with such ferocity she stumbled back. One quick tug and she fell down. Hun-Kamé had noticed nothing. He was still speaking with Xtabay while Casiopea tried to pull the tendrils off her. They were as tough as ropes, and more slippery.

"I have the precious item you seek. The index finger from your left hand. Let me return it to you, and that portion of your power, but assure me you'll crown me as your own queen. Assure me with a kiss," Xtabay was telling Hun-Kamé.

A couple of paces from Casiopea there was a side table, crystal vases crammed with flowers set upon it. She scrambled up and reached for one of the vases while a third tendril wrapped itself around her midsection, squeezing her tight and digging into her flesh. Casiopea smashed the vase against the floor, shards bouncing around her. She picked up one piece of sharp glass and cut the tendril wrapped around her mouth. The plant let out an unpleasant hiss, uncoiling from her.

Xtabay, in turn, let out a gasp and touched her arm, where a scratch had suddenly materialized. She glared at the girl.

"Be care—"

Casiopea's words were muffled by yet another tendril, which struck her and began knotting itself around her head. Xtabay clearly did not wish for her to speak, or maybe she just wanted to suffocate

Casiopea. Either way, this was not good, and she pulled at the tendril, pulled with all her might.

Meanwhile, Xtabay kept speaking to the god. She raised a hand, as if to touch Hun-Kamé's face, and Casiopea realized there were vicious thorns running along the woman's arm. She meant to kiss and simultaneously scratch Hun-Kamé with the thorns.

Casiopea tugged at the tendril around her head and the plant shivered, but it would not relent. In fact, Casiopea felt that it was laughing quietly.

It made her boiling mad. She bit down on it as hard as she could. The plant hissed again in anger—and Xtabay hissed in equal anger, clutching her hand, the marks of teeth showing on her unblemished skin. Casiopea managed to peel the tendril off her face.

"Hun-Kamé!" she yelled. "Don't listen to her!"

When the name escaped Casiopea's lips, Hun-Kamé turned his head to look at her. He had heard nothing of the commotion happening in a corner of the room, but Casiopea's voice sliced through the magic Xtabay had been weaving, as if a hand had shoved away a cobweb. The knots of power, which had remained invisible, glowed blue for a second before being extinguished. This minor act of destruction also had the effect of knocking Xtabay down. She lay on her knees on the zebra rug, stunned.

Hun-Kamé straightened himself up and walked to Casiopea's side. The plant had slackened its grip on her, but when the god approached, it blackened and recoiled entirely, as if it could not withstand the anger of the Death Lord. And angry he did look, eye as dark as coal, brushing off a stray leaf that had caught in Casiopea's hair. He offered her his left hand, so that she might find purchase on him and stand up.

"Are you injured?" she asked. "Do you need me to help you?"

"Perfectly fine," he said. "Although I was about to ask that question."

"Oh. Nothing is broken," she assured him.

"I see. Just a scratch here," he said, touching her forehead for a second, wiping away the mark like he'd wiped away the stray leaf, "and gone again."

By the couch Xtabay, head down, spoke words of power, but they fizzled, a fire without tinder, impossible to spark.

"Your trickery won't work with me," Hun-Kamé told her, but he did not bother even glancing at the woman.

"It almost did," Xtabay said, her voice now a venomous hiss, no sweetness to it. She nursed her injured hand, the red, angry mark of Casiopea's teeth stark upon it.

"Return my property," Hun-Kamé replied coolly.

"It will not change anything," Xtabay told him.

Nevertheless, she complied, walking toward a bookcase where she kept a black box with two green jade lines running down its sides. Xtabay opened the box and offered it to Hun-Kamé, kneeling down before him, in what Casiopea thought was a clear display of mockery.

"For the Lord Hun-Kamé," Xtabay said, as she threw the lid of the box open, "from his humble servant."

Cushioned in black velvet rested the finger. Just like the ear, it was well preserved, as if it had been cut off a few minutes ago. Hun-Kamé pressed the digit against his hand, and it fused with his flesh. Then he motioned for Xtabay to stand up. She did.

"Who has the next piece of this puzzle?" he asked.

"You think I know?"

"My brother wishes to crown you, Xtabay. I think he would have told you."

"You cannot make me speak the answer."

"I have undone your spell," Hun-Kamé said.

"No, not you, you vain and naïve lord, *the girl*. Did you lose one eye or go entirely blind?" Xtabay said, mocking him. "You did nothing."

True, he had not. It had been Casiopea's voice that quenched the spell, an act of will, though her essence mixed with that of a god, and thus it was partly his magic that had given her the ability to perform the task. Partly, but not wholly.

"Then give *me* the answer," Casiopea said, feeling tired, the beginning of a headache drumming inside her skull. She wanted this matter over. She pressed forward to stand inches before the woman.

"You undo one spell and you think you can command me?" the woman said, scoffing.

"I'm suspecting that's the way it works. And if it's not the way, then I'll start smashing all your plants and flowers to bits until you are nicer to me. I think you wouldn't like that," Casiopea said.

"You would not dare."

"I would very much dare," Casiopea said.

"She is a savage," the woman told Hun-Kamé.

"The Lady Tun has a very distinctive personality, but I would not go as far as that," Hun-Kamé said. "And she makes a fine point: do you want us to smash a few things around your home? Burn these flowers and plants?"

"Of course not, my lord," Xtabay said, lowering her head and clutching her injured hand. "There is an uay in El Paso, the Uay Chivo. He serves Vucub-Kamé."

Hun-Kamé turned as if to leave, motioning for Casiopea to walk with him, but Xtabay spoke again, her hard eyes watching them intently. She looked as beautiful as she had when they had entered the room and yet she was also diminished.

"You should let it be, Hun-Kamé," the woman said, and she sounded empty now. "Forget about the throne and disappear. Vucub-Kamé will kill you."

"Gods may not die."

"Yes," Xtabay said with a nod. "Gods may not. Look at your reflection in a mirror."

Hun-Kamé grabbed Casiopea's hand and pulled her out of the

room. When they reached the elevator he dragged the metal door closed with a loud clang.

Downstairs, as he opened one of the double glass doors, Hun-Kamé glanced at his reflection. He saw nothing in the dim outline of his face to cause alarm.

Had he been holding a hand mirror he might have spotted the telltale detail that Xtabay had noticed. His eye, so dark it was like flint, reflected nothing, since it was not human. But the eye had now changed. The pupil, like a black mirror, caught reflections. The street, the cars going down the boulevards, and his young companion. She was rendered in most vivid colors.

Yes, the unweaving of the spell had been partly caused by the god's immortal essence that lay inside Casiopea, giving her the ability to crumple Xtabay's magic with the power of the Underworld. But the other part, the other reason Xtabay's spell had failed—and which Casiopea and Hun-Kamé didn't grasp—was a simpler truth: his vision was already too clouded by Casiopea. When she'd spoken and he'd turned his head, his pupil reflected her and washed away the rest of the room.

Such incidents are not uncommon between young mortals who believe they exist on a deserted island where no one else may step foot.

Hun-Kamé? He was not young, born centuries and centuries before.

And yet he was, upon stepping out of that building in the Condesa, a man of Casiopea's age, his wisdom washing off his skin. Of course Casiopea could not notice this, as she had not noticed how he had no age when they met. He became young and that was that, as if someone had stripped off the dark, coarse bark from a tree, showing the pale core of it.

Chapter 16

After his disastrous encounter with his cousin, Martín immediately ran back to the Hotel Mancera, hoping to meet with her again. He tried to pry the location of her room from the front desk clerk, but the clerk would not budge, unable to even confirm that a woman matching Casiopea's description was staying there. Martín threatened, then he tried to bribe the employee, but the clerk stared at him with the absolute indifference of a capitalino who has seen everything, and much worse. Irritated, Martín planted himself in the lobby, hoping to intercept Casiopea. His cousin never came down, or she'd exited the building already.

Once Martín realized it was futile to maintain his watch, grasping the stupidity of the endeavor, he hurried outside, walking around downtown until he found a vendor who was carrying cigarettes. Casiopea had purchased his smokes, and as he grabbed his lighter he was reminded of this detail, which diminished any pleasure he might otherwise have taken in the cigarette.

Martín went in search of an establishment that served alcohol and found no lack of them downtown, picking a cheap pulquería with a mural of Mexico City's twin volcanos painted on a wall.

There were more dignified establishments, including The Opera, where the revolutionary Pancho Villa supposedly shot bullets into the ceiling one evening, but Martín did not give one rat's ass about the quality of the drinks he was imbibing. Each glass of pulque tasted more bitter than the last, as he drummed his fingers against the table. Women with too much rouge on their cheeks stopped by, hoping to make a few pesos off the surly man in good clothes, but he waved them away, complaining about the faults of the female sex. It all started with Eve and ended with Casiopea, according to him. Serpent, damn viper, that's what she was.

Finally, when night fell, Martín walked back to his hotel, cursing Casiopea under his breath.

"Twenty times a whore and fifty a bitch," he said.

It was in her blood, of course, Jezebel. Not only her gender, but her father's Indian blood committed her to this state—Martín would have never conceived of any genetic ailment in the Leyva side of the family; it had to have been the part of her that was Tun that caused such reckless behavior.

"I'll tell her mother and I'll tell Grandfather, and I'll tell everyone," he promised.

Their whole town would know Casiopea now walked around Mexico City, shameless, almost bald, disobeying the instructions of the family.

Disobeying *him*.

At this, he paused. No, no, no, he wouldn't mention she'd disobeyed him.

He smoked a cigarette and circled the hotel, needing space, needing time, running a hand through his hair.

In his room, Martín splashed water on his face and admitted that he could dally no longer; the god would be expecting news. He clutched the jade ring Vucub-Kamé had given him, and standing in the middle of his room he uttered the god's name.

The lights grew dim as the darkness in the room pooled itself together in a corner, and out of this darkness stepped out Vucub-Kamé. He was clad in white, a cape made of pale seashells falling down his back, and his hair was very light, but he evoked pitch-black darkness nevertheless.

Vucub-Kamé's eyes did not fall on Martín; he seemed as if he were more concerned with other matters.

When Martín first met Vucub-Kamé, he'd had little understanding of the god. Afterward, Cirilo corrected his lack of instruction, muttering his story to his grandson. Cirilo had also explained the character of the Lords of Xibalba and how they should be addressed, including their predisposition for flattery. So, when Vucub-Kamé walked into the room, Martín fell on his knees, head bowed, even if his natural haughtiness made him cringe at such a display.

"Supreme Lord of the Underworld," Martín said. "I thank you for coming. I am unworthy of your visit."

"You must be since your tongue trembles. Have you failed me?" the god asked, but he did not deign to look at the mortal man.

"My cousin, she would not speak to you," Martín admitted, clutching his hands together. "She is a stubborn, ungrateful child. But if my lord would wish it, I will find her and seize her, dragging her by her hair—"

"Such wasteful violence. And what should that accomplish?"

Martín blinked. "She'd do as you wanted, whatever you wanted."

"You cannot force her hand," Vucub-Kamé said.

"I don't—"

"Martín Leyva . . . Martín. When you play chess, do you move your pawns as if they were horses? When you roll the dice do you pretend you tallied four points instead of two? Do you understand?"

Martín shook his head yes, unable to comprehend what the god was about, but knowing at this point he should simply agree.

Vucub-Kamé undid a pouch at his waist and held up four dice

painted black and yellow on each side, the kind used for playing bul. Martín had not played the game—it was the sort of thing taken up by the Indians—but he understood the objective of it was to "capture" and "kill" the opponent's pieces.

"If I thought brute force could grant me what I wish, I would have plucked your cousin from Middleworld already. But since she is a player in this game, I must respect her role. And being a thing not quite human and not quite divine, the girl cannot be dragged by her hair to rest at my feet."

"I . . . Of course not, no."

"Neither can I directly address her at this point, which is why I must use an intermediary, and I'm stuck with you," the god concluded.

Vucub-Kamé motioned for him to stand, so Martín did.

"I will give you a new task, to which you might be better suited, seeing as your cousin is a stubborn creature."

"Yes, my lord," he whispered.

The Lord of Xibalba threw the dice against the floor. They spiraled and fell, all on their yellow side. Around them rose lines like soot, faint. As faint as the silvery thread in a spider's web, from one angle catching the light and visible, from the other invisible. Martín squinted, trying to find a proper shape to the lines. Was this a board game?

"I'll have you head to Baja California, to Tierra Blanca, on the wings of my owl this night. My brother and your cousin will make their way there, eventually, but you will arrive first."

"What will I do in Tierra Blanca?" Martín asked.

"You will learn."

"Ah . . . and what will I learn?"

"To walk the shadow roads of my kingdom. Aníbal Zavala should be able to instruct you."

Martín was not sure what walking the shadow roads meant, but he did know he did not want to be anywhere near Xibalba. It was called the Place of Fear for a reason.

He cleared his throat. "I will do as you say, but why would I want to . . . learn such a lesson? And who would Aníbal Zavala be?"

"My disciple. As for the reason for that lesson, because symmetry in everything is most pleasing, and since it seems Casiopea is poised to be Hun-Kamé's champion, you will be mine. Cousin against cousin, brother against brother. I hope you can appreciate the symbolism."

"Do you mean to pit me against her somehow?" Martín asked.

"She may still have a chance to show me the proper deference. If she will not oblige me, however, I will be prepared," Vucub-Kamé declared.

"And I must know how to walk the shadow roads, if she doesn't change her mind about you."

"You must have an advantage. She won't know how to navigate the roads."

Looking at the spidery lines on the floor, Martín realized it was not a board but a circle, and within this circle an intricate labyrinth branched off in many directions, paths that led to dead ends multiplying. He thought he could make out the shapes of pyramids, statues of great size, causeways, and tall columns. A black drop, like ink, fell upon the labyrinth, and it followed one of the paths, the correct one that led to the center.

It was like spying the solution to a puzzle in the back of the newspaper. But if it was cheating, Martín was not going to complain. He had never felt bad about having an advantage over anyone.

"I think I understand," Martín said.

The Lord of Xibalba had not looked at him all this time, his pale gray eyes fixed on another point in the room. When Martín spoke, the god turned his eyes toward him.

"I would hope you do. It is infinitely important that you emerge victorious against your cousin in the coming contest. Fail me and I will grind your bones into dust," Vucub-Kamé said, his voice impassive. The threat was in his eyes, quicksilver as he fixed them on Martín.

Martín felt as if an invisible hand gripped his throat and squeezed it, sharp nails digging into his skin. He could not breathe, could not move, could not even blink, there was only the oppressive hand wrapped around his neck. It was the same feeling people sometimes have when they sleep, as if an unseen force is weighing them down. The night hag, the dead man crawling. The nightmare that rides mortals. Except he was wide awake.

This sensation lasted hardly a minute, but the dread of the touch sent Martín's heart pounding with terror, and when it subsided he fell to his knees.

Vucub-Kamé smiled at Martín, and he spoke sweetly, like the worm whispers to a man in his coffin.

"Do not be too upset, Martín. I favor you, even if you reek of cheap pulque and discontent. We have, after all, much in common, both of us having to deal with the most obnoxious relatives possible. When this is over I believe we will be good friends, like your grandfather and I were friends. Fate has brought us together. Thank her for this nicety."

"Yes, my lord," Martín rasped, rubbing his throat and bowing his head.

The god held out his hand and the dice jumped back onto his palm. The map dissipated, rising like the smoke of an extinguished candle. Then the god stepped back into the shadows from which he'd emerged, blending with them, his white cape and white clothing and pale hair sinking into darkness.

Martín continued to rub his neck, and he threw his head back, chuckling, because he could already hear the flapping of wings announcing the arrival of Vucub-Kamé's gigantic owl. The god wasted no time. What the hell. It was not as if Martín had anything important to do. He could sleep off his binge drinking in Baja California as efficiently as in Mexico City. Though at this point he had sobered up considerably.

"Casiopea, if I ever see you again . . . oh, dear God, I better not see you again," he muttered.

All this had started because of her. She had opened the stupid box, she had made a god rise from his prison, and now it was her stubborn refusal that was condemning Martín to sink into the paths of Xibalba. Not fifty times a bitch, a hundred.

Chapter 17

Mortals believe gods to be omnipotent and ever-knowing. The truth is more slippery; their limitations are multiple, kaleidoscopic, and idiosyncratic. Gods cannot rudely move mortals like one moves a piece across a game board. To obtain what they wish gods may utilize messengers, they may threaten, they may flatter, and they may reward. A god may cause storms to wreck the seaside and mortals, in return, may raise their hands and place offerings at the god's temple in an effort to stop the hurricane that whips the land. They may pray and bleed themselves with maguey thorns. However, they could also feel free to ignore the god's weather magic, they could blame the rain or lack of it on chance or bad luck, without forging the connection between the deity and the event.

A god can make the volcanos boil and cook alive the villagers who have made their abodes near its cone, but what good is that? If gods destroyed all humans, there would be no adoration and no sacrifice, which is the fresh wood that replenishes a fire.

Vucub-Kamé had limitations and he had ways to counter them. He could not visit the mortal realm in the daytime and he could only wander it for a limited amount of time at night. But he had his owls, his powers of foretelling, and his alliances. Although he could be rejected, he seldom was.

Casiopea's refusal, then, struck him as somewhat novel, even amusing. As he drifted into Xtabay's room, brushing past the billowing curtains, he was actually in a pleasant state of mind. There would be another chance to address the girl. Twice and even thrice she might turn from him, for three is the number that marks women's hetzmek. He was not vexed like Martín was vexed. He knew himself in control of the story.

"You honor me with your presence," Xtabay said, bowing her head and kneeling before him, bejeweled as always.

What an entirely lovely and spiteful creature she was, her mortal beginnings forgotten, the imprint of a shell in the sand long erased. Vucub-Kamé held out his hand, indicating she could rise, and Xtabay did, an artful smile across her face.

"I gather my brother has visited you," he said, unable to sense the dormant essence of Hun-Kamé, which Xtabay had until now kept locked in a box. In its corner, Xtabay's green parrot sat in its cage and hid its head under its wing, as if shielding itself from the god.

"He visited me not long ago," Xtabay replied with a frown. "Along with his awful handmaiden."

Vucub-Kamé walked around the chamber. No trace of his brother remained, yet he had been here, and this made him want to let his steps fall in the place where Hun-Kamé's steps had fallen. They had not seen each other in decades, and now they were but days from again encountering each other.

He allowed himself to picture Hun-Kamé as he'd been, long ago, walking through the jungle with a serpent wrapped around his neck, while Vucub-Kamé shadowed him, an owl on his shoulder. For a moment the memory was sweet. How they had enjoyed their excursions to Middleworld! Until mortals ceased in their worship of the gods and Hun-Kamé in turn ceased to care about the world of men.

Vucub-Kamé did not lose his taste for it, though, and in time it dominated his thoughts. He longed for the adoration of the priests and suplicants, and when he told his brother as much, Hun-Kamé chided him for not grasping the ephemeral nature of all things. The chiding became quarrels, and Vucub-Kamé drew inward, the worm of anger gnawing at his heart.

He turned away from the memory, focusing on the now.

"He did not remain long."

"No."

"Then your charms proved of no use, no matter how much you may boast of your magic," Vucub-Kamé concluded.

There had been the possibility his brother would halt or be injured before he reached Tierra Blanca, easing Vucub-Kamé's triumph. Then again, there was the warring desire that Hun-Kamé should reach Baja California in a robust state, ear and finger and necklace in his possession, making his final downfall more amusing.

"He is the Lord of Xibalba," she said, her voice sharp around the edges, the emphasis on "the," reminding Vucub-Kamé who was the firstborn child and who was the pretender, the traitor.

"Watch your pretty tongue," Vucub-Kamé replied, everything about him sharp, not only his voice. "You wouldn't want to lose it."

"Lord, I serve you with every breath of mine, do not look at me with anger. It was but a slip of the tongue," Xtabay said. "A tongue that I wish to keep."

"A slip. Or you would rather serve my brother?"

Xtabay turned her head to stare at him.

"I have done as you said. I left behind the jungle to live in this distant city where my power waned—"

"Not waned since you were in possession of Hun-Kamé's finger. Do not dismiss the might of his essence, nor the baubles and diversions I've provided you," Vucub-Kamé said. He enjoyed when his generosity was acknowledged and bristled when it was not appreciated. He had kept Xtabay in splendor, ensuring her watch would be more than bearable.

"No," Xtabay admitted. "I will not. But you know well I do not belong here, and it has been an unpleasant chore for me to remain, and yet I've done so since you said he would come one day seeking me and you wanted him to follow your route."

"He must. And knowing this, I feel you might have thought to curry favor again with the Lord," he said acridly.

She had been an esteemed courtier in the Jade Palace, often attending Hun-Kamé. She could spin a good story, and her malicious antics in Middleworld amused the Lords of Xibalba. Sometimes she dragged a poor, helpless man down the Black Road, to the city. Such mortals could not remain long in Xibalba, but the lords laughed as the man was subjected to terrible sights or feasted like a prince before the food turned to ashes in his mouth.

Vucub-Kamé, of course, suspected Xtabay of treachery even if such treachery was unlikely.

"I am wounded by your accusations," she said.

Xtabay pressed the tips of her fingers against the god's mouth, then ran a hand over his brow, as if seeking to smooth the creases there, attempting to erase his frown. He would not allow her such intimacy and stepped away, circling her.

"How did he escape you?" he inquired.

"As you pointed out, my magic was not sufficient," Xtabay replied.

"Yet you told me it would be. That is why I picked you for this task."

"I told you I might be able to slow him down, that I might be able to distract him for a while. But he seems distracted enough by the girl he drags around with him."

Xtabay sounded displeased but not insincere. She looked over her shoulder at him.

"I do your will, Vucub-Kamé. When you hatched your scheme,

did I not assist you? I *could* have courted favor with Hun-Kamé back then and revealed your whole sordid trap. Instead I concealed your plans, found the mortal man you needed."

"You did," Vucub-Kamé conceded.

Vucub-Kamé stood behind Xtabay, letting a hand trail down her hair, the inattentive gesture of a master with an annoying pet rather than a lover, although they had at one point been lovers and he had offered her godhood, a seat by his side, in order to sway her hand and secure her assistance. Gods have appetites, more voracious than those of men, and how quickly they turn from one pursuit to another, like uncorking a wine, taking a sip, then tossing the rest down a drain.

There was no measure of affection between Vucub-Kamé and Xtabay at this point. When they had plotted together, he had enjoyed the plotting, but now that it was all done and arranged, he'd grown disenchanted with her and she with him.

"Did he say anything interesting?" Vucub-Kamé asked, ceasing in his half-hearted caress. He was bored already and yearning to return home. Xibalba called to him; he was tied to the shadow realm. Xtabay was not bound to Xibalba, since she had not been born there, and did not feel that same invisible chain around her waist. Middleworld interested him, yes, but only because it housed within its borders the mortals who might adore him. It was Xibalba he loved, Xibalba and himself and no other.

"We hardly spoke. My magic was of no use, it could not hold him, and I gave him the box. He asked who held the next piece of him, and I said it is the Uay Chivo."

"And he did not inquire any further?"

"What would he inquire about?" Xtabay asked, sitting on her couch, her bracelets clinking as she pressed a hand against her forehead. "He was rather in a hurry. I could tell he is growing weaker, becoming more human."

"I thought my brother would have more stamina," Vucub-Kamé said.

Perhaps Hun-Kamé would not make it to Baja California, after all. Who knew. If he was truly diminishing, consumed like a quickly burning candle, his encounter with the Uay Chivo could prove difficult. The uay was much more . . . forceful than Vucub-Kamé's other associates.

"Apparently not. If you should have seen him when he left, you would not have believed it, he moved like someone who has never walked the Black Road. That girl was reflected in his eye."

Vucub-Kamé had been serene, but when Xtabay said those simple words a shiver went down his spine. He had a talent for soothsaying. He read fortunes in the blood of myriad creatures, but sometimes an augury would present itself without being requested. The words were unpleasantly close to an omen. They made him pause and stare at Xtabay.

"What is it?"

"Quiet," Vucub-Kamé ordered, seized with a mad need.

He moved toward the parrot. The bird shivered. Vucub-Kamé stretched out a hand, opened its cage and grabbed the bird, snapping its neck.

"Now why did you have to—" Xtabay began.

"I said quiet," Vucub-Kamé replied.

His voice was more dangerous than the knife that materialized in his hand and Xtabay, who had risen from her couch at the indignity of having her pet treated this way, sat again, folding her hands. Vucub-Kamé sliced the parrot in two and dropped the body, feathers and blood scattering on the floor wildly.

Before, he had not been able to observe his triumph, even if he could see Hun-Kamé's arrival in Tierra Blanca. But now even this arrival was missing. A hundred branching futures wove before him, and the more he pushed and tried to see through the chaos, the more they tangled, they knotted, they broke before his eyes. When he did glimpse something, it was the young woman's face he'd seen before and then, for a second, his brother on the black throne. Hun-Kamé, crowned anew.

This image, brief as it was, shocked Vucub-Kamé so much it made the scars on the palms of his hands vibrate with pain, as if they were being burned a second time. The knife slipped from his hand, turning to smoke when it touched the floor.

It was not possible. He was the ruler of Xibalba now! Nothing could change this, nothing could ruin his plans.

And the branching paths, as if to soothe the daykeeper, offered him another brief glimpse, this time of Vucub-Kamé on the obsidian throne.

But the balm was not sweet. He was unsettled.

Vucub-Kamé knocked down the parrot's cage and turned to Xtabay.

"Like a man," Vucub-Kamé said. "He walked like a man and she in his gaze. I hope he enjoys this human state, since he will never be a god again."

"Vucub-Kamé," Xtabay began, perhaps wishing to inquire about his state of mind.

But he'd had enough of Middleworld and sank into a pool of shadows, descending the nine levels to his kingdom without another word. He walked to his throne room and sat on his massive obsidian throne.

Vucub-Kamé pressed his fingers against the cold rock. His hands were warm, the scars hot with the memory of his treachery.

He needed to feel the glasslike rock under his fingers, as if to assure himself it was there, it remained his, it would not vanish.

Ah, there is none more fearful of thieves than the one who has stolen something, and a kingdom is no small something.

Chapter 18

Their route cut through many states, the train lurching across mountains and ravines, snaking around colonial mining centers and pine forests, before finally reaching the desert. For a while she had pressed her hands against the glass, trying to document the sights and commit them to memory—the types of trees, the colors of the houses, and the shapes of clouds—but in the end it was too much.

The passengers were as varied as the landscape. A man with chickens in a cage, a group of schoolgirls in identical dresses, three rakish looking young men in a state of inebriation, all headed to different sections of the train. At each stop vendors walked by the windows, hawking their wares, even though they had taken the evening train and Casiopea had not expected this much activity.

At least it would be a comfortable voyage. The ads for the train company promised the finest accommodations possible, and Casiopea realized they were not kidding. Their compartment was one of the largest, with enough space for a bed—not berths, a bona fide double bed—and two plush lounge chairs, a folding washstand, a drop table, a dresser with an oval mirror, and a window with dark orange curtains that matched the bed's covers.

There was much to admire in the compartment, from the varnished wood paneling to the finely woven brown-and-tan rug, but Casiopea decided her focus would be the bed. She was tired and took off her shoes, falling back over the covers, not bothering to change.

Hun-Kamé also kicked his shoes off and lay next to her. Ordinarily this should have alarmed her modesty because, well, it was a bed. It was one thing to share a compartment, as they'd done, and another to be sleeping literally next to a man, no division between them.

"There's a bit of the devil in every man, even if he may act the part of the saint," her mother had warned her. And of course, the follow-up: don't give a fellow any ideas.

Recalling her mother's admonishments, Casiopea thought of constructing a border between their bodies, a wall of sheets and pillows to demarcate the territory. Then again, he wasn't her fellow, and she was too exhausted by their encounter with Xtabay to care what ideas were circling his head. Instead of building a wall, she pressed her head against the pillow and promptly went to sleep.

When Casiopea woke up, a light rain was splattering the windows of the car. It was dark outside. She sat up and glanced at Hun-Kamé, who was asleep, his body turned in her direction.

He wasn't merely lying there. He was sleeping, his chest calmly rising and falling. After he had said he didn't sleep.

Alarmed, Casiopea tapped his shoulder, and he groaned and shifted and opened his eye, his face tangled with dreams. But only for a few seconds, because he sat up quickly enough, frowning, alert.

"Sorry," Casiopea said. "You were . . . I thought you didn't sleep."

"I don't," Hun-Kamé replied in a clipped voice.

He frowned even more now and looked so upset Casiopea wished she hadn't said a thing, hadn't woken him. There was a certain darkness upon Hun-Kamé at all times and it was not the blackness of his hair, the ravenlike eye, it was all about him, as if aside of being clothed in a suit and tie he was also dressed in shadows. Now the darkness intensified, the night without stars settling on the covers, in the space between them, even if the light fixtures shone as brightly as when they'd walked into the compartment.

"It's the mortal element you provide me with. It has been turning me more and more human. And then the distance between us and Yucatán does not help; I grow weaker with each kilometer. My brother knows this, no doubt expecting such a change will help his plans come to fruition. I don't know how much time we have left," he said.

Time. Yes. She remembered the bone shard. She spread out her fingers and held her palms up, looking at her hands. She had forgotten she was dying, he was a disease, a parasite. How easy it was to forget! He made her forget not through arcane sorcery but with his mere presence.

"It's making you human and it's killing me," she said.

"Yes, but it hadn't been quite like this before. It's getting worse."

"Oh," Casiopea whispered, placing her hands on her lap. Oh, for she couldn't think of anything better to say. It wasn't even that she was frightened, she was more . . . dismayed. It didn't seem fair. No, it wasn't fair at all. She'd glimpsed the world outside with no chance to sample it.

Well, I won't die yet, she promised herself. *I have plenty of things to do. Swim in the sea, dance at a nightclub, drive an automobile, to name a few*. Casiopea was pragmatic, yes, but now that these things were possible, although not probable, she was not going to dismiss them and pretend she did not want them.

She clutched her hands together, and as the train stuttered, slow-ing down, she raised her head, looking at him, he who might condemn her to an early grave.

"Why did your brother do this to you anyway?" she asked.

Somehow, they had not discussed it. Hun-Kamé did not venture his thoughts often unless she asked, and she had not thought to go down this painful avenue, but at this point she thought it her right to inquire.

"Have you never heard of family quarrels? You don't get along with your cousin, Martín. If you had the chance, wouldn't you be rid of him?" Hun-Kamé asked with a shrug.

"If you mean I'd harm him greatly . . . I don't know. I've never wanted to be rid of Martín . . . I wished to be away from him; that is different."

"Come, girl, if you could have your revenge on him, you would," he insisted. "You'd strike him and cut him with thorns."

"I'm not a girl," she countered, offended. "And no. I'm not . . . I don't need to cause Martín pain to be happy."

Casiopea considered her cousin. The cruelties he'd inflicted on her, the punishments she'd endured because of him. If the tables were turned, would she not seize the chance to torment him? Hadn't she wished he would fall down a well? But those had been the half-formed ideas of a child. Her mother had been right: it was not as if her cousin's misfortune could bring her joy.

"It did no good that time I hurt him," she said, shaking her head. "I won't be hitting him or cutting him, or anything of that sort. I'd be like him if I derived joy from the misery of others. I'm not like Martín"

Hun-Kamé was frankly confused by her words, as if it had never occurred to him one could be this magnanimous. Not that she hadn't bickered with Martín, not that she hadn't hit him hard that one time, but none of this had ever pleased her. She'd wanted Martín to let her be.

"My brother does derive pleasure from the misery of others, we all do. We are lords of Xibalba, kindness is not in our nature. But of course, that wasn't all that drove him to cut my head off and toss me in that chest. My brother wants a new empire."

"What do you mean?" she asked.

Hun-Kamé rested his back against the headboard and spread his hands, the gesture expansive.

"The chu'lel births gods, but the prayers of men are like a fan that makes the flames rise higher. It increases our power. Picture it, if you will, as a feast. Without the prayers and the beliefs of men, the food is bland and tasteless, but add a pinch of it and it is like the spices that flavor a delicious meal.

"Men ceased to worship Xibalba a long time ago, but Xibalba remains because the well of power from which we were born is deep. I believe the oceans may lick the land and devour it, and the Black Road of Xibalba would exist. Yet our sturdy kingdom of shadows was not enough for my brother."

"What else could he want?"

"He wanted a return to the old ways. The prayers of men to flow anew. Salt in our dishes. He was not content with ancient glories. I kept away from Middleworld. It is not our kingdom, and although I was aware of some of the changes in our peninsula, it did not interest me to see what new palaces and trinkets mortals fashioned."

The god had not been surprised by any of the things they'd witnessed in the city. Neither the trams nor the automobiles, nor the dresses women wore and the hats men sported, caught his eye. She had assumed he had experienced this before. Not the automobiles, but the trains certainly, and the buildings and some of the tastes of people. But perhaps he had not; it might have mostly been vicarious knowledge.

"But Vucub-Kamé, he became fascinated with the world of men and he became interested in a spot in Baja California, a place where the chu'lel also converged. This convergence was not quite as powerful as in Yucatán, but interesting nevertheless. He had been speaking to a mortal man, Aníbal Zavala, and Zavala had a theory both points could be stitched together."

"Stitched?"

"Connected somehow. Xibalba could draw on the power in Baja California. That was the general idea. But I refused to listen," Hun-Kamé said, shaking his head.

"Why?"

"Vucub-Kamé's idea violated the natural order of things. It was fueled by greed and fear."

"What would a god fear?"

"Irrelevance. Eventually, the eternal sleep our godhood grants us," Hun-Kamé said. "Since I would not partake in his mad action, Vucub-Kamé decided to dispose of me, and he managed it, for a while. But after I regain my throne, he shall pay dearly for this affront. I spent a few decades in that box. He will spend centuries, no, millennia in the prison I will fashion for him after I hack off his head and limbs."

The darkness Hun-Kamé carried grew in intensity and it brought with it a chill, like touching ice. It made Casiopea feel as if she were tasting frost, and from her half-parted lips there escaped a soft plume of her breath, dissolving almost instantly. She closed her mouth, frowning, and crossed her arms.

"You wouldn't do such a thing, not truly, would you?" Casiopea asked.

"Do you think me kind?" Hun-Kamé replied. "He cast me into an unbearable torment. I wished to cry in the dark but had no voice. I wished to move but was a pile of timeworn bones. I was and was not, like an insect dashing against a glass dome. He will taste the same misery."

"If you know such a thing is unbearable, then why would you subject anyone to it? Even him."

Hun-Kamé gave her an amused look. "Virtuous child who has not known the true measure of unhappiness, how could you ever imagine the breadth of my enmity? What games do you think gods play?"

Casiopea thought Hun-Kamé was mocking her and yet, when she looked carefully at him, she realized there was a wild earnestness about him. "Did your brother obtain everything he wanted, then?" she asked. "The connection he dreamed of?"

"Had he done it I'd know and you'd know it too. The world would not be the same at all," Hun-Kamé said. "But I suspect trickery awaits us in Baja California. I am not stupid. He has seeded the road and wants us to find him, and therefore I suspect his dream may not be forgotten."

"How would the world be different?"

"It would run with the blood of sacrifices and the adulation of mortals. The cenotes would be piled with gold and corpses. Men would be painted blue and their bodies riddled with arrows, although, certainly, the supreme offering is the severing of the head."

She had seen this imagery in books, had read about the wooden rods displaying hundreds of human skulls at the entrance of the temples, the bloodletting rituals involving shells and obsidian blades, but these were practices long forgotten.

"Surely that wouldn't happen now?" she said. "You wouldn't have a . . . a man riddled with arrows in the middle of Mérida?"

"That is precisely what my brother would have, and not simply Mérida. He would engulf many cities north and south of our peninsula. He desires power, more power than he's ever tasted, more than we were ever meant to have. Incense is not enough for him. He'll burn the land, the forests, swallow the smoke that rises from it."

In that moment Hun-Kamé was again cold, boundless. And, of course, dark. The chill of Hun-Kamé was the chill of the grave. Her grave, perhaps. Why worry about the sacrifices of others when she was scheduled for her own death? And yet, she worried, for the picture he painted in her mind was vivid and for a moment even more real than their compartment. It was crimson and black, and an obsidian throne upon a pile of bones, and the stench of rotting flesh in her nose. She felt like gnawing at her nails or covering her eyes, like a girl.

She shook her head. "You ought to have said all this before."

"I assumed you realized this was greater than you and me."

"Liar," she muttered.

He bristled at that, and she guessed he'd give her some grand speech about how this is what gods do, they keep their mouth shut and don't go spilling all their secrets to lowly mortals.

"I thought you'd be afraid," he said instead, after a minute.

"I am!"

"Hence why I didn't say it. If you were a hero you'd know this is the way things go. It is patan. When Hunahpu and Xbalanque descended to Xibalba they realized—"

"There were also *two* Hero Twins and they were divine," she said, interrupting him. "So maybe that helped them know the rules and . . . and kill monsters. Did you think I'd run off if you told me? Is that it? I would not."

"I know you won't run away, but I didn't want to burden you with all of this. To sour your days more than I have already," he said most politely.

She felt this politeness masked his true feelings. That he did see her as a coward, as unworthy. She knew about patan. Not just tribute, but duty and beyond duty, the obligation that carves your place in the world, and she wasn't about to disregard it. But her hands were trembling.

Maybe she *was* a coward. Cuch chimal, dragging her shield on her back and retreating from battle. She bit her lip.

"I'm not useless," she assured herself more than him. "I can be brave."

"I am not implying you aren't brave," he said. There was something heavy and dark in his gaze as he looked at her, something quiet too, that muffled his voice.

He leaned forward, inclining his head. He didn't seem like a powerful lord then, and she couldn't explain the change, only that in the past few minutes, as they spoke, he'd become more tangible. He was very handsome, with that wonderful voice of his. But he was distant, like the face in an old painting staring at her across the ages. It was beauty you couldn't hold. Then he looked to her, for a moment, very much a man, which startled her.

He drew back, leaned back and away from her, eyebrows furrowed.

"You need not consider my brother and his schemes. I will prevail and you will be rewarded for your assistance as was promised," he said dismissively. Now he was not looking at her and he was a great lord.

He changed. He was always changing, a thousand tiny ripples, tiny tessellations and dark reflections. It threw her out of balance, and her breath burned in her mouth.

"With the finest jewels and treasures of the earth, which your servants will fetch at your command," she said, not meaning to sound bitter; she merely remembered what he'd told her when he'd given her the silver bracelet. She gazed down at her wrist, running her hand along the piece of jewelry.

"With your heart's greatest desire," he said simply.

Ah, the ocean lit by the moon, night swimming in its depths; the automobile she wished to drive, curious about that beast of metal that roared upon the roads; the pretty dress reaching her thighs, made for dancing at clubs where they played all the music they mentioned in the papers, and which she'd never heard.

But when she looked at him to say *may I have all that?* the joy she felt, like a child who opens her Epiphany presents, was scattered.

It was nothing he did or nothing he said, since he was doing and saying nothing, just sitting at her side.

There was silence, a quiet that stretched out forever and was no more than a few minutes long. An emptiness that made Casiopea rub her arms, which filled the heart he'd spoken about. She waited for him to talk because she had no words and did not want to find them now lest she say the wrong thing, but he was prone to silences. She realized he would feel no need to talk.

So, yes, perhaps she was bitter, and beneath her bluster she was scared, and in turn perhaps he kept secrets, which only made it worse.

She sighed, raised her head, admired his profile for a second. She spoke, her voice as light as she could make it.

"Do you think they'll have opened the dining car yet?" she asked.

"We can find out," he said and they rose.

He brushed a few wrinkles from his suit, and she fixed her hair. He offered her his arm.

The dining car was empty but the tables were all set, with spotless white linens and gleaming glasses. Casiopea rested her chin against her hand and looked out the window, at the stars, which were fading. She longed. Not for one specific thing but for everything; she had longed for a long time. He'd made this longing worse: it followed her quietly, this awkward feeling under her skin.

"What do you dream about?" he asked.

"Sorry?" she replied, turning her head away from the window.

"When you dream, what do you dream about?"

"Oh. I don't know. Lots of different things, I suppose," Casiopea said with a shrug, tracing the rim of a glass with a hand.

"Do you dream about the things you see on the streets during the daytime and the people you know?"

"Sometimes."

She wondered what he was going on about. He looked rather

serious, and he rubbed his chin. She noticed the trace of stubble on his cheeks. Had he needed to shave before? He'd seemed very pristine to her, a statue in his perfection.

"I think I dreamed tonight. It's difficult for me to understand it since I am unused to the activity."

"My father had a book and it claimed that dreams can have secret messages. If you dream you are flying it means one thing and if you dream your teeth are falling out it means another. I do hate it when my teeth fall out in dreams," she said.

"I dreamed about you," he said, the voice deliberate, cool.

Casiopea coughed so loudly she thought the entire train had heard her, every single person in every berth and the conductor to boot. And then she blushed so brightly she seriously considered slipping under the table. She grabbed her napkin, tossed it on her lap, and fidgeted with it instead, unwilling to look at him.

"What is the matter?" Hun-Kamé said. "You are very strange sometimes."

"Nothing is the matter with me. You dream about me and nothing is the matter," she said, lifting her head and almost shouting at him. Couldn't he see how mortified she was?

Now he looked irritated, as if she'd been mean to him. But she was not trying to be mean; it wasn't the sort of thing she'd expected to hear.

"I shouldn't have dreamed, not about you or teeth or whatever men dream. I feel like I'm standing on quicksand and I'm sinking fast. I'm forgetting who I am," he admitted.

He looked utterly lost. She patted his hand, which rested against the mahogany table, in sympathy, not knowing what else to do.

"You'll be yourself again soon," she promised.

He looked down at her fingers resting on top of his. He seemed surprised, and she felt abashed, thinking she'd done something wrong. But when she attempted to pull away her hand, he gave it a squeeze and he nodded.

"I dreamed you walked the Black Road of Xibalba," he said. "I did not like this. It is a dangerous path. And I was glad when you woke me. It is not that I think you a coward, Lady Tun, it is that I wish you no harm."

He slid his hand away, and she stared at the empty plate before her. "I suppose there's nothing to do but hope for the best."

"Yes, I suppose so," Hun-Kamé said thoughtfully, grabbing his napkin and unfolding it. A server had walked by and filled their glasses with water. Casiopea guessed they would begin the breakfast service soon.

"Have I told you," he said suddenly, "how beautiful are the mountains in the east of my kingdom? They are made of different layers, first a layer of sturdy jadeite, then a layer of vibrant malachite, and finally a layer of pale pink coral. Even your stars would envy their beauty."

It was a strange comment. Was he attempting to distract her? A light danced in his dour eye. It was muted. The light of a half moon instead of the sun, but it made her lean forward, quick and eager.

"You say that because you have not seen them streaking the sky," she replied.

"Are they made of malachite and coral?"

"Well, no."

"Then they do not compare."

She smiled at Hun-Kamé. He smiled at her too. What was this? A simple act of mimicry? No. The smile, like his laughter, like the errant dream, came from his heart. Did he realize it? No. Does everyone who has been young and foolish realize the extent and depth of their emotions? Of course not.

What about Casiopea? Surely the sonnets, the turns of phrases in poems, had schooled her somewhat. But then, like him, she had lived vicariously, had seen the world from a distance. The yearning inside her was impossible, like when as a child she'd wished to pluck a shooting star from the sky; it was wildly familiar and new at the same time. And she didn't want it; she could recognize a fool's errand even if she could not name it.

The train pressed forward and the glasses tinkled and he looked at her as if he'd not truly seen her before. And maybe, he had not.

Chapter 19

The heat in El Paso was different from the heat in Yucatán. It was a dry, crackling heat, slipping in under the collar of Casiopea's dress, threatening to bake her like a loaf of bread. Men and women fanned themselves with their hats, with newspapers, as they made their way through customs. It was a long wait. Prohibition had turned many a law-abiding citizen into a smuggler of spirits. A case of whiskey bought for thirty-six dollars in Piedras Negras or another northern town could fetch thrice that price in San Antonio. And there was always a fellow willing to attempt to introduce many a weird artifact into the United States, especially exotic pets—a man was caught attempting to carry a Chihuahua in his luggage, while another drugged six parrots to keep them quiet during the crossing. More than a dozen passenger trains stopped daily in El Paso, and that meant customs agents.

Casiopea watched the people ahead of them, standing on her tiptoes, trying to measure the length of the line. She was nervous. She loathed the prospect of being asked questions in a language she did not understand, although, she imagined, it would not be too difficult to fetch someone who knew Spanish, if the necessity arose.

Many of the people in the city hailed from Mexico. Some had come because they had been pushed by the revolution, others had been there since the time when the territory was still part of Spain, and others were recent additions: priests and nuns escaping the government's persecution as well as Cristeros intent on one day becoming martyrs.

The line moved forward and it was their turn. When the agent spoke, she discovered she knew what he was saying; more than that, she could answer him. The words came to her as easily as if she'd been speaking English for ages.

The agent nodded at them and let them through. Outside, the sun blaring at them, Casiopea blinked and turned toward Hun-Kamé.

"I understood what he said," she told Hun-Kamé. "How is that possible?"

"Death speaks all languages," he replied.

"But I am not death."

"You wear me like a jewel upon your finger, Casiopea," he said and offered her his arm with a practiced aloofness. She took it, her hand careful as she touched his sleeve.

They made their way to the Plaza San Jacinto. The locals called it the Alligator Plaza for the critters that swam in a fenced pond there. All streetcar lines went down this square; it served as the town's beating heart, and the hotels clustered around it.

There were several places where a visitor could lodge in comfort these days. El Paso had ballooned in the past decade, transforming from a rudimentary collection of businesses and scattered homes to a full-blown city. The Sheldon, a four-story redbrick building that faced the plaza, was one of the best-known hotels in the American Southwest. During the Mexican Revolution, both journalists covering the happenings and revolutionaries involved in the fray lodged there. And the year before the Hotel Orndorff, also located by the plaza, had opened its doors, astonishing everyone with its extravagant price tag. This was the place Hun-Kamé picked for the duration of their stay. They booked adjacent, though not interconnected, rooms, as had been the case in Mexico City, and the front desk employee handed them their keys.

As soon as Casiopea reached her room, she proceeded to take a shower. This was her favorite amenity at the hotels: the nice bathrooms and the hot shower. She changed into a clean dress, realizing she must send her other clothes to be washed. Then she knocked on Hun-Kamé's door.

A few days before she would not have dared such a thing, but now she simply walked in and sat at the edge of his bed, comfortable in their familiarity.

"What now?" she asked. "Do we head out?"

"Yes. First I need to phone Loray," he replied.

"Is that about the wire he needs to send you?"

"And more."

Hun-Kamé lifted the heavy phone receiver and asked for the operator. He had also changed, switching the gray traveling suit for a navy jacket and trousers. He looked dapper. She watched him as he stood by the window, and she smiled. But the smile slid off her face as she wondered if she should be so familiar with him. She pivoted between conflicting desires, notions she could not even articulate.

Hun-Kamé placed the receiver down and turned to her, sliding his hands into his pockets.

"He is wiring me money; it should arrive come morning," he said.

"You don't seem too pleased," she replied.

"I was hoping he'd know where I can find the Uay Chivo."

"And he doesn't."

"No, but he had a suggestion."

She recalled Loray's suggestion that she cut off her hand. Somehow she didn't think whatever he'd told Hun-Kamé was very nice. Odds were it involved her too.

"I don't have any more hair you can cut, if you mean to use that to map your way," Casiopea replied, touching the short bangs across her forehead. When she looked in the mirror she did not quite recognize herself, the hair hitting her cheekbones.

"I could not summon ghosts right this instant even if I tried," he replied.

"But the illusions, you make those. And the trick with the languages," she protested.

"I told you. I'm far from home and I am not growing stronger. A little more and even that power may be beyond me, who knows."

He said this, but to her he looked no different than the day before. He stood tall and straight and strong, no weakness in his form. She, on the other hand, could feel a headache coming. Casiopea dragged a hand across her forehead. She'd slept on the train and still felt tired. She was an energetic girl, used to getting up with the dawn and working hard, and yet that day she was as frail as a lady who had never lifted a finger in her life.

"Do you have any ideas? Do you even know what the Uay Chivo looks like?"

"Like a sorcerer, like a goat," he replied staidly.

Casiopea did not think there was a half man, half goat with burning eyes casually walking around the streets of El Paso; the creature of legend from the southern peninsula's jungles waiting to catch a tram.

"What aren't you saying?" she asked, eyeing Hun-Kamé carefully; between his smooth, concise words lay a thorn.

"There is a witch," he said. "She will know about the Uay Chivo."

"What is the catch?"

She'd learned by now there was one and there was no point in mincing words, pretending she didn't expect it. Best to pluck the truth out.

"She'll want to be paid. And she won't take a coin," he told her.

Casiopea pressed her lips together, looking down at the floor.

"It's blood," he said.

"Of course it is," she said, her hands clutching the covers. "I can imagine it's not your blood."

"No."

"Then there's no choice, is there? I have to do it, as usual. You don't do anything. Well, fine, here, have the blood," she said, rising and offering him her wrists. "Have it," she continued, lifting her wrists. "What? I feel like I should sleep for three days straight, but no matter. What's a bit of blood at this point."

He said nothing, and she slapped his chest, furious at his dour expression. At this he did react, by catching her wrists, although he did not seem upset. He held her hands.

"I know I ask many things of—"

"You ask everything!"

"You will be repaid," he said, touching the silver bracelet, as if reminding her of his generosity, the possible avenues of wealth offered to her.

Casiopea rolled her eyes. "My heart's desire. And what if I can't—"

She clamped her mouth shut. What if she couldn't have what she wanted. She wasn't even sure what she'd ask him for if she could. Anyway, she needed him to remove the stupid bone shard. And when had there been a god who was not demanding? Tribute was to be expected, and she wouldn't have him saying she'd been a coward.

Casiopea pulled her hands away.

"We should find the witch, then," she said.

"If you want to, you could rest," he offered, gracious.

"No. Might as well get going," she said, wishing to get everything over with.

Hun-Kamé shrugged, which salted her wounds. Cross as she was, she failed to notice that he had not rebuked her for her anger, that he had not thought to remind her of his rank and importance and her comparative insignificance as he surely would have done a few days before.

The cool, protective bubble of the hotel broke as soon as they stepped out of the building. They took a trolley and stepped down after a few stops, reaching a flower shop with the name "Candida" written by its entrance in cursive letters. When they walked in a silver bell jingled, announcing their arrival. It was a narrow, dark little business perfumed with a wild mix of scents: lilies, peonies, and dewy fresh jasmine.

A woman sat behind a counter, her gray hair pulled back in a bun. She was a small, wrinkled lady, wearing a pink apron with her name—Candida Cordero—in the same script as the store's front. Her glasses were thick. She was working on a piece of embroidery.

The fairy tale books of Casiopea's childhood, replete with European fancies, contained old women with magic powers, but in those books they were hunched and wore capes. The folktales of her town, on the other hand, provided a different picture of warlocks and witches. There was a town in the north of Yucatán where they said all the inhabitants were witches, creatures who shed their skin to become animals, prancing around the cemetery or the roads at night. These people were young and old, men and women. Huay Pek, the dog witch, Huay Mis, the cat witch. But neither version of the witch looked like the woman in front of her. She was far too mundane, too sweet in her pink apron, stitching flowers.

"Seeking roses for your sweetheart?" the woman asked, without looking at them. "Red for passion and yellow for friendship, but

lavender is for love at first sight. The hue you pick makes all the difference."

"We don't need flowers," Hun-Kamé said.

"Nonsense. Everyone can use the charm of a flower. Besides, why
else would you be here? It's a flower shop."

"A friend recommended your shop."

"But is he a good friend?"

"It was the Marquess of Arrows."

The woman nodded, reaching for her scissors and cutting a
thread. She stopped to admire her handiwork for a moment, then
turned the embroidery hoop in their direction so that they might see
the roses she had been working on.

"Well. That's a name you don't hear around these parts very
often," the woman said, setting down her embroidery. "What's that
crazy Frenchman up to these days, hmm?"

"He sends his regards, from the south."

"Decked in green, with a pack of cards nearby."

"Likely."

"Ha. You would not believe the trouble he can get himself into
when he has the chance. Marquess. Demon."

Candida adjusted her glasses, pushing them back by the corner
of their frame, and looked at them for a good, long minute.

"I can't quite tell your hue, young man. But . . . not *that* young,
are you? You, dear boy, are decked in black. Boy and not-boy. What
strange darkness do you carry?"

"The hint of the grave, of Xibalba."

"Ah, sympathy flowers," the woman said, smiling a gap-toothed
smile and clasping her hands together. "But then my shop is too
modest to accommodate you, for I think you are a great lord."

Ordinarily, Hun-Kamé looked like a very polished man, but
when she said "lord," he stood even straighter, more rigid, and Ca-

siopea could not only picture his royal diadem—onyx and jade, no doubt—she thought she might touch it. She wondered if she would ever see him in his throne room, if he would stand there the way she pictured it, if his image would be reflected on the walls of the chamber, which would also be of onyx. Of course she couldn't, she wouldn't; Xibalba was his realm, and as soon as he returned to it she'd never hear of him again. And what would she do? Left in a border town like this, staring at the sky.

"I am Hun-Kamé," the god said.

"And what would the lord want of me?" Candida asked.

"You would know the other witches and warlocks nearby."

"Yes, but which one do you seek?"

"The Uay Chivo."

The old woman made a face and smacked her lips, as if she'd tasted an unpleasant dish.

"Him. You should buy a bouquet instead. Much prettier than that old goat and also smells nicer."

"I must insist. I'm afraid I don't need flowers."

"Does your friend not like them? Girl, are you allergic to them? Say that isn't so."

Casiopea shook her head. Hun-Kamé did not bother speaking. Realizing that her jests were not amusing them, the woman let out a loud *hmpf*.

"Well, then, if that is your wish . . . Seven drops of blood is the price. Will you pay?"

"I . . . I will," Casiopea said.

Casiopea had been standing behind Hun-Kamé, his second shadow. Now Candida beckoned Casiopea closer. She hesitated, took a few steps, brushing by vases stuffed with flowers.

"Let me see. A daisy by the side of the road. Closer, closer. And who are you?"

"It hardly matters who I am," Casiopea replied, irritated by the

woman's grandmotherly tone. Besides, it was true. She was the
token he used to pay for his passage.

"Modest too. Sit, sit right next to me."

The woman patted a chair behind the counter. Casiopea did not
sit there, instead leaning against the counter, raising her head, a
small act of defiance.

"You're too thin, girl. Why, you're almost all bones," Candida
said. "Oh, look at those dark circles under your eyes. Are you not
sleeping well?"

"Don't play with me. Have your blood," Casiopea replied, extending her hand, wrist up, like she'd done with Hun-Kamé.

"You'll lose your sweetness if you keep like this," the woman
said, clicking her tongue, disapproving. "Come here, lamb."

Realizing there was no point in refusing, Casiopea went behind
the counter and carefully sat down on the empty chair. The old
woman caught her chin with one hand and squeezed it a little, like
she imagined a fussing aunt might do, though Casiopea would not
know—her aunts had paid scant attention to her.

The old woman released her and leaned back.

"Seven drops is no small thing. Seven hours and the dreams
youth dream, then. I can tell there are lots of dreams in that head of
yours. Will you give me the seven drops?"

"I . . . suppose."

"You must be certain. We can't have halves here," the witch said,
sounding serious.

"I'm sure," Casiopea said.

The woman smiled. She grabbed her pincushion and procured a
white porcelain dish from somewhere under the counter, setting
them side by side. She gestured to Casiopea.

"You want me to prick myself with that?"

"Well, darling, some people prefer thorns and it can be arranged,
but isn't this much more efficient? Mmm?"

Casiopea frowned, but she grabbed the pincushion and pulled out a long silver pin. She held it carefully and pressed it against her little finger. Blood welled. She let a drop fall on the dish. Another fell. The rest she had to squeeze. When she was done she handed the witch the dish with the blood.

"Here," Casiopea said. "It's yours."

"Thank you, dear," the witch said, setting the dish aside. "You are a tiny, darling thing. Come, I'll give you something too, for your troubles. How about a lavender rose?"

The woman reached toward a shelf where bunches of flowers were kept and grabbed a single rose, handing it to Casiopea.

"For your sweetheart, eh?" Candida said, smiling. "And now, you rest, and I hope those dreams are sweet too."

"I don't know what you mean," Casiopea said, grabbing the rose. She had no sweetheart and no use for flowers.

The old woman kept smiling at her. Casiopea felt exhausted. She sat back, and as she did she closed her eyes and fell asleep.

Chapter 20

The road to Xibalba was a ribbon of black ink, staining the land. The land itself was a gray desert, and when Casiopea turned her head to look at the heavens she realized there were no stars, no moon. Yet the land was bathed in a soft, hazy light and here and there, by the road, she saw plants that looked more like glowing anemones than any ordinary vegetation, shining and shifting as she passed them.

Above her something huge flew, flapping its wings and stirring a wicked breeze. When Casiopea noticed this, she grew afraid and hurried down the road. There were stone pillars at certain intervals, and she crouched next to one of them, scanning the sky. But the flying creature had vanished.

Casiopea, realizing she was alone, began walking the road once more. It had no end. At length she came upon a lake that glowed an eerie blue, as if all the stars had fallen into the water and nestled in its bottom. She stretched out a hand and touched the surface of the lake, its luminescence rising, as if to meet her hand. She looked at her fingers, bathed in the blue glow, and smiled.

It was then she noticed a drop of blood falling into the blue pool of water, creating ripples upon its surface. Casiopea held up her wrists, realizing the blood emanated from there, two slashes like bracelets decorating her arms. The blood welled thicker, faster, and as it fell the lake turned red.

She stepped away from the pool of water, hurrying back to the black road, but the black road had disappeared. Instead, a path of the deepest crimson branded the land, like a hot iron. When she stepped on it, she began to sink, as if she'd stepped in quicksand. Down she went, and even though she tried to crawl her way out, she could find no purchase, and as the road closed above her head she tasted the copper flavor of blood in her mouth. There was nothing but the beating of her heart, fear clawing at it, in the depths of Xibalba. And high above in the land of men, a king sat on an obsidian throne upon a pile of bones as tall as a mountain, and his eyes were gray as smoke and she knew him as Vucub-Kamé.

Casiopea gasped, staring at the ceiling. The room was dark, and she could hardly see anything. Then came the click of a light.

She turned her head and saw Hun-Kamé sitting by her bed in a chair. Casiopea pushed herself up on her elbows. Her throat was parched and she struggled to find her tongue.

"What happened?" she asked.

"You fell asleep," he replied simply.

"At the shop?"

"Of course."

"How long did I sleep?"

"Seven hours, as promised. Night has fallen."

He had tucked her under the covers and Casiopea attempted to shove them away so she could stand and take a look out the window, as if to confirm this fact, but as soon as she pulled the covers and made to move, a shiver went through her body.

"Wait," he said, stilling her, his hand on her shoulder. "Do you need anything?"

"Water," she croaked.

He returned with a glass, pressing it into her hands as he sat down on the bed. Casiopea drank it. It hurt going down her throat, but she was very thirsty. She gave him back the glass, and he set it aside on the night table. Casiopea rubbed her wrists, almost expecting to find gashes along them, but the only thing adorning them was her silver bracelet.

"Was your dream unpleasant?" he asked.

"I . . . I dreamed of Xibalba," she said. She did not speak of the blood, nor the road that turned red, superstitious fear holding her tongue, as if by describing this incident she might bring misfortune to herself—and her luck, it was black! Somehow she identified the dream as a portent, and her heart knew not to tempt fate by solidifying it with words. He must have sensed this too; instinct made him frown, an uncomfortable silence extending between them

"Did you get what you needed from the witch?" she asked, wishing to dissipate the fear that clung to her body.

"Indeed. I have the Uay Chivo's address and the assurance that he keeps what I seek in his studio, behind a safe with three locks."

"But you can open the locks."

"Yes."

"Do we go now then?" she asked, already squaring her shoulders.

"Why don't you rest?" he replied.

"I slept for hours," she protested.

"But you did not rest."

"I say we go now."

She made a motion as if to stand up, but he shook his head, his hand bidding her to halt in her efforts.

"He will be there tomorrow, no need to leave tonight," he told her.

"Tomorrow I might be dead," she countered, unable to conceal the edge of panic on which she danced. The dream had brought with it the whiff of the grave, the undeniable reminder that the sands of her life were being spent, that she needed to dislodge the bone shard.

"Not tomorrow," he assured her.

"Would you even tell me if it was tomorrow?" she asked. "Or would you keep quiet?"

"I have not lied to you. Why should I deceive you now?"

"You didn't tell me all. You didn't say your brother means to rule and have offerings brought to him and . . . and all that."

"I might have said it sooner, but I've said it now. You can trust me."

Casiopea tried to grab the glass again, fumbled the job, and he lifted it instead and pressed it against her hands. There wasn't much water left, so when she'd taken a couple of sips he dutifully filled it again, ensuring her thirst would be sated. She settled the glass on the night table.

"The Uay Chivo is a man, not a god, but he commands magic. I expect treachery from him and we must be alert; we will be unable to afford any distractions. We shall venture forth tomorrow night. Now, refrain from overexertion. Rest. Do not be afraid, fear will blind you."

"It is easy to be unafraid if you are immortal," she said. "Not if you are human."

"Fear is generous and does not exclusively lodge in the hearts of mortals."

"And what do gods fear?" she asked.

She'd asked the wrong question. Hun-Kamé had a rigid preciseness about him at all times; in that instant he seemed to become a wooden statue, even the dark eye growing hard. He would not answer, she realized, just as she had not spoken about the road of Xibalba or the blood. Some things are simply not said.

"I'm better now," she said, picking an innocuous comment to distract them both. "We could fetch ourselves supper."

"I can ask them to bring us food. What would you fancy?"

"I don't know. We should phone the front desk."

Casiopea turned her head; noticing the lavender rose by the phone, her fingers reached for the long stem, the delicate petals.

"My rose."

"The witch gave it to you, so I thought I'd bring it with us," he said. "You paid for it, after all."

"But you didn't put it in water. It is beginning to wilt," she replied.

And again, the wrong thing to say, she realized, the reminder of death, putrefaction, the slim limits of existence, like a mantle over her shoulders. She sagged back against the pillows, tossing the rose onto the side table where she'd found it and pressing her hands against her temples, seized with a sudden burst of pain.

"Casiopea?"

"My head is throbbing. My mother used to tell me 'Everything will look better in the morning,'" she said. "Only it didn't look any better, and I'm afraid it won't look better tomorrow. It's much worse . . . the ache. The ache in my hand and now in my head."

"That is why I said to rest," he told her.

"Rest, rest . . . It's so annoying. You look . . . you look quite well. Amazing," she said.

It was true. He did appear quite sleek and stylish. She remembered reading an ad that said most men look well in a navy double-breasted jacket. Of course he was magnificent; the wide lapels and slightly fitted waist only served to emphasize his strong shoulders and granted him a comfortable swagger. No doubt she looked half dead—which she *was*, very likely—and silly and panicky, unable to quench the anxiety in the pit of her stomach. Stupid, stupid dream. And she was stupid, too, for making such a fuss. She bit her lip.

"You shouldn't look that good," she muttered accusingly.

"I'm not feeling entirely well, either, if you must know."

"Why, what's wrong?" she asked.

He shrugged. She felt like pinching his arm. He couldn't sit there, looking pensive, saying nothing. Her head was going to burst if he did.

"You have to tell me," she said.

His back was tense, his brow furrowed, and when he spoke it was he who sounded as if he'd just woken from a strange dream. The words were stilted, which was unlike him. When he talked, he did it well. He carved each sentence with a graceful assurance. Each word was a jewel.

"It's hard to say. Sometimes . . . when we are talking, it's as if . . . I forget," he mumbled.

"What do you forget?"

Such quiet. The quiet between stars. She thought she could almost hear her blood moving through her veins and her heart was loud as a drum, and when she touched the covers the rustle was like dragging a piece of furniture across the floor.

"Will you say something?" she asked again. "You're making me nervous. As if I wasn't nervous already."

"I forget everything. My brother, my palace, my name," he said hastily. "*Everything*."

That wasn't exactly the answer she was expecting, and the weight of it was tremendous, this single word, like a stone.

"That sounds awful," she replied.

"It's not awful. That's the problem. There's a second when I think it would be fine to forget myself, it would be the easiest thing in the world. But if you forget yourself once you'll do it twice, and thrice, and soon—"

He stopped talking. His face, it was brittle. She'd come to associate him with a steadfast harshness, the strength of obsidian.

"What if my name wasn't mine?" he asked. "What if my name was an entirely different one?"

Vaguely she recalled he'd mentioned a secret name when they were in Veracruz, but he had not been pleased when he said it.

"I don't understand," she replied and would have asked him to elaborate, but he gave her a look like a man who is learning a new language and can't find the correct word in the dictionary. And with that she grew quiet.

He raised his hand, two fingers in the air, touching her forehead, then running the fingers down her hairline.

Casiopea was used to spending time with Hun-Kamé in close quarters, and he'd clasped her hand during the train ride, but she thought they'd never sat this close. And the touch on her forehead, it wasn't more personal than the brief touch of his fingers upon her own. Yet it was different. She'd thought he'd held her hand out of sympathy, and now . . .

"I'd like to count stars with you. I don't know where I even got this idea, but it's there," he said.

The dust speaks louder when the wind stirs it, but she heard him anyway and knew not what to say, and everything she'd said so far had been stupid, so why would a few words help at this point?

She stared at him, mystified, unable to produce a coherent sentence. She stretched out a hand, as if to touch him like he'd touched her, a hand on his brow.

Abruptly Hun-Kamé stood up, took her left hand, and kissed her knuckles, like she'd thought gentlemen might do, the kind of gesture fit for films or poems.

"I'll let you be, Casiopea Tun," he said.

She nodded. He was off to his own room. Casiopea kicked off the bedsheets and stared at the hand he'd kissed. She thought of one hundred things she might have replied, but of course he'd long left her.

Chapter 21

artín hated feeling out of place. It was the whole reason he'd had himself shipped back to Uukumil rather than follow through with his expensive education. In Baja California he was immediately out of his depth and he knew it.

Tierra Blanca, it turned out, was a vast complex, a hotel and casino by the sea built in a peculiar style, recalling the Mayan elements of Martín's homeland but also the Art Deco movement. He felt both confused and intimidated as he walked down the hallways of this building, the scale of the project making his home in Yucatán, which he'd thought very elegant, pale in comparison. Besides, there was the basic shock of finding out that he was at a hotel. He had hardly believed his eyes when the owl dropped him off at its perimeter, the night ominous and punctuated by the buzzing of insects. When he'd gone inside and inquired about Aníbal Zavala, they told him he was expected.

Fortunately the hotel employees allowed Martín to check in to a room, comb his hair, and dust his jacket, which would have to satisfy his vanity for now. Martín took great pains to look the part of the gentleman, though he lacked in gentility.

Afterward, an employee came looking for him saying Zavala wanted to speak to him.

The office he was ushered into had very high ceilings carved with gigantic masks, more than six feet tall. The curtains were embroidered with geometrical patterns, and the desk by the window appeared to be a thick tree trunk that had not been properly turned into a desk: too many of its bumps and roots and its original organic quality were visible.

Behind the desk sat an older man, his hair gone gray, dressed in a mustard-colored suit with a dark brown bow tie. He had a tidy mustache, and all about him there was an air of order and mild manners that concealed something else.

"Welcome to Tierra Blanca. I am Aníbal Zavala," the man said, rising from behind his desk and approaching Martín, who was trying to take the whole trip, the building, the room, in.

"I'm Martín Leyva," he muttered, shaking the man's hand.

"You've had a chance to clean up somewhat, I assume?"

"Yes. I have a room."

"Good."

Aníbal reached toward a wooden box on his desk and took out a fat cigar, carefully clipping it and lighting it with a wide, warm smile. He did not offer Martín a smoke, and Martín stuffed his hands in his pockets, feeling offended and unable to complain.

"Do you know why you are here?" Aníbal asked.

"Vucub-Kamé said I should meet with you."

"And more than that?"

"He said I need to learn the shadow roads."

"Do you understand what that means?"

Martín shook his head as Aníbal's cigar began to glow a dull orange and he took a puff.

"Do you understand the mechanics of the realm of Xibalba?" Aníbal asked.

Martín was reminded of the headmaster at his school, whom he had loathed for his strictures, and did not bother shaking his head this time, merely stared at the man, hating the conversation already, as he did when any situation made him uncomfortable. His tactic would have normally been to strike back, but he forced himself to bite his tongue.

"I see," Aníbal said. "Well, I suppose we should go over the basics."

The older man ran a hand against a bookshelf, plucking a book and placing it on his desk. Martín looked at the tome, which was rather large and old. On the page there lay several concentric circles.

"Xibalba is made of nine levels. Through these levels descends the Black Road, which reaches a wall made from the thorns of the ceiba tree. Beyond this wall begins a causeway that leads to the gates of the Black City and allows access to the Jade Palace. By the palace is a lake where the World Tree quenches some of its thirst, and at the bottom of the lake dwells the First Caiman, which swam in the primordial seas and whose head was severed when the world was newly born."

Aníbal turned a page, tapping his finger on a two-page illustration depicting a lake with a tree, and beneath the tree, a caiman. The perspective was all off, it was not tri-dimensional, lacking in depth, and Martín had trouble understanding it.

"Few living mortals have made the journey down the Black Road. It is a dangerous and long path. It may take years to reach the gates of the Black City. Of course, the Supreme Lord does not expect you to walk the road for years. We must expedite your path."

"How would you do that?" Martín asked.

Aníbal turned another page, and now came a drawing that resembled the labyrinth Vucub-Kamé had shown him, an arrangement of black lines branching wildly, turning back and forward.

"Certain sorcerers and priests, and sometimes certain ordinary mortals—though these only in their dreams—have found their way to the Black City with more haste. They've done so by slipping through the shadows."

"What?"

"If you look at the road, carefully, there are spots where you can sense gaps. You can jump from gap to gap, walking the road with more ease. But you must be careful. The Black Road is treacherous. It is changing, rearranging itself. It does not lie still. It hungers."

"For what?"

"Destruction, pain. Keep your thoughts and your feet on the road, do not go astray. The Land of the Dead is vast. It's easy to get lost."

Martín looked at the page, but as he did, a curious sensation came upon him, as if the lines he was observing were not really fixed. The ink was running on the page. A path that he could have sworn snaked to the left in reality bent to the right.

"What madness," he whispered.

"If you look carefully, Martín, and if you focus your will on it, the road will take you to the heart of Xibalba, to the palace."

"Easier said than done, I'd wager."

"You'd wager correctly. I'll help you familiarize yourself with it."

Martín was not brave. His reticence kicked in and he raised both hands, bidding Aníbal to halt. A futile gesture, but one born of instinct.

"Wait. I'm not even sure *why* I'm here. Vucub-Kamé spoke of a contest and Casiopea—"

"A race. If it comes to it," Aníbal replied. He was put off by Martín's words.

"Yes, but why some ridiculous race? I don't—"

"The games of gods, of course. Do you honestly think Vucub-Kamé and his brother would face each other with shield and mace?"

"I don't see why not. It all sounds stupid."

Casiopea's mythology books showed illustrations of men with spears or tridents or another weapon. He had not paid attention to these tomes, but glimpsed their pictures nevertheless. And there were also the bits of Mayan legends he'd heard. Again, he had not paid much attention to these, but he thought the gods fought sometimes. He had, at any rate, the impression of tremendous violence.

"Your grandfather taught you nothing, I gather."

Of course he had not. Damn old mummy of a man slobbering in his room with his aches and complaints. He didn't say it, but Grandfather liked Casiopea better, which was a slap in the face. Now he felt he was being slapped again, by another old man.

"My grandfather is guarded," Martín replied. "Is that my fault? He explained how he assisted Vucub-Kamé, which I think is quite enough."

"Hmmm. But not *why*."

Aníbal rested his back against the desk, carefully holding his cigar between his fingers, as if examining the wrapper.

"Gods move pieces across boards, young man. That is what you are now. Your grandfather was one piece, one move, in a series of moves. It's your turn now, and it is an honor."

"It sounds like bullshit to me," Martín said acidly, rubbing a hand against the back of his neck. He had had quite enough for a single evening. His old instinct to bully someone whom he perceived frailer than him, for Aníbal at least looked frailer, an old man, an unpleasant authority figure, was rising.

"Such language. Besides, you haven't even asked what you are playing for."

"What?" Martín asked.

Martín noticed that the cigar had now developed a head of ash on the tip and needed to be rolled against an ashtray, but Aníbal did not seem in a hurry.

"To the world outside I simply built and own this hotel. Do you think me an ordinary businessman?"

"I guess not."

"How am I different?"

"How am I supposed to know?" Martín shot back.

Aníbal opened his mouth, and out curled the cigar's smoke, rising as high as the ceiling, twisting, and expanding, acquiring a shape. It danced above Aníbal's head, alive, vital, its shape that of a four-legged animal.

"I'm a sorcerer, but more than that, a priest. A loving servant of the Lord of Xibalba."

Aníbal flicked his finger against the cigar, and the accumulated ash rose, combining with the smoke, to further define the animal above him. It was a dog, and when Aníbal flicked his finger again, the smoke and ash rained on the old man, settling like a mantle on his shoulders. Aníbal then opened his left hand and ash fell on the floor, the labyrinth that had been contained on the page now reproduced there, its lines spreading and dancing around Martín's feet. He took two steps back, but the ash rose knee-high and he realized he could not move back or forward.

"Xibalba, it is here and it is there, the Black Road reaches far and wide. Mortals stand, breathe, walk upon Xibalba and do not even know it, having forgotten their allegiance to the Place of Fright. But we will change that. They will know the name of their Supreme Lord."

"All right, I get the point," Martín replied. Now his tone was mellowing as he realized the old man was more dangerous than he'd thought.

"Do you?"

Beneath his mild-mannered face, Aníbal hid a bleak interior, and his eyes were two prick points of glowing red, as if someone had lit them with a match.

"You are playing the one game that matters, Martín. It's the game of creation," Aníbal said. "Temples will rise for Vucub-Kamé and there will be rejoicing and there will be sacrifice."

The ash and smoke came together, forming a dark temple, and then another, until there were dozens of them surrounding Martín. Even someone as obtuse as he could understand the meaning of such an apparition. He bowed his head, afraid, but also aware there was no escaping this fate, that he'd walk the road and he'd somehow ensure Vucub-Kamé's victory, and with it the world would change.

The old man carelessly let his cigar fall on a silver ashtray and yawned.

"Well, we should begin now. Don't you think? After all, your cousin will be here soon," Aníbal said.

Martín shivered. Any living man who will face the Land of the Dead will shiver, but he nodded his head too.

Aníbal closed his fist, and the ash and the smoke formed a wide circle, onto which he stepped and motioned for Martín to join him. Martín obeyed, watching as the gray ash turned black. Beneath them the floor melted, as if it were made of tar, and Martín closed his eyes. He was afraid, like when he'd been a small child and thought monsters lurked under his bed; only now they did, and he assisted them.

Chapter 22

The outside of the Uay Chivo's house was unassuming; its pale blue paint had peeled and the potted plants at the windows were wilting. The inside was a different story. First of all, Casiopea was certain the interior was too spacious, as if extra rooms could exist within the limits of this home, breaking all laws of physics. Second, it was filled with peculiar, unsettling items. The studio they wandered into had two large stone statues of goats, fitting considering the name of the sorcerer who owned the place, and creepy since the goats were carved in a very realistic style, their huge blind eyes making Casiopea frown.

On the shelves there sat multitudes of jars stuffed with herbs and dried plants, others filled with bits of starfish and corals. Some contained whole specimens: fish, snakes, lizards, scorpions, carefully preserved. Bottles glinted with their multicolored liquids and powders, here a green, there a vivid red.

There was a metal safe, which Hun-Kamé manipulated, revealing a small chest, and inside this chest an even smaller box. The house was dark, nobody was home, but the eyes of the stone goats did not allow her to relax. They'd tricked a god and invited themselves into the abode of a spirit, but they had not stolen from anyone yet. This audacious act seemed to Casiopea more perilous than their previous encounters, even if the house was quiet and empty.

"Why is it taking you so long?" she asked, watching Hun-Kamé as he worked his magic.

"All three of these boxes are made of iron, which annoys me, and therefore I proceed more slowly than I'd like," he replied.

"Please hurry. I think I heard something."

"I am doing what I can. It's not just the metal. He cast protective spells. There are locks upon locks."

With a click, Hun-Kamé finally opened the third box to reveal . . . nothing. There came thin, malicious laughter, and Casiopea turned around to find two young men, their hair slicked back with too much pomade, and an older gentleman standing at the doorway, looking at them. It was the older man who had laughed, a gray-haired fellow in a long gray coat who leaned on a cane decorated with the silver head of a goat, a cigarette dangling from his lips.

"Welcome to my home. I suppose proper introductions are not necessary," the man said.

"Yet introductions are always proper," Hun-Kamé replied.

The old man's steps proclaimed his identity as loudly as if he had yelled it at the door. For there could be no denying that this was the Uay Chivo. His gait was odd, and there were the eyes too, with a strange spark in them, the tilt of the head, and all about him this . . . stench: tobacco and ashes, covered up with a cloying cologne.

"You behave improperly, riffling through my things. I doubt you found anything worth your while."

One of the men helped the Uay Chivo out of his coat and placed it on a chair.

"Maybe you were looking for this?" he asked.

The old man pointed to the necklace he was wearing, now revealed after the removal of the coat. It looked heavy and was made of jade beads and a spiny oyster shell. "The boxes were for show. I carry it around my neck."

Hun-Kamé did not seem perturbed by this revelation. "We are indeed looking for my property," the god replied simply.

"And did you think it would be that easy to get your claws on it?"

"I was hoping it wouldn't be too complicated."

The sorcerer grinned at them, pointing the head of his walking stick at Hun-Kamé, shaking it as he walked slowly toward them.

"Then you'll be sorely disappointed," the Uay Chivo said. "I've been expecting you. Only a fool would not have guessed this fact."

"A wise man would choose the words he uses with me."

"Wisdom! And yet you, dear lord, have been most unwise, or I wouldn't be wearing the necklace of a Death Lord. I'm afraid I won't bow to the likes of you."

"No, you bow your head low before my brother," Hun-Kamé replied. "Kiss the dust he steps on, I suspect."

"I do the will of the Supreme Lord of Xibalba," said the Uay Chivo, and so confident he must have been in the support of Vucub-Kamé that he stepped forward and pressed the tip of the cane against the god's chest, a threat and the stamp of his authority.

He reminded Casiopea of her grandfather.

"My younger brother is a usurper, gaining his throne with deceit. You do the will of a liar," Hun-Kamé said.

"Does it matter? Power is power."

Hun-Kamé slid the cane away with one hand, a gentle motion, as if he were removing a piece of lint from his well-tailored suit.

"I know you, Uay Chivo. You are one of the Zavalas. Carnival magicians with delusions of grandeur," Hun-Kamé said casually.

The god was all quiet elegant contempt and his words held no threat. It was as if threats would be beneath him at that moment, as if he would not waste his breath on a creature as humble as the sorcerer. The Uay Chivo must wave his cane and snarl, but Hun-Kamé would not. It was a double humiliation, in words and gesture, the mark of the deepest scorn. And the old man knew it. He stepped back, gripping his cane tightly with one hand, his face red.

He handed his cane to one of the young men who stood next to him and took a deep drag from his cigarette.

"Carnival magicians, huh?" the Uay Chivo repeated.

The sorcerer inspected his cigarette with great care. Flames curled out from his mouth, resting there, hot against his lips, before he spat them out and pushed them away with a wrinkled hand, tossing a fireball against Hun-Kamé. The impact of it sent the god crashing against the floor, toppling a side table and a vase in the process.

Casiopea leaned over him.

"Does that seem like the work of a carnival magician?" the sorcerer said triumphantly.

"Hun-Kamé," Casiopea whispered urgently, touching his neck, his chest, his brow. The fireball had not ignited his clothes, yet his skin felt feverish to her touch. His eyes were closed. She shook him a little.

The sorcerer's assistants were holding knives in their hands, cutting their palms, and the Uay Chivo had started speaking, weaving words and a spell together. Casiopea, not knowing what to do, held Hun-Kamé in her arms and watched as the men pressed their bloodied hands against the floor, tracing a circle around them, the blood bubbling and sizzling, as if water had hit a hot pan.

Despite her fear, which was real and alive, sharp enough to make her fingers tingle, Casiopea chased away panic. It would do no good to cry or scream. She knew no magic, she realized that she could not undo this spell; therefore she merely drew Hun-Kamé closer to her, as if she might protect him with her touch. She clutched him and stared at the men who circled them not with her face deformed by terror but with a more distant look.

A wall of fire rose from the spot where the blood had fallen. It was a fire born of a strange flame, blue in its cast. One moment it was solid, the next as flimsy as a spider web, yet it shivered as a flame would. The sorcerer tossed a handful of ash against it, and the fire acquired an almost violet hue.

The old man and the young ones were pleased with themselves; they chuckled and yelled a few obscenities in their triumph.

Casiopea, knowing nothing, unable to understand the nature of the spell, extended an arm, intending to touch the wall of fire.

"Don't," Hun-Kamé said, grabbing her arm.

He had finally opened his dark eye and stared at her. Casiopea felt such stupid joy in this, in the realization that he was not grievously injured—although he couldn't have died of such an injury, immortal as he was—that she almost spoke an inane term of endearment before she was cut off by the laughter of the sorcerer.

"You won't be able to get out, but it will hurt like the devil if you try," Hun-Kamé whispered in her ear. "Hotter than blazing coals."

Casiopea pulled her arm back, nodding.

"What was that?" the Uay Chivo asked. "Speak up. Or have you been rendered speechless by my magic?"

Hun-Kamé did not appear aggrieved. His eye was cool, though it was a tad too dark, too flat, a pool of ink directed at the silver-haired sorcerer.

"Your magic is thin, like watered-down pulque, no bite to it. Do you think your spell will hold? I can already see the strain it causes you," Hun-Kamé said, and his voice had the same flatness of the eye.

"Strain? Not with this lovely necklace in my possession," the Uay Chivo said, touching the jade beads, the sharp points of the oyster shell.

"Your face tells a different story, flushed like a fool's."

The Uay Chivo was indeed flushed, beads of sweat on his forehead, streaming now down his narrow, angry face, as if he'd been running for a while. Even his voice sounded breathless. The accusation made it worse, the face growing redder. The sorcerer bit into his cigarette with such strength Casiopea thought he'd snap it in two.

"I don't have to hold you forever, Hun-Kamé. I only have to slow you down. By the time you reach Baja California, if you ever reach it, you'll be weak as a kitten," the Uay Chivo said.

"Don't count on it," Hun-Kamé said, and his voice was like the dead of night, utterly still, it clouded everything, it dimmed the lights for a moment. Even the flames that rose around them grew softer before leaping up and shimmering violet-red as the sorcerer tossed another handful of ash at the barrier.

"Enjoy your time in my house," the Uay Chivo replied.

But when he stepped out of the room, he bent over his cane with a great deal of effort, and one of his assistants walked by his side, speaking in his ear. The other assistant remained, obviously meant to guard them.

Casiopea and Hun-Kamé sat next to each other quietly. The guard wrapped his hand in a handkerchief and crossed his arms, sitting down on a chair and watching them intently. At length he grew bored or tired and closed his eyes.

"How will we get out of this?" Casiopea asked in a whisper.

"I imagine with some effort," Hun-Kamé replied laconically.

Casiopea raised an eyebrow at his words. "Was that a joke?"

"I suppose it was."

"It wasn't very good."

"I don't have much practice with them."

She smiled at him and he smiled back. Minutes passed before he half turned away from Casiopea, regarding the wall of flame.

"The spell is sound enough, but there is a solution to every riddle," Hun-Kamé said. "If I thrust myself against the flames, I'd simply scorch my body and writhe in pain. But I won't do that, not exactly. What we need is that guard to come here, right next to the barrier."

"What do you propose?"

"Have you any practice at playing the damsel in distress?"

"I could manage."

"Good. The man is tired; so is the Uay Chivo. Magic takes a toll. Exhaustion may engender mistakes. I will cast an illusion, make myself disappear. You must make a ruckus. Say I've run off and get him as near as you can."

"That is all?"

"I'll manage the rest."

Casiopea nodded. Hun-Kamé stood up, and he slowly lifted his hands. He was there, but then an inky darkness lifted from the floor, enveloping him in the blink of an eye, and he disappeared. The guard who was supposed to watch them had his eyes closed; he had witnessed nothing. Casiopea hoped for the best, took a deep breath and cried out.

"He's gone! He's left me, he's gone!"

The guard was startled awake and stood up, his hand immediately going to the hilt of his knife.

"He's escaped!" Casiopea cried.

The man's eyes went wide. He opened his mouth but did not seem able to believe the sight, the girl alone in the circle of fire, hands pitifully pressed against her face.

"He went away, like a puff of smoke, left me here. Please, come, see," she babbled.

The man looked like he was about to bolt out of the room. Casiopea pointed to the floor. "See! All he's left behind is a jewel, a tiny diamond, like the coin you toss a beggar."

Creative, her tongue, schooled by books and poems. The words, along with her distraught expression, must have done the trick. The guard rushed forward, stood by the rim of fire, and bent down to look at the nonexistent diamond Casiopea was pointing at.

All of a sudden the guard was pulled forward, Hun-Kamé became visible again as the man was violently flung against the floor, the top of his head falling inside the circle of fire. Blood welled from the man's temple and Hun-Kamé dragged him around, following the circle's contour, whispering several words. It was as if he were wiping chalk off a slate, the wall weakening, dissolving with each word and each drop of the man's blood. Every single link in a spell is precious. Topple one, the others will fall, and this is exactly what Hun-Kamé did. He wrote over, crossed out, he eliminated a single link, and the violet fire ceased to burn.

Once the barrier was gone, Casiopea bent down, pressing a hand against the man's neck, relieved to feel a pulse beneath her fingers.

"Thank God, he is not dead," she said.

"What if he was?" Hun-Kamé replied with a shrug, smoothing the lapels of his suit. "He is only a man."

"I am only a woman. It doesn't mean you can chop me down like a weed, without any care or thought; neither can you chop him."

"You forget, maybe, who I am."

"I think you are a nobleman, and killing a man who need not be killed would be ignoble. Am I mistaken?" she countered.

Behind his handsome, polished stillness, there lay a hard and ugly core. Her naïveté allowed her to glimpse it, but she could not fear it. He'd been kind to her, and she therefore expected his kindness would extend to the entire world. He must have realized this and rather than reply with a harsh word he raised a palm up politely.

"You are gracious. I will be gracious, for your sake," he told her.

At that point she noticed that Hun-Kamé's hand, which he'd used to get hold of the guard and thrust briefly into the barrier, was blackened, as if it had been charred. This distracted her from the meaning of his words, which, had she analyzed, she would have found rather shocking, since he'd said he meant to please her. He did this thing for her.

"Are you hurt?" she asked.

"It is not a nice sensation, but soon remedied," he replied and shook his hand, bits of blackened skin flaking off, revealing a whole and perfect hand again, which now reached for the knife the guard had dropped. "But I suspect there will be more fire and pain. Come, we need to find the Uay Chivo. I can't leave without that necklace."

They headed up the stairs quietly. The house had been a tomb when they entered it, and it had returned to its stillness, their steps almost soundless. At the end of a hallway they glimpsed a man standing in front of a door and retreated. It was the other guard.

"What now?" she whispered.

"Same as before, I'll make myself hard to spot."

As he said this, the inky darkness shrouded him and he disappeared, but when she peered down carefully at the shadows she noticed that they were darker than they should have been, a thing of velvet. This velvet piece of darkness drifted around the corner and away. Casiopea pressed her lips together and waited.

Hun-Kamé came back a couple of minutes later and guided her to the door the sentinel had been guarding, only the man was now sprawled before it.

"Alive," Hun-Kamé pointed out, half in jest. "Never say I was not generous to you."

"If anyone asks, I'll say you are the most generous of all the gods I've ever met."

"Your jokes are no good either," he replied.

But he was smiling again; the practice of it made it easier.

He turned around and fiddled with the door, unlocking it as he'd done with the boxes. The Uay Chivo's room was crammed with many bottles, jars, and sundry objects, just as his study had been filled with odd specimens. In the room there were two goat sculptures that matched the ones downstairs, but the sculptures in this room were made of a dark, rich wood. There was also a four-poster bed, heavy and ornate. On it slept the old man, his hands against his chest, covering the necklace.

They moved quietly, but no sooner had they taken three steps than the wooden goats turned their heads in their direction, staring at them. The room grew warmer.

"What a pair of brazen fools you are," the Uay Chivo said, rising from the bed. "Walking into my inner sanctum like one walks into the maw of a beast."

"Rethink whatever it is you are planning," Hun-Kamé said.

The admonition had no effect. The sorcerer held up his hands. The goats charged at them. Casiopea was able to move to the right and jump behind a table, putting it between herself and one of the magical beasts. This slowed down but did not deter the goat. It glared at her with its blind eyes, lowered its head, then rushed forward, shoving the table with brutal strength. Casiopea was thrust back, the goat pinning the table and her against the wall.

She could do little except watch the animal as it glared at her and tried to push the table harder, pressing her like an insect, sending splinters jumping through the air as it bored into the wood, into the wall behind her, and squeezed the girl. Casiopea thought she would die, her lungs would burst, for surely no one could withstand this and survive.

The goat, frustrated with the slow progress of such an endeavor, now attempted to chomp at whatever part of Casiopea's body was visible and available. It happened to be the face, and if it didn't bite off half a cheek, it was because she managed to lower herself a few centimeters, evading its maw, though this angered the goat, which kicked the furniture and squeezed her harder against the wall.

She could not scream. Her breath seemed to have escaped her

body; it hovered in an empty space, and no plea of help rose from her lips.

Hun-Kamé shot forward and plunged his knife into the creature's head and yelled a word. A ripple, a crack, ran down the goat's head, and it split into two pieces, and those pieces jumped in the air, the knife jumping with them, and the wood split into more pieces. It dashed against the walls, dashed against the floor, shivering, twisting, and growing still.

Hun-Kamé pulled the table away and pulled Casiopea toward him.

She felt boneless, a flower with a broken stem, and if he had not held her she would have fallen to her knees. On the opposite side of the room she spotted the remains of the other wooden goat. She took a breath and pressed a hand against her throat.

"That knife, where has it gone?" Hun-Kamé said.

Before he could add anything else, he was shoving her away. Casiopea fell on her knees and watched as a long rope of fire whipped him, tangling around his limbs. Hun-Kamé ripped it away, but even as he did the sorcerer was rushing toward him. He was a man, old, his gray hair wild, and then in an instant he wasn't. He had changed into the shape of a monstrous goat, as big as a horse, its black horns sharp, the hoofs heavy and shiny as steel, the eyes red. The goat snorted, opened its mouth, and out poked the tongue of fire, whipping Hun-Kamé and tossing him against one of the bed's posts, snapping the post in two in the process.

Pain shot through her arm, and she curled her fingers into a fist, unable to rise to her feet. The pain cleaved her, it made her eyes water, and she watched the goat rearing up and smashing Hun-Kamé like a rag doll. But he'd said a knife. He'd said a knife, and she forced the fingers to uncurl.

"A knife," she whispered and once she said it, it became the only thing that could matter, and the pain in her arm diminished. She ran around the room, tossing bits of furniture away even as she struggled to regain her breath. At last she spotted it in a corner, half hidden by a curtain, but when she stretched out a hand to retrieve it, the broken mouth of the wooden goat statue, which lay nearby, attempted to bite her fingers. Casiopea let out a loud yelp and used a chair's leg to smash the chomping piece of wood, smash and smash until it did not move. She kicked it aside.

Her hand curled around the handle of the knife. Other bits of wood began to shake and tossed themselves against her body, trying to scratch and harm her. Casiopea blindly stabbed at the wooden remains of the goat, she kicked them away and managed to climb on a desk, shielding herself from the attack.

At this point the room was in more than shambles, furniture toppled and ripped to shreds, feathers from cushions spread upon the rugs. The Uay Chivo was stomping in fury, breathing out fire that scorched the god's body and although it touched him and left no permanent mark, Hun-Kamé looked like he was out of breath. The goat pressed forward and gave Hun-Kamé a monstrous shove. The god lost his balance and fell on his back.

It was then that he caught sight of her and made a grasping motion.

The knife. She tossed it in his direction, and he caught it in his left hand. The goat was springing forward again, but Hun-Kamé jumped to his feet and as the animal reared its head back, baying, Hun-Kamé sliced a swift arc through the air, cutting, almost completely severing, the animal's neck.

It was a feat of impossible strength for a man, and it was even more impossible that as the goat lay shivering on the floor, its blood seeping out through the enormous gash on its neck, it attempted to stand up and managed to kneel. A man, kneeling now, not a goat, but Hun-Kamé struck a second time, and the head was detached from the body.

Casiopea turned her face, the taste of bile and blood in her mouth.

When she looked again, Hun-Kamé had snatched the jade necklace from around the dead man's neck, clutching it in one hand. A white, foul smoke lifted itself from the corpse. Casiopea coughed and her eyes watered.

The smoke had no face, but it did have a mouth, and the mouth spoke blistering words.

"You think you've defeated me, Xibalban? My lord will raise my bones before two nights have passed."

"And we will be long gone by then," Hun-Kamé replied.

"Ah, yes, run. Run to meet your destiny. But you may find yourself outmatched in Tierra Blanca, and I will be avenged, one way or another. Vucub-Kamé brings a new era with him; you are the dregs of the old one."

"And you, meanwhile, are dead."

The Uay Chivo's mouth snarled, but it could not bite, it could not harm anymore, and as the blood of the sorcerer cooled, like diminishing embers, the smoke dissipated.

She jumped off the desk.

Hun-Kamé placed the necklace around his neck and turned to her. On his cheeks and forehead, on his hands were the black burn marks left by the goat, but they crumbled away in the beat of a heart, the skin flawless again. Yet he reached for her and leaned against her, like a man who has been injured in a nasty brawl, like she had leaned on him before.

"Are you all right?" she asked.

"As well as can be under the circumstances," he said, although he sounded breathless.

Casiopea nodded, wiping her mouth with the back of her hand.

"You cut your lip," he said.

"That explains the taste," she muttered. She had no idea at what point that had happened. "It'll go fine with the other bruises."

"What bruises?" he replied.

His fingers grazed her lips, the lightest touch, there and then gone. She realized he was merely casting his magic, healing whatever cuts and abrasions she sported, no alternate agenda aside from this, but her heart leaped up.

"There. A useful trick, don't you think?" he said.

"Yes, but it would help if you could also mend clothes," she said. He looked a complete mess, the furthest from a god one could imagine, his hands dirty with soot and his hair wild. Which didn't matter one bit, because that heart of hers was dancing, and she smiled.

"Let us leave this city," he told her, shaking his head. "And let us sleep."

"I couldn't agree more," she replied. "And maybe . . . maybe, we could buy some aspirin before that."

His lips curled, his eyes grew lighter. He returned the smile. He hadn't smiled at her before, or if he had it had not been like this, his face clumsy and unadorned. The artless shape of the smile endeared him to her. She chuckled despite all the aches in her body, which did not fade as quickly as the shape of the bruises.

Chapter 23

They slept nearly a whole day as the train sped west, the most direct route to Baja California actually taking them across the United States rather than Mexico, following the border. Her sleep was dreamless and Casiopea was thankful. She did not wish the image of the dead sorcerer to haunt her, nor did she want to envision the Black Road and the gray soils of Xibalba. A deep sleep in her twin berth was a blessing.

When they awoke they sat by the window. The land and the sky and the cacti were bright streaks of color. An arid sight, so different from the lush jungles of the south, the blue pools of water where she'd cooled herself. Baja California was closer now and with it the feeling that something important would happen. Portents in the air, in the clouds, if she'd known to read the signs.

Hun-Kamé was quiet and kept his distance despite their narrow quarters. He had a sour look, and sat very firmly on the lounge chair that faced their berths. It made her nervous, this stasis, even if she knew his silences. It chafed Casiopea, making her want to spring up and pace around in counterpoint.

Something was amiss. Their triumph against the sorcerer should have brought them joy. Instead, he wallowed.

The sun burned the windows; the heat was a white heat, like a sheet. Back in Mérida she could hide in the cool patio of the house, but there was no hiding on this train, and despite all the niceties it contained, it was hot as an iron in there. She opened the window a bit—dirt and cinders would blow in, but she needed to cool herself—and looked at Hun-Kamé over her shoulder.

The train let out a long whistle.

His gaze was on a faraway point she could not reach.

"What is it?" she asked, unable to stand it any longer.

"He seeded the path for us, but now I wonder what will flower," Hun-Kamé said. At least he'd spoken up, breaking the silence.

"I don't understand."

"My brother left behind all these pieces for me to retrieve, drawing me farther from the heart of my empire, from the Yucatán. A calculated game, which has not bothered me until this point, but now I wonder . . . if I'd first found the eye instead of the necklace, it might be better. This, around my neck. I thought it would be enough, I *wanted* it to be enough, but it's not enough . . . My strength ebbs."

He pressed a hand against his throat. He'd cast an illusion and the jade necklace now appeared an ordinary tie, but it was there. She perceived it without seeing it. "And you look weaker too, more frail," he muttered.

He had not gazed out the window, the scenery did not concern him, but now he turned his gaze there, ignoring her. He spoke as if talking to the desert, the sand and the sky, not to her.

"I must return home. Every second away is unbearable. Xibalba needs me and I need it. At times I think if I spend much more time in this land I will not be able to return to where I was . . . to who I was." He shook his head "You wouldn't understand."

"I do understand."

"Please," he said dismissively.

His poised indifference offended her. He was being rude, cruel, and rather than accepting this as the whim of a god she spoke, harsh and loud.

"You don't realize it, do you?" she asked. "You don't see the way you are turning my world upside down. I was someone in Uukumil, someone I may never be again."

"I'll remove the bone shard as soon as I have my throne back, I won't waste a second," he said, and the words were like a blow. She raised her head high.

Casiopea stood right in front of him, so that he could not glance out the window and ignore her. She almost felt like grabbing him by the lapels of his jacket to emphasize her point. "It's not the bone shard," she said "It's everything. I have no idea where I'll go after this, what I'll do. Did you ever even wonder about that? You'll return home, but I've forsaken mine. My family won't take me back."

"It is not the same."

He stood up. The desert heat shrank the boundaries of their compartment, drawing him closer to her. She thought about a story Mother had told her one time when she was bad, about wicked girls combusting into balls of fire. She could swear she was about to be scorched, but she stared at him.

"I can feel the taint of your mortality in me, and I must scrub it off, soon," he went on.

"You talk as if I'm poisonous," Casiopea protested.

"You are," he said, careless and cold. "And I'm poisonous to you, killing you with every breath you take. If you had any common sense you'd understand why I grow weary. If I had my eye back I might be stronger, if I was in Mérida . . . but I am here, incomplete. You are not foolish, you must have some idea . . ."

As he spoke, the words grew sharper, and she realized something, hearing him speak, something that ought to have been obvious from the moment they had woken up and he'd sat, morose, in his corner of the compartment. "You are afraid," Casiopea said in wonder.

Afraid of death. Of life? How to define it. It was clear then, the nervousness, the way he stood, the timbre of his voice. And why wouldn't he be? Immortal, suddenly faced with the possibility of mortality, of all his plans gone asunder. Casiopea was not able to summon much fear for herself, although she was aware that she was dying, that he was drawing her essence away, and when he was full she'd crumple, a wilted flower. For the moment she was more interested in his reaction.

He jerked his head up, annoyed, and did not reply.

"You should have told me. I thought you feared nothing," she said, pressing on.

"Quiet now," he said, his voice low. "The things you name grow in power."

She closed her mouth and stared at him, wondering what black luck she was inviting by speaking as she'd done. There was magic to be reckoned with and the rules of gods she didn't comprehend. She'd made him speak, and maybe she ought to have let him be quiet, as he'd wanted.

"I'm sorry," Casiopea said in a whisper.

"It is no matter," he replied, casually, and she realized there was pretense in his voice; he was rattled but would not show it openly.

Casiopea nodded, but his distress was palpable, a frightened creature that circled the room.

"Let's see what they are serving in the dining car. It's probably something disgusting, like roast beef," she said, because she'd had a chance to look at the menu and had been dismayed by all the American dishes.

She took him by the hand and before he could object, dragged him out of their compartment. But rather than stopping in the ornate dining car, with its silver and crystal and porcelain, she kept going until they reached the observation car. There were tables, arranged with stationery so people could pen letters to their families, plush chairs, and panoramic windows offering an excellent view of the receding tracks. The observation car served drinks and light food, functioning as a lounge, but right that moment there was no service and there were scarcely any other people there. Everyone must be having a proper dinner in the dining car or else had turned in for a nap. It made perfect sense to sleep the evening away.

Casiopea sat down, and Hun-Kamé sat next to her. For the moment the thought of food was forgotten, and she rested her head against the glass.

"Well, if we are going to sit here doing nothing, we could have stayed in the compartment," he said after a while. "What's the reason for this excursion?"

"Not everything needs a proper reason. I wanted to get out of there," she told him. "Do you want to go back?"

"I suppose not. One compartment is as good as another."

The rattle of the axles was very loud. *Clack clack clack.* Casiopea smiled.

"I like the train, but I think I will fall in love with the automobile," she said, tapping her foot to this rhythm.

"Why is that?"

"This heads in one direction, back and forth in a line. But can you picture an automobile? Cutting in whatever direction you will, winding down roads. Did you see them in the city? You could do as you pleased in one of those," she said, thinking of the vehicles that had rolled before their eyes, providing an exciting chaos to the streets in downtown Mexico City. Along with the night swimming and the dancing, this was one of her secret, deepest wishes.

"You want to go back home," she said. "I don't want to go back. Not for a thousand years, and yet . . . I don't know what I'll do if I'm not taking care of Grandfather and fetching the groceries. I've never seriously thought of it, and now it seems I should. Or maybe not, maybe it's too soon. Maybe there's no point in talking about automobiles when I don't know if I'll live to be nineteen. But it would be fun, wouldn't it? To ride one. Maybe to ride it with you."

He tossed her a strange look she'd never seen before. She catalogued all his looks and thought she knew them by now. This look she did not recognize. It reminded her of the movement of a match as it strikes the box.

"With me?"

She felt abashed, tried to shrug it off. "It's only daydreams."

"Casiopea," he said. His voice had a deep, pleasant rumble to it. He let his hand fall upon hers.

Again she had the sensation that she was in the belly of a whale, swaying gently, as she had had during the ride from Mexico City to El Paso. She recalled that Jonah was thrown into the sea to appease God, and he lay nestled inside the creature, but she could not remember, for the life of her, what had happened to him.

His thumb stroked over her knuckles. and Hun-Kamé leaned down in what she took to be a motion to kiss her. He had been afraid and uncertain, and now he was composed, and it was she who felt a shiver go down her spine.

She remembered a story she'd read or heard—she could not much remember where—about men who took advantage of women on trains, using the privacy of the compartment as a means for mischief. It might have been the priest who issued the warning during a sermon, it was the kind of thing he might lecture them about. Ride a train and find yourself with a bold, strange man. Kiss a man and soon enough he'll be taking liberties with you. Wait a little and you'll be carrying a bastard baby to be baptized at the church, with a single surname to his name.

Yes, men could be brazen on a train.

And so could women, she mused. She was, after all, here, with him. Chasing adventure, a fancy. Chasing *something.*

There was tightness in her throat, and the sun shone harshly through the window, making his dark eye even darker, as if he objected to its light and conjured more shadows. Since she'd cast away seven layers of decency already, she decided one more would not matter, and if he attempted a kiss she'd allow it.

"I like your daydreams, dear girl," he said quietly.

"I've never said them aloud before," she told him.

It was true. She'd pressed all her fantasies like dried flowers in books, carefully hidden where neither Martín nor Cirilo would see them. Rarely, late at night, had she allowed herself to contemplate them. If she'd declared them in a loud voice Casiopea would have let them take root inside her, and she could not have that. Instead, she polished them in secret, precious bits that they were, but bits and not wholes.

She understood now, his paucity with words.

He did not kiss her. He hovered next to her, pressed his forehead against her own instead, which was worse than any liberty he might have taken, more raw.

"Words are seeds, Casiopea. With words you embroider narratives, and the narratives breed myths, and there's power in the myth. Yes, the things you name have power," he said.

Casiopea clenched her hands together, and her heart clenched too, and she nodded solemnly, though she also sighed when he drew away from her.

They were quiet and they were foolish, both of them, thinking they were treading with any delicacy, and that if they somehow moderated their voices they'd stop the tide of emotion. The things you name do grow in power, but others that are not ever whispered claw at one's heart anyway, rip it to shreds even if a syllable does not escape the lips. The silence was hopeless in any case, since something escaped the god, anyway: a sigh to match the girl's own.

Chapter 24

Vucub-Kamé walked in the gardens of his palace, past ponds filled with minuscule glowing fish, until he reached a lake of considerable size. He set a hand upon one of the ceiba trees growing next to the lake, bigger than any of the other trees, its massive roots dipping into the water. The ceiba trees in Xibalba had a silver cast, but this particular one was brighter than the rest, its leaves more luminous, almost iridescent.

The lake was special too, its waters never reflected anything. Not a leaf nor a branch, nor the figure of the Death Lord circling it. Though curiously clear, the waters seemed bottomless and no fish swam there: only the Great Caiman, in its depths, which had traveled the seas when the world was young and teemed with the fury of chaos. Shards of chaos remained in the water, which was why it rejected reflections and why Vucub-Kamé could not read portents in its depths. Curiously, auguries function following the principles of order.

Or not so curiously. After all, prophecy traces clean paths. Vucub-Kamé's ability lay in witnessing the arrow of what might be, of following the thread of order among what others thought was simple chance. Men also had this gift, but being a god, his power was unparalleled. Yet the more time passed, the more disorganized his visions of his own future became.

Vucub-Kamé had not tried to divine the future since leaving Xtabay's home, but he had been considering the facts as he knew them, considering them very carefully. And pacing, pacing beside the lake and wondering about the strength of chaos upon his finely laid plans.

Vucub-Kamé was alone, the attendants of the god having been dismissed for the time being. Yet now two men approached the Death Lord, bowing low when they reached him. Aníbal and Martín. He'd sent for them. After they had abased themselves sufficiently, Vucub-Kamé bid them rise.

"How do you find my kingdom?" Vucub-Kamé asked Martín. The heavy obsidian necklace around his neck accentuated the harshness of his face, giving his words an added weight.

"It's interesting," Martín mumbled. He was prosaic and, lacking any desire for the fantastic, he would have rather kept his eyes shut the whole journey. Best ask a slug what it thinks of the architecture of a city.

"Do you think you can walk its road alone?" the god asked, aware now that there was no need for formalities and polite inquiries with the Leyva boy, and somewhat irritated by this since the vanity of gods extends to their constructions, and surely he desired to hear a long exultation of the beauty of the Black City.

"Martín progresses," Aníbal said.

"Quickly, I hope."

Aníbal inclined his head, a deferential nod. Vucub-Kamé began to walk again and the men trailed behind him, dogs waiting for scraps from their master. In the trees black birds stared at the trio but did not sing. The god had been irritable as of late, so they wisely kept their mournful melodies to themselves.

"Your brother is dead, Aníbal," Vucub-Kamé said casually. "The problem with the old goat is he is always underestimating the difficulties of certain tasks."

Vucub-Kamé turned around to stare the Zalazar man directly in the face. The god did not appear displeased, but the wind that had been tugging at his pale hair ceased, growing shy.

"Listen with care. Hun-Kamé and the girl will arrive in Tijuana soon. You, Leyva, will meet them there."

"I?" Martín asked. "What for?"

"Because I set the tone from the very first step and because I want to offer certain terms to your cousin."

"What terms?"

"The details don't concern you. You'll meet them and kindly escort them to Tierra Blanca. And you, Aníbal, will be polite too. No gnashing of the teeth or foolish revenges."

"They killed my brother," Anibal said.

"As if that was but a temporary condition."

"It's the principle, my lord, and you know precisely how—"

"I know precisely how much of an idiot you can be sometimes," Vucub-Kamé replied, his voice harsh. "But I am not interested in stupid displays of pyrotechnics and whatever rough magic you command. Hun-Kamé and the girl will be received like honored guests. *Especially* the girl."

Aníbal Zavala had assisted Vucub-Kamé in overseeing the construction of the structure in Tierra Blanca, as well as in the manufacture of the axe that had robbed Hun-Kamé of his head. Yet that did not mean the god would treat him kindly if he were to disobey.

"Casiopea?" Martín scoffed.

"Bind that tongue of yours. You may speak when I ask a question."

Vucub-Kamé's eyes were the color of ashes that have lain in the hearth for a long time, all warmth leached from them. Had Martín been paying more attention he might have noticed this before speaking, but he was not a man of subtleties. Now the eyes had grown colder, and Martín snapped his mouth shut.

"Your cousin will be like our dearest friend; she will be offered delicacies and gifts. You will speak kindly to her and attempt to make her see, once more, how much easier it would be to side with me. You understand now, boy?"

"Yes," Martín said.

"Make sure that progress you spoke of turns to certainty," Vucub-Kamé said, turning his gaze to Aníbal.

He did not even bother ordering them away. The men bowed and left of their own accord, the impatience of the lord encouraging them to flee like scared buzzards.

Vucub-Kamé stood by the lake, alone now, to weigh his worries. It had occurred to him that he had found the kink in his plans: Casiopea Tun.

She was the seed of all this trouble, having opened the chest in the first place. Despite this, Vucub-Kamé had considered her as a minor piece in the game—someone had to open the chest, it did not matter to him who did, nor when.

But Vucub-Kamé had begun to worry about the exact value of the mortal.

Symbols are of importance both to sorcerers and gods, and Vucub-Kamé ought to have identified this particular symbol before. Casiopea, like certain tiny, colorful frogs in the jungle, was more dangerous than one could imagine at first glance.

She was, after all, the maiden, and there is power in this symbol.

One time the Lords of Xibalba had executed two mortal men when the men challenged them to a game of ball. The bodies of the mortals were buried under the ball court in Xibalba, but the head of one of them was placed on a tree. A maiden approached the tree, and when she reached up toward it, the head of the dead man spat into her hand. Pregnant in this magical way, she gave birth to the Hero Twins who returned to avenge their dead father, and eventually succeeded in restoring him to life.

Although mortals mangled the story in the telling—for the tale concluded with the defeat of the Lords of Xibalba, and the gods persisted—there was a smidgen of truth to the myth. But what mattered was not the veracity of the story, but its power. The symbol. The hidden meaning. A woman and rebirth and the restoration of something lost. A vessel, a conduit through which everything is made anew.

There she was, the girl, accompanying Hun-Kamé, and it could mean she was nothing, strictly an ordinary girl with ordinary thoughts and the weak flesh of all things that will die. Or she could be something else. How to tell, there was no clue. There was magic in the air, the dance of chaos and fate, and Vucub-Kamé grew grayer in his discontent, wondering how to dislodge this bit of sand that had sunk into his eyes and irritated him greatly.

The girl.

Had Vucub-Kamé been able to kill Casiopea, no doubt he would have. But it was impossible, with her human body protected by the strength of a god.

He had thought to bribe the girl. That was why he'd sent Martín to find her in Mexico City, hoping he'd convince her to side with him. He could offer her the bounty of the seas, strings of pearls and jewels from the earth, the kind of promises that make fools of men. Or else a way with magic, the capacity to weave necromantic spells and bid the dead speak. Power, too, over an entire city, an entire length of coast—he might even keep his end of the bargain.

Vucub-Kamé could attempt to sway her this way, but he suspected she would turn him away.

What to do, then.

Vucub-Kamé's owl had brought him an interesting tidbit that day.

Before, the owl had captured Hun-Kamé's full laughter in a white shell. This time it brought two shells. Tucked neatly inside a black snail shell lay Casiopea's sigh. It was a delicate thing, like a nocturnal butterfly. Pretty too. In strokes of crimson and blue it painted a picture of the most exquisite heartache.

Vucub-Kamé was able to somewhat re-create the mind of the woman who had breathed this sigh. He could not know everything, but he drew conclusions, and they were sharp and accurate since he was, after all, a daykeeper, used to teasing stories out of the smallest leaf and pebble lying on the road.

He thus surmised that Casiopea Tun, rather than being drawn by treasure chests and pageants of power, was infatuated with his brother. Hun-Kamé was the prize she desired.

Vucub-Kamé knew he must play upon this weak point, but he had not quite determined how he might accomplish it. Now, however, as he pondered the waters of the lake, his thoughts solidified.

If Hun-Kamé she wanted, Hun-Kamé he could grant, in a fashion. Truly, there was no other way they might expect to be together, for otherwise such an exercise would be immediately doomed.

And Hun-Kamé? Would he not oppose such a scheme if he were made aware of it?

But, ah, there was the matter of the second shell. This one was yellow. Hidden in it was another sigh. The mind of the one who had uttered this sigh, Vucub-Kamé could not re-create as fully as in the case of Casiopea: it was Hun-Kamé's sigh, his immortal Xibalban essence shielding naked thoughts and desires. However, enough of the mortal element was audible to Vucub-Kamé that, although haltingly, it painted a different picture. Not exquisite in its construction, nor light like Casiopea's, but crude like an unfinished carving. The sketch of a man in that sigh.

Here was the mortality that afflicted Hun-Kamé, and that Vucub-Kamé had thought would lead to a contest and a decapitation. Now he glimpsed another path, more subdued but less onerous. Left or right the road splits, what did it matter the direction it took if Vucub-Kamé obtained his crown?

Because Hun-Kamé's sigh made one matter clear. That, unbelievably, immortality weighed on him, it chafed, he struggled against it.

Has a god ever abdicated his eternity for a woman? No. Such idiocies cannot be expected of anything immortal. But mortals descend into paroxysms quite often. And what was Hun-Kamé now but half a fool, his voice young, his eye almost bereft of shadows? He sighed and he yearned, and in that yearning lay a weakness to exploit.

Both of them stupid puppets of harmless flesh.

Vucub-Kamé tossed the shells into the water. They caused ripples, but in those waters he could see no futures, nor did he intend to. The gesture was one of defiance against the chaos that conspired against him.

"It is my kingdom, for me alone and for me to keep," he told the water.

Silver eyes and a smile like the edge of the voracious sea, Vucub-Kamé whirled away and walked back to his palace.

Chapter 25

The tracks changed in Mexicali. The rail became a narrow gauge, and this smaller train they had swiched to rattled painfully, finally reaching Tijuana. It was terribly hot: they called the road south of Tijuana the "road to hell" for a reason. Even the shade of the whitewashed shed that served as the train "station," with a few benches and little else for show, offered no solace. Hun-Kamé and Casiopea fanned themselves with their hats and contemplated the border town.

Prohibition had been good to Tijuana. Avenida Revolución, the artery of the city, was jammed with hotels and establishments selling curiosities to the tourists. There were rows of eateries, many advertising themselves in English. Peddlers walked around the streets trying to entice the newcomers with their wares. At a corner, a man stood with a donkey painted as a zebra, offering to take photographs of children riding on its back for a low fee.

The number of saloons had doubled in the span of a few years. Gambling clubs mushroomed: Monte Carlo, the Tivoli Bar, the Foreign Club. Raunchy establishments mixed with others that promised a glimpse of "old Mexico," a false creation more romantic than any Hollywood film. But what did the tourists know? The Americans streamed into Mexico, ready to construct a new playground for themselves, to drink the booze that was forbidden in Los Angeles, San Diego, and San Francisco, but flowed abundantly across the border. Lady Temperance had no abode here. The longest bar in the world was in Tijuana, and it charged fifteen cents for a beer. Even as far away as New York people talked about casinos like the Sunset Inn, where one could win or lose a fortune playing faro and monte. There was music too. Dancers, even magicians pulling rabbits out of hats.

Everyone visited Tijuana, jamming the crossings at Calexico and San Ysidro. Gloria Swanson, Buster Keaton, Charlie Chaplin, they all ventured there. Rich men in tweed suits from back east, very formal, would let loose upon the dance floor. Wild types with a thing for jazz hustled their way through town. Criminals, prostitutes, liquor runners, and the cream of the crop, crammed together, smoking cigarettes, pushing back tequila, slamming down the dollar bills.

Casiopea and Hun-Kamé found their way across this haven of hedonism and into one of its hotels, where they spoke to a clerk who said that they'd need to hire an automobile to get to Tierra Blanca.

"It's the damn best hotel and casino in this state. You head off down the coast, past Rosarito," the clerk told them. "There's cars willing to drive you down in the morning, but they get scarce at night."

Since it was now nighttime, and since they were both tired from their adventure in El Paso—although at this point Casiopea was always tired, not for any reason—Hun-Kamé booked two rooms. The clerk assured them he'd fetch them an automobile in the morning.

Casiopea lost no time in slipping into her nightgown and falling upon the bed. The room was cramped and stuffy. There were also too many pillows, and she shoved them to the floor.

She had evaded Xibalba the previous nights, but now the nightmare returned. She saw the Black Road, the gray landscape with its strange plants. Casiopea had the sensation she was not alone, the rustling of wings alerting her to something strange in the air. Again she arrived at a lake of pure blue, glowing softly, and then there was the blood welling from her wrists. The blood ran down her body, the skin sloughed off her bones, leaving the pulsating flesh, and birds with mighty beaks pecked at her, tearing chunks of meat. They pecked her bones clean and then those bones were laid beneath the obsidian throne, and Vucub-Kamé sat on this throne with a necklace made of human skulls around his neck.

She woke up screaming. The rooms were connected, and Hun-Kamé must have heard her because he rushed in, looking startled. At first Casiopea said nothing. She was terribly embarrassed. She'd roused him, and he seemed entirely unsure of whether he should speak or dash out.

"What is it?"

"I died," she told him, her mouth trembling, although she had meant to say "I had a dream, I'll go back to sleep," even if the dream had followed her, the room eerily quiet, the shadows much too dark. On the floor, a pillow might have been a wild creature ready to strike, and the wallpaper, it was the foliage of a distant jungle.

"I was in Xibalba."

The name, so soft, like an insect's wing, and his face, upon hearing it, strained, uncertain. She kicked the covers away and stood up, her voice hoarse.

"What happened there?"

She shook her head. "There was blood, my blood. The road

turned crimson with it. I don't want to say more; you told me we shouldn't speak about certain things."

She rubbed her left hand, which ached, and looked down at the floor, careful to avoid the too-dark shadows in the corners, which resembled black wraiths. She knew, if she stared at them, they might shift and grin at her. There was the memory of death in the darkness, dream-death, but not any falser for its oneiric nature.

"It hurts again?" he asked.

"Yes," she said. Not just the hand. The head, her body, pain like a current running through her. Pins and needles in her arms and legs, a sour taste in her mouth. The pain came and went, but it didn't end.

He reached out and held her hand. The ache diminished and he released her. She looked up at him. "I apologize for the discomfort, both the physical pain and the pain gazing upon Xibalba may cause you," he said. "I know that contemplating my kingdom of dust and smoke is no simple thing for a mortal."

"'Yesterday a dream; tomorrow dust. Nothing, just before; just after, smoke,'" she replied.

It was an automatic reflex. In her desire to soothe herself she'd stretched her mind, looking for something familiar, and ended up finding the old tome with Quevedo's sonnets. A poor choice, but one made in haste.

"Pretty words," he said. "What do they mean?"

"It's a poem, from one of my father's books. It was titled 'He indicates life's essential brevity, unexpected and with suffering, assaulted by death.' I don't think I'd mind if life was brief if only . . ."

"If only what?" he pressed her, when she didn't speak.

"You'd laugh."

"I don't much laugh at you."

Ordinarily, she wouldn't have said a word to him, to anyone, but her fear clung to her like a spider web, and in her attempt to shake it off she forgot she should have been mortified about speaking so plainly. Babbling, truly. In the end, what did she care? And had she not told him so many things already?

"I'd like to dance. The dances we couldn't dance in Uukumil. My mother, she said a waltz had been fine in her day, but now she's heard people dance too fast. But I'd like to dance fast."

She wouldn't know where to start, couldn't imagine how they did the Charleston, but words were whispered, even in towns like Uukumil, about the dances and the shoes and the dresses the girls wore. Enough to seed the idea in her mind, let it take root.

"And what else?"

"Swimming at night, in the Pacific. To taste the water, taste the salt. To see if it tastes any different from the water of the Yucatán."

He chuckled at this.

"You said you wouldn't laugh!" she chided him.

As she spoke, the sounds of the city returned. The distant, strident note of a trumpet blasted the night, the laughter of pedestrians spilled against their window, and the room became ordinary: the headboard, smooth and lacquered, the pillows on the floor a pale lump of cotton, the wallpaper a pattern of rhomboids. Casiopea and Hun-Kamé were ordinary, too, sitting in the semi-darkness of any spring night. They'd scared away whatever odd shadows had crept by their side.

"I don't laugh out of malice. As I've said, I like your daydreams. I'll tell you what, when this is over, I'll give you many gifts so that you may go dancing and swimming as you wish," he declared and made a motion with his hand, tossing upon the floor dozens of black pearls, which rolled under the bed, a chair.

She caught one, and it dissolved into nothingness between her fingers, an illusion, like others he used. Now it was Casiopea's turn to chuckle.

"They're not real. You're giving me fake pearls. It's like handing me a slice of cake and taking it away."

"It's merely an amusement, for the time being. But I will pay you back, when it is all over."

"When it is over," she repeated, and she couldn't help the uncertainty in her voice.

The Black Road, the blood on her hands were gone but not forgotten. The hand hurt, with its bone shard that was death, and she knew herself minuscule and mortal.

"I won't lie to you," he said. "I don't know what awaits us in Tierra Blanca. My brother is a liar and a traitor, and if he lopped my head off once, no doubt he will attempt to do it again. You have been brave, and you might have to be braver."

"I won't stop now, not when we are almost there," she replied, not wishing him to assume her worries meant she'd falter at this point. "And afterward, when you are a god, we'll laugh at all the trials we went through. Maybe they'll even tell stories about us, like with the Hero Twins."

She smiled. Casiopea thought this would reassure him, but instead he was rattled; he looked away. She'd been scared and now it was his turn to look anxious. She felt his dread, as if it were scraping against her skin, but it was a different sort of dread. She feared death, Xibalba, the bone shard in her hand. He feared something else.

"Listen to me, there're not many hours in the night left. Everything will change soon," he said, hurriedly, as if someone were chasing him. As if to emphasize this, he began pacing, back and forth he went. "Tomorrow I may be someone else. I'll regain my throne, I'll change. Six hours, sixteen, maybe not tomorrow, maybe sixty hours, but no matter, soon. I'll look at you with different eyes. You must trust me, now, when I speak to you, will you?"

He kept talking, unwilling to give her a space to raise her voice, his words apparently of the utmost urgency.

"I deal in illusions. It is my gift. But it's not an illusion. Who I am right this second with you. Do you understand? I can't say it any better. Remember me like this, if you choose to remember me at all."

"You'll forget me," she said. It was obvious in that instant what he was trying to get at, the fallibility of a god's memory, and he stood still at last.

"No, not forget . . . but it won't be *me* remembering and *I* won't . . . it's a heart here, inside this body," he said, pressing a hand against his chest "But this is not my body, Casiopea. It's this suit I wear, for a moment, and the moment will cease. And when that happens . . ."

"You will be like a stranger to me," she concluded, and *her* heart, troublesome thing that it was, stuttered.

"Yes."

"There is no 'after,' " she whispered.

It wasn't fair. But there wasn't an "after" in stories, was there? The curtain simply fell. She was not in a fairy tale, in any case. What "after" could there be? He, sending her a postcard from the Land of the Dead? They would become pen pals? Maybe in the end what would happen is she'd hitch a ride back to her town and spend her days sweeping the floors of her grandfather's house, nothing to show for all her efforts. Back to the first square on the board. If she didn't end up keeling over in the next few hours, if buzzards didn't rip her flesh.

"You'll have your black pearls. Your heart's desire," he said. He sounded charitable and for once she despised his politeness. Better that he had offered her nothing.

She laughed at his words. She had never desired pearls. He didn't know her, she thought. He didn't know her one bit.

Chapter 26

She woke to an ache so deep in her bones and such copious sorrow that she thought she would not be able to rise from bed. The world outside seemed muted and gray, which she thought fitting. Had it not been gray for her since birth? The burst of colors she had experienced during the past few days was the anomaly.

The mirror revealed the face of a sickly girl, her eyes heavy.

A *dying girl*, Casiopea thought. She inspected her left hand, trying to find the point where the splinter lodged.

There came a knock on the bathroom door. Hun-Kamé said something about leaving soon.

Casiopea jutted her chin up and put on a short-sleeved yellow dress with a small flower corsage pinned to the waist.

When they stepped out of the hotel, Martín was waiting for them. Casiopea was so surprised she almost dropped her suitcase. Hun-Kamé did not seem bothered by the unexpected appearance of her cousin, who leaned against a sleek, black automobile. Next to Martín stood a chauffeur in a neat white uniform.

"Good morning. We've been sent to pick you up. Lord Vucub-

Kamé wants to speak to you," Martín said, folding the newspaper he had been reading.

"How gracious of him," Hun-Kamé replied. "We could have made our way on our own."

"No need. Please get in."

The chauffeur held the door open for them.

"Should we?" Casiopea asked, grasping the crook of Hun-Kamé's arm.

"It will make no difference," he replied.

They sat in the back, Martín riding in the front. They did not talk. Casiopea's cousin fanned himself with the newspaper as the car rolled out of the city and continued down south. Even this early in the day it was already warm.

The sun bleached the land around them and leached the life out of Casiopea, who lay listless in the back of the automobile, once in a while running her hands through her hair.

She was so tired now, and she did not want to think what this meant. She tried not to pay attention to her throbbing hand, which she pressed against the window.

There came into view a white building surrounded by a lush greenness that defied the desert heat, twin rows of palm trees leading toward its front steps. An oasis, if she'd ever seen one. Casiopea blinked, blinded by the building's whiteness.

It was a precise, powerful structure. They'd been in nice, fancy hotels, but this was beyond fancy. It seemed . . . it seemed almost like a temple, a palace like the ancient ones in Yucatán, although there was nothing in it that fully imitated the Mayan buildings she was familiar with. Not quite. The resemblance was in the boldness of the three-story building or the whiteness of the walls, which made her think of limestone, of salt. As the automobile stopped before the front entrance, she was able to make out the carvings decorating the exterior. Fish, sea stars, sea turtles, aquatic plants. The double door, which a porter held open for them, was made of metal, a lattice of water lilies.

The lobby had a similar marine theme. The ceilings were extremely tall, as if giants, rather than men, were supposed to walk the halls. The floor was tiled blue-and-white, with powerful Art Deco accents here and there: in the chandeliers, the lines of the furniture, the painting behind the front desk. The elevators, she noticed, were flanked by stylized stone caimans. There were floor-length mirrors spanning the lobby, duplicating the entrance, magnifying it, and milky-blue windows that changed the light filtering in, as if they were gazing up from the bottom of a waterhole up to the heavens.

There were frescoes, the walls painted in the brilliant shade of blue they called Mayan blue, the truest blue you've ever seen. Oceans filled with marine creatures appeared on those walls, the flora and fauna painted in rich reds and intense yellows, fringed with geometric shapes. Above them, the ceiling was silver and gold, with the glyphs for earth and water repeated over and over again.

It was like tumbling into another world, the textures on display—stone, glass, wood—coming together in a mixture so heady it was impossible not to stop and gawk.

"Come along," Martín said. "No need to check in, it's all been arranged."

"What has been arranged?" Casiopea asked, regaining the capacity for speech.

"Your stay."

They went into the elevator, all gleaming metal—the glyphs there again—and got out on the third floor. The porter had attached himself to them and carried their bags. When they reached the end of a hallway, Martín unlocked the doors and motioned for them to step in.

They stood in a vestibule, the sofas yellow, the walls blue. A table in the center with lilies on display. At each side a door. Martín opened one, then the other.

"Your rooms," he said.

Casiopea took a tentative step into one of the bedrooms. The yellow and blue scheme also reigned here. The windows were huge and led toward a balcony. If she stood out there she might smell the ocean, its salt. They'd come so far! She had not even realized the magnitude of the trip until now, all the states they'd crossed, the cities that had gone past their window, to reach this point at the edge of the sea.

She felt such joy then. This was one of the things she'd dreamed about. An ocean offering itself to her. It was the postcard in the old cookie tin, it was that breathless feeling she'd carried hidden in her heart. She stepped out, onto the balcony, and gripped the railing with both hands. She could hear them talking from where she was standing.

"You are to have dinner with Zavala tonight at eight," Martín said. "He's asked that you make use of the stores downstairs to outfit yourselves. Zavala has dinner in the main ballroom. Travel suits and ordinary dresses will not do."

"Very well. And my brother, will he grace me with his presence tonight during dinner?" Hun-Kamé asked.

"I wouldn't know. I'll see you at eight. If you need anything, do ring for it," Martín said, making his exit.

Casiopea turned and went back into the room, leaning against the balcony door, watching Hun-Kamé. He walked around, looking at the ceiling, inspecting the windows, all the finery, his hands behind his back. He was smiling.

"Vucub-Kamé is up to his clever games. Very, very clever, my brother."

"I don't understand."

Hun-Kamé continued his inspection, now running his hands along a wall, scratching with a nail its blue paint. Casiopea saw the expensive room and the elaborate décor, but he was clearly finding something unusual about the setup. "I told you about the chu'lel, remember? Vucub-Kamé wanted to connect two points of power together. Look at this place. Look at the glyphs, the shape of it, each wall, each angle, it sings with magic. It's not an ordinary hotel."

Casiopea cocked her head, staring at the motifs on the ceiling and the walls. It reminded her of the images in history books, drawings of temples in the midst of the jungle or the ruins dotting the peninsula where she'd grown up. "It's a pyramid without being a pyramid," she ventured.

"Precisely," Hun-Kamé said, looking very pleased, although she wasn't sure why he would be so happy.

"You said he had not connected the two points of power."

"No, he hasn't. This place is thrumming with potential, it's a sleeping beast, one of your engines before it's been set in motion."

In her dream there had been an obsidian throne, the Lord of Xibalba on it. Now she recalled other details: piles of bones as tall as houses, littering the land, skulls that formed walls, blood slick upon the earth. Yes, she had glimpsed something that was not, but which could well be.

"Why hasn't it been set in motion?" she asked.

"Isn't it obvious?" Hun-Kamé replied. "There must be a mortuary chamber somewhere. He intends to kill me and rule across this whole vast expanse of land; my blood is bound to be the final stone. Oh, I can feel it."

"Why aren't you afraid, then?"

He smiled even more, as if she'd made a particularly clever joke. "Because, Casiopea Tun, he hasn't killed me yet, has he?"

"He could come barreling down that door, ready to fight you," she said, pointing in that direction. It was unlikely, but there was no sense in dismissing the possibility either.

"Gods don't fight each other with shields and swords. That would be improper."

"He cut off your head."

"I'm aware of it. When I am done with him I'll have this place hauled off, bit by bit, into the sea, not a speck of his work left behind. How glorious that will be. The misery of his cries when he gets to enjoy a few centuries in a carved box, and the added misery of watching his creation crumble into nothing."

"That's your plan, then. You're going to do exactly the same as he did to you," she said, taken aback by the harshness of his words. "It hardly seems right."

"It's always been the plan."

Casiopea stepped away from Hun-Kamé, rubbing her left arm. The ache reached far beyond the wrist, a constant though dull pain, but worse when it came to her hand. "Then gods don't fight with swords, but they can be as petty as men," she mused.

"Do not chide me. I've waited too long for this vengeance, and I intend to enjoy it."

"It's unnecessarily cruel."

"Then maybe I should rap his fingers with a ruler instead, what do you say?" he asked her. "What would you have me do, hmmm?"

"I don't know," she admitted. She could not even begin to imagine how the conflicts between divinities played out, but she had not liked the sight of the decapitation of the Uay Chivo, even if he'd risen afterward, a strange cloud of smoke that spoke to them. She did not fancy observing the decapitation of Hun-Kamé's brother, either.

Hun-Kamé sat down on a chair, which was upholstered in a vibrant yellow, crossing his arms. He was shy of twenty, an angry boy and nothing more. Casiopea shook her head and took a seat across from him.

"You've never told me what he was like, before your fight," she said. She had not asked. Likely she wanted to imagine Hun-Kamé as a unique creature, no other like him, even if this was illogical, since the existence of his sibling proved this a false notion.

"What?" Hun-Kamé replied.

"You and your brother couldn't have always hated each other."

He frowned. "We are both different principles of the same thing. It was impossible for us to exist in constant hatred any more than the moon can despise the stars."

She looked at Hun-Kamé and found herself thinking of her own family, of Martín. Had Martín always hated her? Did she truly hate him? The anger that had felt so hot in Yucatán had cooled down during her trip.

"My brother wanted more," Hun-Kamé said. "There is a stasis in eternity, but he did not . . . I am the senior of the two, ruler of the night. He questioned me, spoke when he shouldn't, did not show the appropriate deference. It was there, the resentment. That is not the same as hate."

"You didn't speak about it?"

Hun-Kamé scoffed, and she thought again about Martín. Had that not been what Martín wanted? That Casiopea show the appropriate deference, that she be quiet? Back in Yucatán, had her resentment not knotted and grown, poisoning her gut? She realized, with a shock, that she might have more in common with Vucub-Kamé than with his brother.

"What?" Hun-Kamé asked, frowning.

She raised her head, and she looked at him, and she thought he'd pulled her away from all that. Unintentionally, yes, but he'd granted the distance she'd needed from Uukumil, from Martín and everyone. But Vucub-Kamé had been meant to reside eternally in Xibalba, by his brother's side, wrapped in his quiet rage.

"Maybe it hurt, for him," Casiopea said. "Watching you have the last word, having to follow each of your commands."

"Are you saying it was right of him to do this to me?" Hun-Kamé said, rising from the chair and pointing at his face, at the eye patch that hid the empty eye socket.

She stood up, echoing him. "It was wrong. But I have the feeling you were cruel. That who you are now is not a reflection of who you were before."

"Anyone who expects sweetness from the grave is a fool," he declared.

"Not sweetness. But . . . I don't know, kindness. It's strange, perhaps it is because I am dying that I do not want others to die too. I want everything to live."

This was true. She could hear the gulls outside, the waves crashing against the rocks, and the sun filtering through the windows shined brighter than it had ever shined before. It was the memory of that old postcard, that childish joy, which made her happy; it revived her, and her face was not muted nor gray.

He looked at her with a visage as cold as ice. He allowed her nothing, and yet his expression softened, his chance to echo her.

"I've told you the words you speak have power, and yet you don't seem to comprehend me, do you?"

Casiopea shook her head slowly. There he was, so near she might press her fingertips against his chest. Had he moved closer to her or had she breached the space between them?

"I am someone else when we are together. I am kinder . . . I want to be kinder," Hun-Kamé said. He sounded embarrassed when he spoke, transformed into someone very nearly innocent. "Was I cruel? I was a god; you might as well ask the river if it is gentle in its path, or the hail whether it hurts the land when it strikes it. At times, I can barely recall it."

He was not lying. Looking at his face no one could have said it was the face of a being that has existed beneath the earth for centuries upon centuries. Looking at his face anyone would have thought

Who is this confused fool? and kept walking. Even his beauty was now tempered, not the handsomeness that had sliced her so painfully when she'd first looked at him, but the good looks of a young man one could find in many cities, in many streets.

"That is the magic you make, you see?" he told her, his voice low.

Hun-Kamé did not look at her when he spoke. She could tell by his expression that he was looking at Xibalba. The memory of Xibalba, realm of shadows that glistened in his mind and could not be denied.

It lured him. It was him.

There was no point in pressing her hand against his chest.

"My brother, he'll try to trick us," Hun-Kamé said, his tone changing. "He'll play on our weaknesses. We must not let him win. Believe nothing he promises—he is a thief, a cheat, and a liar. Remain at my side, no matter if he threatens or flatters."

She felt the bone shard in her left hand and stepped back from him, nodding.

Chapter 27

ierra Blanca had all the conveniences one could ever desire. A barbershop, a spa, a pool, and a multitude of shops that offered fur wraps, perfumes and colognes, pipes, glassworks, clothes, magazines, for the enjoyment of the well-to-do and their hangers-on. Fabulous amounts of money could be spent on authentic Japanese kimonos and French silks, tweed jackets and embroidered blouses. The idea was that the guest should never want for anything, should never have to leave the premises, that the world would come to Tierra Blanca.

Martín had not been exposed to this level of luxury and palatial tastes, and found himself stiffly uncomfortable as he waited for Casiopea to walk out of the clothing store she'd gone into. He was relieved when she came out, bearing a couple of bags.

"Let me help you," he said, stretching out a hand.

Casiopea, instead, froze and looked at him warily. "What are you doing?"

"Are you headed back to your room?"

"I'm going to the hairdresser," she said. "What does it matter to you?"

"I want a word with you. Please."

She did not seem too happy with the idea, but she nodded, and they scooted to the side of the store's front door.

"What now?" she asked.

"I have a telegram for you, all right? Read it," he said, holding it up.

Casiopea took the piece of paper and unfolded it. The missive was from her mother. Casiopea frowned.

"You put her up to this?" she asked when she was done reading.

"No. I telegrammed Grandfather to let him know how I'm doing, and she decided to also send a message. She's worried about you. As far as she knows, you ran off with a man and Grandfather sent me to find you."

"Is that supposed to make me feel guilty?"

The telegram had been a spontaneous occurrence, like he'd told Casiopea, but Martín had thought it might benefit him. He shrugged, but knew it had had the required effect. Casiopea looked rattled.

"If you felt guilty, you'd have listened to me in Mexico City."

"Right. I'm sorry, I don't want to keep talking to you."

"Relax. I just passed the telegram on to you. Did you want me to toss it away instead?" he asked.

Casiopea twisted the handles of the bags she was carrying. She was quiet.

"Vucub-Kamé wanted to talk to you in Mexico City, yes, and maybe you could have saved me a trip if you'd spoken to him back then. But you've got another chance now," Martín said and raised a hand. "Now wait before you start saying you don't want to hear anything else, because I'm telling you this for the sake of both of us, all right?"

"As if you'd do anything for my sake," she countered.

"*Both* of us, I said. If you don't want to believe in my goodwill, believe in my selfishness. Look, these gods don't care a lick about us.

I'm trying to keep my head in its place. Will you listen to what I've got to tell you?"

Casiopea hesitated, nodding uncertainly. Martín took his cousin's arm and directed her down the hallway. He didn't want to keep standing next to the shops, speaking in the shadow of the mannequins. The casino had tennis courts, beautiful gardens, and if you walked down a series of steps toward the beach, an excellent view of the ocean. Martín guided her to the gardens, following a row of palm trees. No cacti in sight, a profusion of flowers and lush greenness greeted them instead: it was meant to make patrons forget about the relentless desert awaiting not far beyond the rows of manicured trees.

"Zavala is going to propose a contest tonight. Vucub-Kamé will want to meet with you later and make another offer, a bit of a deal," he said. He had wondered how to speak to her this second time around and decided to be direct, no half-truths or tricks. Or the bare minimum to achieve his purpose.

"What offer?" Casiopea asked.

"I don't know the terms, they wouldn't say, but Vucub-Kamé will be generous to you. He . . . it would be best if you take Vucub-Kamé's offer, because the other option, that first one, is no good."

"Why not?"

"There's a road, all right? The Black Road, it runs through Xibalba. They'll have us walk it."

"You and I?"

"Yes. A contest."

They stood by a stone fountain, water spilling from the mouth of a stone frog resting at its top. It made him think of home, their courtyard there, the parrot in its cage. All he wanted was to go to Uukumil. He'd never desired the world; it was Casiopea who had wanted that.

"Look, Casiopea, I don't . . . whatever shit competition they have planned, it scares the hell out of me. So if for once in your life you'd do as you're told and . . . I mean, that asshole you're hanging out with, it's not like he—"

"What are you talking about? I always do what I'm told," she interrupted him.

"No, you don't. Not without a fight," he said.

It was true. She was willful, daggers hidden beneath her muttered yeses, her eyes fixing on him, slick as oil. Like now, the way her mouth curved, a painting of defiance without uttering a single sound.

"Is that why you hate me?" she asked.

"Why does it matter?" he replied.

He thought of the dark little girl who had arrived in Uukumil one afternoon, stepping down from the railcar with her hair in a pigtail and her pretty mother at her side. He had been curious, then, instead of hostile. She was a poor relation and therefore Martín did not know how to talk to her, whether it was proper to play together, so he kept a cautious distance. That mild courtesy became ice one spring.

"Do you remember the day after I came back from school, when they expelled me?" he told her, the memory loosening his tongue. "I went to talk to Grandfather, and he was in his room, of course, and you were there, reading the newspaper for him."

Sitting with her simple navy dress and the pigtail that reached her waist. Martín had felt wretched as he walked into the room and realized he'd have to explain himself in front of her, which increased the humiliation, but his grandfather had ordered him to speak up and did not bother to dismiss the girl.

"I was scared, but I had to tell him what had happened. I thought he'd hit me with the cane, but instead he sighed and he turned to *you* and he said, 'Why couldn't you be a boy?' And I knew then exactly what he thought of me."

"It wasn't my fault," Casiopea said.

"It was. It doesn't matter if you intended it or not, we were meant to be enemies from then on."

Casiopea now, with her hair cropped so short and a sharp yellow dress, seemed ages away from the big-eyed girl in the chair, but something of the child remained, hurt at one of his taunts.

"I wanted you to be my friend," she admitted.

"I'm sorry about that," he told her, and it was the most honest thing he'd ever said to her, likely the kindest too. Although . . . if he had stretched his mind far back, there had been an afternoon, shortly after her arrival in Uukumil, when they had gone hunting for bugs behind the house. Digging with sticks and getting dirt under their nails. Until his mother came out and pulled him inside with a few sharp words.

Poor relations. Didn't make sense to mix with them, especially when that relation bore a resemblance to the maids. *Look at her*, his mother said, *might be a full Indian girl if one did not know any better. Shameful*. Martín could only nod at his mother.

"So now . . . now I'm supposed to do what? Bend the knee before Vucub-Kamé because you are sorry?" Casiopea asked, her voice sharp, making him raise his head.

"Because it's the smart thing to do, all right?" he shot back.

"You won't even tell me what Vucub-Kamé has planned."

"They won't tell *me*. They are evasive. It's not surprising. Grandfather told me nothing growing up, not a single word about Xibalba or the Black Road."

"But you do know there will be a contest."

"Something of the sort. Casiopea, neither one of us should be in the Land of the Dead. Take whatever he offers, all right? What's the matter, don't you want to go home? Think of your mother if you'll think of nothing else."

Martín patted his jacket and lit his cigarette. Gestures like this helped him feel more secure; they reminded him he was alive, which was a great worry to him lately, having seen Xibalba. No man can remain quite the same after observing the Place of Fright.

"I want to get out of this without any more trouble," he told her. "I want to go home."

It was he who slipped back this time, becoming the child in Grandfather's room, sniveling and afraid of the wrath of his elders, twisting the cuffs of his shirt. As he twisted his cuffs, his fingers slid upon the ring of the Death Lord and a change came upon him. He dropped the cigarette.

He felt a voice course through his body without warning. He did not hear it, it was merely there, inside him, as though he were an instrument and someone else was playing him. Ice rushed through his veins, made his eyes shine as bright as polished stones.

"When he no longer needs you, Hun-Kamé will abandon you on the side of the road," Martín said, and this voice was not his own. It was much too intense, much too bitter. It was not Martín at all, even if it sounded like him. Somehow, it was Vucub-Kamé. "He will give you ashes and vinegar, for he is not generous. You'll have faced foes and trials, and be left with nothing."

"I'm not helping him in order to obtain a reward," she replied.

"But it isn't *fair*, is it? Your family will lose everything they have, and you will return home empty-handed. If you can even find the way back. If you even live through it. All he does is take. Take and take some more, doesn't he?"

He raised a finger, pressed it against his lips, and smirked. "Don't deny it. He takes your life, your blood. Why can't *you* take something for a change?"

She must have noticed the change in him, the glimmer in his eyes.

"Vucub-Kamé . . . he's here, isn't he?" she whispered.

"Yes, he's here," Martín muttered.

Casiopea spun around, as if trying to find the Death Lord, but of course Vucub-Kamé wasn't standing anywhere in sight. Martín bowed his head and placed his hands on Casiopea's temples.

A fog enveloped him. It blotted his eyesight, it filled his brain. He was there and he wasn't. When he touched Casiopea the fog lifted for a moment and a thousand colors danced in his eyes. Blue and crimson and yellow and white. In that moment, in that swirl of colors, he saw her dead by a lake. Then a different sight, but no less gruesome: a monster with bat wings ripping off her head. Other grisly deaths followed. The final sight was of Martín plunging a knife into her side. Through all these visions Vucub-Kamé sat on his obsidian throne, unblinking, superimposed, a shadow at the edge of his vision. There. Triumphant. Always.

She gasped. He knew she saw it too. And he knew they were being shown things that might be.

"Name your price, it will be granted. Should you want glory or gold, the Lord of Xibalba can give it to you. But do not consider only the benefits of your abeyance, but pause to think about the dangers of your defiance."

He released Casiopea and she stumbled back. Her eyes were watery and dark.

"Kiss the lord's ring and you shall be his favorite courtier," Martín said with that voice that was not his own. He raised his hand, offering the ring for her to see.

Casiopea looked at him in fright, like when they'd been small and he was cruel to her, and Martín did not know why he felt ashamed then. Of who he had been, who he was. But there was no time to think about this, because she was shaking her head.

"No," she said, also with that childhood stubbornness.

A terrible pain seized him; it went from the bottom of his spine to his skull, and he grimaced, gnashing his teeth. Vucub-Kamé could not speak more than a few words through this intermediary, and poor Martín shivered as the overwhelming presence that had invaded him departed.

"Martín?" she said.

"It has passed," he mumbled.

"Do you want to sit down?"

There was a stone bench nearby. She tried to get him to go to it, but he could not. His legs felt weak, and a sob lodged in his throat. "No, no . . . Casiopea, can we simply get out of here? Can we simply *leave*?" he begged her. "Can you take me home?"

That is what he desired more than anything. Home, without monsters or gods or journeys.

"Oh, Martín," she said.

Casiopea set a hand on his shoulder. For a moment he thought she was going to accept he was in the right, that she'd do the bidding of Vucub-Kamé, but then he noticed that her sympathy was not a sign of soft weakness.

"No," she said, but kindly this time.

"God. Stop being pigheaded!" he yelled, shoving her arm away, more furious at her warmth than her refusal. "It's exactly like I said, you do something stupid! You never do as I say!"

Casiopea took a step away from him, but she did not seem too worried about his fury.

"I am a man," he said, jabbing a thumb against his chest. "I am your elder. I am going to be the leader of the family. What are you? Who do you think you are?"

"I've never been anyone," she replied.

"He'll kill you!" he yelled. "Maybe he'll kill us both! Is that what you want?"

She did not answer him. He watched her rush back inside the building and did not follow her. Martín sat by the fountain, listening to the stone frog gurgle. He tried to convince himself that Casiopea was a stupid girl, that if they were to compete she would lose. That he had the upper hand, having seen Xibalba and walked through its road. That Vucub-Kamé would necessarily win this contest, and then Martín would be returned home, rewarded like a prince. He tried to count the gems and the gold he'd obtain. He tried and he did a good job of it, even if his hands shook.

Chapter 28

You could not, they'd told them, enter the main ballroom without a tuxedo and an evening gown. There was a strict dress code. And so Casiopea and Hun-Kamé set about making themselves presentable, courtesy of the owner of Tierra Blanca, who had ordered they be treated with the utmost care.

She settled on a dress of pale cream, sheer chiffon with a floral design, rhinestones and silver beading splayed down the front of the bodice. The back of the gown was scandalously low, the kind of dress society ladies and movie stars wore when they were photographed for the papers. Not that she'd ever thought they'd want to take her picture and caption it. But now! Now she twirled in front of a mirror and watched the beading of her outfit sparkle like tiny twinkling stars.

They washed and combed her short locks and rouged her cheeks. When she met Hun-Kamé, her hair like lacquer and her eyes lined dark with kohl, she looked as elegant as any of the celebrities who crowded the casino. He looked very fine too, the tuxedo and bow tie giving him a severe yet appealing air, and she fancied that he was a

bit like this when he sat in his throne room. A jewel, cut and polished to perfection.

He nodded at her, seemingly pleased, and gave her his arm.

They walked into the ballroom, and a few heads turned their way,
curious, wondering who these two were. Movie people, come from
Mexico City? Fortune hunters made a note of them as they were guided
toward Zavala across the vast dining room, which was made to seem
vaster thanks to the profusion of floor-to-ceiling gilded mirrors, each
one separating the tall windows that opened to one of the gardens.

Great chandeliers illuminated the patrons, and were organic in
their look, recalling the branches of trees. The floor was oak, perfect
for dancing, and the walls were painted the intense blue Casiopea
associated with Yucatán, but the pillars carved with pre-Hispanic–
inspired figures that seemed to support the room were all white. It
was truly a palace, and she felt like a lady who is to be presented at
court for the first time.

Upon a raised platform, shaped like a shell, a band played, the
members attired in identical white outfits.

There, not far from the band, was the table where Martín and an
older man sat together. The man was idly smoking a cigar, looking
bored and decadent, oblivious to the music and the people around
them, but seeing them he stood up in greeting. Martín followed suit.

This could only be Zavala. The resemblance to the Uay Chivo
was plain enough and it made her uncomfortable, as she recalled
the death of the man. Casiopea sat down. A waiter approached
them and poured champagne into long-stemmed glasses.

"Hun-Kamé and Casiopea Tun. Thank you, thank you so much
for meeting with me. Did you find your rooms adequate?" Zavala
asked. "I do hope you are having a grand time. That dress looks
lovely, my dear."

Zavala spoke with the kindness of a doting grandfather, his voice mild, but having spent her childhood next to a tyrannical man, Casiopea could spot the unpleasantness in the warlock, like cigar smoke may cling to a jacket.

"Thank you," she said.

"Fine things suit her, don't they, Martín?" Zavala asked, although he did not turn toward her cousin, who had not deigned to utter a word of greeting to her. "And you? How do you like the place, Hun-Kamé?"

"It is gaudy," Hun-Kamé replied.

"Well, we couldn't exactly have a pyramid, could we? This is a modern adaptation."

"Is that what you are calling it?"

"Power flows through this building and even more power will flow through every tile and every wall, spreading across the land, bringing back the might of Xibalba. The name of the Supreme Lord will be on every man's lips and they will lance their tongues and offer their blood to Vucub-Kamé," he said, the mask of the kind patriarch yanked away, the magician, the priest, unveiled.

"Not while I remain," Hun-Kamé said.

"We shall see."

Hun-Kamé picked up one of the glasses and took a sip. She followed suit, drinking too fast, the sweetness of the champagne alien to her. Martín stared at her, and she almost apologized, the old custom, before remembering that his disapproval did not matter.

"Well, did we come to hear you speak the same inane words you have spoken for decades?" Hun-Kamé asked, setting his glass down.

"If you were wiser you'd have let me assist you and overseen the design of this fabulous palace. But you are stubborn," Zavala said, again speaking like a kindly father might, chiding a recalcitrant son. It had no effect on Hun-Kamé, whose face was hard.

"And you are nothing but an upstart warlock almost as deluded as my brother. Tell me why we are here."

Zavala held his cigar between his thumb and his index finger and stared at them, grinning, flashing a row of yellowed teeth. His face, if you looked at it carefully, was slightly jaundiced. They said that when Montejo attempted to conquer Yucatán he had captured Indians and thrown them to his pack of dogs, to be devoured. That's what Zavala reminded her of. He devoured people.

"We are here to discuss terms," Zavala said.

"Oh?"

"You don't expect your brother will sweep in and you will skewer him with a sword, do you? The conflicts of gods don't often play out that way. At least, not these days, and not with you in this state. You look . . . diminished."

Hun-Kamé sat proud and dignified. He did not protest Zavala's words, perhaps because they were true, or more likely because he thought it beneath him to answer such a charge.

"The Supreme Lord proposes a contest, the girl serving as your proxy and this young man here representing Vucub-Kamé," Zavala said, slapping Martín's shoulder. Her cousin was not pleased with the physical contact, grimacing.

"What kind of contest?" she asked.

"In ancient times we might have had two mortals face with shield and bladed weapons. Or perhaps play the ball game, the loser to be sacrificed upon the sacred court. Alas, I don't think it would be quite fair, seeing as neither of you are ball players, nor are you warriors."

Casiopea almost chuckled. Martín could ride a horse, but little more than that. He had no interest in sports, and while the other children in their town might eagerly chase a ball across the street, he did nothing of the sort. At least Casiopea had the strength developed from going to and fro around the house; the constant scrubbing of floors and the carrying of boxes stuffed with fruits and vegetables into the kitchen had developed her muscles—though these days, she felt tired and spent.

"The Supreme Lord suggests a more appropriate game. Whoever walks the Black Road and reaches the World Tree in the heart of Xibalba first wins. It is elegantly simple."

It did sound simple, and if she had not seen the Black Road in her sleep she might have readily agreed, but the dream of blood and death made her curl her hands in her lap, clutching a bit of the fabric of her dress between her fingers. She recalled her meeting with her cousin, the visions she'd had in the garden. She could not pretend these were mere dreams. She had felt the touch of magic; she'd seen portents.

Vucub-Kamé was warning her. Or threatening her. And though she tried to dismiss it all as tricks, as ridiculous attempts to intimidate her, Casiopea knew there was some truth in the words he'd spoken and the things he'd shown them.

"Now, there are rules," Zavala said. "First of all, Hun-Kamé's magic may not protect you in Xibalba. You will be vulnerable to the elements and the piercing kiss of the blade. The same will go for Martín. No assistance can be provided; you will walk the road alone with an obsidian knife to keep you company. We are fair, after all."

"What happens if I get there first?" Casiopea asked.

"The Lord Vucub-Kamé will kneel before Hun-Kamé and let him lop off his head for his intransigence. But if you should lose, dear girl, then it is Hun-Kamé's head that will roll, and you will face an unpleasant life and an even more unpleasant afterlife, shackled inside the Razor House."

She recalled the story of the Hero Twins and their journey through the houses of Xibalba. The Razor House was filled with knives, which flew through the air and sliced the flesh, but the twins had offered the knives the bodies of animals. As a result, the knives did not cut their skin. But that was a story, likely told to comfort mortals, and Casiopea did not think she'd be granted such a respite.

"You look upset, darling," Zavala said, his voice full of mock kindness. "Would you like more champagne?"

"I'm fine."

Zavala ignored her words, instead filling her glass to the brim again. She did not touch it, watching as her cousin finished his drink and fidgeted with a napkin.

"Well, one must always bet to win the game, and this is an important game, Casiopea. Being the champion of a god is no easy task. Now, you two don't need to accept the proposal right this instant. Vucub-Kamé wishes to speak to you. He has a more magnanimous idea."

"He has some trap he wishes to spring on us," Hun-Kamé replied. "A trick of his."

"Tricks, tricks, what an unkind thing to say. It may be he wishes to make amends, hmmm?" Zavala said. "Whatever he wants, he cannot address you directly unless you allow it, Hun-Kamé. Therefore, will you speak to him? He will visit you, if you agree."

"As if we have a choice."

"You have a choice. That is the point," Zavala said.

"If I said no, what would he do? Place notes under my door?" Hun-Kamé asked. "We are at the end of this journey, after all, and must greet each other at last. He may show his face, if he wishes it."

"Then it is accepted and arranged. Go back to your rooms. He will be there."

Though the words were uncomplicated and mundane, Casiopea knew by now that every sentence spoken might carry hidden, magical meanings, and so it was in this case.

Zavala raised a glass, as if toasting them, and smiled at her. "You must know, dear girl, that Vucub-Kamé can be kind. Up to a certain point. But if you two force his hand . . . then it's the Black Road. Tell me, honestly, do you fear death?"

Her eyes darted away, and she took Hun-Kamé's hand in one fluid motion, rising to her feet with the quickness of an arrow.

"I think we should dance," she said. It was the first thing that

popped into her head, the excuse so that she wouldn't have to answer the question.

Casiopea guided him toward the people dancing without sparing
Zavala a single look. She felt her conviction faltering when he placed
a hand against her waist. She did not know the steps to the song,
which was slow and sweet, like syrup. She wanted to look down at
her feet, to make sure they were moving in a somewhat coordinated
motion, but she knew this would seem clumsy. Not that he was
looking at her: his head was raised, as if peering above her shoulder.

"Your brother made me an offer today," she said, finding a rhythm.
"He spoke, somehow, through my cousin, and promised glory or gold.
And he showed me, too, what might happen to me. He showed me
death and Xibalba."

"He has the power of prophecy, but not all his visions come to
pass," Hun-Kamé said.

"But I had already dreamed it, before, during the journey."

He'd not been worried before, but now a frown creased his brow.
His mouth grew tight.

"I am afraid," she said. "You were right, if I was a hero I'd know
this is the way things go. I wouldn't hesitate to risk my life to save
the land, to save you. I'd charge ahead. But I'm scared, and if we go
up those stairs . . . maybe I won't refuse him a third time. And . . .
and so I wish we could just keep dancing."

Hun-Kamé did not reply, sinking into one of his hard silences.
She might have been worried if the music hadn't been so divine, the
swaying to the song so languorous. Had she not wanted to dance?
Not quite to this song, not quite in this ballroom next to women in
silks with diamonds in their hair and men with their bow ties and
crisp jackets; these were unexpected elements to her fantasy. And of
course she had never pictured her dance partner when she chanced
to think of dances. She'd swatted the idea away too quickly, and her
partner remained an amorphous figure. Even if she'd been able to

picture a boy, he would never have come close to the man guiding her in the dance.

Therefore she danced, because she'd desired the dance and because if she paused to rest she might begin questioning herself. *Do you fear death?* Yes, she did.

Hun-Kamé danced, she thought, to distract her. Or else, to show them all—Vucub-Kamé, Zavala, Martín—his disdain, his aloofness.

But when she chanced to look aside, catching a glimpse of their reflection splayed across a mirror, she did not observe any disdain or aloofness.

In Uukumil, when she'd gone to fetch a few items from the general store, on an occasion when she forgot to bring her shawl and conceal her hair with it, she'd caught the eye of one of the boys who worked there. He was the shopkeeper's assistant, and on that summer day he was carrying a heavy sack of flour in his arms. When she walked in and began reading out the list of supplies, he lost his hold on the sack and dropped it, the flour spilling over the floor. Casiopea remembered three children, who were also in the store, giggling at the mishap, and she'd blushed because the boy had stared at her. Not a normal stare, if there was such a thing, but a startling look of eagerness.

Casiopea recognized the look on Hun-Kamé's face: it was that same look, more engrossed if anything, heavier than the brief flicker of a look she caught in Uukumil before she mumbled an apology and stepped outside the store.

This look went to her head. It was stronger than the champagne and she gripped his hand tight and she would have stumbled if he hadn't held her against him.

"I wish we could keep dancing too," he said.

Chapter 29

They walked up the stairs of the hotel, avoiding a group of drunk patrons who, between giggles and shoves, were making their way down the wide staircase. It was a somber march for Casiopea and Hun-Kamé, almost funerary. When Hun-Kamé placed the key in the door's lock, she thought to turn around.

But they'd danced, and now they were here, and they needed to keep going.

He turned the key.

Shadows had invaded the vestibule. Hun-Kamé and Casiopea walked into one of the bedrooms, and there were pools of darkness so vivid they looked liquid, as if someone had left a window open and the night had dripped against the wallpaper and elegant furniture, making the bulbs of the lamps dim.

A lazy plume of darkness rose in the middle of the room and a man stepped out from it, clad in a white cape. He resembled Hun-Kamé, his skin dark, the face proud. His hair was very pale, the color of the fragile crust of salt that forms upon the seawater when it evaporates. The eyes were devoid of color, not dark like Hun-

Kamé's, but a silken gray. Therefore the brothers mirrored and did not mirror each other.

"How long, our parting," Vucub-Kamé said, his voice also silken, the curve of his lips not quite forming a smile.

Hun-Kamé did not say anything, but Casiopea felt his anger like a hot coal. If she reached out and touched his hand she feared he might scorch her.

"Long enough for you to construct this monstrosity," Hun-Kamé replied, at last.

"Monstrosity? Hun-Kamé, you are caught in the past." Vucub-Kamé smiled fully. But the smile did not reach his eyes. "Do you think I could build a temple in the middle of Baja California? They have outlawed the Christian churches—not that I mind—and now they pray to idols of aluminum and Bakelite. We need new trappings, new acolytes. And blood, of course."

"So, not everything is new."

"Blood is the oldest coin. Blood remains."

Hun-Kamé took several steps until he was standing in front of his brother. They were of the same height and stared each other in the eye.

"I told you not to defy the wisdom of eternity. Your scheme is ignoble. If ever Xibalba should rise anew, it shall rise by the will of fate and not by cheap sorcery," Hun-Kamé said. "You will pay for your treason."

"I paid long ago, swallowing each one of your offenses."

"We all play our roles," Hun-Kamé said. "My role was to rule over Xibalba."

"Over Xibalba, not over me. I was not born to be your slave."

"Enough with your nonsense."

"You expected me to gnaw at scraps, to drink spoiled wine. One time we were *gods*, not shadows. Until they, the twins—"

"The Hero Twins defeated us and we were humbled, as we had to be humbled for our pride was great," Hun-Kamé declared.

"Then I shall build great temples and paint them with blood until our defeat is washed away! Until we are humbled no longer!"

"Enough, I said."

Hun-Kamé's voice was imperious and well rehearsed. She imagined they'd had similar conversations before. She imagined, by the tone Hun-Kamé employed, that the conversations ended with Vucub-Kamé's acid silence. Not on this occasion.

"Has he told you what it was like?" Vucub-Kamé asked, turning toward Casiopea and moving in her direction. She saw Hun-Kamé shift uncomfortably, but Vucub-Kamé blocked her line of sight with his body.

"The burning of the most precious incense, the sweet blood of priests, the sacrifices in the cenotes littered with jewels, the ball game concluding in glorious decapitation," he said.

Casiopea almost thought she could see it, could taste it. The night skies like velvet darkness, pierced by the stars, the murals in the palaces, waterholes so blue you'd think them inked with the leaves of the añil, and the devotion of men, like a wave, a sound, this force that made the land quiver. The adoration of mortals filling one's lungs. Then that same adoration receding, the emptiness it left, the way the azure remained on the walls of temples, weathering the assault of time, but everything else faded until it felt as if you'd fade too.

"The world was young then, it smelled of copper and brine," Vucub-Kamé told her, almost wistfully, and she thought even though he stood before her, he wasn't there, his eyes far off, gazing into the land of his memories.

Slowly he looked down at her, tilting her head up as if to better examine goods at the market, and it reminded her, oddly enough, of the town's butcher, his eyes on her as he tried to tip the scale. Now this god weighed her flesh on a scale of a different sort. "Young, as you are young. Look at you, like the dawn," he said. "You can't understand, of course, but one day you'll want to be new again," he continued. "You'll wish to return to this moment of perfection when you were the embodiment of all promises."

Vucub-Kamé took a strand of her hair between his fingers. He was so close to her she thought his eyes were not gray, but lighter, the shade of bones that have been pecked clean by wild animals.

"You've refused me twice. Will you do it a third time and risk my wrath, I wonder? Three is a special number, for it is the number that represents women and I ask what shall you represent? Shall you perhaps be the fruit, plucked too soon and left to rot upon the ground? You are, as I've said, so young."

There was Xibalba deep in his gaze, and the promise of her death. And deeper yet she saw the bones of men that would litter Middleworld if his schemes came to fruition; she saw the splash of blood on stones; she felt the fright and the pain of mortal beings.

She looked away.

"Stop your nonsense," Hun-Kamé said, moving to stand by Casiopea's side, his arm brushing against hers, his fingers pressing against her knuckles.

"My nonsense? You'll pit her against the Black Road, brother," Vucub-Kamé said.

"I did not conceive the challenge," Hun-Kamé replied, his voice unpleasant, his body tense.

"It does not matter. One way or another, you are killing her before her time. Such cruelty."

Vucub-Kamé spoke with the most delicious mockery, Hun-Kamé replied with a haughty silence.

"It does not have to be this way. The lot of us, we could be friends," Vucub-Kamé said, looking at her again with the same care he'd granted her all through their meeting. She felt she was being weighed anew.

"What do you mean?" she asked cautiously.

"I'd like to offer you life instead of death," Vucub-Kamé said, sliding past them, and picking an apple from the bowl of fruit that had been set by the window. "It's a simple trick. You cut your left hand off."

"I know how that goes," Casiopea said. "I cut it off and sever the link between Hun-Kamé and me, and then he'll be so weak he won't be able to fight you, and you win."

"I must admit that did cross my mind. I'm thinking something more complicated, but beneficial for all parties. Don't just cut the hand. You *kill yourself*."

He paused, as if to allow her to perfectly understand the meaning of his words. She scoffed. Did he imagine she was mad? Or so exhausted she'd simply admit defeat? She was tired, her body pained her, her hand ached, and there was a weariness of her spirit, as if it was being ground down bit by bit, and yet she was not so tired she'd stop at this point.

"Kill yourself, and as you die offer yourself to me in sacrifice," he continued, tossing the apple in the air and catching it. "Those who pledge themselves to the Lord of Xibalba are invited to dwell in the shadow of the World Tree."

"I don't see how that is any better for me," Casiopea said. "I'd be dead, and then you could harm Hun-Kamé."

"Oh, Hun-Kamé offers himself afterward, too; he pledges his allegiance. He kneels down and I cut his head with my axe. Then his blood spills upon the floor and I collect it, using it as the mortar to complete my spells. But as weakened as he will be after you die, and as changed as my brother is, the Hun-Kamé who will walk into Xibalba will be very much a mortal man."

Vucub-Kamé squeezed the fruit and it shrank, blackening and rotting in the blink of an eye, until he was holding nothing but ashes, which he displayed on his palm for her to see.

"I have the power to restore mortals who worship me," Vucub-Kamé said.

As he spoke, the ashes in his hand formed themselves back into an apple, as crisp and red as it had been seconds before. Not a scratch on it.

"Gods don't . . . they don't become mortal," Casiopea said. "They don't die."

"There are two warring essences in my brother's body in this instant. Separate his immortal elixir from the mortal substance coursing from his body, and why not? I lop off his head, he resurrects. He'd open his eyes and be a man," Vucub-Kamé said. "Free to walk Middleworld, to dream the dreams men dream. And you, too, Casiopea, alive again. I am offering you what no one else can offer. Give up your quest. And you, my brother, give up your claim. Give yourself to me, and in giving, grant me all you are."

Vucub-Kamé took a half dozen steps and carefully placed the apple back in the bowl.

"I'm offering you your secret wish," Vucub-Kamé said simply.

Casiopea felt as if she'd swallowed a goldfish whole and it swam in the pit of her stomach. She pressed a hand against her body, thinking this might soothe her, but it did no good, because she opened her mouth and sputtered silly words, anyway, unable to control her shaky voice.

"What do you mean?" she asked.

"He knows what I mean," Vucub-Kamé said with that same slice of a smile he'd smiled before, circling them. "You know what I mean, Casiopea. I mean the chance to live a life in Middleworld, a whole, long, happy life, even to love. Are you not tired of your denials?"

Vucub-Kamé stood immobile, watching them with his strange, inhuman eyes, as firm as a cliff against the ocean's spray, so cold she shivered. Next to her Hun-Kamé wrapped an arm around her shoulders, as if to keep her warm, keep her from trembling.

"You don't have the capacity to accomplish such a thing," Hun-Kamé declared.

"If the whole of your blood spills upon this place, if this ultimate sacrifice is performed, every stone and every bit of metal in this building will thrum with the might of Xibalba. Bow before me, brother. Give me your blood and forget yourself. If you will it, it will be."

Conviction, symbols. Casiopea thought the pale-eyed god spoke truth; that this could happen, this scared her more than any foe they'd met during their journey.

"I must ask again if you want her to walk the Black Road. Or maybe you'd prefer my most generous alternative," Vucub-Kamé said, his voice light and sly.

No, she thought. She wasn't entirely sure why Vucub-Kamé was offering this and what was happening, but she'd say no. She'd seen bones and ash and death. She was afraid, she wished to live, and yet she was no fool. She could not agree to this. She opened her mouth, struggling to put this into words.

"We need time to consider it," Hun-Kamé replied instead.

Casiopea was so startled she gripped his arm and looked up at him. But Hun-Kamé was busy staring at his brother, and Vucub-Kamé stared back at him.

"Time is precious. How much time do you think this darling girl has left? How much death poisons her veins? Answer me *now*."

"Give me an hour," she said.

She saw a glimmer in Vucub-Kamé's eyes, an intense, cold flash, like the edge of a blade, directed at her.

"A single hour," she insisted. "Surely a great lord can grant an hour." If words have power, then requests must have power too, she guessed and she guessed right. Vucub-Kamé nodded reluctantly.

"One hour, then," he granted her. "Think about it carefully. Reject me and you'll face the Black Road. I doubt you wish for that."

Vucub-Kamé summoned shadows, and the shadows wrapped him as warmly as the cape he wore, then collapsed on the floor, the god vanishing and the darkness that had infected the room disappearing. The lights were bright, the room ordinary.

"Come, we need to go down by the sea," Hun-Kamé said, clutching her hand.

"Why?" she asked.

"Because my brother would surely spy on us here, but he has no dominion over the sea. That belongs to others. Let's go," he urged her.

Chapter 30

Not many people visited the beach, despite the wide stone steps that led down to it. Most guests preferred the comfort of the swimming pool and the shade of its umbrellas, the waiters walking by with drinks on a tray. At night, the beach was absolutely deserted. The full moon lurked in a corner of the sky, guiding their way, but a cloud drifted over its surface, muffling its light. Strangely, this illumination resembled the night-sun of the Underworld, rendering all things half hidden, as if to aid their secrecy.

Despite the lack of proper light, Casiopea could see Hun-Kamé's face clearly. It is possible her vision had sharpened since she shared some of the god's essence, revealing secrets tucked in the dark, or she had grown so accustomed to Hun-Kamé she could conjure his features with ease.

"Come into the water," he said.

"Our clothes will be ruined," she told him, her shoes in her hands.

"It is necessary," he said and walked toward the waves, ankle deep. "The cenotes we may roam, but the ocean with its currents and its tides, that was never ours. The salt will keep our secrets. My brother can't hear us here."

She placed the shoes on a rock and went into the water. It was cold; the waves struck the land with a stark precision, violent almost. The water, in the daytime, was of a precious blue-green, but it had now turned gray and she waded into this grayness.

"You have a plan, yes?" she told him. "Some way to defeat him?"

"I have nothing beyond the two options he has offered us," he said, sounding solemn.

"But then . . ."

She'd assumed he would reveal a plot of some sort, a trick they could employ, like the Hero Twins, who burned the feathers of a macaw to avoid the peril of the House of Gloom and fed old bones to the jaguars so they would not be devoured. That's the way stories went.

"What do you think my name is?" Hun-Kamé asked abruptly.

The wind was picking up and whipped at her expensive dress, and the sea was loud, and the lights from the casino were far. Casiopea shook her head.

"I know your name," she said.

"No. Not the name I told you. If you'd seen me on the street, if you'd met me while you walked through the city and you'd looked at me over your shoulder, what name would you have given me?"

"Are we playing a game?" she asked, exasperated.

"I told you we all have different names. You are Lady Tun, you are Casiopea, you are the Stone Maiden, and deep inside your heart you have a secret name. Grant me a name and it will be yours and mine alone."

"I don't—"

He was standing close to her, but he moved closer, and she stared at him.

"I could be a different person. If you gave me a name, who is to say it is not mine? If I had an ordinary name, I could have an ordinary story," he said. "I could swear I first saw you in Mérida, standing in the middle of the street."

It was too cold out there, and she without a jacket, the tips of her fingers tingling. Casiopea wanted to rub her hands against her arms, but did not move.

"It's all symbols, the stories we tell; if you give me a name I could die and I could open my eyes again, and I'd remember that name."

He was determined and grim, and something else entirely, which she did not recognize, and then his face softened. "I wouldn't be a god. I . . . I told you already, I hardly remember myself sometimes. I could forget it all."

But we've come this far, her mind protested. Her tongue, however, was unwilling to voice the thought. Her mouth caged the words.

"Gods don't die and yet, at times, when I've sat next to you I thought I'd die, this pain in my chest that I can hardly understand except it's you, caught there," he told her, more than a little bewildered, very quietly, the waves almost drowning out his voice. "Have you ever felt anything like that?"

Casiopea's breath was a burning coal. She did not reply, tentatively raising her left hand, where the splinter lay, where he'd marked her, brushing away a lock of hair from his forehead.

"Yes," she said finally.

He leaned down, pressing his lips against her neck, before grasping her face and kissing her on the mouth.

He was untested, raw, worse than Casiopea. She'd at least found kisses on the printed page. But it was nice, the kiss, and he was the handsomest man she'd ever seen. He wanted her. She hadn't thought . . . had not allowed herself to think she might be wanted like this.

But this plan! To become mortal!

Madness. He'd gone mad.

But who was to say she had *not* met him in Mérida? That the story Martín had told her family had not been the truth? Who would look at Hun-Kamé, devoid of his supernatural sheen, and think *There goes a man who was a god?* They'd simply say, "Look now, look at this pretty couple, look how he holds her hand and she kisses him. Like they are the air each other breathes."

His mouth against her own, the imprint of his smile against her cheek, and she knew she wanted nothing other than this man. Not the god, but the man, with the dark brows, his long nose, the slender hands that rested against her back. She had already picked a name for him—Francisco, like that poet who wrote about life and death and loving—and might have said it, sealed the bargain this way, but a nagging detail tugged at her, made her open her eyes and look at him. The eye patch, the missing eye, the bit of him that wasn't there hitting her like the waves hit the shore.

Casiopea understood the strength of narrative and the strict rules that govern a sonnet. The rhyme scheme constant, like the tide. There is a way to things. And, long ago, so very long ago, she recalled a word: patan. It was this that stalled her.

"You told me we must not let him win," she reminded him. "What happens in Middleworld, with your brother now all powerful?" she asked. "Blood and sacrifice, and—"

He shook his head. "The glory he desires. The rest, does it matter?" he told her. "It doesn't matter, if there's you and me."

She wished she could repeat his words, like the parrot in its cage back in Uukumil. But she remembered what he'd told her: the cenotes would be piled with corpses, men riddled with arrows. She'd seen it, it was no illusion, and she couldn't quite make up her mind, she couldn't be heedless, even if her resolve was crumbling.

"Vucub-Kamé would do wickedness upon the land, and there might be pain, but we'd be together and we'd go far away. The world is wide. What matters what happens to a fraction of it?"

"But—"

"My brother can have the halls of Xibalba and the black throne," he said. "We can have each other."

He kissed her again, and it lasted forever. Casiopea thought there'd be nothing left of her when he moved away, it wouldn't be *he* who was erased and granted a new identity. And when she pressed a hand to his hair she was sure nothing but love mattered, there was only the two of them in this place by the sea.

"You'll lose me otherwise," he said, in a whisper.

"I want you to stay with me."

"Then make me stay."

She was dazed and breathless, leaning forward into the touch of his fingers, and it would be the easiest thing in the world to simply whisper a new name for him. It lingered heavy on her tongue, the name.

Francisco.

He was there; he raced through her bloodstream, and she saw no way to deny him.

"I want to dance with you, to the fastest music possible. I want to learn the names of stars. I want to swim in the ocean at night. I want to ride next to you in one of those automobiles and see where the roads go," he said, laughing, as he held her face between his hands.

She clung to him, felt his hammering heart under her palm. It was real, he was real, this was real, and the rest was just . . . stories. Children's stories. There was no magic, no gods, no quests. She could convince herself she had imagined it all and then it would be that way. A wisp of a nightmare and the reality of them.

But . . . stories. She knew poems and she knew stories and to recognize shapes in the stars when learned men cannot make out constellations. She knew this story, and it must have a different ending. Mythmaking. It was the treacherous weight of mythmaking, of patan, that pulled her up, made her push back.

"It would not be fair," she said, and the words were like a knife: they seemed to hurt him. He lifted his hands, beholding her.

"Fair? Nothing is fair in the universe."

"But I *want* it to be fair. I do not want the wicked to triumph, the innocent to be slaughtered by your brother. I do not want to turn back."

"Don't be foolish. You cannot have a perfect, happy ending," he said warily.

"But, Xibalba—"

"I do not care about it."

Casiopea looked at him. His gaze was the gaze of a naïve young man, but behind it she caught the flickering darkness of Xibalba even as he attempted to deny himself and kiss her a third time. She turned her head.

"You are the Lord Hun-Kamé, and you do care about Xibalba. And life may not be fair, but *I* must be fair. I can't turn away," she said.

The words, they bruised him. A light dimmed in him, and his naïve, young face was not that naïve anymore. Lord of Xibalba again, old as the stones in the temples deep in the jungle.

"I wish you were a coward instead of a hero," he said, speaking bitterly, like old wood cracking, snapping in two, making her ache.

"I don't think I'm much of a hero."

"And yet you are," he said, his gaze deepening, becoming a velvet black as he tilted her face up. She thought he'd kiss her. He did not.

He walked past her, farther into the water. It reached his knees and she followed him, wondering what he was doing, where he was headed. He turned abruptly, and she realized he did not know where he was going, he was simply moving with the sea, troubled and adrift.

"I can't protect you in Xibalba," he said, his voice anguished. "How can I let you go there?"

"Would I have a chance?" she asked. "A real chance?"

"I can't assure victory. The Black Road is dangerous. You'll be alone, you may feel lost, but the road follows the commands of the person who walks it, and it will listen to you since you are also part of me."

"How can I speak to it?"

"Command it as you'd command a dog, and look carefully. The road may seem a single solid line, but there are shadows where it becomes dimmer and you can jump through the shadows. Do not fear it. Fear will make it more difficult. And never step off the road."

She nodded, taking a quick breath. "I won't," she promised.

"The greatest peril is inside your heart. If you focus, if you are steady, you will find the way to the city. Picture my palace and you will arrive at its doors."

"I've never seen your palace."

"You have, you must have glimpsed it in my gaze."

She recalled the times they'd spoken of Xibalba. He had said his palace was like a jewel, and he had mentioned the ponds surrounding it.

"There are silver trees near it," she said tentatively. "And strange fish swim in the ponds."

"They glow, like fireflies," he said.

"Your palace has many rooms."

"As many rooms as the year has days."

"Painted yellow and blue," she continued.

"And there is my throne room and my throne, of the blackest obsidian."

"You sit on the throne, a diadem of onyx and jade upon your head."

The phantom image they built of the palace was nothing but that, a fragile creation of the imagination, and yet it was solid. Casiopea saw the palace and she knew she pictured its true likeness even though she had never walked its hallways.

She took a long, deep breath.

"I can do it," she said.

"Then there's no more to it," he concluded. His voice had recovered its customary coolness. "You've made your choice."

"No, there is no more."

He nodded and moved back toward the sand, trousers sodden. Casiopea's lips tasted of salt; her throat was dry. She spoke before he set a foot on dry land.

"Wait a few minutes," she said. "They won't miss us for a few minutes, and this is the last time I will see you, isn't it? Either way."

"Yes," he said. "I'll be a god again, or dead."

"Then wait a few minutes," she said. It was stupid to try to extend the reach of time, it did them no good. She'd refused him, besides. And yet.

Casiopea looked up at the sky with its multitude of stars. Then she looked at him, standing in profile. Feeling her gaze on him, he turned to her and smiled a crooked smile. He drew her against him, and then he tipped his head up, to look at the stars that he'd never bothered to survey before.

Chapter 31

They dallied like this by the sea, the waves splashing against their legs, attempting to make the minutes stretch, until all time had been spent. A hotel employee greeted them at the top of the stairs that led into the hotel. He informed them Zavala wished to speak to them.

Casiopea and Hun-Kamé were ushered into a windowless room decorated with intricate carvings. Bone-white were the walls of this chamber, though the floors were black, and polished with such intensity they reflected the columns and the frieze and the walls, as if one were walking upon an ocean of ink. Although it might be used for one casino function or another—a dance, a lavish party—the place had the quiet air of a temple.

As if to reinforce this impression, in the middle of the room there were two heavy wooden chairs with high backs, fit for priests or kings, or both. Between them a rough stone pedestal had been set, and on it rested a huge axe.

Vucub-Kamé sat on the chair at the right, but when they walked in, he rose and walked in their direction, his cape trailing down his back. The cape was a curious creation, made of bones and owl feathers, stitched with the silk of moths, standing stiff and strong despite its delicate components. When he moved, the bones rattled and laughed.

Behind Vucub-Kamé stood Zavala—looking more yellow than before, his white clothing contrasting badly with his jaundiced face—and Martín, who also wore white.

"Your time is up," Vucub-Kamé told them. "Will you be wise and take my offer, or foolish and reject it?"

"I'll walk the Black Road," Casiopea said.

Vucub-Kamé did not appear surprised nor annoyed by the answer. He looked down at her with his pale eyes, impassive.

"You reject me at every turn," he said. "Very well. I'll teach you humility."

She said nothing, chose to stare back at him rather than regaling him with her fear.

"You may have a blade and a gourd filled with water for your journey, but nothing more," Vucub-Kamé declared.

She saw then that he'd set up two tables with these items, the obsidian knife and the gourd. She wore an evening gown not fit for traveling, but when she held the knife her clothes changed, the pale cream chiffon became plain cotton, transforming into a black blouse, a long black skirt, and a black shawl, like the ones she might have worn back home. At her waist was a belt, with a sheath for the knife. The gourd had a cord, which she might place around her neck or tie to the belt, but as she held it, her fingers twitched, and there came the pain brought by the bone shard, as if it had dug deeper into her flesh.

"Allow me to assist you," Hun-Kamé said, looping the cord around her belt. When he was done, he held her hand between his. "We could—"

She felt she might faint, but she shook her head firmly. "It'll pass, it always does," she said, and tried to play the part of the fearless hero, even if she did not quite feel up to the role.

Her performance must have been acceptable, because he nodded.

"Let's not waste any more time," Vucub-Kamé said, though he sounded more bored than eager to begin the game. "Your champion looks ready."

"A minute," Hun-Kamé replied.

He grasped her hand, tighter, and she thought he might bid her goodbye, he might kiss her one last time. He leaned forward.

"Xibalba will attempt to confuse you," Hun-Kamé told her in a low voice. "But you must not let it. The road listens to you, you don't listen to it."

He let go of her. This was his farewell. She could not help the drop of disappointment, even if they had already, for all intents and purposes, parted ways by the ocean.

Hun-Kamé sat down on the chair on the left. Vucub-Kamé sat on the matching chair, his bone cape clacking, looking indolent. She imagined the brothers had been like this in Xibalba, side by side, in a fabulous underground throne room.

"Shall we begin?" Vucub-Kamé asked, looking ahead, his eyes empty.

"We will," Hun-Kamé replied, and he also looked ahead, but his gaze settled on her.

Zavala lit a cigar and stood before the twin gods, taking a puff.

Casiopea glanced at her cousin, and he replied with a wary look, but no words were exchanged. What was there to say?

Zavala opened his mouth and spat out a violent cloud of smoke and ash, which enveloped Casiopea and Martín.

The smoke was substantial, and the room grew darker, but it did not bother her throat, she did not cough. As the smoke thickened, it erased the borders of the room, the contours of the brothers' faces, Martín's silhouette, the carvings on the walls. It even wiped away the floor on which she stood. Casiopea rested upon a surface and yet she stood on nothing; she might have been floating, no angle to guide her eyes and give her a sense of perspective.

Slowly the world recovered its contours and she found herself upon a lonely road. Above her head there was an odd, starless sky, and all around her stretched a desolate grayness. She had descended into Xibalba.

Casiopea took a deep breath and began her journey. She walked for many minutes, but when she looked ahead the land was exactly the same, and behind her there was only the road, the gray desolation. Hun-Kamé had told her it was not possible to determine how long it would take her to reach the city. Time and distances were not the same as in Middleworld. Now she understood what he meant, because she had made little progress; it was as if she'd walked the span of three steps in an hour. Even worse, she could not spy the gaps Hun-Kamé had mentioned.

Casiopea pressed the gourd against her lips and took a sip. She walked slowly, looking down at the road, trying to see if there were spots where it was different, but it was all a deep blackness, like obsidian.

As she walked she noticed that this land was eerily quiet. No wind, no rustle of the gray sand by the road. It was so quiet that she began to hear the beating of her heart, the movement of the blood through her veins; each step was like the trampling of the elephant. But this was the only noise: it all came from within her and had a disorienting effect. She paused a couple of times to sip from the gourd, and the sloshing of the water was as loud as the rapids of a river in this desert of silence.

She could hear her lungs, the breaths she drew, and she began to walk faster, hoping to find a source of noise, an end to the silence. But when she walked the road was the same, it did not change, and neither did the absolute stillness of the land. It was like being encased in amber.

Casiopea sped up her pace, then she ran. Her heart thundered inside her chest and she had to stop, out of breath, the sound of Casiopea drawing air as loud as a hurricane.

Once she had recovered, the stillness wrapped around her and she discovered she was standing at a crossroad. Casiopea spun around, trying to determine which direction she should follow, but no matter where she turned the gray desert was the same, and the roads had no end. They did not curve, they were four straight lines. Hun-Kamé had said nothing about this.

In the stories of the Hero Twins there had also been four roads that intersected, but they had different colors, green and red and black and white, one for each corner of the earth. This was not the case, and each path could lead to doom or her objective.

"East lies the answer," said one of the roads to her.

"West is the city," replied the other road.

"North you should go," cried the third.

"Turn back, you go in the opposite direction," concluded the fourth.

Casiopea did not know how the roads spoke, but they did, in an insidious whisper, a bothersome buzzing, which made her grimace. Their voices came from inside her head, too, just like every other sound. She squinted, trying to discern which path was the appropriate one. The roads spoke.

"I hear her heart beating in fear," said one road.

"I hear the blood in her veins, cold from the madness which assails her."

"I hear her breath catching in her throat."

The voices were like a steady drop of water falling on her skull, a form of clever torture, terribly distracting. One could not concentrate when they spoke, but it was even worse when they were silent, the quiet hitting her like a wall.

"There are monsters in this land."

"There are places crafted with the sorrows of men."

"There are traps made of blood and bone."

She placed her hands against her ears, but the voices were within her, and they laughed at Casiopea, making jokes, telling her to follow each one of them.

She spun in a circle and knelt down, tired and overwhelmed, her fingers aching again. Casiopea clutched her left hand, where the bone shard lay, and the silver bracelet Hun-Kamé had gifted her clinked against her wrist, a soft noise, which in the quiet of the land was like a note from a cymbal. She recalled then what he'd said: the road listens to you.

Slowly she stood up and dusted her clothes, the rustle of the fabric like a knife that scratched the land, and the roads laughed louder, drawing echoes inside her head.

Casiopea gritted her teeth and opened her mouth.

"I am headed to the Jade Palace," she told the roads. "You will show me the way."

The roads did not wish to comply, and they yelled terrible curses at her, promising to eat her bones and spit them out, but she held her left hand up, and she remembered how Hun-Kamé spoke, sure of himself at every turn, and her mouth reproduced his iron tone.

"Show me the way," she demanded.

The roads wavered, physically shaking, making Casiopea almost lose her balance. Like tongues they wagged and went quiet all at the same time.

She noticed then that the road to her right possessed a section with a slightly different coloring, not black like obsidian. Instead it was black like bone char, more velvet than silk.

Casiopea stood upon this section of the road and, not knowing what to say, she simply repeated her destination.

"The Jade Palace," she said and took a step forward.

For a second she was in a pocket of shadow, black the world

above and below, and then she had stepped back onto the road, which was bordered by mounds of earth. More mounds in the distance. The land had changed: it was no longer the flat grayness she had walked through. The silence had broken too. There were weeds by the road, on the mounds, and animals there, crickets and snails, which made the dry plants rustle.

She found another patch of shadow and then another, and she stepped through these, and with each leap she took, the land changed and she progressed in her journey until she was moving past pale stone pillars, a few of which stood proud and tall, while many had fallen by the side of the road, broken into two or three pieces, some missing large chunks, others almost intact.

The pillars had faces on them, and she paused to look at them, thinking they represented warriors. But this was a wild guess. There might have been a hundred or a thousand pillars bordering the road. At one point she sat next to one of them, drinking from the gourd and massaging her feet, but she did not dally long.

Then the road dipped. In the middle of the road there rose a pillar, but this one was made of dark stone, and when she looked at it more carefully she realized it . . . breathed. It was alive. It was not a pillar at all.

Martín, due to his previous experience in the Underworld, was able to wander the Black Road with more ease than his cousin. Nevertheless, his previous travels had been conducted in the company of Zavala. Alone, he found the journey more taxing. He had begun the competition walking at a brisk speed, but he grew tired and slowed down. The path he followed felt sticky and warm. He was sweating and cursed under his breath.

The sights around him were dispiriting. The road cut through a luxurious patch of jungle, the leaves of trees jade green. But the birds in the trees were fleshless, eyeless creatures that cawed angrily. Other animals stirred in the foliage, and the more Martín walked through the jungle, the more he felt disturbed, worried a jaguar would lunge out from the darkness and eat him.

The road was like tar against his shoes, holding him back, until he could barely advance three paces without great effort. "Take me to the Jade Palace," he told the road. "Take me to the Jade Palace fast."

But the road, malicious, smirked, and sweat dripped down Martín's collar. He strained to move forward, and he was still entirely too slow.

A loud rustling in the trees startled him, and Martín clutched his knife.

Martín looked up and saw a monkey, staring at him.

"Idiot thing," he whispered, placing the knife back in its sheath. "Go off!"

A second monkey peered at the man, then a third. A dozen pairs of bright yellow eyes stared at Martín. He began to walk away, slowly, since the road felt like tar.

And then a monkey threw a stone at him. And another. Martín yelped; he raised his arms and shrieked as the stones rained on him. One cut his cheek and another hit him between the shoulder blades. The monkeys hollered, gleeful.

"I'm headed to the Jade Palace!" Martín yelled. "I'm headed there by the will of Vucub-Kamé!"

The monkeys continued tossing their stones, but the road released its hold on the man, and Martín was able to run away from the screeching creatures.

In Middleworld, Vucub-Kamé rested his chin against the back of his hand and observed the shifting ashes on the floor, which rose and traced the contours of the Black Road, allowing them to witness the progress of both champions. Casiopea had lagged behind her cousin, but she was now moving at a decent speed. However, she had found a significant obstacle.

Hun-Kamé shifted in his seat, leaning forward, as if to get a better look at the unfolding scene. He looked worried. As he should be. In a stroke of good luck Casiopea had gleaned one of the secrets of the Black Road and had learned how to navigate it, but her luck had run out.

Xibalba counted many frightful creatures, obstacles, and snares. Casiopea had chanced upon one of the most imposing ones, and she quivered.

"You should have taken my offer," Vucub-Kamé told his brother. "There is no champion in her; she's a scared girl."

Vucub-Kamé's eyes had grown translucent, like a sastun, because in the ashes he divined his future and his triumph.

Chapter 32

It was not a stone pillar. It was a bat. Twice as tall as Casiopea, its wings were folded against its bony body. Its skin was very dark; it glimmered, as if it had been carved from a single stone. The bat's face was crude, made of primordial, half-formed fears, and its eyes were closed. It did not dream, since no entity of Xibalba dreams, but it stood in a trance similar to sleep, awaiting wary pilgrims. These days there were not many, the road had grown dusty with disuse, but in centuries past it had gloried in chasing men through the dark lands, and sometimes, it had flown to Middleworld, to drink from the armpits and the chests of mortals.

Thus he roamed across Xibalba and waited, Kamazotz, who is the death bat that withers the crops.

There was no way to avoid the creature. It blocked the narrow path Casiopea was on. If she followed the road, she'd find herself right next to it, and Casiopea did not think it was a good idea to approach the monstrous bat. In the tale of the Hero Twins a bat-god had ripped off the head of one of them. She was not interested in finding out whether he was fond of doing this.

Casiopea watched the bat as it slept, its body rippling with its breathing. She took a step forward.

"It will hear you if you go near it, and attack," said a low voice. "It's blind, but your movements will alert it to your presence."

Casiopea looked down in surprise and saw a bright green snake by the road. It had two heads and four eyes, which it fixed on her. She did not think it poisonous—she'd seen ones like this back home, though they obviously lacked the second head. She knelt down next to it and frowned. "What are you?" she asked in a whisper.

"Only a snake," said one head.

"Oh," Casiopea said. "How is it that you look . . . different from the snakes I know, and you speak?"

"I speak because we are in Xibalba and because you are not an ordinary woman. I recognize you. You carry the seal of Hun-Kamé in your eyes," replied the other snake head.

"You know him?"

The snake was offended by the question and proudly raised both of its flat heads.

"He was our lord, and then he was betrayed. Vucub-Kamé has brought imbalance to Xibalba, and only the return of Hun-Kamé may restore the scales of duality. If you are here, bearing his invisible standard, then the lord must be nearby."

"I'm on a quest."

"As must be," the snake said, looking prim. Snakes, after all, have a great sense of decorum and order.

Casiopea glanced again at the bat that blocked her path. Hun-Kamé had told her to stay on the road, so she did not dare leave the path. Besides, even if she tried to put some distance between herself and the road, the bat might hear her.

"You wouldn't have any ideas about how to get past it, would you?" she asked the snake. "I need to reach the World Tree."

The snake thought for a minute. "My sisters and I could distract it. But you'd have to be fast."

"You'd help me?" Casiopea said. "That's very generous of you."

"Yes, for we are both daughters of the earth," the snake said loftily. "Besides, I like the silver bracelet you wear on your arm. You could give it to us, to seal the bargain. One must give, after all, in quests like this."

Casiopea touched her wrist, looking at the silver circle she wore. Hun-Kamé's gift, the only piece of jewelry she'd ever owned, and the one item she'd expected to keep, a reminder of her journey. And of him. She bit her lip.

"Here, then," Casiopea said, shaking her head and setting the bracelet on the ground next to the snake.

The snake looked happy. It blinked, rubbing both of its heads against Casiopea's hand, like a cat. Then it called to its sisters. There were three of them, jade green, also possessing two heads each, and when they saw the silver bracelet they were pleased, since all snakes appreciate jewels, precious metals, and mirrors. Their vanity causes them to spend many minutes chasing their reflection in their surfaces, but one must not think poorly of snakes for this reason, since they are kind, thoughtful creatures.

Once they had looked at the bracelet, the snakes turned their attention to Casiopea, whispering among themselves.

"We will scatter in different directions," the snake told her, "and when the road is clear, run away. But be quick about it."

"I have no desire to remain here," Casiopea said. "Thank you."

She stood up and readied herself. The snakes slithered away, following the road. At first the bat paid them no heed. It slept on, its arms resting across its chest, its eyes closed. But as the snakes shifted sand and dirt, making the tufts of grass bordering the road shiver, the bat stirred. It raised its head and spread its wings with one thunderous movement that resembled the sound of a whip, and it pushed itself into the air, flapping it wings and attempting to find the source of the noise.

It seemed to be even bigger in flight, and for a few startled heartbeats Casiopea did not move. Then, regaining her wits, she dashed forward.

She ran, attempting to find the shadow gaps in the road, but there were none. The Black Road did not cease, no matter how hard she looked.

The bat, which was chasing a snake, turned its massive head and changed its mind, deciding to follow instead this new sound. It flapped its wings, gaining speed, and Casiopea attempted to run faster. She'd had plenty of chances to go down and up stairs, run to and fro around her house, and she was a nimble girl, but the bat fast approached her.

Casiopea began to run in a zigzag, hoping this might throw the creature off. She'd seen moths do this in the late hours of the day, to trick bats and avoid becoming their dinner, but although it bought her a few moments, Kamazotz loomed closer. She spotted two columns that had collapsed at an angle, tangling together, leaving a space beneath them. Casiopea threw herself to the ground and rolled under the columns.

The bat dove down, attempting to snatch her head like it had snatched the heads of heroes in ages past, and instead it struck a column. The claws hit the column with such force they left gouges on the rock. The bat flew up and down, striking the column again and again. In her hiding place Casiopea felt the stone shiver as it was incessantly pummeled. She undid the cord of the gourd and waited until the bat rose, ready to come swooping down against the column, then she tossed the gourd away with all her might. The gourd rolled upon the road, the water inside it sloshing. The bat, attracted by the noise, moved in its direction.

Casiopea stood up and began running. Again, the sound of her shoes hitting the road made the bat turn around and seek her out. In no time it had found her.

The Black Road extended solid and firm before Casiopea, no chink in it, and behind her, above her, the bat flapped its wings, readying to snatch her head away with its razor-sharp claws.

I'll die, she thought. *Horribly, I'll die.*

But she shook her head, shook the thought away.

She saw it then, wavering, the shadow that indicated a gap, and leaped forward.

She did not name her destination—there was no time for a sound to leave her throat—and she tumbled into a perfect darkness and tumbled out onto the Black Road again.

She raised her head, but above her there was nothing except the strange non-sky of the Underworld. Behind her the road was quiet. No columns, broken or intact, bordered the road. She'd left the bat behind.

Casiopea lay on the ground until her heart had regained its regular rhythm. Then she stood up and began walking again.

Martín reached a river filled with blood. The sight of it was disgusting, and he was forced to turn back, find another gap in the road, and jump forward again, because the trick in Xibalba was that although the road seemed a straight line, it branched and moved. It constantly changed. However, once Martín jumped forward again, he found himself by a river of pus, impassable.

"Damn you!" he yelled. He turned back a third time and finally was able to keep moving forward. At this point the road was not sticky anymore, so he moved with more ease, but he had bruises on his arms from the monkeys, and although his cheek had stopped bleeding, it ached mightily. More than that, his pride had been injured, and he was disheveled, a scared miscreant stumbling down the Black Road.

Bones protruded from the earth, like broken teeth. Some were white, some were yellow, and some were a rotting black, with pale pink or vermillion meat clinging in strings to them. They varied in size, as small as a clump of daisies, and others as tall as a person. And they carried a foul stench that made Casiopea press her shawl against her face.

The stench attracted black vultures, which perched atop the bones. Their wrinkled, featherless, dark heads turned in Casiopea's direction, and their eyes, made of opals, reflected the young woman, but they left her alone and did not attempt to impede her path. More unpleasant were the flies, which swarmed around the bones. These came in greens of different shades, the delicate green of bottles and glasses, and the milky green of jade, and finally the dark green of the jungle. Clouds and clouds of flies flew up in the air when she walked by, buzzing noxiously. She pressed her shawl against her face and held her breath, the perfume of carrion making her eyes water, until the flies were thick against the bones, like a cloud. But then, slowly, the flies and the stench faded.

The bones that greeted Casiopea were now pecked clean, pale, naked, rising very high. No longer did they clump like tiny daisies, the smallest bones reached her shoulder; they extended as tall as trees, and where before they had bordered the road, now bones erupted in the middle of the black path she followed. First it was a bone or two, until she was walking by four large bones, then five, all in a row.

Casiopea drew the shawl from her face and looked ahead. A wall of bones greeted her. It gleamed under the sunless sky of Xibalba. Although tall, the wall was not impassable. There were gaps between the bones, large enough that someone might squeeze between them.

Perched high above the bones, a few black vultures gazed at the woman.

"Very well," Casiopea said, a sigh punctuating the words.

She walked through the gaps. Sometimes she had to duck her head, and her progress was slow. But otherwise all was fine. Until the vultures yelled suddenly and flew off. Casiopea raised her head. She could see nothing from where she was, the bones as thick as the canopy in the jungle.

She kept going. But then she heard it: a loud scraping noise and a rumble that almost made her lose her footing. The bones were moving. The gaps between them were disappearing.

Casiopea scrambled forward, hurrying to escape this trap. The bones clacked against each other, and she pushed at one protrusion, which resembled a gigantic rib, managing to make it rock a little to the left, allowing her to squeeze through. The bones clacked louder, closing in like a mouth. There was a gap, small enough that she might scrabble out if she got on her knees, and this she did. The ground was harsh against her knees, scratching them, but Casiopea hurried. The bones descended, ready to crush her whole, and she rolled out of the maw. Her shawl tangled with the bones, but she tore it off her shoulders and left it behind, landing on her back and peering up at the sky.

The wall of bones showed no gaps anymore. It stood white and silent, the clacking having ceased. Her shawl, trapped between two bones, moved with the wind, like a flag, before the bones seemed to pull it in, swallowing the cloth whole.

Better it than me, she thought.

Casiopea stood up, rubbing her palms against her skirt, and walked away from the wall of bones. She had lost her bracelet, her gourd, and her shawl, retaining only her knife. She thought this did not bode well, but she was no soothsayer, and had neither a divining stone nor eighteen kernels of corn to peer into the future.

A black vulture flew down to land on the road next to her and stared at Casiopea curiously.

"I'm headed to the Jade Palace," she told the bird and knew she must move on. There was nothing more to do. One foot before another, and the Black Road like fresh tar.

The gods sat each in his chair. On the floor the ashes kept changing and reshaping the scene the twins observed, showing both travelers. Martín, aided by his previous experiences on the Black Road, was moving in an efficient fashion through the shadows, increasing his speed.

The ashes on the floor rose and traced the image of Casiopea. She'd had a harder time at it, but she'd evaded the monstrous Kamazotz and the maw of bones. If Vucub-Kamé had been a betting man, he would have bet against this outcome.

Vucub-Kamé sank his nails into the wood of his chair, making it groan. Quickly he turned his head and stared at his dark-haired brother, who in turn was utterly concerned with the movement of the ash-girl across the land.

"Who is she?" Vucub-Kamé demanded, standing up, furious, but with the cold fury of a Lord of Death, the words ice.

"What do you mean?"

"How is she doing it?"

"There is no trick, if that is what you are implying. I have not cheated," Hun-Kamé said.

Of course he had not. He could not have. The girl had moved slowly, clumsily, at the beginning, but she had now gained speed and might soon be overtaking Martín. It was her own doing, the firmness of her resolve, and Vucub-Kamé again thought about the meaning of symbols. The maiden, a bracketed promise.

"You must be cheating in some way," Vucub-Kamé said, offended. "She is a weak thing to manage on her own."

"You are a poor judge of others," Hun-Kamé replied and looked at his brother, his one eye inky black.

Bah! And yet, had they not all failed Vucub-Kamé? Old Cirilo, the cunning Xtabay, the Zavala twins with their midnight sorceries. It came down to Martín now. The young man was not the fine blade a god might have wanted to wield, but a coarser weapon, a heavy mace. Who cared?

"I'll see her dead," Vucub-Kamé told the ash, and his cold anger froze into an invisible arrow of ice, and when he breathed out, the arrow slid from his lips and into the mind of Martín, who sat on the stump of a tree, which had fallen by the road.

The man was wiping his forehead with a handkerchief, exhausted by the trip, feeling rather depressed by the landscape of Xibalba. He wet the piece of cloth and dabbed his cheek with it, feeling the sting of a bruise. Around him there were black trees without any leaves, their naked branches stretching up to the heavens, and logs ripe with rot, like the one that served as a seat for him.

Martín pressed his hand against his head, and the ring he wore stung, biting into his flesh.

Vucub-Kamé's thought reached him as if it had been his own. It echoed in his skull.

Kill her, Vucub-Kamé said.

"Kill her," Martín repeated. His voice had no color; it was bleak and brisk and old.

The echo died away, and Martín twisted the handkerchief between his hands.

"Lord, please," he said, but the presence had abandoned him. He sat alone, with the dead trees as his only company. The instructions had been clear.

He could already feel his cousin approaching, even if he did not understand how he could sense her. Somehow Vucub-Kamé must have engineered her arrival, steered her from her course. Or it might not have been the Lord of Xibalba; the Black Road did have a mind of its own.

No matter. He felt her.

It was as if she were an insect, making the silk of a spider web vibrate.

This, in turn, made him the spider.

Martín clutched the handkerchief.

Chapter 33

Trees, so close together at times they formed a lattice, bordered Casiopea's path. Yet the trees were invariably shrunken, dead, and their branches stood ghostly white against the gray sky.

The road was steep; it led up a hill, and she had trouble managing it. At last she reached a clearing. A clump of trees lay to her right, but she could see below, far away, the Black City.

A monumental causeway cut through a ring of thorns that rose around the city, like a defensive stone wall might have shielded mortal towns, though this metropolis need not shield itself from any foes. All the buildings were made of black stone, honoring the city's name, but of a glossy black that shifted and shimmered. Pillars and stelae rose in the plazas, long staircases decorated with pale glyphs led to multiple platforms. Serene, sober, monochromatic, that was the city. Except for the Jade Palace at its center, aflame with color and unlike any of the structures Casiopea knew back home.

The palace had four levels, each level receding slightly from the previous one, their façades decorated with elaborate geometrical patterns that created a palpable rhythm, like the beating of a drum. These terraces were connected by an imposing central staircase. Impossibly, the whole structure was made of a pale green jade, like a giant jewel, as Hun-Kamé had said. It looked like the palace she had imagined when they stood by the sea.

She looked at this strange city, sculpted from the stray dreams of restless mortals, and took a deep breath.

A rustle came from the clump of dead trees, and Casiopea turned her head, expecting to find a snake or another animal, and instead stared at her cousin. Martín was grim and tired as he stopped and also looked in the direction of the city. He took a sip from the gourd dangling from his neck and wiped his mouth with the back of his hand. He offered her a sip. She took it, cautiously.

"God. I feel like I've been walking forever," he said. "Do you feel the same way?"

"A little," she replied, handing him the gourd back.

Martín drank more, but there was no more to be had. Irritated, he took off the gourd from around his neck and tossed it away. It rolled down the side of the hill.

"Casiopea, you shouldn't go any farther," he told her.

"It's a competition. We are competing to see who gets there first. I can't stay here," she replied, guessing he meant to fill her with doubt.

"Yes, you can, if you know what's good for you. Vucub-Kamé does not want you moving any closer to the city."

"I don't care what he wants. We have a deal, and I am not going to give up now."

Martín had not looked at her this whole time. Now he turned his eyes toward her. His face was parched, not a physical thirst but a spiritual one. He looked haunted.

"Casiopea, I can't let you go on. So . . . sit down here and wait," he said, running a hand through his hair. It was slick with sweat. He had a scratch on his cheek, he was dirty, and his hair was a mess, as if he'd been walking for days on end. The journey must have taxed him. She was tired, too, and would have loved to sit down and rest.

"And what? Let you win?" she asked.

"Vucub-Kamé needs to retain the throne, the whole family depends . . . God, they depend on that. Your loss . . . it would be the best for everyone."

"For you and him, maybe."

"Trust me. You don't want this. And I'll talk to Vucub-Kamé," he promised. "He's not going to kill you; you are a Leyva, after all."

"Don't try that again. I've never been a Leyva. You made sure I knew that."

"I'm sorry! All right? I'm sorry! But for God's sake don't take it out on me, on us, now. Casiopea, tell me you won't go on."

She thought he'd keep his word, he'd do as he'd promised when they spoke in Mexico City: call her "cousin," let her walk beside him. Even buy her dresses and trinkets, take her to dances in Mérida like he did with his sisters on occasion. He was desperate, after all.

Although she would have liked this, once upon a time, she would not relent.

"I'm headed to the palace," she said, as much to him as to herself.

"God. You never quit, do you?" he yelled, and there was a dangerous anger in him.

Casiopea attempted to run, but he was very quick and rushed at her. She did not know how to fight and could barely gasp as he cleaved her against the ground. She raised her arms, trying to push him back, and their limbs thrashed as they struggled.

He meant to beat her, she thought. Teach her a lesson, like their grandfather with the cane; like Martín himself had done before. A slap or two. But then he raised his knife and she raised her hands, trying to shield her face; she kept the knife at bay, trapping his wrists with her fingers and holding him in place. And she couldn't even yell at him: he was heavy, he crushed her. It was as if she'd forgotten how to breathe. She thought she'd die in this strange place, by the shrunken trees, their white branches whispering to the wind.

With his hair in his eyes and with his fury, her cousin was unrecognizable. He was a monster from the myth, more terrifying than Kamazotz because she'd feared Martín for a long time, because she'd dreamed it might end like this somehow, that he'd commit himself to violence, long before she ever initiated this quest.

"Martín, please," she managed to croak, and she thought he would never budge.

But then he stood up, and he scrambled away from her, trembling, as if it had been he who had been pinned down against the dirt, a knife in front of his eyes. Casiopea blinked and pushed herself up.

"I can't," Martín said. "You stupid, stupid girl, I can't!"

He was crying. She'd seen him cry when they were younger, when she'd hit him in the head. Blood had welled, so much blood, and he'd wept. Now he cried again, even though *he* had been attempting to hurt *her*. Noticing her gaze on him, he turned abruptly toward Casiopea, and Casiopea raised her arms. She thought he might attempt to finish what he had started.

Instead of the bite of the knife she felt his hands on her. He shoved her away with such force she rolled down the hill. She landed on a clump of weeds, no damage done. The ground was soft clay and the hill small. A trickle of a stream ran nearby.

"Stay there!" he warned her, and then he disappeared from sight.

Casiopea stood up and waited for a few minutes before climbing back up, but when she reached the top of the hill she found the road had vanished and she was standing upon a long, muddy flat. She turned around, trying to spot the road. It was nowhere to be seen.

Another stream flowed near her. Or perhaps it was the same one she'd seen before, even though that would have been impossible.

But Xibalba did not respect the topography of Middleworld; distances here were extended and compressed.

Trees, yellow and rotting with age, poked out from the mud. Mud cones served as nests for strange birds that resembled flamingos but did not have their colors. They were gray. Not the gray of the flamingos when they are young, before they have eaten enough of the shrimp that give them their vivid pink hue. A darker sort of gray, like soot.

Not knowing what else to do, Casiopea began to walk. The birds, when she went by, raised their heads and stared at her and flapped their wings, making sounds that resembled a hiss, but they did not attempt to get close. She kept a hand on her knife.

She decided to follow the stream, even if any direction would have been the same now that she'd lost the road. When she grew thirsty, she knelt down and drank from it.

The souls of the dead, when they made their way to Xibalba, forgot themselves and were lost if they journeyed beyond the Black Road, and she began to lose herself too. She thought she had been walking for weeks, blisters on her feet, shoes caked with mud, her clothes askew, her hair in disarray.

When she looked over her shoulder, back to the place where she'd come from, she saw nothing but the mud cones and the trickle of water rolling through the land. She blinked, realizing the oddity of water rushing in the open: she'd never walked by a river before, they were all underground, back in northern Yucatán.

It was hard for her to remember Yucatán, though she'd spent her entire life there.

It was equally difficult to remember her bedroom, the books she used to read, the poetry she'd learned, the names of stars, her mother's face, her father's stories. Had it been hours in Xibalba? Could it have been years? She looked at her hands, and they were the hands of a young woman, but the more she stared at them, the older they became. Brown spots appeared upon the back of them, and she moved slowly, her spine weighed down by age.

Had she been young? Once upon a time. Stories began like that, but she'd never had the chance to imagine fairy tales, busy on her knees scrubbing the floors. Was that the way she'd lived? Every day, cleaning the house, helping carry fruits and vegetables to the kitchen, shining her grandfather's shoes.

It had been like this. She'd grown up, grown into a woman. Still the same routine. Still in Uukumil. Fetch this, fetch that. The brush and the soap and her hands cracked from all the housework. Her mother had died, and she'd stayed in Uukumil. Martín married, had children. But Casiopea did not, since she was a poor relation, there by force of charity. Her hair had hints of silver, then it went all white. She'd died an old woman, her breath sour, her eyes cloudy with cataracts.

She never set a foot outside the town. In her youth she'd dreamed of fast dances, the lure of the automobile. But she never saved enough money, never had the courage to move to Mérida. She'd grown resentful, then bitter, until she knew nothing but the taste of spite.

She'd died and somehow she'd ended here. In this place where birds that lacked flesh and feathers followed her journey with their empty eye sockets and she sank into the mud, her skirt crusted with the wet earth.

But then, there had been . . .

Hadn't there been something else? The memory scratched against her skull, stubborn. Casiopea scratched her head in turn, felt stray wisps of hair against her fingers, the dryness of the scalp. She squinted and could not focus her eyes well. She was an old woman, after all.

And there had been . . .

There had been a poem that described exactly what she was feeling. This poem, read long ago, in a musty book, pages missing from it.

And it had said . . .

"'He indicates life's essential brevity, unexpected and with suffering, assaulted by death,'" Casiopea whispered.

She remembered. She'd told Hun-Kamé about this poem when they were in Tijuana. But that had not been years ago, it had been a few days ago. She was not old. She was a young woman, and when she raised her hand and looked at it she saw the skin she knew, unblemished by the passage of time.

She remembered her quest too.

She was headed to the palace, to find the World Tree.

Casiopea blinked. All around her the land was a blinding white, which made her shield her eyes for a moment. The mud flat and the birds were gone. She stood upon a salt flat instead, dotted with phosphorescent plants that swayed gently to a soft breeze.

Xibalba had attempted its tricks again.

The river had disappeared, and Casiopea began to follow the odd phosphorescent plants. They were placed in a row, each one chained to the next. There were also anemones and plants that looked like curious orchids, but were made of travertine. In the distance she spotted mountains of corals. She looked up, and a school of sightless fish flew above her head, as if they were birds, as if they had forgotten they were supposed to dwell in the deepest of waterholes, beneath the calcareous soil.

Her body ached, but the hand ached worst of all, and she pressed it against her chest. She could almost feel the time running out, like a gigantic beating heart that palpitated quietly across the land.

The salt was cool and inviting. She pressed on, and when her shoes were lodged full with salt, she took them off and continued barefoot. She was headed nowhere, and nowhere she went, hoping to find the Black Road even if she knew, within her, she could not.

She walked past towering pillars of seashells, pressed together like bricks, and reached a lake. It glowed a soft blue, like in her dreams.

The wind had dried Martín's tears, which hurt more than the bruises on his body, more than his parched throat. He raced down the causeway that led into the Black City, raced past graceful buildings carved from onyx. In the windows of some of those homes stood people with white masks who regarded him curiously, and he encountered and ignored soldiers, priests, and commoners who also walked down the same road, who turned their heads to glance in derision at a mortal man who dared to navigate their knotted city.

Casiopea stood by the lake while the wind tugged at her hair. Forward, beyond the water there was only salt, and going around it might take a long time. She was forced to sit by the lake and catch her breath. Her body did not hurt anymore, but she knew this was a sign that the end was approaching. There would be no more time.

She felt the strength ebbing from her, and around her, like a vibration, she could also feel Martín's steps upon the Black Road as he walked into the city, as he went past the black houses and black monuments and approached the Jade Palace.

She was dying. The mirage of her old age had been an illusion, but this was real, this death nibbling her fingers.

She was too far from the Black Road to ever reach the World Tree on time.

Casiopea grabbed the knife and sighed, turning it between her hands.

She remembered Loray's advice. Cut off the hand, serve Vucub-Kamé. And Vucub-Kamé's offer. Die and offer herself to him. She'd be invited to dwell in the shadow of the World Tree. Hun-Kamé would perish. But he'd perish anyway, and if she performed this one gesture Vucub-Kamé would look at her kindly.

He might be merciful.

Betrayal was in her nature, after all. Her grandfather had been disloyal.

She had dreamed this moment, the slicing of the wrists. It was the arrow of fate. She had been foolish to think she could win this challenge. Unlucky Casiopea, born under a bad star, could not prevail.

Casiopea clutched the knife, tight. Desperate, scared, wishing to weep her sorrow, she waded into the lake until the water reached her thighs. The knife was in her hand. The obsidian blade was sharp, unnaturally perfect, it was like a black mirror. She caught her reflection in it.

The Black Road grew more convoluted the farther Martín walked around the city. It led him down alleys with dead ends, it dragged him next to magnificent temples and through a market where men sold jaguar pelts and featherless birds, their bones inked with dozens of colors. Gamblers sat on woven mats and threw dice, moving red and blue pebbles across a board. They laughed, showing Martín their pointed teeth.

"Damn it," he cursed.

But he caught a flash of green in his right eye and, turning, beheld, not so distant, the unmistakable silhouette of the Jade Palace.

Martín smiled.

She could hear Martín's steps upon the stones of the Black City. She could hear his breath and she could feel inside her the last shreds of time wilting away.

Casiopea was scared. The fear was like a cloak lined with lead; it held her stiff in its arms. It would not let her move. She was bound in its coils. Live, live, she wanted to live. She wanted a way out.

It was as Hun-Kamé had told her: life was not fair. Why should she be fair? Why should she suffer? This was not even her story. This kind of tale, this dubious mythmaking, was for heroes with shields and armor, for divinely born twins, for those anointed by lucky stars.

She was but a girl from nowhere. Let the heroes save the world, save kings who must regain their crowns. Live, live, she wanted to live, and there was a way.

Who was to say she couldn't serve a death lord, as her grandfather had? Vucub-Kamé had promised Casiopea would be his favorite courtier. She might even become like Xtabay, with jewels on her fingers and her ears, much admired and respected.

Why not?

"I pledge myself to the Supreme Lord of Xibalba," she told the blade, her voice wavering.

She raised her arm. And she could see Hun-Kamé dead, the head separated from the body, the body falling. And she could see the future Vucub-Kamé envisioned: his expanded kingdom, the world tasting of smoke and blood, and darkness blotting the land.

Then she remembered the long road she'd traveled, the obstacles she'd overcome, and what Hun-Kamé had told her when they stood by the sea. It rang in her ears so clearly: *And yet you are.* She also recalled the ways his eyes had deepened, the velvet blackness, that third kiss he did not share. He didn't need to. He loved her, she knew it. She loved him back.

She could not betray him. She could not betray herself. She could not betray the story.

Mythmaking. It's greater than you or I, this tale.

Maybe she was not a hero with a shield and a divine provenance, but it's the symbolism that matters. She gripped the knife tight.

"I pledge myself to the Supreme Lord of Xibalba, the Lord Hun-Kamé," she said, this time with aplomb. Casiopea slid the knife against her throat.

K'up kaal. The cutting of the throat. The proper way to die. Vucub-Kamé's suggestion of the slashing of the wrists would have been inadequate.

Proper or no, the pain was raw; it roared through her body and she opened her eyes wide. The blood welled. It soaked her shirt and she trembled. She let go of the knife, she did not attempt to press her hands against her throat, did not attempt to stop the flow of blood.

Instead, she remembered what she'd told Hun-Kamé at the hotel: that she wanted everything to live. And her lips, they repeated this request, not life for herself but for all others.

Casiopea sank to her knees, slid into the water, the lake swallowing her whole.

The lake was perfectly still. She might never have been there at all.

K'up kaal.

In the deserts of Xibalba men walked and cried for mercy. In the swamps skeleton birds shrieked. In caves like honeycombs mortals tore their hair out, having forgotten who they were. In the Black City the noble dead who had made proper preparations for the Underworld, decking themselves in serpentine and jade and placing the correct offerings, sat on their couches and drank a black liqueur.

Xibalba was as it always had been.

Then the snakes and the jaguar and the bats turned their heads, because the land held its breath. The men in the deserts paused in their cries, the skeleton birds ceased their shrieking, and the lost mortals stopped their gnashing and their tearing, the noble dead held on to their cups tightly.

Martín, approaching the main entrance to the Jade Palace, stumbled and stood motionless. He did not understand why, only that he must pause, that a force greater than himself demanded he be anchored and he dare not even turn his head.

In Middleworld, in the casino by the sea, the ground shook. The chandeliers clinked. Huge cracks spread across many mirrors and windows in the hotel. The guests who were watching the roll of the dice and the employees working their shifts let out a gasp, thinking an earthquake was assaulting the peninsula.

The two Lords of Death, who had been sitting in their wooden chairs, stood up and held their breath, just like the land did. Aníbal Zavala watched as the map of ash that showed the Land of the Dead trembled like a leaf, and though he ordinarily would have coaxed it to regain its shape with his sorcery, he could not.

Vucub-Kamé stumbled, as if he echoed Martín's stumble, and Hun-Kamé pressed a hand against his throat.

On its pedestal, the iron axe that had lopped off Hun-Kamé's head, and which hungered to cut it again, trembled too. It twisted, as if it were made of paper, and it was shredded into pieces, minuscule bits of iron dashing against the walls of the chamber.

At the same time the map of ash collapsed upon the floor.

It was as if the land opened its lips and breathed again, and was made anew.

Chapter 34

They emerged under the shadow of the World Tree. Vucub-Kamé and Hun-Kamé, Zavala and Martín. Even if they had wanted to keep away, they could not have stayed behind. Xibalba drew them in and demanded their presence by the lake.

At first, there was nothing to see; it was like stepping into an austere, silent chamber. The World Tree rose, majestic, impossibly high, like no natural tree could rise. Without any warning a ripple cut across the water and from the lake emerged a monstrous being. It was very old, its body shone slick, like the starry night, a whirl of galaxies and the dust of dead suns coating its scales. It was the Great Caiman, blind creature of the depths.

A long time ago the caiman had been dismembered, sacrificed. But it had risen again.

Destruction brings renewal.

Casiopea had flung herself into the water, and the sacrifice had been noted, echoing through Xibalba. She had woken the caiman, which seldom stirred from its dark abode, massive and roughly carved and so awe-inspiring that upon seeing the creature, Zavala fell to his knees. Martín followed suit. Vucub-Kamé did not move an inch.

"It cannot be," whispered the god.

Vucub-Kamé had foreseen many futures, but he could never have foreseen this. He knew himself already defeated, but the extent of the defeat burned like the fury of the whip. It was as if the universe decided to humble him by conjuring this vision, this being. Vucub-Kamé looked at the palms of his hands, burned by the axe he'd wielded. Burned for no reason. Such a joke! He had achieved nothing.

Slowly the caiman reached the shore of the lake. Each of its mighty footsteps made the ground tremble. It opened its jaw, and in its mouth it carried a bundle of cloth. The caiman deposited the bundle on the ground, then lumbered back into the water.

In the silence of its departure stood the gods and the mortals, immobile, until Hun-Kamé stepped forward.

The bundle of cloth was crimson, the kind of mantle that might be used to wrap a corpse. Hun-Kamé knelt next to the bundle and tugged at one of the corners. There, like a broken flower, lay Casiopea. Her throat bore the cut of the knife, her clothes were caked with blood, her eyes were shut. Her black hair was plastered against her skull.

"It is trickery," whispered Vucub-Kamé, and his palms itched as if he'd lacerated them anew. "You have cheated."

"It is her victory," replied Hun-Kamé, with such anger Vucub-Kamé lowered his proud head.

Hun-Kamé looked again at the girl. Gently he gazed at her and even more gently he touched her, a finger upon her brows, sliding down her cheek, touching her lips, until he pressed a hand against her neck. The gash on her throat became a line of red cinnabar, then he brushed away this line of red dust and the skin was healed.

Slowly Casiopea opened her eyes, as if she were stirring from a deep and long sleep. He stood up and helped lift her to her feet, and when she rose, her soiled clothing was replaced by a bright crimson dress with black fringes that reached her ankles, a black sash around her waist. In turn, his clothing changed, the jacket and trousers he'd used in Middleworld dissolving. A black loincloth replaced his old outfit, a cape made from the wings of black moths fell upon his shoulders, and on his chest rested his jade green necklace.

Casiopea blinked, swaying for an instant, and looked at Hun-Kamé attired in his magnificence. When she spoke her voice was low.

"What happened?" she asked.

"You won the race," he told her. "You saved me."

"I died," she whispered, her hand splayed against her throat. She glanced at the ground and then back up at him. "I got here first?"

"It cannot be denied," Hun-Kamé said, and he turned to his brother.

Vucub-Kamé stood with his head lowered, but now he extended a hand forward, and on the palm of this hand materialized a black box, decorated with skulls. He offered this box to Hun-Kamé. He did not do so with any joy, but even a god is bound by rules, and Vucub-Kamé could not hold the throne any longer.

"No, it cannot be denied. She reached the World Tree first, the Great Caiman served as witness to it. Your reign is secure. I offer you that which I took," he said.

Hun-Kamé grabbed the box and slid it open. In it sat his missing eye, like a jewel against velvet. He must reintegrate it into his body, complete the process that had begun in Yucatán. Before this, though, he spoke to Casiopea.

"I owe my kingdom to you and my gratitude," he told her. "I promised you your heart's desire, and you may have anything you wish. If you ask for the jewels of the earth, I will grant them. Should you wish to avenge yourself against your treacherous cousin, his blood will be spilled."

She glanced at Martín, who was on his knees, his forehead pressed against the dirt. Same as Zavala. She shook her head.

"I never wanted jewels," she said. "And I'd like that Martín be allowed to return home."

"Very well," Hun-Kamé said. "As for you, my brother—"

"I submit to you," Vucub-Kamé replied, scarred palms up, toward the sky. "Take your vengeance. You've earned it."

Vucub-Kamé sank to his knees, his head bowed, like a war captive, under the shadow of the World Tree. He offered no resistance, the defiance had been drained from him, and the color had vanished from his eyes. They were as pale as pearls, and his clothes, mimicking his debased state, withered, becoming moth-eaten tatters fit for a beggar.

Hun-Kamé looked at Vucub-Kamé with a hard face, the face of the blade against the jugular, but when he leaned down it was to clasp his brother's shoulder.

"I've desired nothing except your death," he said, "and yet now I do not find the need for it. I was unkind to you and you returned the unkindness, but I cannot perpetuate a cycle of sorrows."

At this, Vucub-Kamé did raise his head. He tried to read deceit in his brother's voice, but could not find it.

"It is the remaining mortality in your veins that renders you like this," he said, wary.

"Perhaps. Or the wisdom to understand the order of duality should not be challenged," Hun-Kamé said, and then, quietly, "Or the fact that despite my bitterness you are my brother."

Hun-Kamé looked down at his brother's scarred hands, and Vucub-Kamé beheld Hun-Kamé's face, the empty eye socket.

The nature of hate is mysterious. It can gnaw at the heart for an eon, then depart when one expected it to remain as immobile as a mountain. But even mountains erode. Hun-Kamé's hate had been as high as ten mountains and Vucub-Kamé's spite as deep as ten oceans. Confronted with each other, at this final moment when Hun-Kamé ought to have let hate swallow him, he had decided to thrust it away, and Vucub-Kamé slid off his mantle of spite in response.

Casiopea had given herself, after all, and Hun-Kamé ought to give too.

Hun-Kamé handed Vucub-Kamé back the box, and Vucub-Kamé hesitated for a moment before carefully grabbing the missing eye and placing it in his brother's eye socket. Then Vucub-Kamé lifted his hands, and a crown knit itself between his hands, the royal diadem of onyx and jade, which he placed on Hun-Kamé's head. Around Hun-Kamé's waist there was now a leather belt decorated with large incrustations of matching onyx and jade.

The brothers were both exactly the same height, and when they looked at each other, their eyes were level, dark and light. They were eternal, never changing, and yet they had changed.

"Welcome to your abode, Supreme Lord of Xibalba," Vucub-Kamé said.

The wind, whispering in the branches of the World Tree, repeated these words.

Crowned anew, Hun-Kamé might have been expected to make his triumphant entrance into the palace, to bask again in the glory of his kingship. Courtiers filled cups brimming with liquor, the incense burners perfumed the air of the throne room. A hundred exaltations waited to be spoken.

Await they must a little longer.

He returned to the girl.

"Come," he told Casiopea and took her by the hand. His power restored, he did not need the Black Road to walk between shadows, as she'd done, and he simply slipped into that space between spaces and out into a distant corner of his kingdom.

This was the desert of gray. Nothing grew here. It was the outer edge of Xibalba, where the Black Road begins, even if the borders of Xibalba are ever-changing and no cartographer could ever draw an accurate picture of it. Nevertheless, it was the border of his realm.

"Soon you must return to Middleworld," Hun-Kamé told her. "And I must become a god."

"Are you not a god yet?" she asked.

He shook his head. "One last thing remains," he said, taking her hand between his, and she knew he meant the connective thread of the bone shard, binding death to life. It was there.

"After this . . . there is no way for me to stay?" she asked.

"You live," he told her soberly.

"I died, moments ago," she countered.

"Yes, and I have returned you to your life. Nothing living can remain for long in the Land of the Dead. It will invariably wither."

"And you cannot exist in the land of the living."

"No. You forget, besides, my mortality comes to an end. With it, my heart."

Casiopea nodded. She understood, and if tears prickled her eyes, she quickly rubbed them away. Hun-Kamé, likely wishing to soothe her, spoke.

"You've asked for nothing, but I wish to place before you these gifts. Let me grant you the power to speak all tongues of the earth, since death knows all languages," he said. "And let me give you also the gift of conversing with the ghosts that roam Middleworld. Such necromancy may be of value."

No show of power accompanied his words, and when the words were said, nothing more remained but to bid each other goodbye.

He pierced her with his gaze, but his face grew softer as he looked at her, like a man who still lies dreaming. He smiled.

He cupped her face between his hands and then he pulled her so very close to him. She slid a hand upon his chest, felt there the heart he'd spoken about.

She stood on her tiptoes and kissed him, willing him to remember her. It was impossible, like asking the ocean to remain in the palm of one's hand, but he was somewhat mortal. He was, despite his gleaming garments and the restitution of his power, more mortal than he'd ever been, and he kissed her back with the absolute belief in love only the young can possess.

He kissed her knuckles and closed his eyes for a moment. His hand fell upon her throat. No mark of the wound she'd inflicted remained, but he traced the invisible line nevertheless, before opening his eyes and looking at Casiopea.

Then he pulled out the bone shard that lay deep within her flesh, the last piece in the puzzle of his immortality.

The dark thread that bound them snapped. She stared at him as he placed a hand on his chest and gasped. His heart was grinding to dust beneath the palm of his hand, and it hurt to see this, but she did not look away.

When there was but a gray speck of his heart left, he bent down and kissed her again, briefly, a brush of lips. A grain of dust may contain a universe inside, and it was the same for him. Within that gray speck there lived his love and he gave it to Casiopea, for her to see. He'd fallen in love slowly and quietly, and it was a quiet sort of love, full of phrases left unsaid, laced with dreams. He had imagined himself a man for her, and he allowed her to see the extent of this man, and he gave her this speck of heart, which was a man, to hold for a moment before taking it back the second before it faded.

As he straightened up, his eyes all darkness, a curious thing happened. The speck did not fade, instead turning vermillion, and it lodged behind those dark eyes, unseen. But Xibalba, so intimately connected to its lord, must have seen, must have known. Xibalba sensed the echo of this silent goodbye.

The inhabitants of this realm, who had been startled when the land held its breath, now had a second chance to be surprised. Such a dark place, Xibalba, built of bitter nightmares and fever dreams, with the stones of sorrow; a land where lost souls could never find the proper road. But the Lord Hun-Kamé had dreamed a different dream, and this dream that was now nothing but a speck subtly transformed the land.

There were no flowers in Xibalba. Trees and weeds and the strange orchids that were not orchids dotted the Underworld, wild desert anemones grew upon its white plains, but there were no flowers in its jungles, its swamps, nor its mountains. Yet now flowers bloomed in the most astonishing of places, across the gray desert. Tiny, red flowers, as if demonstrating for Hun-Kamé what he could no longer demonstrate, so that Casiopea, instead of observing the cold face of a stranger as he'd warned her, beheld instead the appearance of the red flowers, like the ink of a love letter. The stars, when traced by the human eye, formed constellations, and the flowers, linked together, spoke to her. They said, "My love."

Hun-Kamé bowed his head to her, like a commoner instead of a lord.

Then he took Casiopea's hand again and wrapped her in his cloak for a second. It was like slipping into an absolute blackness, the darkness of the garment blotting out Xibalba, and within another second she had slipped into her hotel room. Alone.

Chapter 35

Grief arrived, eager to keep her company, and she clutched her hands together and raised them to her lips, head bowed. Yet as Casiopea stood in the middle of the room she did not consider her heartache for long, because the sound of crying reached her ears, startling her. It was as if someone else gave voice to her unhappiness. Cautious, she approached the doorway of the room Hun-Kamé had occupied and found Martín sitting on the floor. Her cousin wept.

Casiopea leaned down next to him, slowly, like one might when dealing with a scared child.

"What is it?" she asked.

"Grandfather is going to kill me when I get back to Uukumil," he said, sniffling. "You might as well have asked Hun-Kamé to cut off my head."

"Grandfather won't kill you," she said with a sigh.

"Why didn't you ask him to murder me?"

"You didn't kill me either," she replied.

He hunched his shoulders. His clothes were dirty, his hair a mess. She recalled how much he'd prided himself in his nice clothing, in his freshly polished boots. She had polished those same boots, swallowing her tears when he said cruel things. It was his turn to be miserable. Yet even though she'd pictured a scene like this when he was bad to her, it did not please her to witness it.

"Yeah . . . well . . . I'm not a killer," he muttered.

"Neither am I."

Casiopea went to the bathroom and fetched a towel. She handed it to Martín and sat down in front of him. He hesitated, but took the towel and cleaned his face.

"I'm horrible to you," he said when he was done. "I'm a terrible person."

"Maybe you could stop being so horrible, then."

Martín bunched up the towel and gripped it tight, blinking back further tears.

"I'm . . . I'm thankful, you know. For your asking him to send me back here. And I'm sorry. About everything. Will you accept my apology?"

He looked shattered, his voice thick with shame. Casiopea thought he meant it. But it wasn't that simple. He'd left scars. She did not trust him. She didn't want to hate him either. It was pointless now.

"I can't forgive you in an instant," she said.

"Well . . . maybe one day, maybe after a while. After we go back to Uukumil. Although I don't want to go back to Uukumil, but I must. Oh, the old man is going to be so mad at us," he mumbled.

"If you don't want to go back, maybe you shouldn't?"

"Where would I go?" Martín asked, looking rather shocked.

Casiopea shrugged. "I don't know. Maybe you can find your forgiveness on the way there."

Martín was quiet. She stood up, and he shoved his hair away from his face, his eyes red.

"You're not headed back, are you?" he asked her.

"Not yet."

"Then I suppose this is goodbye."

"Yes. So long, Martín," she said.

In the end "so long, Martín" is what she had yearned to say all along, and there was more satisfaction in it than any elaborate revenge fantasy she could have conjured. They were headed in different directions, and this was sufficient.

Casiopea returned to her room and curled up on top of the covers. She was tired, not only the weariness of the road, but a spiritual ache. When she woke up it was morning and Martín had left. He'd scrawled a note for her, saying he'd likely travel to Guadalajara. There was money with the note, his final apology. She stuffed the bills into her suitcase and packed her clothes. While arranging her things she realized that she still had her old shawl, the one she'd worn in her village. A flimsy, cheap piece of cloth that had seen better days, but she placed it around her shoulders. It had traveled with her, weathering distances and foes. She thought it might bring her luck.

When she was done packing, she went to Hun-Kamé's room and stood there, feeling its emptiness. On the nightstand lay the hat he'd worn; in the closet, his suits. She ran her hands over the clothes, but there was nothing of him left, not a strand of hair. She might have imagined him, dreamed him.

She knew it had not been a dream.

Casiopea checked out and noticed the lobby looked different. The luster of it was gone. It was a feeling, as though she were standing in an empty shell. She asked for an automobile to drive her to Tijuana. The clerk apologized and said it might take a few minutes. There had been a small earthquake and problems with the water. Several guests had left.

Casiopea went outside to wait by the hotel's front door. She looked at the sky. Then there came an automobile, and she grabbed her suitcase. She recognized it as the vehicle that had delivered her to the hotel. But the chauffeur was different. He wore a green jacket and a matching flat cap. It was the man she'd met in Mérida, Loray.

"Good morning," he said as he stopped the automobile. On the lapel of his jacket he wore a silver pin in the shape of an arrow and his eyes were forest green, the color of the hunt. His raven was perched on his shoulder.

"Good morning," echoed the bird.

Casiopea approached the automobile, frowning. "What are you doing here?"

"Hun-Kamé kept his bargain and allowed me to walk the Black Road. I've finally been able to leave Mérida behind."

He leaned out the window to give her a friendly smile, which she did not return. "That doesn't explain why you are here."

"Oh, well. He thought you might need a ride, and I very nicely offered to see to that. Jump in."

Casiopea clutched the handle of her suitcase with both hands and held it in front of her, but did not move. The man sighed theatrically.

"Look, despite whatever you've heard about demons, we're not that terrible. Besides, I'm not interested in your soul. Unless you're selling," he said, and he got out of the automobile, opened the trunk, and motioned for her to toss the suitcase in. "That was a joke."

"You're not funny."

He rolled his eyes at her.

"I'm hilarious. Come on. You can't stay here. Zavala has run off with his tail between his legs and this place is going to wither away pretty soon. There's no magic left in it. The tiles are going to crack, windowpanes will fall out, and there will be a million roaches. Don't lay your foundations with magic. It's too difficult to keep it going.

"Now, this is Zavala's automobile and technically I'm not supposed to be driving it. So, would you like a ride in a stolen vehicle, or are we going to waste a bit more time?" he concluded.

Casiopea shuffled her feet, but she moved toward the back of the automobile. He attempted to put her luggage in the vehicle for her, but she would not have it and shoved it in without his assistance. He closed the trunk and went to the passenger's side of the automobile, holding the door open for her. Casiopea sat down.

They drove in silence, and Casiopea contemplated the pleats of her skirt.

"Hun-Kamé sends a gift, by the way," Loray said and reached into his jacket pocket.

He took out a small black bag and handed it to her. Casiopea opened it and found it was full of black pearls. She smiled. Hun-Kamé had kept his promise. Her smile turned sour and she flinched, the pearls rattling against each other.

Loray looked at her from the corner of his eye.

"I'd think you'd be happier," he said. "That must be worth a pretty penny. I wonder what black pearls go for these days. We could find out in Tijuana."

"What? Should I pawn them to satisfy your curiosity?"

"I didn't say that," he replied lightly.

She had a feeling he took everything lightly. The raven on his shoulder turned to look at her and nodded, as if he were agreeing with her assessment. She wondered what Hun-Kamé had told Loray about her, or if the pearls had been delivered with a stern silence. Whether they were merely the result of the god settling his account very precisely, or if this final measure of attention for Casiopea possessed some warmth.

She chose not to dwell on this. It was not the kind of thing she wanted to discuss with a stranger. Perhaps, one night, she would ask the stars, she would ask the dark, and the dark might whisper back an answer.

"Where are we headed?" she said.

"I can drop you off anywhere you want. But myself, I'm going somewhere where they speak French. It's a gorgeous language and I haven't heard it spoken widely in a few decades. I'm trying to figure out whether New Orleans or Quebec is more appetizing. What do you think?" he asked her.

"I don't know anything about either."

"Do you like gumbo, that's the question."

"I don't know what that is."

"Want to taste it?"

"Taste," the raven said. It hopped down from Loray's shoulder and onto the back seat of the automobile.

"Are you asking me to tag along?" she told him.

"Well, you're in my automobile."

"Is it your automobile if you stole it?"

"Right of possession, girlie," he said cheerily.

Casiopea ran a hand down the dashboard, considering the situation. She did need a ride, and she wasn't too inclined to remain in Tijuana, even though she had not planned her next stop. Going home was out of the question. She wanted to remain in motion.

"Why would you take me with you?" she asked.

"For a lark. Also, I can't read a map to save my life. Can you read maps?"

"Of course," she said. She had spent enough time contemplating Grandfather's atlas and tracing routes with her fingertips.

"Good. I have no sense of direction."

"You called me a soiled parcel," she reminded him.

"Lady Tun, I tried to make it up to you by getting you nice dresses. By the way, very fetching skirt. I appreciate someone with a sense of color."

Casiopea wasn't ready to concede. She let out a *hmpf* and gingerly placed her hands on her lap.

"So . . . want to go to New Orleans or Quebec?"

"I don't know if I want to make up my mind now," Casiopea said.

"Take it from me. Now is always the answer. Besides, do you have anything better to do? Mope around for a decade or two?"

Casiopea drummed her fingers against her skirt and chewed her lip. The dramatic poetry she'd read would have called for this and more. There was sadness in her, of course, but she didn't wish to crack like fine china either. She could not wither away. In the world of the living, one must live. And had this not been her wish? To live. Truly live.

Loray took out a silver flask from his jacket and pressed it against his lips. He offered her a swig, and she declined.

"Should you do that? Drive with one hand?" she asked, alarmed.

"I'm a demon, remember? Don't worry," he replied, tipping his head back.

"I know you're a demon. That's why I'm worried."

"Oh, small potatoes. I won't steal your soul, promise."

Casiopea slumped back against the car seat, watching his hands upon the wheel, the feet on the pedals. She'd wanted to drive an automobile; she had confessed this truth to Hun-Kamé. Here was an automobile, at last.

"Would you teach me?" she asked.

"What? To steal souls?" he said, raising an eyebrow at her.

"To drive!"

"What if you crash the car?"

"It looks like a straight line," she said, scoffing and pointing at the dusty path they were traveling. There didn't seem to be any art to moving the vehicle down the road. He certainly handled it in a casual way.

"Same with life, and then it branches off."

"I want to drive."

"But now?" he asked, looking doubtful.

"Now is always the answer."

Loray had a constant look of mischief about him, and her answer made him give her an even more mischievous smile.

"Got me there," he admitted. "But if you drive, who is going to handle the maps?"

"Show me how to drive a bit, and I'll show you how to read a map properly."

He removed his cap and smirked. "After this you must call me your friend, you know?"

"We'll see."

He stopped the automobile, just stopped in the middle of the road and got out. She pushed her door open and they switched places. Casiopea sat very straight, contemplating the wheel. The sun had reached the highest point in the sky, and there wasn't a single shadow in sight, the desert burning bright, the sky a canopy of blue. No other vehicles were on the road. She felt bold.

"What do I do first?" she asked.

"First," said the raven.

Loray took a sip from his flask and mimed the turning of the automobile keys, then he explained how the vehicle worked. Casiopea chuckled as the automobile began to move. It was a long road, and she feared the automobile would get away from her and she wouldn't know how to stop, but she smiled.

Glossary

There is no such thing as a homogeneous Mayan language. There are twenty-nine recognized Mayan languages spoken throughout Mexico and Central America. The way these languages are represented in Latin script has changed over time. Therefore, if you open a nineteenth-century Mayan dictionary you may find the spelling of a word is different from a contemporary dictionary.

In this novel, I have used a modernized spelling of most words. As an example, the names of the Lords of Xibalba are commonly spelled Hun-Camé and Vucub-Camé in older texts, which I've rendered as Hun-Kamé and Vucub-Kamé (they could also be Jun-Kamé and Wukub-Kamé, although this spelling is rare). The names translate, at any rate, as One Death and Seven Death.

Gods of Jade and Shadow is inspired by the *Popol Vuh*. Many elements of Maya mythology are woven throughout this novel, some more explicitly than others. However, this is a work of fantasy and should not be considered an anthropological text. Nevertheless, I provide a simple glossary below, which may be of interest to readers.

aluxo'ob—Trickster spirit that can cause mischief, but with certain offerings may be appeased and protect the crops.

balché—A fermented drink made from the bark of a tree, which is soaked in honey and water. The Lacandon utilized it in ceremonies, where ritual intoxication was practiced.

bul—A board game, played with kernels of corn. Bul can also be used to refer to any game of chance, such as dice.

caiman—A reptile, member of the crocodilian order, found in marshes and swamps.

ceiba—A tropical tree. When young, the trunk of the ceiba is deep jade green and as it ages the coloration changes to a more grayish tone. In Maya mythology, the ceiba is a world tree that connects the planes of existence.

cenote—A waterhole. Like caves, certain cenotes were considered entrances to the Underworld and were of ritual importance.

charro/a—A traditional horse rider from central Mexico, easily recognizable by their elaborate outfits.

chu'lel—Vital energy. All animals and inanimate objects possess it.

cuch chimal—To be defeated, to bear one's shield on one's back in retreat. A Nahuatl loanword.

daykeeper—A soothsayer who interprets the calendaric cycle.

divine caste—Upper-class families of European descent who dominated the politics and economy of Yucatán.

haltun—Crevices in the calcareous rock soil where rainwater gathers. Stone trough.

henequen—A fiber plant woven since pre-Columbian times. It was the bedrock of the economy of Yucatán.

Hero Twins—Two brothers who journey to Xibalba and, among other things, avenge the death of their father and uncle at the hands of the gods of the Underworld by besting them in several competitions. They are tied to the idea of cycles, of birth and rebirth.

hetzmek—A ceremony marking the first time the baby is carried on the hip. For females it takes place on the third month of their birth. Three is associated with women because three stones hold the comal women use to make food.

jade—Jade was associated with corn, hence with life. A jade bead was placed in the mouth of corpses as part of funerary rites. Jade was also associated with royalty.

kak noh ek—Fire tail star. A large comet or asteroid. The precolonial Maya don't necessarily distinguish between comets, asteroids, and meteors the way we do. For example, comets are defined by their size with "kak noh ek" meaning a large fiery star. Smaller ones are named chamal dzutan, which literally means warlock's cigar. But when this cigar is discarded it can become a meteor, and there is such a thing as halal ek (a fast-moving star). Other terms were also employed. In the novel, I utilize kak noh ek because in my narrative it was a "large" celestial body that gave birth to the gods of the Maya, but one could argue halal ek/u halal ek dzutam or another term might also be appropriate.

Kamazotz—The Death Bat. A creature that resides in Xibalba.

kuhkay—Firefly. Associated with stars and cigars, due to their burning tip.

k'up kaal—Beheading or cutting of the throat. Ritual decapitation is present in many Mayan monuments and accounts. Players of the ritual ball game were decapitated, an offering that echoes events in the *Popol Vuh*. Sacrifice, in all shapes and forms, is part of the Maya universe.

Mamlab (plural; singular Mam)—Huastec deities associated with rain and thunder. When the rivers overflow with rain, they use the bellies of swollen animals that have drowned in the currents to play the drums.

Middleworld—In Ancient Mayan cosmology, Earth is the land where humans reside.

patan—Tribute, duty. But also a virtue. Even kings pay tribute to the gods.

Popol Vuh—A narrative of the creation myths of the K'iche' people originally passed down through oral tradition.

pulque—An alcoholic drink.

royal diadem—Mayan kings wore a white headband with a jade carving in the middle called sak hu'unal as a sign of their lordship. Upon ascending the throne, a king would also have been presented with a scepter (k'am k'awiil).

sacrifice—Stingray spines and other instruments were used by Mayan no-bles in order to draw blood that would nourish the gods. When the Hero Twins defeated the Lords of Xibalba, they ordered that humans would no longer give them proper sacrifices, only croton sap and "dirty blood." Sac-rifice by humans is the engine that drives the universe, and proper sacrifices must always be made. Indeed, the reason humans were chosen to inhabit earth is so that they could provide such sacrifices.

sascab—White, soft, unconsolidated limestone. Extensively used for build-ing by the Maya.

sastun—Stone mirror. A stone used for divination.

suhuy ha—Place of virgin or pure water; water meant to be used in rituals.

tun—Stone. Also, year. Stones are associated with time or cycles, since they are used to commemorate events.

Uay Chivo—Literally "ghost goat." An evil sorcerer who can take the form of a goat. In Mayan tales, sorcerers can take multiple forms including cats or dogs.

Xaman Ek—The god of the North Star, who guided merchants.

Xibalba—The Mayan Underworld, full of terrifying sights, such as a river of blood and a river of pus. The Yucatec Mayans referred to the Under-world as Mitnal. Owls or dogs are associated with death, hence the mes-sengers of Xibalba are four fearsome owls (Chabi-Tucur and Huracán-Tucur are mentioned in this novel).

x'kau—A common black bird, similar to a magpie. *Quiscalus mexicanus*, in Spanish zanate.

Xtabay—A mythological creature that has the appearance of a beautiful woman who seduces men and drives them to their death.

zaca—A drink mixed with ground corn, used in religious offerings.

Acknowledgments

I must thank David Bowles, who looked at an early draft of this novel and corrected the Mayan vocabulary I used. A heartfelt thanks also to Eddie Schneider, my agent. And finally, thanks to my editor, Tricia Narwani, and to all the people at Del Rey who have made this book possible.

Read on for a sneak peek at

MEXICAN GOTHIC

by Silvia Moreno-Garcia

A reimagining of the classic gothic suspense novel, a story about an isolated mansion in 1950s Mexico—and the brave socialite drawn to its treacherous secrets.

Coming in summer 2020.
Enjoy this special preview!

Chapter 1

The parties at the Tuñóns' house always ended unquestionably late, and since the hosts enjoyed costume parties in particular, it was not unusual to see Chinas Poblanas with their folkloric skirts and ribbons in their hair arrive in the company of a harlequin or a cowboy. Their chauffeurs, rather than waiting outside the Tuñóns' house in vain, had systematized the nights. They would head off to eat tacos at a street stand or even visit a maid who worked in one of the nearby homes, a courtship as delicate as a Victorian melodrama. Some of the chauffeurs would cluster together, sharing cigarettes and stories. A couple took naps. After all, they knew full well that no one was going to abandon that party until after one A.M.

So the couple stepping out of the party at ten P.M. therefore broke convention. What's worse, the man's driver had left to fetch himself dinner and could not be found. The young man looked distressed, trying to determine how to proceed. He had worn a papier-mâché horse's head, a choice that now came back to haunt him as they'd have to make the journey through the city with this cumbersome prop. Noemí had warned him she wanted to win the costume contest, placing ahead of Laura Quezada and her beau, and thus he'd made an effort that now seemed misplaced, since his companion did not dress as she had said she would.

Noemí Taboada had promised she'd rent a jockey outfit, complete with a riding crop. It was supposed to be a clever and slightly scandalous choice, since she'd heard Laura was going to attend as Eve, with a snake wrapped around her neck. In the end, Noemí changed her mind. The jockey costume was ugly and scratched her skin. So instead she wore a green gown with white appliqué flowers and didn't bother to tell her date about the switch.

"What now?"

"Three blocks from here there's a big avenue. We can find a taxi there," she told Hugo. "Say, do you have a cigarette?"

"Cigarette? I don't know even where I put my wallet," Hugo replied, palming his jacket with one hand. "Besides, don't you always carry cigarettes in your purse? I would think you're cheap and can't buy your own if I didn't know any better."

"It's so much more fun when a gentleman offers a lady a cigarette."

"I can't even offer you a mint tonight. Do you think I might have left my wallet back at the house?"

She did not reply. Hugo was having a difficult time carrying the horse's head under his arm. He almost dropped it when they reached the avenue. Noemí raised a slender arm and hailed a taxi. Once they were inside the car, Hugo was able to put the horse's head down on the seat.

"You could have told me I didn't have to bring this thing after all," he muttered, noticing the smile on the driver's face and assuming he was having fun at his expense.

"You look adorable when you're irritated," she replied, opening her handbag and finding her cigarettes.

Hugo also looked like a younger Pedro Infante, which was a great deal of his appeal. As for the rest—personality, social status, and intelligence—Noemí had not paused to think too much about all of that. When she wanted something she simply wanted it, and lately she had wanted Hugo, though now that his attention had been procured she was likely to dismiss him.

When they arrived at her house, Hugo reached out to her, grasping her hand.

"Give me a kiss good night."

"I've got to run, but you can still have a bit of my lipstick," she replied, taking her cigarette and putting it in his mouth.

Hugo leaned out the window and frowned while Noemí hurried into her home, crossing the inner courtyard and going directly to her father's office. Like the rest of the house, his office was decorated in a modern style, which seemed to echo the newness of the occupants' money. Noemí's father had never been poor, but he had turned a small chemical dye business into a fortune. He knew what he liked and he wasn't afraid to show it: bold colors and clean lines. His chairs were upholstered in a vibrant red, and luxuriant plants added splashes of green to every room.

The door to the office was open, and Noemí did not bother knocking, breezily walking in, her high heels clacking on the hardwood floor. She brushed one of the orchids in her hair with her fingertips and sat down in the chair in front of her father's desk with a loud sigh, tossing her little handbag on the floor. She also knew what *she* liked, and she did not like being summoned home early.

Her father had waved her in—those high heels of hers were loud, signaling her arrival as surely as any greeting—but had not looked at her, as he was too busy examining a document.

"I cannot believe you telephoned me at the Tuñóns'," she said, tugging at her white gloves. "I know you weren't exactly happy that Hugo—"

"This is not about Hugo," her father replied, cutting her short.

Noemí frowned. She held one of the gloves in her right hand. "It's not?"

She had asked for permission to attend the party, but she had not specified she'd go with Hugo Duarte, and she knew how her father felt about him. Father was concerned that Hugo might propose marriage and she'd accept. Noemí did not intend to marry Hugo and had told her parents so, but Father did not believe her.

Noemí, like any good socialite, shopped at the Palacio de Hierro, painted her lips with Elizabeth Arden lipstick, owned a couple of very fine furs, spoke English with remarkable ease, courtesy of the nuns at the Anglo—a private school, of course—and was expected to devote her time to the twin pursuits of leisure and husband hunting. Therefore, to her father, any pleasant activity must also involve the acquisition of a spouse. That is, she should never have fun for the sake of having fun, but only as a way to obtain a husband. Which would have been fine and well if Father had actually liked Hugo, but Hugo was a mere junior architect, and Noemí was expected to aspire higher.

"No, although we'll have a talk about that later," he said, leaving Noemí confused.

She had been slow dancing when a servant had tapped her on the shoulder and asked if she'd take a call from Mr. Taboada in the studio, disrupting her entire evening. She had assumed Father had found out she was out with Hugo and meant to rip him from her arms and deliver an admonishment. If that was not his intent, then what was all the fuss about?

"It's nothing bad, is it?" she asked, her tone changing. When she was cross, her voice was higher-pitched, more girlish, rather than the modulated tone she had in recent years perfected.

"I don't know. You can't repeat what I'm about to tell you. Not to your mother, not to your brother, not to any friends, understood?" her father said, staring at her until Noemí nodded.

He leaned back in his chair, pressing his hands together in front of his face, and nodded back.

"A few weeks ago I received a letter from your cousin Catalina. In it she made wild statements about her husband. I wrote to Virgil in an attempt to get to the root of the matter.

"Virgil wrote to say that Catalina had been behaving in odd and distressing ways, but he believed she was improving. We wrote back and forth, me insisting that if Catalina was indeed as *distressed* as she seemed to be, it might be best to bring her to Mexico City to speak to a professional. He countered that it was not necessary."

Noemí took off her other glove and set it on her lap.

"We were at an impasse. I did not think he would budge, but tonight I received a telegram. Here, you can read it."

Her father grabbed the slip of paper on his desk and handed it to Noemí. It was an invitation for her to visit Catalina. The train didn't run every day through their town, but it did run on Mondays, and a driver would be sent to the station at a certain time to pick her up.

"I want you to go, Noemí. Virgil says she's been asking for you. Besides, I think this is a matter that may be best handled by a woman. It might turn out that this is nothing but exaggerations and marital trouble. It's not as if your cousin hasn't had a tendency toward the melodramatic. It might be a ploy for attention."

"In that case, why would Catalina's marital troubles or her melodrama concern us?" she asked, though she didn't think it was fair that her father label Catalina as melodramatic. She'd lost both of her parents at a young age. One could expect a certain amount of turmoil after that.

"Catalina's letter was very odd. She claimed her husband was poisoning her, she wrote that she'd had visions. I am not saying I am a medical expert, but it was enough to get me asking about good psychiatrists around town."

"Do you have the letter?"

"Yes, here it is."

Noemí had a hard time reading the words, much less making sense of the sentences. The handwriting seemed unsteady, sloppy.

> . . . he is trying to poison me. This house is sick with rot, stinks of decay, brims with every single evil and cruel sentiment. I have tried to hold on to my wits, to keep this foulness away but I cannot and I find myself losing track of time and thoughts. Please. Please. They are cruel and unkind and they will not let me go. I bar my door but still they come, they whisper at nights and I am so afraid of these restless dead, these ghosts, fleshless things. The snake eating its tail, the foul ground beneath our feet, the false faces and false tongues, the web upon which the spider walks making the strings vibrate. I am Catalina Catalina Taboada. CATALINA. Cata, Cata come out to play. I miss Noemí. I pray I'll see you again. You must come for me, Noemí. You have to save me. I cannot save myself as much as I wish to, I am bound, threads like iron through my mind and my skin and it's there. In the walls. It does not release its hold on me so I must ask you to spring me free, cut it from me, stop them now. For God's sake . . .
>
> Hurry,
> Catalina

In the margins of the letter her cousin had scribbled more words, numbers, she'd drawn circles. It was disconcerting.

When was the last time Noemí had spoken to Catalina? It must have been months ago, maybe close to a year. The couple had honeymooned in Pachuca, and Catalina had phoned and sent her a couple of postcards, but after that there had been little else, although telegrams had still arrived wishing happy birthdays to the members of the family at the appropriate times of the year. There must have also been a Christmas letter, because there had been Christmas presents. Or was it Virgil who had written the Christmas letter? It had, in any case, been a bland missive.

They'd all assumed Catalina was enjoying her time as a newly-wed and didn't have the inclination to write much. There had also been something about her new home lacking a phone, not exactly unusual in the countryside, and Catalina didn't like to write anyway. Noemí, busy with her social obligations and with school, simply assumed Catalina and her husband would eventually travel to Mexico City for a visit.

The letter she was holding was therefore uncharacteristic in every way she could think of. It was handwritten, though Catalina preferred the typewriter; it was rambling, when Catalina was succinct on paper.

"It is very odd," Noemí admitted. She had been primed to declare her father was exaggerating or using this incident as a handy excuse to distract her from Duarte, but that didn't seem to be the case.

"To say the least. Looking at it, you can probably see why I wrote back to Virgil and asked him to explain himself. And why I was so taken aback when he immediately accused me of being a nuisance."

"What exactly did you write to him?" she asked, fearing her father had seemed uncivil. He was a serious man and could rub people the wrong way with his unintended brusqueness.

"You must understand I would take no pleasure in putting a niece of mine in a place like La Castañeda—"

"Is that what you said? That you'd take her to the asylum?"

"I mentioned it as a possibility," her father replied, holding out his hand. Noemí returned the letter to him. "It's not the only place, but I know people there. She might need professional care, care that she will not find in the countryside. And I fear we are the ones capable of ensuring her best interests are served."

"You don't trust Virgil."

Her father let out a dry chuckle. "Your cousin married quickly, Noemí, and, one might say, thoughtlessly. Now, I'll be the first to admit Virgil Doyle seemed charming, but who knows if he is reliable."

He had a point. Catalina's engagement had been almost scandalously short, and they'd had scant chance to speak to the groom. Noemí wasn't even sure how the couple met, only that within a few weeks Catalina was issuing wedding invitations. Up until that point Noemí hadn't even known her cousin had a sweetheart. If she hadn't been invited to serve as one of the witnesses before the civil judge, Noemí doubted she'd have known Catalina had married at all.

Such secrecy and haste did not go down well with Noemí's father. He had thrown a wedding breakfast for the couple, but Noemí knew he was offended by Catalina's behavior. That was another reason why Noemí hadn't been concerned about Catalina's scant communication with the family. Their relationship was, for the moment, chilly. She'd assumed it would thaw in a few months, that come November Catalina might arrive in Mexico City with plans for Christmas shopping and everyone would be merry. Time, it was merely a question of time.

"You must believe she is saying the truth and he is mistreating her," she concluded, trying to remember her impression of the groom. *Handsome* and *polite* were the two words that came to mind, but then they'd hardly exchanged more than a few sentences.

"She claims, in that letter, that he is not only poisoning her but ghosts walk through walls. Tell me, does that sound like a reliable account?"

Her father stood up and went to the window, looking outside

and crossing his arms. The office had a view of their mother's precious bougainvillea trees, a burst of color now shrouded in darkness.

"She is not well, that is what I know. I also know that if Virgil and Catalina were divorced, he'd have no money. It was pretty clear when they married that his family's funds have run dry. But as long as they are married, he has access to her bank account. It would be beneficial for him to keep Catalina home, even if she'd be best off in the city or with us."

"You think he is that mercenary? That he'd put his finances before the welfare of his wife?"

"I don't know him, Noemí. None of us do. That is the problem. He is a stranger. He says she has good care and is improving, but for all I know Catalina is tied to her bed right now and fed gruel."

"And you said she was the melodramatic one," Noemí said, examining her orchid corsage and sighing.

"I know what an ill relative can be like. My own mother had a stroke and was confined to her bed for years. I also know a family does not handle such matters well at times."

"What would you have me do, then?" she asked, daintily placing her hands on her lap.

"Assess the situation. Determine if she should indeed be moved to the city, and attempt to convince him this is the best option if that is the case."

"How would I manage such a thing?"

Her father smirked. In the smirk and the clever, dark eyes, child and parent greatly resembled each other. "You are flighty. Always changing your mind about everything and anything. First you wanted to study history, then theater, now it's anthropology. You've cycled through every sport imaginable and stuck to none. You date a boy twice then at the third date do not phone him back."

"That has nothing to do with my question."

"I'm getting to it. You are flighty, but you are stubborn about all the *wrong* things. Well, it's time to use that stubbornness and energy to accomplish a useful task. There's nothing you've ever committed to except for the piano lessons."

"And the English ones," Noemí countered, but she didn't bother denying the rest of the accusations because she did indeed cycle through admirers on a regular basis and was quite capable of wearing four outfits in a single day.

But it isn't like you should have to make up your mind about everything at twenty-two, she thought. There was no point in telling her father that. He'd taken over the family business at nineteen. By his standards, she was on a slow course to nowhere. Noemí's father gave her a pointed look, and she sighed. "Well, I would be happy to make a visit in a few weeks—"

"Monday, Noemí. That is why I cut your party short. We need to make the arrangements so you're on the first train to El Triunfo Monday morning."

"But there's that recital coming up," she replied.

It was a weak excuse and they both knew it. She'd been taking piano lessons since she was seven, and twice a year she performed in a small recital. It was no longer absolutely necessary for socialites to play an instrument, as it had been in the days of Noemí's mother, but it was one of those nice little hobbies that were appreciated among her social circle. Besides, she liked the piano.

"The recital. More likely you made plans with Hugo Duarte to attend it together, and you don't want him taking another woman as his date or having to give up the chance of wearing a new dress. Too bad; this is more important."

"I'll have you know I hadn't even bought a new dress. I was going to wear the skirt I wore to Greta's cocktail party," Noemí said, which was half the truth because she had indeed made plans to go there with Hugo. "Look, the truth is the recital is not my main concern. I have to start classes in a few days. I can't take off like that. They'll fail me," she added.

"Then let them fail you. You'll take the classes again."

She was about to protest such a blithe statement when her father turned around and stared at her.

"Noemí, you've been going on and on about the National University. If you do this, I'll give you permission to enroll."

Noemí's parents allowed her to attend the Feminine University of Mexico, but they had balked when she declared she'd like to continue her studies upon graduation. She wanted to pursue a master's degree in anthropology. This would require her to enroll at the National. Her father thought this was both a waste of time and unsuitable, with all those young men roaming the hallways and filling ladies' heads with silly and lewd thoughts.

Noemí's mother was equally unimpressed by these modern notions of hers. Girls were supposed to follow a simple life cycle, from debutante to wife. To study further would mean to delay this cycle, to remain a chrysalis inside a cocoon. They'd clashed over the matter a half dozen times, and her mother had cunningly stated it was up to Noemí's father to hand down a decree, while her father never seemed poised to do so.

Her father's statement therefore shocked her and presented an unexpected opportunity. "You mean it?" Noemí asked cautiously.

"Yes. It's a serious matter. I don't want a divorce splashed in the newspaper, but I also can't allow someone to take advantage of the family. And this is Catalina we are talking about," her father said, softening his tone. "She's had her share of misfortunes and might dearly need a friendly face. That might be, in the end, all she needs."

Catalina had been struck by calamity on several occasions. First the death of her father, followed by her mother's remarriage to a stepfather who often had her in tears. Catalina's mother had passed away a couple of years later and the girl had moved into Noemí's household: the stepfather had already left by then. Despite the warm embrace of the Taboadas, these deaths had deeply affected her. Later, as a young woman, there had been her broken engagement, which caused much strife and hurt feelings.

There had also been a rather goofy young man who courted Catalina for many months and whom she seemed to like very much. But Noemí's father had chased him away, unimpressed by the fellow. After that aborted romance, Catalina must have learned her lesson, for her relationship with Virgil Doyle had been a paragon of discretion. Or maybe it had been Virgil who had been more wily and urged Catalina to keep mum about them until it was too late to disrupt any wedding.

"I suppose I could give notice that I'll be away for a few days," she said.

"Good. We'll telegraph Virgil back and let them know you are on your way. Discretion and smarts, that's what I need. He is her husband and has a right to make decisions on her behalf, but we cannot be idle if he is reckless."

"I should make you put it in writing, the bit about the university."

Her father sat down behind his desk again. "As if I'd break my word. Now go get those flowers out of your hair and start packing your clothes. I know it'll take you forever to decide what to wear. Who are you supposed to be, incidentally?" her father asked, clearly dissatisfied with the cut of her dress and her bare shoulders.

"I'm dressed as Spring," she replied.

"It's cold there. If you intend to parade around in anything similar to that, you better take a sweater," he said dryly.

Though normally she would have come up with a clever rejoinder, she remained unusually quiet. It occurred to Noemí, after having agreed to the venture, that she knew very little of the place where she was going and the people she would meet. This was no cruise or pleasure trip. But she quickly assured herself that Father had picked her for this mission, and accomplish it she would. Flighty? Bah. She'd show Father the dedication he wanted from her. Perhaps he'd come to see her, after her success—for she could never picture herself failing—as more deserving and mature.

Chapter 2

When Noemí was a little girl and Catalina read fairy tales to her, she used to mention "the forest," that place where Hansel and Gretel tossed their breadcrumbs or Little Red Riding Hood met a wolf. Growing up in a large city, it did not occur to Noemí until much later that forests were real places, which could be found in an atlas. Her family vacationed in Veracruz, in her grandmother's house by the sea, with no tall trees in sight. Even after she grew up, the forest remained in her mind a picture glimpsed in a storybook by a child, with charcoal outlines and bright splashes of color in the middle.

It took her a while, therefore, to realize that she was headed *into* a forest, for El Triunfo was perched on the side of a steep mountain carpeted with colorful wildflowers and covered thickly with pines and oaks. Noemí sighted sheep milling around and goats braving sheer rock walls. Silver had given the region its riches, but tallow from these animals had helped illuminate the mines, and they were plentiful. It was all very pretty.

The higher the train moved and the closer it got to El Triunfo, though, the more the bucolic landscape changed and Noemí reassessed her idea of it. Deep ravines cut the land, and rugged ridges loomed outside the window. What had been charming rivulets turned into strong, gushing rivers, which spelled doom should anyone be dragged by their currents. At the bottom of the mountains farmers tended groves and fields of alfalfa, but there were no such crops here, just the goats climbing up and down rocks. The land kept its riches in the dark, sprouting no trees with fruit.

The air grew thin as the train struggled up the mountain until it stuttered and stopped.

Noemí grabbed her suitcases. She'd brought two of them and had been tempted to also pack her favorite trunk, though in the end she had judged it too cumbersome. Despite this concession, the suitcases were large and heavy.

The train station was not busy and was barely a station at all, just a lonesome square-shaped building with a half-asleep woman behind the ticket counter. Three little boys were chasing one another around the station, playing tag, and she offered them some coins if they helped her lug her suitcases outside. They did, gladly. They looked underfed, and she wondered how the town's inhabitants got by now that the mine was closed and only the goats provided the opportunity for a bit of commerce.

Noemí was prepared for the chill of the mountain. The unexpected element was therefore the thin fog that greeted her that afternoon. She looked at it curiously as she adjusted her teal calotte hat with the long yellow feather and peered onto the street looking at her ride, for there could hardly be any mistaking it. It was the single automobile parked in front of the station, a preposterously large vehicle that made her think of swanky silent film stars of two or three decades earlier—the kind of automobile her father might have driven in his youth to flaunt his wealth.

But the vehicle in front of her was dated, dirty, and it needed a paint job. Therefore it was not truly the kind of automobile a movie star would drive these days, but seemed to be a relic that had been haphazardly dusted off and dragged onto the street.

She thought the driver might match the car and expected to find an elderly man behind the wheel, but a young fellow of about her age in a corduroy jacket stepped out. He was fair-haired and pale—she didn't realize anyone could be *that* pale; goodness, did he ever wander into the sun?—his eyes uncertain, his mouth straining to form a smile or a greeting.

Noemí paid the boys who had helped bring her luggage out, then marched forward and extended her hand.

"I am Noemí Taboada. Has Mr. Doyle sent you?" she asked.

"Yes, Uncle Howard said to pick you up," he replied, shaking her hand weakly. "I'm Francis. I hope the ride was pleasant? Those are all your things, Miss Taboada? Can I help you with them?" he asked in quick succession, as if he preferred to end all sentences with question marks rather than commit to definite statements.

"You can call me Noemí. Miss Taboada sounds so fussy. That's the sum of my luggage, and yes, I'd love some assistance."

He grabbed her two suitcases and placed them in the trunk, then went around the car and opened the door for her. The town, as she saw it from her window, was peppered with winding streets, colorful houses with flower pots at their windows, sturdy wooden doors, long stairways, a church, and all the usual details that any guidebook would call "quaint."

Despite this, it was clear El Triunfo was not in any guidebooks. It had the musty air of a place that had withered away. The houses were colorful, yes, but the color was peeling from most of the walls, some of the doors had been defaced, half of the flowers in the pots were wilting, and the town showed few signs of activity.

It was not that unusual. Many formerly thriving mining sites that had extracted silver and gold during the Colonia interrupted their operations once the War of Independence broke out. Later on, the

English and the French were welcomed during the tranquil Porfiri-ato, their pockets growing fat with mineral riches. But the Revolution had ended this second boom. There were many hamlets like El Triunfo where one could peek at fine chapels built when money and people were plentiful; places where the earth would never again spill wealth from its womb.

Yet the Doyles lingered in this land, when many others had long gone. Perhaps, she thought, they'd learned to love it, though she was not much impressed by it, for it was a steep and abrupt landscape. It didn't look at all like the mountains from her childhood story-books, where the trees appeared lovely and flowers grew by the road; it didn't resemble the enchanting place Catalina had said she would live in. Like the old car that had picked Noemí up, the town clung to the dregs of splendor.

Francis drove up a narrow road that climbed deeper into the mountains, the air growing rawer, the mist intensifying. She rubbed her hands together.

"Is it very far?" she asked.

Again he looked uncertain. "Not that far," Francis said slowly, as if they were discussing a matter that had to be considered with much care. "The road is bad or I'd go faster. It used to be, a long time ago, when the mine was open, that the roads around here were all in good shape, even near High Place."

"High Place?"

"That's what we call it, our home. And behind it, the English cemetery."

"Is it really very English?" she said, smiling.

"Yes," he said, gripping the wheel with both hands with a strength she would not have imagined from his limp handshake.

"Oh?" she said, waiting for more.

"You'll see it. It's all very English. Um, that's what Uncle Howard wanted, a little piece of England. He even brought European earth here."

"Do you think he had an extreme case of nostalgia?"

"Indeed. I might as well tell you, we don't speak Spanish at High Place. My great uncle doesn't know a word of it, Virgil fares poorly, and my mother wouldn't ever attempt to stitch a sentence together. Is . . . is your English any good?"

"Lessons every day since I was six," she said, switching from Spanish to English. "I'm sure I'll have no trouble."

The trees grew closer together, and it was dark under their branches. She was not one for nature, not the real thing. The last time she had been anywhere near a forest had been on that excursion to El Desierto de los Leones when they went riding and then her brother and her friends decided to do some practice shooting with tin cans. That had been two, maybe even three years before. This place didn't compare to that. It was wilder here.

She found herself warily assessing the height of the trees and the depths of the ravines. Both were considerable. The mist thickened, making her wince, fearing they'd wind up halfway down the mountain if they took a wrong turn. How many eager miners hunting for silver had fallen off a cliff? The mountains offered mineral riches and a quick death. But Francis seemed secure in his driving even if his words faltered. She didn't generally like shy men—they got on her nerves—but who cared. It was not as if she'd come to see him or any other members of his family.

"Who are you, anyway?" she asked, to distract herself from the thought of ravines and cars crashing against unseen trees.

"Francis."

"Well, yes, but are you Virgil's little cousin? Long-lost uncle? Another black sheep I must be informed about?"

She spoke in that droll way she liked, the one she used at cocktail parties, and that always seemed to get her very far with people, and he replied as she expected, smiling a little.

"First cousin, once removed. He's a bit older than me."

"I've never understood that. Once, twice, thrice removed. Who keeps track of such a thing? I always figure if they come to my birthday party we are related and that's it, no need to pull out the genealogy chart."

"It certainly simplifies things," he said. The smile was real now.

"Are you a good cousin? I hated my boy cousins when I was little. They'd always push my head against the cake at my party even though I didn't want to do the whole mordida thing."

"Mordida?"

"Yes. You're supposed to take a bite of the cake before it is cut, but someone always shoves your head into it. I guess you didn't have to endure that at High Place."

"There aren't many parties at High Place."

"The name must be a literal description," she mused, because they kept going up. Did the road have no end? The wheels of the car crunched over a fallen tree branch, then another.

"Yes."

"I've never been in a house with a name. Who does that these days?"

"We're old-fashioned," he mumbled.

Noemí eyed the young man skeptically. Her mother would have said he needed iron in his diet and a good cut of meat. By the looks of those thin fingers he sustained himself on dewdrops and honey, and his tone tended toward whispers. Virgil had seemed to her much more physical than this lad, much more present. Older, too, as Francis had indicated. Virgil was thirty-something; she forgot his exact age.

They hit a rock or some bump in the road. Noemí let out an irritated "ouch."

"Sorry about that," Francis said.

"I don't think it's your fault. Does it always look like this?" she asked. "It's like driving in a bowl of milk."

"This is nothing," he said with a chuckle. Well. At least he was relaxing.

Then, all of a sudden, they were there, emerging into a clearing, and the house seemed to leap out of the mist to greet them with eager arms. It was so odd! It looked absolutely Victorian in construction, with its broken shingles, elaborate ornamentation, and dirty bay windows. She'd never seen anything like it in real life; it was terribly different from her family's modern house, the apartments of her friends, or the colonial houses with façades of red tezontle.

The house loomed over them like a great, quiet gargoyle. It might have been foreboding, evoking images of ghosts and haunted places, if it had not seemed so tired, slats missing from a couple of shutters, the ebony porch groaning as they made their way up the steps to the door, which came complete with a silver knocker shaped like a fist dangling from a circle.

It's the abandoned shell of a snail, she told herself, and the thought of snails brought her back to her childhood, playing in the courtyard of their house, moving aside the potted plants and seeing the roly-polies scuttle about as they tried to hide again. Or feeding sugar cubes to the ants, despite her mother's admonishments. Also the kind tabby, which slept under the bougainvillea and let itself be petted endlessly by the children. She did not imagine they had a cat in this house, nor canaries chirping merrily in their cages that she might feed in the mornings.

Francis took out a key and opened the heavy door.

SILVIA MORENO-GARCIA is the author of the critically acclaimed novels *Mexican Gothic*, *Untamed Shore*, *Gods of Jade and Shadow*, *Signal to Noise*, *Certain Dark Things*, and *The Beautiful Ones*, and the science fiction novella *Prime Meridian*. She has also edited several anthologies, including the World Fantasy Award–winning *She Walks in Shadows* (aka *Cthulhu's Daughters*). She lives in Vancouver, British Columbia.

silviamoreno-garcia.com
Facebook.com/smorenogarcia
Twitter: @silviamg

About the Type

This book was set in Sabon, a typeface designed by the well-known German typographer Jan Tschichold (1902–74). Sabon's design is based upon the original letter forms of sixteenth-century French type designer Claude Garamond and was created specifically to be used for three sources: foundry type for hand composition, Linotype, and Monotype. Tschichold named his typeface for the famous Frankfurt typefounder Jacques Sabon (c. 1520–80).